KOREAN ODYSSEY

Dale A. Dye

"Korean Odyssey is just what we would expect of Dale Dye. Well plotted and fast paced with credible characters, historically accurate with just enough technical detail, and the unmistakable ring of authority. Dye's description of the 1950s Marine Corps will resound among warriors of any war."
—Barrett Tillman, award-winning author of *When the Shooting Stopped: August 1945*

"The Forgotten War comes to life as these Marines jump from the page, as real as life, complete with flaws and courage. The veteran will appreciate the details and history, while the layman will become educated as to the horrors of the Korean War and the bravery of our Marines who fought it."
—Colin D. Heaton, author of *The Star of Africa: The Story of Hans Marseille, the Rogue Luftwaffe Ace Who Dominated the WWII Skies*

"Excellent writing and a very enjoyable read....this one is special. I have read a couple of other novelized versions of the campaign, but none rang true in the Jarhead sense of behavior, lingo, and combat experience like Dye's work here."
—Lieutenant Colonel Vic Taylor, USMC (Ret).

"Dale Dye proves himself once again to be as good a storyteller as he was a soldier during his own distinguished military career....Dye manages to combine the pacing and plotting of Stephen Hunter with the angst-rattled soldier's sensibility of Phillip Caputo."
—Jon Land, *USA Today* bestselling author of the Caitlin Strong series

Also by Dale A. Dye

Korean Odyssey

DALE A. DYE

WARRIORS PUBLISHING GROUP
LOCKHART, TEXAS

KOREAN ODYSSEY

A Warriors Publishing Group book/published by arrangement with the author

PRINTING HISTORY
Warriors Publishing Group edition/November 2022

Cover Image: Rifle Platoon from Easy Company, 5ᵗʰ Marines, 1ˢᵗ Marine Division.
Pusan Perimeter, Korea, by David Douglas Duncan, August 1950.
(Harry Ransom Center, The University of Texas at Austin.)

ISBN: 978-1-944353-44-5
Library of Congress Control Number: 2021931935

The name "Warriors Publishing Group" and the logo
are trademarks belonging to Warriors Publishing Group

PRINTED IN THE UNITED STATES OF AMERICA

10 9 8 7 6 5 4 3 2 1

Here's a long overdue salute to the rock-hard and resilient men of the 1st Marine Division who endured the Frozen Chosin in the Freezin' Season. A few of those Marines took the time to pass along their wisdom and spirit to me before I had to endure my own combat crucible in Vietnam. They have my eternal gratitude and respect. And they deserve yours.

Foreword

THEY CALL KOREA the forgotten war. It is, I suppose, except for a handful of military historians and a dwindling number of veteran survivors. It was not an event that carried the absorbing worldwide interest of World War II, a bloody global clash that ended less than five years before the war in Korea began in the summer of 1950. Most war-weary and isolationist-leaning Americans didn't give Korea much thought until friends, sons, and other relatives began to be wounded or killed in significant numbers. Not many citizens understood the stated reasons for sending American soldiers to fight: Support an unprepared ally in South Korea that had been cruelly invaded by their North Korean neighbors and blunt the spread of worldwide communism. As the war escalated, particularly after Chinese combat formations got involved, many Americans vocally disputed the call for American sacrifice in a place as remote and unfamiliar as South Korea.

American involvement in the Korean War had shaky underpinnings from the start. Harry S. Truman, the U.S. President who ordered troops into South Korea, finagled his decision past Congressional oversight and inevitable dispute by calling it a "police action," thus sidestepping the requirement to ask Congress for a declaration of war. None of that meant much to the soldiers and Marines who found themselves on short-notice orders to head for combat in Korea. And few of those shorthanded, undertrained, and mostly garrison troops were anywhere near prepared for the ordeal that followed. Therein lies the story in my view as an author, amateur historian, and Marine combat veteran of later wars, also mostly controversial and undeclared.

In my early years as a Marine, I knew a number of Korean War veterans. Some of them offered hard-learned tips and valuable training based on their experience. And some of that played a big role in keeping me alive when I faced my own combat crucible in Vietnam. Their stories of combat in Korea, some embellished but many gospel, stuck with me over two decades in uniform and I often wondered why more wasn't written about the war in Korea. That conflict never really spawned the flood of literature that World War II and the Vietnam War did. Even the currently unresolved, controversial, and ambiguous conflicts in various part of the embattled Middle East seemed to have more written about them. I consider that a disservice to Korean War veterans—not to mention a sorely missed literary opportunity. Hence, this book.

And this book is a novel full of departures from the record of actual events during the Korean War. There are any number of good books and historical monographs that adhere to strict recounting of events in Korea circa 1950-53. This book is not one of them. I was compelled by my storytelling instincts to narrow the focus primarily to one Marine rifle company from initial spool-up at Camp Pendleton through the end of the Chosin Reservoir Campaign. I chose to end the story there because what happened after that brutal campaign in the winter of 1950 was less interesting than what came before. And I needed to cap the book at a readable length. Simple as that.

The main characters I created to serve with Able Company, 1st Battalion, 5th Marines, are entirely fictional, although I admit that most of them are admixtures and vague reflections of real Marines I knew and admired somewhere or sometime in my two decade active-duty career. Other characters are real people directly or peripherally involved in the Korean War. In a few places, I quote them directly from the historical record, but in most instances I take the liberty of relating what I believe they would have said or thought given the situations they were facing. I'm a novelist. I get to do that.

Historical nitpickers—on the off chance that any of them read this work—will likely complain that that the business of sweeping up support troops for service in rifle companies and the call-up of Marine Reserves actually took place after the first draft of Marines went to Korea as the 1st Provisional Marine Brigade and not prior to it as I relate in this story. They may also complain that some of the actions I've attributed to Able Company 1/5 were actually fought by other units of the 1st Marine Division. They'd be correct—and I'd be pleading guilty quite happily. I have attempted to convey the sense of the time, the struggle of an undermanned Marine Corps, and the initiative of men who knew when it was time to shit-can the rulebook. This story is meant to absorb and entertain, with only a respectful nod to historical accuracy.

A word about jargon here as I have always loved the way Marines talk or used to talk. When my Marines speak in this book, they use the Naval terminology that was so common among Marines for many years after World War II. For instance, it was entirely common and appropriate to address lieutenants as Mister. Marines did not re-up or reenlist, they shipped over. And there are so many other terms that I love—and still use—because they comprise a special language unlike the Army-speak and help to define Marines as soldiers of the sea, the formation we were established and designed to be. Much of that salty, colorful language has disappeared in a more modern Marine Corps and it saddens me.

And finally, to those hidebound Leatherneck readers who might insist that the Corps would never send a man into combat without benefit of molding and shaping at boot camp, I beg to differ loudly. One of my close friends, former Corporal Barry Jones, now deceased, was a rifleman with the 7th Marines in Korea and he never set foot on a grinder at Parris Island or San Diego. He introduced me to several others who had the same experience—or lack of it—before they found themselves in combat in Korea.

That's it for this briefing. Any questions? No? Very well, carry on. Read. Enjoy.

I. WAR CLOUDS

Korea – 25 June 1950
38th Parallel

WATCHING A LONE hawk swooping on thermals through a pale blue sky, Master Sergeant Pak Chun Hee wondered if the bird was an omen. His mother always said hawks carried hints, information picked up by their sharp eyes as they soared high above the country and the people who lived there. She had promised to teach him to read those hints, but a drunken Japanese officer put an end to all that. In fact, Pak thought as he shrugged his shoulders to settle the weight of his pack and ammunition, that Jap bastard put an end to nearly all of the Pak family of Uijongbu. He rubbed idly at the spot on his left hip where the Nambu bullet had penetrated on that ugly day. The Jap was in a raging fury, and his aim was shaky when he finally turned the pistol on a teenaged boy. It was a painful wound but not lethal, not like the well-aimed rounds that killed Pak's father, mother, and sister.

The hawk flapped dark wings to brake his descent and settled on a stretch of rusting barbed wire near a sign that proclaimed this was the Military Demarcation Line, the border between north and south, established by yet another slew of foreigners when that war ended and the Japanese were finally driven out of Korea. His eyes automatically went to the *hangul* characters on the black and yellow triangle, but he could read the English printing below it that said the same thing. He'd learned the language fairly well after an American officer from the post-war occupation forces picked him from a long line of war orphans and put young Pak to work as a houseboy and general go-fer. Two years later, Pak joined the Army of the Republic of Korea and found a new home.

He was a soldier now, a good one with responsibilities to the platoon of mostly teenaged conscripts kneeling behind him and waiting for orders. They gabbed and teased one another, trading sticky rice balls like kids on a holiday outing. It was just a couple of years in uniform for them, no real danger, and a fairly nice posting with the 3rd Infantry Regiment of the Capital Guard Command. They had no idea how lucky they were to be born in the south. A little shift in the geography, a misdrawn line on the map of post-war Korea, and those kids might be serving the *In Min Gun*, the North Korean People's Army, eating rats rather than rice.

"On your feet! Play time is over," Pak barked, but he couldn't hide a smile as he watched his soldiers rise and shoulder their tools and the heavy spools of spare wire. He pointed at a hill mass to the west and then at the fence line. "Check every meter of the wire from here to that hill over there. Any breaks or sections that need replacing, let me know right away." As they started to walk the wire, Pak tossed a rock at the hawk and watched it flap away, heading north. He was tempted to take a catnap, but Master Sergeant Pak had duties to perform on this still summer day. He pulled at the young soldier carrying their radio, halting him, and pointed at a shady spot below a line of tall boulders. "Your lucky day," he said. "Sit over there and let me know if there are any messages."

His soldiers knew their job. It was simple enough and they'd patrolled this border area a number of times before, so they didn't need much supervision. Pak pulled his binoculars from their case on his equipment belt and surveyed the North Korean valley below the high ground. A recently resurfaced road led from the tall mountains to the north, across the valley and then petered out before reaching the wire barrier. Heat waves shimmered and shook above the black ribbon, but there was no traffic on the road and nothing visible in the valley it bisected.

Pak was about to call in a routine situation report when he spotted a flurry of movement with his peripheral vision. He turned to look and saw a kettle of hawks bolt into the sky as if they'd been spooked by something or someone in the valley. And then he heard the unmistakable roar of diesel engines coupled with the creak and clank of steel tracks. Tanks?

He grabbed his field glasses and focused on the road. They *were* tanks, North Korean T-34s, maybe ten or more from what he could see through belching exhaust smoke and the plumes of dust they raised swerving onto the black-top road. He spotted a North Korean officer in the lead vehicle waving some sort of signal flag, and the following tanks roared to the flanks forming an assault line. It looked like a stampede of elephants as the tank gunners swiveled their 85mm cannons right and left searching for targets. The tankers maintained high speed and gave no indication that they intended to stop at the end of the surfaced road. Pak understood then that he was probably witnessing the first action of a war everyone in South Korea knew must come one day when the communists in Pyongyang got hungry enough to start it.

Master Sergeant Pak Chun Hee grabbed for the radio handset and called his headquarters. A bored watch-stander in Seoul had barely responded when a wall of fire erupted all around Pak and his men. Artillery or heavy mortar rounds began to detonate all along the fence line. Pak was hit by a burst of shrapnel and spun into the dirt before he could get his rifle off his shoulder. An ambush party of NKPA soldiers swooped down from the rocks belching rounds from their burp-guns. The platoon radioman was nearly cut in half and fell on top of Pak leaking gouts of warm blood all over his leader. Peeking out from under the dead soldier, Pak watched the *In Min Gun* soldiers putting kill shots into his men who were splayed and dying, bleeding into the dirt all along the wire. It was chaos, bedlam, and butchery.

The ground beneath Pak trembled as a T-34 crashed through the wire followed by a long stream of other tanks and trucks. The North Koreans were in a hurry now that the war had started, and their haste to push south likely saved his life. Fighting to remain conscious, Pak saw the NK infantrymen who were killing his wounded and defenseless soldiers form up to follow the armor south toward Seoul.

PRESIDENT HARRY S. TRUMAN stood at a window polishing his spectacles and gazing out toward the rose garden. Washington was sweltering on a late June summer day, and the temperature outside was nearly matched by the atmosphere inside the Oval Office. Behind the President, under pillars of pipe and cigarette smoke, were the members of his Kitchen Cabinet, his most trusted advisors. There was some muted chatter and the clatter of coffee cups. Nothing beyond standard pleasantries. None of them wanted to upstage the President who was due to begin this emergency meeting as soon as Chairman of the Joint Chiefs of Staff, General Omar Bradley, arrived with the latest updates on the situation in Korea.

Senior National Security Advisor George Elsey, a hold-over from FDR's administration, hung up a phone and cleared his throat. "Mr. President, General Bradley just entered the grounds." He moved toward his place in the circle of advisors gathered around an ornate coffee table and sat. "Two minutes..."

The President nodded and moved to sit in his padded easy chair. He'd had the old piece of handmade furniture shipped to the White House from his homestead in Independence, Missouri. The chair had always been a comfort to him, a place where he could do his best thinking. And today's strategy session demanded good thinking. America was facing a serious international crisis. The President reached for a coffee cup and eyed the assembled staff. They were all here as he demanded: Vice President Alben Barkley, Secretary of State Dean Acheson, Secretary of Defense Louis Johnson, Attorney General James McGrath, and Elsey. They'd likely have differing opinions, bound to be some arguments, but Truman would allow that, hear them out fairly, even though he'd nearly made up his mind.

Hearing footsteps outside the door, the President replaced his coffee cup and glanced at the Resolute Desk behind him, an ornate, heavyweight fixture made from the oak timbers of HMS *Resolute*, a gift from Queen Victoria to President Rutherford B. Hayes in 1880. Lots of monumental decisions had been made by men sitting at that desk, and it looked to the current President like he would have to make another one very shortly. As General Omar Bradley swept into the room, followed by an aide carrying his briefcase, President Truman noted the sign he'd placed on the Resolute Desk the day he become America's chief executive: The Buck Stops Here. *Indeed it does*, he thought, nodding at the Chairman of the Joint Chiefs and pointing at the coffee service.

"It's a mess, Mr. President." General Bradley gulped coffee and shuffled through a stack of messages his aide handed him. "No doubt about that. So far, we've identified at least four North Korean divisions involved, and they are driving straight for Seoul."

"And the South Koreans?" The president crossed his legs and scratched at an ankle. "How are they doing?"

"Pardon my candor, sir..." Bradley shook his head and lit a cigarette. "But not worth a damn. The North Koreans are hell bent for leather on this one. They're pushing through Syngman Rhee's troops like crap through a tin-horn."

Secretary of Defense Louis Johnson confirmed the general's opinion. "Not to put too fine a point on that, Mr. President, "but the ROK troops are being crushed like a bunch of empty beer cans. I don't know how General Bradley would describe it in military terms, but I'd call it a rout. We're going to have another communist country in Asia if we don't do something in a hurry."

"We damn sure don't need that." President Truman pointed at his Secretary of State. "Dean, we better hear what you have to say."

"Well, you've all heard my opinion before..." He glanced around the room and gently placed his coffee cup back in its saucer. "The Korean Peninsula lies outside our worldwide sphere of influence and interest. However, I suppose that's neither here nor there given the current situation. We need to watch our language carefully here, gentlemen. I'm assuming when Louis says *we*, the reference is to the United Nations, isn't it? The Security Council voted nine-zero in passing a resolution that calls this North Korean invasion a breach of the peace."

Truman leaned forward with his elbows on his knees and glared at his assembled advisors. "Listen, we can paint lipstick on this pig all day long, but there's no doubt in my mind that the damn Soviets are behind it. They were behind the turmoil in Greece, and they're behind this thing in Korea. This is nothing more or less than another attempt to spread communism worldwide."

Vice President Alben Barkley kicked back in his chair and nodded in agreement. "The President's right about that. This is a clear challenge to the Truman Doctrine. Our policy is to contain communist expansion whenever and wherever it occurs. And if this thing in Korea isn't an example of communist expansion, I don't know what the hell is."

National Security Advisor Elsey scratched his balding pate. "If nobody else is going to mention it, I guess I'd better. It's important to consider the political implications here. You all know this administration stands accused of being soft on communism. If we don't do something concrete, Senator McCarthy and his ilk will be getting a lot of ink in the very near future."

"I don't want to hear about Tail Gunner Joe in this conversation, George. The hell with him and his cronies over on the Hill. I'm concerned much less about public opinion than I am with stopping this aggression in Korea. It's a damn puppet show in my opinion. The Soviets are pulling the strings, and the North Koreans are doing just what Moscow tell them to do. Now, the Russians have got their eyes locked on Korea, and they're not above rattling the atomic saber to back it all up. I'll just be damned if we'll lose another allied country to communism on my watch."

Attorney General James McGrath poured himself coffee and cleared his throat. "I guess it's time for the lawyer to chime in," he said turning to look directly at Truman. "Mr. President, is it your intention to go to Congress and ask for a declaration of war against North Korea? From an international legal perspective, that will be a difficult proposition at best."

Truman slipped off his glasses and pinched the bridge of his nose. "Jim, if we do it right, we won't have to argue the issue before Congress. We go for a United Nations mandate. Any action we take carries their authority as a worldwide organization of which we are a member. It's not war *per se*, it's something like...well, something like a police action where we're the meanest cop on the block. I'm due to meet with the UN Foreign Affairs and Foreign Relations committees in about an hour. I think I can sell that."

"At least it won't look like we're taking unilateral action in Korea," the Vice President said. "I think it's important to convey an image of international effort here through the UN."

The President felt himself getting hot under his starched collar and began to drum the arm of his chair with the fingers of his right hand. "I don't much give a damn what it looks like at this point, Al." He replaced his spectacles and swept his eyes around the room. "Now, you all get your heads together and draft a statement outlining our position for the press. The bottom line should be clear and unmistakable. The United States is not going to let this situation in Korea stand unchallenged."

As the assembled advisors began snapping briefcases and shuffling papers, General Bradley interrupted. "Before I go, sir...assuming your intent is to send U.S. military forces in to shore up the South Koreans, you should know we are in pretty poor shape militarily in that part of the world. We've been cutting capabilities and manpower to the bone since the end of the last war."

Truman was midway back to his desk when he heard that assessment. He spun around and glared at the general. "Damn it, Brad! Are you telling me we don't have the wherewithal to beat those North Koreans back to where they came from?"

"Not precisely, Mr. President." General Bradley stood and nodded to his aide. "I'm just reminding you that it's been a long time since we had to fight a land war, and we are not immediately and completely ready to do so without some time to train and reinforce."

Shaking his head, trying to get a grip on the frustration he was feeling, the President pointed at the JCS Chairman. "Time is the one thing we don't have, General Bradley. If we're not ready, we better get ready in a hurry." Truman paused to glance at a photo of himself as commander of an Army artillery battery during World War I on the credenza next to his desk. "We did it in my day, we did it in the last war and, by God, we'll do it now. You wind up one of your best field generals and get cracking."

Bradley approached the Resolute Desk as the other cabinet members filed out of the Oval Office. "The logical choice would be General MacArthur in Tokyo."

Truman nodded and picked up his briefing papers for the UN meeting. "Well, he's a pain in the ass, but I guess we go with what we've got. And he's closest to the situation. Let me get this United Nations thing in the bank and then you notify MacArthur that he'll be the likely commander of our efforts in Korea."

General Bradley turned to follow the others out of the Oval Office. "I'll cable Douglas tonight, Mr. President. I'm sure he'll be delighted with the opportunity."

CAPTAIN SAM GERDINE hopped out of his Jeep, stretched, and nodded to his driver. "You head on back to the company area. If the First Shirt is still around, tell him I'll see him before morning formation on Monday. Anything needs my attention, he can call me here at the club."

Corporal Bayliss Thornton straightened the Jeep's wheels and nodded as he ground the transmission into low gear. "Ah reckon Top secured before we left, Skipper. Gunny Bates is likely still there."

"OK, Thornton. Same message for the Gunny. And keep your speed down on the way back. This ain't one of your Kentucky back roads, and there's MPs out tonight."

"Aye, aye, sir." The driver eased out on the clutch and twisted the wheel. "See you Monday."

Gerdine squared his cover and brushed a little dust from his herringbone utility uniform. They were issuing a new green sateen version of the field uniform now, but he preferred his old, worn, and faded herringbones. One look at that uniform and any Marine worth his salt knew right away he wasn't dealing with some rear-echelon pogue. *On the other hand*, he thought, eyeing the line of officers in starched and pressed khakis escorting well-dressed ladies into the Officers' Club main entrance, *I probably should have changed.*

A year or so ago, he would have been among those happy couples, squiring Della into the club for dinner and drinks. But that was then. *And this is now*, he thought, changing directions and heading for a back entrance that led to the club's Stag Bar where officers who didn't have time to change, or didn't much give a damn, would be hitting it hard on this Friday night. Sam Gerdine was a career Marine, but a spit and polish image wasn't going to do him much good anymore. Not with final divorce papers sitting in his desk drawer back at the company area.

Della forwarded the documents two days ago, which meant he'd have to get his status changed in his Officers Qualification Record. Lots of admin involved, pay records, next of kin and all that. And that meant his divorce would be a matter of official record, available for any and all stiff-necked seniors to view with raised eyebrows. A company grade officer in the post-war Marine Corps was expected to be an upright and stable family man. Likely his prospects for promotion were swirling down the crapper. At least he'd go out on a high note. For an infantry officer, commanding a rifle outfit like his Able Company was about the best thing there was to do in service to Uncle Sam's Misguided Children.

Ducking into the muggy atmosphere of the Stag Bar, Gerdine let his eyes adjust to the gloom and spotted the hawk-eyed barkeep who merely glanced in his direction and nodded. Sam ran a hand over his scalp, more to be sure he'd remembered to remove his utility cover than to tame his shock of greying, close-cropped hair. Behind the crowded bar hung a highly polished ship's bell that the barkeep would ring if anyone were dumb enough to enter the joint wearing a hat of any kind. A long-standing Naval Service tradition held that "anyone who enters covered here shall buy the bar a round of cheer." Gerdine couldn't afford that right now. A big chunk of his pay went to Della down in San Diego in the form of child support for their son.

Gerdine slumped against a bulkhead and looked for familiar faces. First Lieutenant Baldomero Lopez, one of his two platoon leaders, mentioned that he'd be going to the club for a couple of pops at liberty call. Unlike his Company Commander who was what the Corps called a Mustang, a former enlisted man who earned a field commission, Baldo Lopez was a Naval Academy grad. And unlike a number of other Boat School officers that Gerdine knew, Lopez was loyal, courteous and a huge admirer of his CO's World War II combat experience.

Sam was about to assault into the mob milling around the bar under a dense cloud of tobacco smoke when he was jostled by a crusty Marine Gunner, a warrant officer he knew slightly from the South Pacific. "Sad Sam Gerdine, the old gravel-cruncher! How the hell you doin'?"

"Doin' fair-to-middling, Gunner." Gerdine struggled to remember the man's name, but it wouldn't come. "What they got you doin' in this peacetime lash-up?"

"I got the rifle range at Camp Matthews, Sam. They're puttin' in new butts, so I cut all my PMIs loose for weekend liberty. That includes yours truly. Lemme buy you a snort."

"In a minute, Gunner. Gotta hit the head."

Gerdine ducked into the toilet and bent over a sink to wash some of the grime from his face and hands. He pried some gun grease out from under his fingernails and ran a paper towel over his face. The guy looking back at him in the cracked mirror was kind of hangdog with deep crows-feet around blue eyes that contrasted brightly with a bone-deep, leathery tan. Maybe a little jowly around the mouth and chin. Never gonna make a recruiting poster, but not bad for 35 at his last birthday. Still, he couldn't see the Sad Sam thing. He'd asked the First Shirt and his Company Gunny to discourage that nickname every time they heard it, but Sad Sam stuck to him like the digits of his service number. He didn't think of himself as morose. Maybe no kind of comedian, but not sad. He had a sense of humor just like everybody else. Maybe just a little disinclined to laugh at the dumb shit everyone else thought was hilarious. Two years with the Old Breed, the 1st Marine Division, knocking around the Pacific, including getting banged up pretty badly on Peleliu will do that to a man. And, he thought with a grin as he tossed the paper towel into a shit-can near the door, it's like the man said: You can't polish a turd.

Gerdine ducked into the crowd, mostly company grade bachelors, lieutenants, and warrant officers blowing off a week's worth of steam with cheap draft beer and off-brand whiskey. He made it through a throng playing liar's dice for drinks and got a double-knuckle of Four Roses over ice. A radio behind the bar was tuned to a San Diego station that played big-band classics. A couple of young second lieutenants were bitching about that, wanting the barkeep to switch stations, but their complaints were barely audible above the chatter and chuckles that marked a roaring start to a weekend liberty. Gerdine sipped whiskey, tuning in and out of a sea story being related by another captain nearby who had survived the Iwo Jima campaign. You always knew a sea story when you heard one because it began with the standard intro: Now this is no shit...

Sam missed the fighting on Iwo Jima and from the sound of the sea story, exaggerated or not, he was damn glad he did. Peleliu had been bad enough. It was on that bloody pile of coral that he won his Silver Star and the field commission. Not that he'd ever expected to survive long enough for either to make much difference. He ordered a backup drink and elbowed his way to the back of the room where it was a bit quieter. He slumped casually against the wall, watching Marines just being Marines. To Captain Sam Gerdine it was like watching a big rowdy family arguing over a dinner table.

"Hey, Skipper!" Baldo Lopez was zealously guarding a pair of beer bottles as he danced his way through the crowd. "How's your drink? Get you one of these?"

Gerdine held up his whiskey glass and rattled the ice cubes. "Beer ain't gonna cut it tonight, Baldo. I'm calling in heavy weapons."

Lopez polished off one of his beers and stuck the empty bottle in a pocket. "Gunny Bates mentioned I might want to keep an eye on you, sir. What's the skinny?"

"He say why?"

"I don't know, Skipper...he said something about a divorce. I didn't want to pry."

"I am now an officially divorced officer, which is a status that is not gonna sit well with future promotion boards. I'm what you might call a casualty of domestic war, Baldo. Don't let it happen to you."

Lopez held up a hand and flashed his Naval Academy graduation ring. "Not to worry, sir. Us ring-knockers are married to the service."

Gerdine snorted into his drink. "Right out of Canoe U and into Able Company, 5th Marines. You're definitely on a roll, Baldo."

"That's gilding the lily, Skipper. My platoon is still about the size of a reinforced rifle squad. We ever gonna get more Marines?"

"Not anytime soon, I'm afraid. Mother Corps is still in what Hairy Ass Truman insists on calling a post-war restructuring. That's what we get for electing a piss-ant National Guard cannon-cocker. He hates the Marine Corps."

"Of course, as a commissioned officer, I'm precluded from making political judgments, sir. But between me and thee, I think you hit that fucking nail right on the head."

"In which case, it falls to us to get drunk."

"Gunny Bates said that was probably what you were gonna do. I think he's worried about you, sir."

"He's just being a mother hen. I'll be OK." Gerdine rattled the ice and drained his glass. "And when you see Gunny Bates, tell him you found Sad Sam wiser but not sadder."

"He didn't mean any disrespect, Skipper. You know the Gunny thinks the world of you."

"He's a good man, a master of creative profanity. Let's re-load and have a drink to Gunnery Sergeant Elmore No Middle Initial Bates, of the fighting Fleet Marine Force."

They were plowing through the crowd when the bell behind the bar rang loudly. It was quiet for a moment as officers looked toward the door to see what numb-nuts had entered wearing a cover. Before the roar could resume, the bartender cranked up the volume on the radio. A silken voice introduced the President of the United States who sounded like he was in the midst of a national announcement.

"In Korea the Government forces, which were armed to prevent border raids and to preserve internal security, were attacked by invading forces from North Korea. The Security Council of the United Nations called upon the invading troops to cease hostilities and to withdraw to the 38th Parallel. This they have not done. In these circumstances I have ordered United States air and sea forces to give the Korean government troops, cover, and support..."

Whatever followed was lost in the babble of shouting voices. All the officers listening knew what had just happened. The Commander In Chief was ordering American troops to go on a war footing. And everyone assembled in the Camp Pendleton Officers' Club also knew that when a thing like that happens suddenly, it is never long before someone sends in the Marines.

Gerdine grabbed Lopez by an elbow. "Get on your horse, Baldo, and beat it back to the company area. I want all hands recalled from liberty right now. No excuses. Get the First Sergeant on it right away. Then round up our officers and NCOs. I'm gonna see if I can find Colonel Murray."

CO of the 5th Marine Regiment, Colonel Ray Murray, waited at the front of a jam-packed Quonset hut for all his officers to arrive. He'd heard the President's announcement while preparing a backyard barbecue at his on-base quarters and immediately ordered an officers' call. It had taken only three hours for his leaders to heed that call, rushing back to the base from scattered locations. Some swayed in their seats showing the effect of a running start on the weekend, but most sat quietly, waiting for The Word, wondering what direction their lives would take in the very near future.

The last few of them were just barging in the door as the Regimental Sergeant Major caught Murray's eye and nodded. All present or accounted for. Now Murray would tell them what he knew about the situation in Korea, which wasn't much more than the broad strokes he'd gleaned from talking to pals on the 1st Marine Division operations and intelligence staffs. The important thing was to let these guys know what he expected of them immediately. No more mark-time training for his 5th Marines. Ray Murray had been a Marine long enough to know what would come for his outfit in short order.

"Gents, I'm told air elements—U.S. and Australian units for the most part—are flying strike missions right now in Korea. That has not had much effect on the North Korean 3rd Division which is currently driving deep into the south. General MacArthur is sending American soldiers from Japan to block the commie thrust, but those are mainly garrison troops with way too much soft living and way too little training. There is no doubt in my military mind that will be getting orders to go to Korea in the very near future."

Murray spoke softly, but his dark eyes flashed as he swept them over the audience, pausing to let his words resonate. Expressions ranged from shock to bewilderment on most of the younger officers. A few of the older men, combat vets from the last war, just nodded or looked at each other with raised eyebrows. Murray began to pace.

"From this moment, we will consider ourselves on a war footing. Don't bother asking me about additional men or more gear. When orders arrive, this regiment will go with what we've got. The Commandant and everyone else at higher echelons knows the manpower situation. They will do what can be done to give us what we need. Meanwhile, the Lord helps those who help themselves, so we will sweep this base for plank-owners, desk-jockeys, homesteaders and support troops. Anyone who can carry a rifle is gonna do so. I can promise you that. What we will do immediately is anything and everything humanly possible to get our Marines ready for war."

Gunnery Sergeant Elmore Bates slammed the phone receiver back into its cradle and ran a finger down the Able Company roster. He plucked a pencil from behind an ear and made tic marks beside two more names. The second lieutenant on the other end of the phone had managed to cajole the Oceanside cops into releasing two Able Company Marines from the lock-up where they'd been jailed after a bar fight. PFCs Benson and Maitland—both of whom would be buck-ass privates come Monday. But he'd let First Sergeant Hammond deal with those peckerheads after he ran them up for office hours.

Bates lit a cigarette, then leaned back in his desk chair and stretched. Korea, he mused, another party with the wily Asian folk. Probably not a lick of difference between them and the Japs he'd faced in the South Pacific. Same tune, different dance. Bates smiled and sucked on his smoke. Didn't matter. War is war. Different enemy in his rifle sights from time to time, but it's mostly the same drill: Kill a shit-pot full of them and try not to get killed yourself. The rest is all details. And he was a Marine, in the war game for the past 17 years, ever since

'33 when gut-busting life on an Oklahoma oil rig drove him into a recruiting office.

Back in those days, Elmore Bates was an hombre, a rootless kid with no middle name, a hardhead whose penchant for rebellion got him tossed out of high school before he could finish. Roughneck, mouthy rebel, hell-raiser. Funny, he'd often thought, that he picked a stiff-neck outfit like the Corps, where discipline was both demanded and sternly enforced. *Snapped the hellion right out of me*, he thought, remembering the ass-kicking, brig time, and punch-outs that molded him from Parris Island, through sea duty aboard a cruiser, a year in Shanghai, and on into a fighting outfit bound for war in the Pacific. That war had been tough and he had spilled some blood, but Elmore Bates thrived. Sergeant, Staff Sergeant, then Gunny when it was all over, and he shipped over for six more years. The Corps dicked around with the rank structure after the war. Bates was carried on the payroll as a Technical Sergeant. But at home in a rifle outfit, he was always the Company Gunny. The billet was Old Corps, and that suited Elmore Bates just fine.

When he spent any time at all thinking about his past, Bates mostly remembered the good times, the fun, the wildness in exotic spots around the world, the stuff of legendary sea stories. Lots of booze and plenty of women in and around all that. Shit, even the bad times were good one way or another. He'd nearly married a couple of women along the way. Probably should have. Maybe had a couple of his own kids instead of spending his time raising other people's offspring.

And here we go again. Gunnery Sergeant Elmore Bates crushed his smoke, picked up the duty roster and smiled as he headed out of the hut to find the CO and report this lash-up standing by for orders.

He ducked out of the Quonset hut and spotted Captain Gerdine conferring with the First Sergeant under the yellow glow of a standing light. He tucked the clipboard containing the recall roster under his arm and looked around at the straggling line of Marines clomping toward their barracks, most of them reeling and half-snockered. A pile of paperwork had kept the Gunny from securing early this evening or he'd be dragging ass back aboard right along with them. Except he would be fully snockered. Gunny Bates was not one to half-step on a weekend liberty. He walked over to join the CO and handed the roster to First Sergeant Leland Hammond.

"I'll be kiss my Marine Corps ass if I know how, Skipper, but it looks like we got the biggest part of our peckerheads rounded up. Two of 'em run afoul of the Shore Patrol but I got Lieutenant Porter to sign for 'em. Should be back aboard shortly."

First Sergeant Hammond adjusted wire-rim spectacles and held the roster under the light. "We got three on ten-days annual leave, so they ain't gonna make it back before middle of next week sometime."

"Check," Gunny Bates nodded. "And we got two more sick, lame, or lazy over in sickbay. We can pry their asses out of there tomorrow morning. I'm guessing we'll have the full complement by 2200 tonight, give or take."

Captain Gerdine just nodded and waved a dismissive hand at the roster. "By full complement you mean half of what we rate by T-O, right Gunny?"

"I mean we got what we had before the shit hit the fan, Skipper." Bates pulled a pack of Pall Malls from his sock and lit one. "We need us some more men if we intend to get this lash-up ready for a shootin' war."

Gerdine nodded and smiled. "Pretty much what Col. Murray said at officers' call. Don't know how he expects us to do it, but he said the days of two platoons per company and two companies per battalion are over. Maybe they'll call up the reserves. Who knows?"

"You finally gonna get an XO, Skipper?"

"We can hope, I guess." He pointed a finger at First Sergeant Hammond. "Until that happens, you're the man, Top."

"I was over at the Staff NCO Club tonight, sir." The First Sergeant said. "The Division Sergeant Major is sayin' they're gonna commence press-gangs all over Camp Pendleton right after reveille on Monday morning. You leave it to me and the Gunny, Skipper. Any swingin' dick that ain't serving in an infantry outfit will be by nightfall."

Gerdine borrowed the Gunny's smoke to ignite one of his own. He waved his hand at the sprawling base surrounding them. "Gonna be a scramble. We ain't the only rifle company short-handed."

"Yeah..." Gunny Bates nodded and smiled. "But them other outfits ain't Able Company of the pogey-rope 5th Marines, Skipper. They'll fuck around with paperwork and all that cheap shit. Me and the First Shirt operate a little different. We see a warm body looks like he can handle an M-1 and he's ours—paperwork to follow—if and when we get around to it."

They were still speculating on their chances in the upcoming manhunt when duty driver Cpl. Thornton rolled up in the Jeep. Corporal Ashford, the Duty NCO, bounded out of the vehicle and grabbed a large leather-bound book from the back seat. He saluted Gerdine and handed him the book. "Damndest thing, Captain." Cpl. Ashford said as he followed the company command group into their Quonset hut headquarters. "Apparently there ain't a single map of Korea anywhere on Pendleton. I had to go to the base library which was just fixin' to close. I cornered the clerk and got that Atlas. The whiny little fart wanted me to sign for it but I told him to go piss up a picket-rope."

"OK, thanks, Cpl. Ashford. Leave it with us. You better get over to the barracks and see all our little lost lambs hit the rack."

At the door Ashford had to sidestep 2nd Lieutenant George Porter, leader of Able Company's first platoon, who barged in with a handful of paperwork. Porter tucked his khaki pisscutter into his belt and handed the papers to the First Sergeant. "Benson and Maitland, Top. Those are the release forms. Both of 'em are here. I told 'em to take a shower and hit the rack."

"Thanks, Mister Porter. I'll deal with those two yahoos in the morning."

Captain Gerdine had opened the Atlas to a map of Korea and was examining it closely. "This won't be much tactical help—no elevations or contour lines—but it's gonna have to do until we find something better." Using his pocketknife, Gerdine cut the page from the spine of the book and handed it to First Sergeant Hammond. "Top, first thing in the morning, post this thing on the company bulletin board where everyone will see it. We'll update it as we get more information on what's happening in Korea. I want an All Hands formation at zero-eight tomorrow morning. We pass the word. From now on, it's double-time all the time in this company."

Porter rubbed a hand over his crew-cut and shook his head. "Skipper, I can barely muster two squads in my first platoon. How am I gonna..."

Gerdine cut him off abruptly. "Listen up, gents. This outfit is not going to war under-manned, under-equipped, and under-motivated. I've been down that road before and it's not gonna happen with Able Company. We *will* get ourselves up to T-O and E. I don't care how we do it, but we are damn sure gonna do it."

FOR FOUR LONG, PAINFUL DAYS after the ambush on the border line, Master Sergeant Pak, the sole survivor of his platoon, struggled southward. He was riddled with shrapnel, the entry wounds swathed in battle dressings. His body was swollen, his joints complaining with every step he took. The rifle slung on his shoulder felt like it weighed a ton, and there seemed to be no way he could carry it that didn't hurt. Small slivers and larger chunks of the mortar round that felled him worked their way out of his body as he hobbled and limped along headed southward.

What he saw along the way was depressing. His army was folding under communist pressure, battered and bleeding, their leadership absent or confused. From what Pak could tell, ROK units north of the Han River were scrambling south in headlong, disorganized retreats. He always seemed to be threading his way through long lines of shuffling, dispirited soldiers.

A wounded man Pak recognized from his regiment said their outfit had been shattered and scattered in brutal battle with the *In Min Gun*. He had no idea if there were any remaining troops from the 3rd Regiment still in the fight, but he doubted it. The soldier had heard that Seoul was about to fall, and orders were being issued to abandon the city. But the man was dazed and babbling, so some of that might be rumor, a reflection of the chaos everywhere around them. Pak needed to find his unit, or some other outfit that was willing to stand and fight. The Han River flowing south of the capital was a prominent terrain feature, a natural military barrier. Surely some ROK units would be holding there, trying to keep the North Koreans at bay. There was a railroad bridge near Uijongbu, his home village. Surely the army would be defending that.

Pak continued moving slowly, steadily south. Everywhere he looked along the way, there were dead bodies, soldiers, and civilians lying where they'd fallen, bloated into grotesque, reeking, and nearly unrecognizable shapes. Many of the villages he passed through were in flames or just smoking ruins. His meager rations had run out long ago and his canteen was empty, but Pak didn't bother to ask for food or water along the route. It was obvious there was none to be had. The *In Min Gun* was living off the land, sweeping through the area like a swarm of marauding locusts.

Master Sergeant Pak Chun Hee struggled to the top of a hill overlooking his home village, stared for a while, and then collapsed on a nearby boulder with tears forming in his eyes. Uijongbu was flattened, a pile of smoldering rubble with only a few larger structures standing. And south of his village, the bridge over the Han was collapsed. Pak could see North Korean tanks and troops on the far side of the river, shooting and shelling everywhere as they pushed into Seoul. Turning to look in the opposite direction, he could see more North Korean units in the distance, already beyond the capital, grinding steadily southward.

He watched a pair of airplanes, summer sun glinting on their canopies, as they circled a North Korean convoy. He couldn't tell the type or identify the markings, but they weren't the MIGs the North Koreans flew. He watched them dive toward the enemy formation, their wings flashing as the pilots fired rockets into the tanks and trucks jammed on the road. The war was not completely lost—at least not yet. Pak levered himself up off the rock, shouldered his rifle, and trundled down the hill, headed south with no particular destination in mind.

"I THOUGHT WE WAS SUPPOSED to get orders or something, First Sergeant." The Marine in the back seat of the Jeep was sitting on his sea bag, still in his cook's white uniform and wearing a sweat-stained paper hat. The two senior NCOs in the front of the Jeep had hustled him out of the galley area so quickly that he hadn't had time to change. PFC Franklin Waters, a reluctant cook, stuck with a military occupational specialty he never wanted, was perfectly happy to get out of the mess hall, but he'd been a Marine long enough to know you were supposed to get orders when you get transferred. Otherwise they could haul your ass up for a court martial. He already had one Office Hours for Unauthorized Absence and he didn't need another one.

The Gunny at the wheel of the Jeep glanced over his shoulder. "Word we got was you wanted to get away from them stew-burners. Ain't that right, Waters?"

"Yeah, Gunny. But there's supposed to be official orders, right?"

The First Sergeant in the passenger seat swiveled around and pointed a finger at the ex-cook. "Waters, we're saving your ass from years of shit-duty in that mess hall with a gaggle of rear-echelon pot-wallopers. You're gonna love duty in a rifle company. Just shut up and let us worry about orders."

First Sergeant Hammond turned back to the notes on his clipboard. "Next one is Jones, Jonathan J. He's listed as assigned to Base Special Services."

Gunnery Sergeant Elmore Bates swung the Jeep left, heading off the main drag toward a sprawl of Camp Pendleton athletic fields. "That the one pitches for the baseball team?"

"That's him. He's a rifleman but they got him handing out jockstraps at the gym. Probably so's he'll be handy for baseball games." Hammond thumbed through the notes on his clipboard. "Says here he's from St. Louis and had a major league shot with his hometown Cardinals."

"Gotta wonder how come a man like that winds up in the Corps..."

"Guy I know in S-1 told me Jones got drunk on a road trip and punched out a cop. You know the drill. Judge says he goes to jail or he goes to the military. No tellin' why he picked the Marine Corps."

"Don't matter," Gunny Bates said as he pulled the Jeep into a parking spot near the baseball field where players on Pendleton's varsity squad were working out. "Guy with a wing like that will be helpful pitching grenades."

Bates turned to their passenger as they climbed out of the Jeep. "Waters, you hustle over to the gym and change out of them mess whites. Put on a utility uniform and then come back to the Jeep and wait."

Bates and Hammond sat on a bench near the dugout watching a tall lanky left-hander throw a variety of breaking balls to a warm-up catcher. Corporal J.J. Jones did, indeed, have quite an arm. Gunny Bates was impressed watching the baseball dive and break sharply before it smacked into the catcher's mitt with a resounding pop. The catcher was also impressed.

"That's the one, JJ! Sinker's working today, man. Howie Polett ain't got nothin' on you."

"Yeah, he does." Jones caught the return throw and toyed with his grip. "Polett's got over a hundred strikeouts already this year. And I'm stuck fuckin' around in the Marine Corps playin' bush league."

"Not anymore you ain't." Gunny Bates whispered and elbowed the First Sergeant. They walked through the dugout gate and headed for the practice mound. Jones eyed them suspiciously as they halted between pitcher and catcher. Bates just smiled at the bewildered Marine as Hammond consulted the clipboard. "Your name Jones, Jonathan J., Corporal, 1815203?"

"That's me, Top. What's the problem?"

Gunny Bates plucked the baseball from Jones' glove and tossed it back to the catcher. "There ain't no problem, Jones— except you're in the wrong place. The right fuckin' place for you is now Able Company, 5th Marines." He turned to point at the Jeep where PFC Waters now sat in a utility uniform watching the practice. "Get in the jeep with that other turd."

Jones stripped off his glove and put his hands on his hips. "I'm being reassigned? Since when? Lemme see some orders."

Gunny Bates took a threatening step up onto the mound. "You're in the Marine Corps, ass-eyes. And good Marines don't ask to see no fuckin' orders, they just obey 'em. Now get your ass in that jeep. We'll go by your barracks so you can pick up your sea bag."

Able Company, including a dozen new men recently shanghaied into the rifle squads with varying levels of experience and motivation, was running assault on a fortified position for the third time. They still didn't have it right. Squad leaders set their men up for another go while Captain Gerdine stood on the hood of his Jeep observing. Lt. Lopez was shaking out a newly formed third platoon full of scatterlings picked up in the sweep of Camp Pendleton's base or support commands. They were dragging ass as their two inexperienced squads maneuvered to the flank of the bunker representing the objective.

Baldo Lopez was crouched near the .30 caliber machinegun that was emplaced to fire support for the maneuver elements. Gerdine jumped off the Jeep and walked toward him as Lopez gave the signal to open fire. Squads to the right and left of the gun lunged forward dripping sweat as they negotiating the steep terrain leading to the bunker. The machinegun, which had been chattering in short bursts, suddenly erupted in a long continuous stream of fire. Smoke was streaming from the red-hot barrel as Gerdine rushed toward the crew.

"No, goddammit!" The CO launched a kick at the gunner's legs. "Short bursts, five to eight rounds!"

The assistant gunner to the left of the weapon rolled clear. "Runaway gun!"

Gerdine snatched the belt of linked ammo that was pouring through the gun and twisted it. When that portion of the ammo belt reached the receiver, the gun suddenly stopped. As did the third platoon which was panting and straining about halfway up the hill.

The machine gunner stood and aimed a vicious kick at his weapon. "This thing is a complete piece of shit, sir!"

"Third time this week, Skipper." Lt. Lopez walked over, signaling for his troops to return to the starting line. "That gun needs to be surveyed."

"Damn sure does, sir." The gunner agreed. "I checked the armory records. This fuckin' gun is older than I am. It's just done wore out."

"I know..." Gerdine turned to Lopez. "I've got a plan."

"Aye, sir. We'll try it again without the fire support."

"No, hold up on that, Baldo. Get your squad leaders to bring 'em in. School circle over by my Jeep."

In a few minutes, the third platoon was kneeling around their company commander, panting and blowing from their exertions. Sweat dripped from under their steel helmets making rivulets through the grime and dirt caking their sunburned faces.

"I know it's been a tough week," Gerdine said. "I know you're all tired, dirty, and pissed off. You can ignore that. Marines are supposed to be tired, dirty and pissed off—especially Marines headed for Korea." He waited for the chuckles, groans, and grunts to subside.

"I got the word just before I came out here, people. We are now part of the 1st Provisional Brigade. And that outfit is headed for Korea. I don't know exactly when we'll move out, but I know when Able Company hits the deck over there, we're gonna be as sharp and squared away as training can make us." He signaled for Lopez and pointed up the hill toward the bunker. "Have your squad leaders set 'em up for another run. Use a BAR in place of the machinegun for this one."

As his senior men prodded third platoon into position for another run at the exercise, Lopez joined Captain Gerdine at the Jeep. "So, Skipper...we're really going?"

"That's the word I get, Baldo. Straight from this morning's S-3 briefing. Apparently, it's turning into a real shit sandwich over there. The commies are rolling south at high port.

They've taken the capital at Seoul. The South Korean President and his cabinet have been evacuated."

"What about the doggies they sent from Japan?"

"They got hammered. Seems like everybody is retreating south under serious pressure. They've formed a U.S. 8th Army under a three-star named Walton Walker. He's facing at least three North Korean Divisions they've identified so far. Walker is bringing in the 1st Cavalry Division. Then we're next. Plan is to make a stand in the far south of the country, around a seaport called Pusan. That's probably where we'll land."

"The whole 1st Marine Division going?"

"Not right away. The brigade will be mostly our 5th Marines under Colonel Murray plus some cats and dogs, armor, arty and an aviation element. We're due to work for 8th Army until the rest of the division gets to Korea."

"I know we go with what we've got, Skipper, but if it's a time crunch, we need to do some re-shuffling."

"Yeah, I know...and there's some good news about that problem. We get to keep all the people Gunny and Top Hammond shanghaied. And I'm told the Commandant is calling up the reserves. There's gonna be a shit-pot full of people flooding in here over the next couple of weeks. We'll get our share."

"That's gonna solve some manpower problems. How about weapons? We've got to do something about these ancient machineguns."

Gerdine nodded and led Lopez toward the rear of the Jeep. He lifted the corner of a tarpaulin as Lopez bent at the waist to identify a case of Johnny Walker. Gerdine dropped the tarp and dusted his hands. "I'll take over for you out here, Baldo. You take the Jeep and a couple of our best machinegunners over to see Master Sergeant Hartman at the regimental armory. He's been hiding replacement guns, parts, spare barrels—and a big thirst for scotch whiskey. I made a deal..."

Salem, Oregon

PAUL RUGGLES MADE a scheduled spot inspection of the roaring machinery on the floor of the Pendleton Sawmill. He waved at a few of the shift men he knew well and made a mental note to have the maintenance guys get after the sawdust piling up on the floor. Everything looked good, timber stacked, planers and rip saws roaring. The number-four band saw needed a new blade, but the crew would make quota for this shift. He'd make a note of the band saw situation and drop it in the plant manager's box at lunch time. He scrunched up on a bench, crossed his legs, and flipped through the work orders on his clipboard. Below them, he kept some of his most recent sketches. He pulled a pencil out of his shirt pocket and added a few strokes to his rendering of old man Simpson, an ancient bark stripper who'd caught Paul's artistic fancy. The guy looked like a cross between Elmer Fudd and Popeye the Sailor Man. The artwork was pretty fair, he thought, not good enough for him to quit a good paying job and make a living at it, but fairly good. And it pleased him, knocked the boring edges off routine work

Paul had been an assistant floor manager at Pendleton for four years. Went to work the year after World War II ended, the year his promising career as a Marine officer turned from exciting to mundane. He never even went overseas and wound up being shuttled from one stateside base to another. It was a sore disappointment. His Forestry degree had gotten him a slot at Quantico, but shortly after he finished training, the war had ended. What he had wanted, the test he wanted to take as a Marine, ended before it could really begin for Paul Ruggles. He was assigned frustrating busy work, helping to rapidly process thousands of returning veterans out of the Corps.

Never heard a shot fired outside a rifle range, and that left him feeling empty, somehow like a slacker, unworthy, robbed by bad timing of a chance to prove himself in the ultimate challenge for a military man. He loved hearing sea stories from veteran officers who had gone to war against the Japanese in the Pacific, but he could never add anything of his own experience. It was too embarrassing, so he applied for an early release. It was granted, and 2nd Lieutenant Paul Ruggles went from active duty into something called the Individual Ready Reserve. There wasn't much to it. He wasn't required to attend monthly drills or annual training exercises. He was just sort of out there in case he might be needed. These days, even with the developing situation in Korea, he didn't think much about it, but there were times when he sat with other mill hands drinking beer after work that he missed what he'd found in the Marine Corps. He missed the colorful characters and the edgy business of training to handle life or death situations, never knowing what lay in store for him at dawn on each day in uniform.

When the lunch whistle blew and crews started shutting down and reaching for their lunch pails, Ruggles dusted his hands and went to the mail and message center where he'd leave a note about the band saw for the Plant Manager. There were a few new work orders in his slot, all routine, but a manila envelope with familiar government markings caught his eye. It was addressed to 2nd Lieutenant Paul E. Ruggles USMCR from the Department of the Navy, Headquarters, U.S. Marine Corps in Washington, DC. He had to read it twice, studying the official verbiage carefully under a desk lamp. Each time, the message was clear and concise. Lieutenant Ruggles was re-called to active duty with a reporting date ten days hence when he was to arrive at Marine Corps Base Camp Pendleton, California for further assignment within the 1st Marine Division.

Pittsburgh, Pennsylvania

THE TROLLEY CAR WAS jammed with Tri-City Steel workers from the mid-shift heading home after work on a payday. Most of them sat smoking and joking with big industrial lunch-pails perched on their laps. As the car made scheduled stops in Pittsburgh's tenement neighborhoods, small groups jumped off and headed for little beer bars that proliferated on almost every street corner. Steve Petrosky desperately wanted to join them. He had a powerful thirst and he had to fight it all the time, especially on paydays.

Even before a shift ended these days, he had to conduct a mental exercise, reasoning with himself, throwing up barriers to what he really wanted to do at quitting time. He'd be half-way through his shift, pushing a handcart loaded with ingots from the receiving docks to the smelter, when he'd start seeing flashing neon lights, tasting cold draft beer, feeling the bite of whiskey on his tongue, and even smelling the stale booze and cigarette smoke miasma of a cozy bar near the tenement where he lived. That's when he'd remind himself that Alma was at wit's end, repeat in his mind her threats to leave with their two kids, if he blew sorely needed money on booze or came home stewed to pass out on the couch. She even tried to keep bottled beer stocked at home for him. It wasn't so much what he drank as how much he drank that caused their problems, according to Alma.

Steve Petrosky had a drinking problem. In reflective moments, he readily admitted that to himself. He'd brought that with him from the Marine Corps. After Okinawa, he needed the booze just to numb himself, wash away memories from that nasty, bloody campaign. But that was a long time ago, five years and a second kid since that time, and he still struggled to keep his craving manageable if not totally under control. Money was short, the plant was crowded with workmen, and promotion to a better paying slot at Tri-City was unlikely for a guy with little formal education. When the arguments started and Alma said she might have to get a job, leave the kids with neighbors, Petrosky started looking around for another source of income.

He was never any good at gambling, and it would be too risky even if he'd learned a thing or two from the hustlers he played cards with while he was on active duty in the Marines. There were some shady deals on offer, mostly pilfering, petty theft or stealing from delivery trucks, but Petrosky wanted no part of anything that might get him busted and jailed. Alma and the kids meant too much for him to risk that.

One day after work when he stopped into Dugan's for just one quick beer, he ran into a Staff Sergeant he knew from Okinawa. The guy had been a solid gunner in one of Petrosky's machinegun squads, a steady hand. Not as good with the guns as Sergeant Petrosky, but a reliable man who could put steel on target. They had a couple of pops and Petrosky learned that his old buddy was now on the Inspector-Instructor Staff at the local Marine Corps Reserve unit. That's how Steve Petrosky wound up rejoining the Corps as a weapons platoon sergeant in that same reserve outfit. Alma wasn't happy at first, but she quit bitching when the paychecks for his reserve time started to arrive. And Petrosky wasn't the only reservist employed at Tri-City Steel. The bigshots at the plant were pretty decent about granting time off to drill. Alma thought the discipline was good for her husband, and she liked it when he wore his uniform with the new Staff Sergeant chevrons. The kids were proud. On the whole, Marine Reserve duty seemed to steady Steve Petrosky's family situation.

He swung down off the trolley car at his stop, glancing only briefly at the smudged windows of Dugan's Bar, and climbed the stairs to his walk-up apartment. The two boys saw him coming from the window overlooking the street. By the time he reached the apartment door, they were racing by him headed downstairs and out for the vacant lot next door where they played with other neighborhood kids. Petrosky opened the door, walked into their kitchen where a pot of cabbage was boiling, and plopped his lunch-pail on the table. He could hear his wife slamming drawers in the bedroom. *Must be folding laundry*, he thought, and jerked open the fridge.

"Alma! No beer in the fridge? I thought you went to the store."

Alma Petrosky, a slight woman with a solid build and greying hair, walked out of their bedroom, dabbing at her eyes with a dishtowel. "No beer in the fridge is the least of our problems," she said plucking an envelope out of her pocket and handing it to her husband. "That came in the mail. You better read it."

There was a lot of familiar military jargon and stilted language, but the message was clear. Staff Sergeant Steven S. Petrosky, USMCR, 554631, was ordered to report to Camp Pendleton immediately for extended active duty.

Alma Petrosky pointed to the Pittsburgh Post-Gazette on the kitchen table. A headline blared: Situation Bleak in Korea. "You know what this means, don't you?" Tears were rolling down her face and she dabbed again with the dishtowel. "It means they're gonna send you to Korea. Jesus, Steve. I don't even know where Korea is!"

"Listen, Alma. Don't worry about it. This is a form letter, that's all. I'll just go out there to Camp Pendleton and talk to the right officer. I got you and the kids. They won't keep me. They'll send me back home. Don't worry about it."

EASY COMPANY OF THE 24th Marines was mustered in the parking lot of the county reserve center. The pavement radiated heat from a blazing summer sun overhead, and a gritty wind blowing in from the city suburbs was rapidly turning their starched uniforms into shapeless khaki bags. The First Sergeant, a KC cop when he wasn't drilling with the reserves, eyed the one young man wearing jeans and a chambray shirt at the rear rank of the second platoon. Abramson, he remembered from seeing the name on a roster, was a new guy waiting for a slot at the San Diego Recruit Depot. Officially, the kid was a drilling member of the unit, just standing around most times, no uniform and clueless, waiting for orders that would send him to boot camp, turn him into a real Marine before he returned to reserve duty with Easy Company. *Well, all that's about to change*, the First Sergeant thought as he saluted the Company Commander and reported all present or accounted for.

The CO, a mid-level exec with the city gas and electric service when he wasn't in uniform, opened a folder and stepped closer to the ranks where he would be sure to be heard by all hands.

"Listen up," he said. "Attention to orders. Company E, 24th Marines is herewith activated. Members of the command are designated augmentees for active duty service with the 1st Marine Division at Marine Corps Base Camp Pendleton, California."

The Captain paused to look over his Marines. Most were stoic. They could read newspapers and hear the reports about Korea on the radio. This wasn't that big a surprise to many of them. Still others showed shocked and disbelieving expressions. He could hear the whispers in the ranks and understood he'd spend the next couple of days dealing with long lines of men waiting to offer every conceivable reason why they couldn't possibly comply with the active duty orders.

"In compliance with this order," he continued, "all hands will be prepared to move out anytime in the next 72 hours. First Sergeant and the Admin Chief will be preparing orders and movement instructions. In the meantime, every man will report back here by 0700 tomorrow morning with a complete sea bag including all uniforms and equipment." He executed an about face and nodded at his senior NCO. "First Sergeant, dismiss the formation."

It was bedlam when the dismissal was ordered. Some of the reservists sprinted for their vehicles. Some stood around in the hot sun, either bitching vociferously or asking questions that had no answers. After the initial shock subsided, most of Easy Company shambled off the hot pavement. Except for 18-year-old Miles Abramson, who stood squinting in the glaring sun, not sure what all this meant to him, or what he was supposed to do about what he'd just heard.

Corporal Ron Edison, owner of a local radio repair shop when he wasn't drilling as an Easy Company squad leader, put a reassuring hand on Abramson's shoulder and offered a handkerchief to mop at the sweat running down the younger man's face.

"What am I supposed to do?" Abramson wiped his face and returned the handkerchief. "Does this mean I go to Camp Pendleton?" The teenager's voice cracked and he looked to be on the verge of tears. "I ain't been to boot camp yet!"

"Something is very screwed up here, Miles." Cpl. Edison took him by an elbow and steered Abramson toward the headquarters building. "Let's go see the First Shirt and find out what we're supposed to do with you."

"I been thinking about this," the First Sergeant said when Edison and Abramson stood in front of his desk. "The way I see it, Abramson here is on an enlistment contract. That means technically he's a Marine and subject to lawful orders."

"Top, he hasn't even been to boot camp. He's not a real Marine yet."

"He's real enough, Cpl. Edison. And he'll get plenty of training out at Pendleton. He goes—and that's that. Let them figure it out. I got enough on my plate right now with the rest of this company. Now get gone, both of you."

Edison walked Miles Abramson out to his car and offered the young man a ride home. "You better tell your folks—and be here tomorrow morning at zero-seven."

"There's just my Mom," Abramson said as he slid into the passenger seat of Edison's Chevy. "She's been expecting me to leave for boot camp. Maybe I'll just tell her that's where I'm going."

"Good idea," Edison said as he started the engine. "Sometimes less information is more, you know?"

Miles Abramson just nodded. "Where do you think I'll wind up, Corporal Edison?"

"Knowing the Marine Corps like I do, Miles, I'd bet you're probably gonna wind up in Korea with the rest of us."

CORPORAL HEYWOOD TRENTON paused beneath the flagpole in front of regimental headquarters and checked his uniform. He'd broken out his best dress greens for this appointment with the colonel. He was buffed, polished, and pressed to Marine Corps perfection. It was vital for him to make not just a good impression but a totally *professional* impression, if he had any chance to get what he wanted. And he wanted it so badly that he jumped the chain of command to Request Mast, a personal meeting, with the regimental Commanding Officer. Any number of people at subordinate levels told him he was wasting his time, just being uppity and troublesome, but Cpl. Trenton was determined to take his shot and friends who had served with the CO told him that Colonel Homer L. Litzenberg, was a fair man.

Trenton took a final look at the burgundy glow on the toes of his dress shoes, tucked his Service Record Book under an arm, and marched resolutely up the steps leading into the regimental Command Post. A Staff Sergeant serving as Duty NCO eyed him up and down for a few moments after Trenton gave his name and then checked an appointment book on his desk. He pointed down a long dark corridor to their right and watched Trenton march into the shadows. "Never gonna fuckin' happen," he whispered and then sat to resume reading Field & Stream.

Trenton rapped smartly on the Commanding Officer's hatch and made a final tug at khaki necktie before he opened the door. He glanced only briefly at the lanky, steely-eyed colonel sitting at a government issue desk in shirtsleeves. Out of the corner of an eye, he noted the colonel's green uniform blouse hanging on a nearby coatrack ablaze with combat decorations and campaign ribbons. Then he kept his eyes locked on the bulkhead over Colonel Litzenberg's head and halted precisely two paces in front of the desk.

"Sir, Corporal Trenton reporting to the Commanding Officer!"

Col. Litzenberg eyed him carefully, nodded, and held out his hand for Trenton's service record book. "Stand easy, Cpl. Trenton. Let me look this over." Trenton snapped into a position of Parade Rest which was standing about as easy as he dared at the moment. The colonel flipped through the pages of the SRB, nodding here and there, pausing to read more carefully at a few places.

"I see you've got your battalion commander's endorsement," he said closing the file and leaning back in his chair.

"Yes, sir!" Trenton could feel sweat dripping down his ribcage. "Favorable endorsement on my request for transfer to Camp Pendleton and service with the 1st Provisional Marine Brigade."

"Trenton...unwind a bit. I like to look in a man's eyes." When Trenton slowly lowered his gaze to meet the colonel's stare, the senior officer nodded and leaned further back in his desk chair. "That's better," he said. The colonel wasn't exactly smiling, but he wasn't frowning either. Trenton took a deep breath. "I'd genuinely appreciate your endorsement, Colonel Litzenberg."

"You know, Trenton, this is the first time we've met face to face, but I know a few things about you." He tapped the SRB folder on his desk. "I know your record. I looked into it when you volunteered for Korea. It's quite impressive, really." Trenton expected the colonel to say quite impressive for a man *like you*, but he didn't.

"Four-oh pro and con marks all the way. Rifle and pistol expert, Good Conduct Medal...and you served overseas toward the end of the war, mostly with support troops. Is that right?"

Trenton merely nodded. All that was a matter of record, right there in his SRB. Colonel Litzenberg continued to stare, drumming his fingers on the desktop in a martial rhythm for a few seconds before he continued. "And you shipped over when the war ended to hang around with us remaining on active duty. That's unusual in and of itself. I was impressed by that. And I was impressed when you were one of the first Negro Marines to join up with a rifle company when the President ordered integration." There was a long silence. Then the colonel seemed to have made up his mind. A slight smile showed. Nothing big or phony, but it made Trenton feel like he might just have a chance.

"Let me ask you something, Trenton...man to man."

"Yes, sir."

"Are you trying to prove something here?"

"Colonel, I'm volunteering for duty in Korea for the same reasons I fought my way into a rifle company back in 1948 when the chance came for people of color to move from support troops into line outfits. I'm a Marine, sir—a good one. And I want to be where the action is."

The colonel nodded and sat forward with his elbows on his desk. "You and a lot of other good Marines, Trenton. I'm a little concerned in your case. I know—and so do you—that the Corps is full of southerners who don't necessarily agree with integration of the ranks. Is that going to be a problem for you?"

"I've learned to deal with that stuff, Colonel. I didn't make these stripes by being a trouble-maker or some kind of crusader."

It was a full two minutes before Colonel Litzenberg finally nodded and broke into a genuine smile. "I believe that brigade headed for Korea can use an NCO like you, Trenton. Your request for transfer is approved. You may carry on."

Corporal Heywood Trenton snapped to attention, took two steps backward and returned the colonel's smile before he executed a perfect about face. He was nearly out the door when the colonel halted him.

"And Trenton...don't screw it up. I'll be heading to Pendleton myself in a week or two and I'll be checking up on you."

Camp Pendleton
San Onofre Area

ABLE COMPANY NOW HAD four skeleton platoons and they were strung out, struggling and panting up the infamous hill that every Marine who'd ever climbed it called Mount Motherfucker. Wearing helmets, carrying weapons, and burdened with heavy field marching packs, Captain Gerdine's Marines were sweating hard and trudging in silence. They were well beyond the early bitching and joking that rattled though the ranks on the lower elevations. At this point about halfway up, they simply kept their eyes down and concentrated, straining to make just one more step up the steep boot-worn trail that led to the top of Camp Pendleton's tallest hill mass.

Captain Gerdine was focusing on training evolutions that built endurance. His men would need a ton of it along with their rapidly improving infantry skills. Korea was a country with lots of mountains, hills, and high ground. If he'd learned nothing else from his combat experience, Gerdine knew you always had to take the high ground. That's where the enemy was in every war he ever studied. That's where the enemy would be in Korea.

Endurance training almost always involved things like stress injuries or heat casualties, and Gerdine was holding back a bit, not pushing as hard as he might have if he could afford routine, temporary losses. He'd only agreed to the Mount Motherfucker effort when Gunny Bates promised to keep the pace slow and steady. No racing up the hill in platoon competition, no showboating among the PT studs. Slow and steady, build the legs and lungs. They had two heat casualties already, and it looked like they'd have a few more.

Weapons Platoon, marching in the middle of the serpentine formation, was climbing with a full load of machineguns, 3.5-inch rocket launchers, and 60mm mortars. They were having a particularly hard time, so Gerdine and Gunny Bates fell back from the point to provide some personal motivation. The Staff Sergeant who was senior man in the platoon was doing the best he could, but Weapons Platoon needed an officer, and second lieutenants were in critically short supply. Able Company had picked up a good number of stragglers and a sprinkling of replacements, but they were still critically short of commissioned officers. Weapons and 2nd Platoon were being run by senior sergeants of only middling capabilities.

As the unit climbed, its commander was stressing about what would happen when they got to Korea and started to take casualties. He needed about 30 more enlisted men, a couple of good lieutenants, and more Navy Corpsmen. Trained Corpsmen would be crucial when the shooting started. And they often didn't last long in combat as Gerdine learned in the South Pacific campaigns.

He rated four Corpsmen in Able Company and planned to steal a few more if he could find them before they shipped out. The two that Gerdine had on hand were good men, but they were rapidly becoming overwhelmed with routine sick calls, plus treating sprains, strains, bumps, and bruises as training intensified in units designated to deploy with the provisional brigade. Colonel Murray was promising more manpower soonest, but that didn't keep Gerdine or the other 5th Marines company commanders from fretting over empty billets.

Gerdine was about to call for a five-minute break when one of his mortarmen shifted the weapon's unwieldy bipod from one shoulder to another. The move, just at a point where the trail bent hard left, caused him to stagger, twist an ankle, and tumble down the slope. Gerdine made a grab for the man as he rolled by but missed. The captain scrambled down the slope shouting for Gunny Bates just as the mortarman slammed into a boulder that halted his fall. The man was dizzy from the tumble but seemed otherwise uninjured until Gerdine lifted him to his feet.

"Ah, shit! Think I twisted my ankle pretty bad, sir."

Gerdine was pulling at the man's boot laces when Gunny Bates came sliding down the slope. "I called for a Corpsman, sir." The Gunny shouldered Gerdine out of the way and pushed the mortarman man down where he could assess the injury. "But it's gonna be a while. Our Docs are way down slope dealing with them heat casualties."

Gerdine picked up the mortar bipod and started to climb back up to the trail where the rest of his Marines were either crapped out or staring down at the casualty. Gunny Bates waved him on and dug in his pack. "I got an Ace bandage in here somewhere, Skipper. Lemme see if I can get this pecker-head mobile."

Lt. Baldomero Lopez was waiting with weapons platoon when Gerdine rejoined the unit. He'd come forward from his trailing third platoon to see if he could help.

"Gunny's gonna try to wrap his ankle," Gerdine said, sipping from his canteen. "Hopefully it isn't much more than a sprain. We'll know more when the Docs get here."

"I been thinking about that situation, Skipper. We damn sure need a couple more Corpsmen."

"That we do, Baldo. But all I get from Navy Personnel over at the hospital is bullshit excuses and sob stories."

"Yessir. I heard what you said at the staff meeting, so I asked around, you know, talked to our two Corpsmen for a while."

"And?"

"Well, they said there's a guy, a second class, who keeps putting in for duty with a rifle company, but he can't get himself cut loose from the hospital. When I took my platoon over there for shots yesterday, I talked to him. Name's Clinton, and he seemed really anxious to get the hell out of the hospital."

"He know he'd likely be heading for Korea?"

"Said he didn't join the Navy to empty bedpans."

"OK, Baldo. When we get off this hill, you go see Doc Clinton. Maybe we can help cut him loose. He's got a home in Able Company if we can swing it."

Hospital Corpsman 2nd Class Arleigh Clinton sat across from Lt. Lopez in the Naval Hospital cafeteria sipping coffee. He was listening to a pitch about joining up with Able Company, 5th Marines, who were critically short of Corpsmen and scheduled to deploy in a couple of weeks. So far, Clinton liked what he was hearing. As a drop-out from Tulane University, more for lack of motivation than any trouble with the pre-med curriculum, he'd joined the Navy after reading an article written by a US Navy Pharmacists Mate who had served with Marines during WWII. The author essentially wound up running his own little medical practice treating patients who loved him and respected him as their personal physician. Clinton liked that a lot. A Navy trained medic was bound to gain a ton of real-world experience in medical matters. So he committed for four years which guaranteed him a six-month training course for Hospital Corpsmen. If he liked the work, he could always get out at the end of his enlistment, complete med school and become a licensed physician.

Clinton's plan looked good until he found himself assigned to the Naval Hospital at Camp Pendleton. Here he was a glorified orderly, rarely getting close to patients, doing piddly work for an asshole of a Chief Petty Officer who ran the enlisted staff like a tyrant.

"I don't know, Lieutenant," Clinton said checking the nearby passageway to be sure his nemesis was nowhere in sight. "My Chief is one hard-nosed sonofabitch. I put in for a transfer to the FMF three times already. He said if he saw one more transfer chit from me, he'd run me up with colors as a malcontent."

"You come to Able Company, Doc, and we'll treat you right. And you'd be senior man. Our other two pecker-checkers are both junior to you."

"Yeah, but the Chief's gotta approve it—and I know he won't."

"We really need you, Doc. Anything I can do to help, just say the word."

"Listen, Lieutenant. Suppose I got shit-canned somehow, you know, tossed out of here on my ass. You think maybe you could rescue me?"

"You're not gonna kill anybody are you, Doc?"

"Nothing like that, sir. But I'd want to think somebody will go to bat for me if I get my ass in a crack in an effort to get the fuck out of this place."

"Like I said, Doc. I'll do anything I can and our Skipper will, too."

Clinton finished his coffee and stood. "Let me work on it, Lieutenant Lopez. Keep an eye out for me over the next couple of days."

Arleigh Clinton walked back to the ward where he was on duty and decided to do it. He'd been dreaming about doing it for weeks. Now damn sure looked like the time. On a trolley just outside the door to his ward, he found a couple of bedpans and lifted the towels covering them. Just what he needed, a couple of juicy turds swimming in urine. Clinton picked up the pans and headed for the sanitary washroom. That would lead him right by the Chief's station where that asshole spent his watch smoking cigarettes and staring at the hospital corridors like a traffic cop.

Clinton stopped outside the Chief's window and lifted the bedpans into sight. "Hey, Chief! Soon as I empty these, I'm gonna put in another transfer chit. Be sure and look for it."

As he expected, the Chief mashed out a smoke, stood and stormed into the corridor. He jabbed at Clinton's chest with a nicotine-stained finger and growled. "Clinton, I told you about that kind of shit, didn't I? I see one more chit with your name on it, and your ass is grass. You'll be a fuckin' seaman deuce before you know what happened to you."

Hospital Corpsman 2nd Class Arleigh Clinton just grinned. And then he dumped the reeking contents of both bedpans down the front of the Chief's pristine white uniform.

Second Lieutenant Paul Ruggles studied himself in the full-length mirror on the back of the door to his BOQ room. His dress uniform still fit nicely and he looked the part of a Marine officer, down to the fresh crew-cut he'd gotten at the base barber shop shortly after checking in at Camp Pendleton. His outward appearance was OK, but Ruggles worried about what was beneath the green cloth. He wasn't too far out of physical shape, and he could improve that when he reached his unit. What worried him was his mind, his heart, what was in his gut now that he was getting a first real shot at leading Marines. Quantico was a long time ago. Things had probably changed, especially in an outfit alerted for combat duty in Korea. Paul Ruggles adjusted the knot in his tie, remembering with a grin that it was called a field-scarf in the Marine Corps...for some unknown reason.

There was a knock on his door, and Paul opened it to see another lieutenant standing in the passageway consulting a clipboard. The guy was blocky, tough looking in his dusty utility uniform bearing gold bars on the collar.

"Your name Ruggles, Paul E.?"

"That's me, Lieutenant, fresh off the bus. What can I do for you?"

The officer stepped inside Ruggles' room and extended a hand. "Name's Lopez. I got the third platoon of Able Company. CO sent me over here to police you up. Ready to go?"

"Gimme a sec," Ruggles said and walked toward the desk where he'd stashed a brand-new briefcase containing his paperwork and some field manuals he'd been studying. "My orders are in here." He shut the lid of the briefcase and reached for his pisscutter.

"Better lose the briefcase, Ruggles." Lt. Lopez put hands on hips and eyed the replacement officer like he was conducting a critical inspection. "All you'll need is a copy of your orders and your OQR." Lopez made a flicking motion with his hand. "And you better broom the dress canvas. Just put on a set of dungarees."

"Oh, Jeez...sorry." Ruggles started pulling at his carefully knotted tie and shrugging out of his dress uniform blouse. "I thought for reporting to the CO, you know..."

"Captain Gerdine's a mustang. He won't be impressed. You're better off if you show up in a field uniform ready to roll. We're not much on the pomp and circumstance these days."

"Yeah, short fuse for the Korea thing, I guess." Ruggles hung up his greens and rummaged around in his Valpak for boots and a utility uniform.

"Short fuse doesn't half describe what we're going through, man. We're up to our asses in unit strength and supply problems with only a couple of weeks until we're due to report for embarkation. Skipper is really cracking the whip."

"Well, I'll sure give it all I've got." Ruggles stood to adjust his web belt and reached for a cover. He grabbed his orders and Officer's Qualification Record and looked around to see if he was forgetting anything.

Lopez opened the door but paused. "Let me give you the skinny," he said, "one lieutenant to another. I don't know where the Skipper's gonna stick you for duty, but it's probably one of our platoons...probably weapons or second platoon. Whatever, you're gonna inherit a command that's like as not manning up with raw recruits, malcontents, shanghaied clerks, and a few brig-rats we managed to get released. As we used to say at Annapolis, Lieutenant Ruggles, you are faced with a leadership problem."

Gunny Bates stood next to First Sergeant Hammond at the 5th Marines assembly point going over rosters along with senior NCOs from other rifle companies in the regiment's first battalion. They were all waiting for a big shipment of replacements to arrive from Camp Pendleton's mainside reception area. Colonel Murray had delivered on his promise to fill regimental vacancies. A convoy of trucks and cattle-cars was due any moment and all the NCOs were speculating about the quantity and quality of the men they were about to receive.

"Let's hope to hell we get a bunch of reservists," Hammond said offering Bates a smoke from his crumpled pack. "At least we won't have to start from square one with them."

"We'll take anything that's upright and breathing," Gunny Bates said pointing at his well-worn boondockers. I got my ass-kicking boots on."

"Skipper seemed OK with the new lieutenants for second platoon and weapons." Hammond sucked on his smoke as Gunny Bates flicked his Zippo under it. "Ruggles and Boyle, one reserve shavetail and the other one fresh out of Quantico."

"Yeah, they're both gonna need to snap in most ricky-tick." Bates pointed at the dust cloud on the horizon where the replacement draft was approaching. "And both them platoons need solid senior NCOs—which we ain't got."

"Maybe we'll get lucky with this draft." Hammond led the way toward the convoy pulling into the parking lot. Each vehicle bore a placard designating the passengers for assignment to one of the 5th Marines subordinate units. To keep infighting and headhunting within reasonable limits, the Division Personnel (G-1) section had done the shuffling before the replacements were released to their new commands.

"That's us," Gunny Bates said pointing at a cattle car marked with a big A. It looked to contain at least 30 Marines staring anxiously at the senior NCOs approaching. "I'll fall 'em in and you check 'em off the roster."

As the dust began to settle, Marines in utility uniforms, struggling with bulging sea bags, began climbing out of the vehicle, stretching and yawning. Gunny Bates approached barking.

"All you people going to Able Company, fall in and let's get this belch organized. NCOs over here on my right, non-rates on my left."

The Able Company replacements began to swirl around in obvious confusion. And then one of the new men began to bark nearly as loud as Gunny Bates.

"You heard the Gunny, people! It ain't that hard." A tall black Marine hopped down from the cattle car and began to shove at the new men. "If you're an NCO...over here. If you're not...over there!"

Gunny Bates watched the group shuffle into two clumps and then approached the man who was barking orders. Two stripes stenciled on his uniform sleeves and herringbone utilities, topped by a sun-bleached cover bearing the eagle, globe, and anchor, and worn salty, low over his eyebrows. This guy had been around a day or two. Bates stepped closer to the tall, black Marine and eyed him up and down. He wasn't expecting anything like this, not in a rifle company.

"What's your status, Sunshine?"

"Name ain't Sunshine, Gunny. It's Trenton...Corporal Trenton. I got orders to Able Company, 5th Marines."

Hammond approached with the roster. "He's for us, Gunny. Name's here. Trenton, Heywood, Corporal, transfer from 2nd MarDiv."

"That you?" Bates never took his eyes off the new man.

"That's me, Gunny. Service Number 552381."

"Uh huh. You got any time in a rifle company, Trenton? Or is this your first dance with us white folks?"

"I been in rifle outfits since 1948, Gunny. Last cruise was with 6th Marines at Camp Lejeune."

Bates took a step back and craned his head as if he'd heard something unbelievable. "You served with Litz the Blitz?"

"His signature is on my orders."

Something caught Bates' eye. A kid in civilian clothes was just climbing off the cattle car. "OK, Trenton. Get over there with them others. We'll talk some more at the Company area."

Bates stormed over to the teenager who was wearing a sweat-stained white shirt and rumpled slacks. The young guy clutched a cheap cardboard suitcase in one hand and was wiping his face with the other.

"And what the fuck is your story, sad sack? You miss the school bus?"

Private Miles Abramson smiled and shrugged. "I don't know what to do, sir."

"Well, the first fuckin' thing you're gonna do is stop calling me *sir*. I'm a Gunnery Sergeant and I work for a living. What's your name, sweetheart?"

"Miles Abramson...sir...uh, sergeant. From Kansas City."

"And what is it you're doing here, Miles Abramson from Kansas City?"

"They told me to get on the bus. I'm sorry. I never went to boot camp."

Bates just stared open-mouthed for a few seconds and then motioned for the First Sergeant. "Top, come over here. You ain't gonna believe this."

"He's on the roster, Gunny." The First Sergeant showed Bates the clipboard and pointed at a name. "Reservist out of 24th Marines, Kansas City."

"I do not believe this shit." Bates poked Abramson in the chest. "Where the fuck is your uniform, shit-heel?"

"They never gave me one."

"Never got a uniform issue, First Sergeant." Trenton shouted from the ranks. He'd questioned the kid in civilian clothes on the trip from mainside. "All he's got is what he's wearing."

Bates just blinked, nodded, and turned to the First Sergeant. "Now this here is a first for me. What the fuck are we gonna do with this little fartknocker?"

"Bring him along, Gunny. We'll get it straightened out back in the area. Somebody will get wind of the fuck up and send him down to MCRD. Meantime, one of our guys can take him over to Quartermaster stores and draw him some boots and utilities."

First Sergeant Hammond finished checking the replacement roster and stood watching as Gunny Bates shoved them and their sea bags into a pair of six-by trucks for the trip to Able Company's area. An NCO approached with his orders in hand.

"First Sergeant...I'm Sergeant Petrosky, reservist out of Pittsburgh. I think there's been some kind of foul-up with my orders..."

Combat Zone
Near Pusan

TWO JEEPS BEARING HEAVY machineguns in pintle mounts and followed by a halftrack carrying a Wolfhound recon element roared into a clearing and braked to a halt in a swirl of dust. Two officers leaped out of the lead vehicle, grabbed a large canvas-covered map board out of the backseat, and trudged toward a battle-damaged cement structure. Parked near a crude sign identifying the Command Post of the 27th Infantry was another Jeep, this one marked with a placard featuring three white stars on a blue field. The man those stars represented was waiting inside the CP for a report from the ever-shifting battle lines. The recon officers had a lot of news for Lieutenant General Walton Walker, and none of it was good.

Walker, a bulldog of a man with square jaw and barrel chest, was puffing on a cigar at the back of the Command Post and conferring with another general, a two-star who commanded the Army division that was now on the point of the 8th Army's blunted spear.

"Let's get to it, gents." Walker nodded to a section of the CP that was closed off from squawking radios and the anxious hubbub of the division staff. He led the party into seclusion, stoked his cigar, and waited for the map to be mounted and uncovered. "First thing I need to know is the status of the Twenty Fourth."

"Not good, sir." A lieutenant colonel from the 8th Army staff who had accompanied the recon mission shook his head. "They're...well, shattered is probably the best way to describe it. We ran into little clumps of them, all retreating, all headed south. I'd have to rate them combat ineffective at this point."

"Piss poor, piss poor," Walker muttered under his breath and walked over to examine the map brought in by the recon element. The light colonel joined him and began jabbing a grimy finger at various locations.

"We went all the way up to Taejon, General. So far we've identified the North Korean 2nd Division as the unit that pushed Wolfhound elements out of that area. Their 3rd Division kicked hell out of the 5th and 8th Cav at Yongdong. Cav elements are regrouping and falling back toward the Naktong River. Just about everybody else along the MLR is under intense pressure. We believe the North Korean 3rd Division is currently holding fairly firm along this line northwest of the Kum River. We're trying to call as much air on them as possible while they're sitting still."

"That won't last..." General Walker dropped his cigar butt and reached in his pocket for a replacement. "What about their strength north of our Main Line of Resistance?"

"I've got something on that, General." The officer commanding the division dug into a folder. "My G-2 says as of 2100 hours last night, we've identified seven North Korean Divisions in the fight north of the Naktong. We estimate about 150 tanks involved in that, all of them T-34/85s. And all their maneuver elements are supported by organic artillery and heavy mortars...about 200 tubes, 75 millimeter and up."

General Walker sighed and struck a match to his fresh cigar. "And that doesn't count all the arty and ammo they've captured from us. Goddammit, we've got to stop this retreating! We're gonna find a place to stand and fight." He traced his cigar along the line of the Naktong River. "We need to muster and regroup, hold for reinforcements. I'm thinking right here at the Naktong."

"Yessir," The Operations Officer tapped a spot on the map near the west coast of the Korean peninsula. "Our most pressing problem in the meantime is right here at Chinju. Their 6th Division is pressing hard in that area. If they take Chinju, they'll be in position to turn our flank and have a straight shot into Pusan."

"We can't risk that seaport, gents." General Walker began to pace and growl. "No matter what happens we keep the port of Pusan open and in friendly hands. I talked to General MacArthur in Tokyo this morning and he's aware of our problems. Elements of the 2nd Infantry Division and a brigade of Marines are due to arrive shortly. We'll fight a holding action at the Naktong and establish a perimeter around Pusan. When we're in shape to do so, we counterattack."

Walker waved his cigar and then pointed it at the senior officers. "I want some fire in the bellies around here, gents. No more ass-kicking contests where we wind up on the losing side."

AS ABLE COMPANY'S third platoon Marines alternated between prone and kneeling positions on the firing line, Gunny Bates and Lt. Lopez observed from the line shack. Targets bobbed up and down from the butts 300 yards from the shooters. It was all M-1s at the range today. Captain Gerdine wanted every man to qualify or requalify with the M-1, no matter if his assigned weapon was a carbine, BAR, or one of the WWII vintage Thompson submachinegun now being pulled from storage for use in Korea.

"Maggie's Drawers!" Gunny Bates spat on the deck and raised his eye from the spotting scope he was using to monitor the shooters. "Mister Lopez," he said with a sigh, "you got some dingers, but that shitbird on target three can't hit a bull in the ass with a bass-fiddle."

"That's Abramson, Gunny, the kid that never went to boot camp. He just learned how to load an M-1. I got a couple of squad leaders working to get him snapped in."

Another red flag waved tauntingly before target number three and Bates stood up from his scope. "If they don't pull him out and send him to MCRD before we ship out, maybe we ought to have him shuffled around—maybe weapons platoon."

"Leave it with me, Gunny." Lopez slid in behind the spotter scope. "We'll get him up to speed."

Bates nodded and left the line shack. Bunched around a folding desk at the rear of the firing line near the rifle cleaning benches, Captain Gerdine and First Sergeant Hammond were poring over the company's organizational chart, and the Gunny wanted to be sure he had some say in assignments for the new men. He had some strong opinions about that. As a Company Gunnery Sergeant he would be responsible for all Able Company men in the field, and he wanted his say about who went where.

"Jackson?" The First Sergeant checked one of the new men on his replacement roster.

"The black kid? PFC. High school grad. Rifle expert. Fairly good pro and cons." Captain Gerdine checked his notes. "He goes to second platoon."

"You made a decision about machineguns yet, Skipper?" Bates hitched himself up onto one of the cleaning benches. "You know Lt. Boyle is straight outa charm school at Quantico. He's gonna need help with them cranky guns."

"Who are you thinking? Petrosky?"

"Yessir. He's a staff NCO. Machinegun experience in the last fracas. Guy I know was with him on Okinawa. Said he's really good with the thirty calibers."

"He's also constantly pissing and moaning about how he never should have been activated." First Sergeant Hammond added. "Wants to go home to the wife and kiddies pretty bad."

"He ain't the only one." Captain Gerdine made a note on the chart. "Petrosky goes to weapons. He'll be Lt. Boyle's new machinegun section leader."

"Sixty mortars are solid," Bates said. "But Weapons Platoon needs a good NCO in rockets. We been hearing the North Koreans got 'em a shit-pot full of T-34's over there."

"I'll get right on that, Gunny." Gerdine opened his pocket-knife and began to sharpen the stub of a pencil he was using. "Just as soon as I can pull one out of my ass." He pointed at the First Sergeant. "Top, see if we can get some time on the 3.5-inch rocket range. You and the Gunny can watch 'em shoot and see if there's anybody might be good enough for a section leader."

"Will do, sir." Hammond eyed the rifle platoon rosters and shook his head. "What's got me worried is second platoon. Mr. Ruggles is a retread Second John, no field experience. He's gonna need a strong hand with that herd."

"I'm thinking Trenton for platoon sergeant, Skipper." Gunny Bates retied the laces on his ancient boondockers. "He comes highly recommended."

"He's only a corporal...and a black one at that." Hammond lit a cigarette and squinted into the sunlight. "I don't know. Second platoon has got more than its share of shitbirds."

"I know Litz the Blitz from the old 4th MarDiv on Kwajalein, Top. If he says Trenton can hack it, that's good enough for me. Gotta be some way we can get him another stripe."

"Might work," Captain Gerdine said making a note on the second platoon chart. "Battalion Commanders got the colonel's authority to make some spot promotions. I'll talk to Trenton tonight and think it over."

Lt. Baldomero Lopez scrawled his name and rank on the release form and slid it back to the sergeant who was serving as duty turnkey in the Camp Pendleton brig. The Sergeant scrutinized the paperwork for a moment and then slid it into a desk drawer.

"He's all yours now, Lieutenant. We'll have him out here in just a sec." The Sergeant picked up a phone and ordered the prisoner brought to the reception area. Lopez could hear cell doors clanging somewhere in the dark distance behind the turnkey's desk as the NCO hung up the phone.

"Should warn you, Lieutenant. You're probably gonna be hearing from one pissed off Chief Petty Officer."

"Way I hear it," Lopez said as he watched a man being escorted out of the shadows by another Marine NCO. "The Chief was pissed on rather than pissed off."

The Brig Sergeant was still chuckling when a buzzer sounded. The barrier door leading from the cellblock swung open and the guard nudged Hospital Corpsman 2nd Class Arleigh Clinton out of confinement. Clinton stood still for a second, blinking in the glow of fluorescent light fixtures, and then nodded at Lopez.

"This mean I'm a free man, Lieutenant?" Clinton was dressed in Navy dungarees and holding onto a bulging laundry bag stenciled with his name and service number.

"In a loose manner of speaking it does, Doc. You're now our new senior Corpsman, but we need to play this really low-key. I've got a Jeep and driver outside. Corporal Thornton is gonna take you and a new man over to draw some uniforms and gear at Quartermaster stores. Then they'll take you back to the company. From that point on, you stay way the hell away from mainside."

"I'm OK with whatever you need me to do, sir. I appreciate the effort to get me sprung from here."

"Thank Captain Gerdine. He made a deal with the personnel officer over at the hospital. But the Chief is still on the warpath. We're gonna have to keep you hidden for a bit. At least until the ship sails."

Corporal Bayliss Thornton, at the wheel of the Jeep, nodded at the Corpsman and jerked a thumb toward the back seat where Pvt. Miles Abramson sat smiling and dressed in a set of Marine utilities draped on his body like an over-large potato sack. Abramson shifted over a bit on the backseat bench and helped Doc Clinton with his laundry bag. Lopez had a few other errands to run while he was mainside, so he just dumped his knapsack on the vacant front seat.

"Thornton, you take these two over to QM stores. Field gear and a uniform that fits Abramson. Utes and boots for our new Doc plus a full 782 gear issue. Then swing by the mainside PX. I'll be waiting for you there. And steer well clear of the Base Hospital on the way."

"Aye, aye, sir. See you then."

Thornton had to brake the Jeep at an intersection where a pair of road guards stopped traffic to let a long line of marching Marines pass. He listened to the platoon sergeant's throaty cadence call for a while and then turned to extend a hand toward Clinton.

"Heard you was the new Doc," he said. "Mah name's Thornton, Bayliss Thornton, Corporal-type, one each. From Kentucky. How 'bout you?"

Clinton took the hand and smiled. "Arleigh Clinton, H-M-Two. Most recently from the brig."

Thornton hooted and shook his head. "Ain't nothin' wrong with that. Thought I might wind up there a couple of times myself. Where you from before all this?"

"Louisiana," Clinton said. "Coon ass born and bred."

"Well, awright! I was afraid you was gonna turn out to be a damn Yankee..." Thornton jerked his head at Abramson as he jammed the Jeep into gear and made a right turn. "Like ole baby brother here."

Abramson stuck out a hand and introduced himself. "Private Abramson. From Kansas City. I haven't been to boot camp yet."

"What the hell are you doing here then?" Doc Clinton shook the younger man's hand and looked him over more carefully. Someone had peeled all the hair from the kid's scalp. Not very professionally. Clinton could see a number of nicks and scabs above the man's ears despite the over-large utility uniform cap that was jammed on his head. And the rest of Abramson's uniform looked like ill-fitting hand-me-downs which, in fact, they were.

"Well, they sent all the guys from my reserve unit out here to join up with units that didn't have enough Marines. I just sort of went along. Nobody told me not to."

"They're lookin' to get him a spot down to San Diego," Thornton added as they pulled into a parking space outside the Quartermaster Stores building. "But I been tellin' him not to hold his breath on that there. I been in the Crotch long enough to know once they got you, they ain't likely to let you go."

"Seems funny they'd send a guy who hadn't even been through boot camp to Korea." Clinton tucked his laundry bag under the seat and followed the two Marines toward the QM warehouse.

"I'd rather go with the company," Abramson said. "They been taking pretty good care of me, you know, teaching me what I need to know...."

"What you need to know, Abramson, is that this here is the Marine Corps." Thornton swung open the door to a big room fronted by a long counter and motioned for them to enter. "And in the Marine Corps it's mind over matter. They don't mind and you don't matter."

Cackling at his joke, Thornton led his charges up to the counter where he shook hands with another corporal that he seemed to know pretty well. "They was supposed to call about these two," he said to the supply man. "We're from Able Company, 5th Marines."

The supply NCO reached beneath the counter and came up with two clipboards. Attached to each was a Navy/Marine Corps Form 782, that outlined the field gear each individual Marine rated. "Master Sergeant got the call this morning," the supply man said. "One Corpsman for full 782 gear issue plus utility uniforms." He shoved one of the clipboard's at Clinton. "And one boot-ass private who needs the same plus some utilities that don't make him look like a walking shit-blivet."

"That's the deal," Thornton confirmed. "How 'bout you take Abramson back there and get him some dungarees that fit? I'll give Doc Clinton a hand drawing his Seven-Eighty-Deuce. Then we'll just switch around."

With Thornton's help and advice, HM2 Clinton drew all his necessary field gear: Steel helmet, webbing, leggings, and a host of other things the Navy man didn't really recognize or understand, plus two canvas saddlebags that he'd use to carry his medical supplies. He had it all stuffed into a waterproof bag when Abramson emerged from the uniform issue area looking decidedly less like a refugee and more like a Marine.

"Your turn, Doc." The supply corporal waved at Clinton. "C'mon back here and try on some boondockers."

Thornton led Abramson into the aisles where field equipment was stored. A bored clerk began to pick items out of the bins and toss them into a bag. Pointing at the clipboard he was holding, Thornton whispered. "You take a look at this here. Be sure what it says on the paper matches what this guy is tossin' in yer bag."

"Looks like it's OK," Abramson said scanning the form on the clipboard. "Some of this stuff, I don't..."

Thornton jabbed an elbow into the younger man's ribs. "Just read out anything you don't understand." Abramson looked at the corporal. He was beginning to see the problem.

"Don't make no big thing out of it, Abramson. I don't read so good that's all."

Abramson took the clipboard and started to review the gear that was thudding into his issue bag. He was pretty sure he understood most of what he was reading and managed to match the majority with what he was seeing the clerk handle. He thought it funny the way items were listed. Pegs, tent, three. Belt, ammunition M-1, unit of issue, one each. Mask, Field Protective, M-9A1 w/carrier, and a lot more. You just had to spot the key word and ignore the backwards syntax. Abramson kind of liked reading the terms in that stilted fashion. Made him feel almost like a real Marine.

"That's it, Corporal." The clerk said pointing at the clipboard. "Needs an NCO's signature to verify he got what he rates. Sign on the bottom and we're done here."

Abramson glanced at Thornton and whispered. "Should I sign it?"

Thornton snatched the clipboard and caught the pen attached to it by a beaded chain. "You ain't no fuckin' NCO, Abramson. And I guess I can manage to sign my name."

When they were back at the Jeep with Clinton stowing the newly issued gear, Thornton grabbed Abramson by an elbow. "Don't say nothin' about this to nobody back at the company. We ain't got what I signed for, Boot, I'm gonna kick yer ass."

It was just after evening chow on a third hectic day of processing and admin work when 2nd Lieutenant Paul Ruggles finally discovered that he was the new leader of Able Company's second platoon. He was anxious to visit the Quonset hut that housed his new command, but the Company Gunny advised him to wait and meet his platoon sergeant first.

Ruggles stood watching a long convoy of trucks rushing by the company area. He knew where they were headed: the Navy docks at San Diego where ships were being loaded for the trip across the Pacific. The vehicles were full of gear, ammunition, and other vital items that would accompany the 1st Provisional Marine Brigade to Korea. In the briefing for Ruggles and 2nd Lt. Arthur Boyle, the other new officer who would take over Weapons Platoon, Captain Gerdine indicated their exact deployment date was still undetermined, but he thought it couldn't be more than a week or ten days from now. That left the new officers little time to get oriented and meet their men, but Captain Gerdine didn't seem like the sort of commander who wanted a lot of conversation on the topic.

A tall lanky Marine bearing three stenciled chevrons on his utility uniform approached and saluted smartly.

"Lieutenant Ruggles?"

"That's me..." Ruggles returned the salute and tried not to show surprise that he was being addressed by a black man. He knew that the American armed forces had been ordered to integrate the ranks, but so far he'd seen only a few black Marines at Camp Pendleton.

"Sergeant Trenton, sir. I'm your new Platoon Sergeant."

Ruggles shook hands with the man. Iron grip but not a strength test. Trenton had dark eyes, a skeptical squint, and a chiseled jawline. Everything about the man told Ruggles he was addressing a seasoned pro. Ruggles squirmed a bit and shuffled his boots in the dirt, not sure how to proceed. He felt like he was a recruit back at Quantico being scrutinized by one of the salty Sergeant Instructors.

Trenton smiled and fell into a loose Parade Rest with his feet spread and hands clasped at the small of his back. "You look a little puzzled, Lieutenant. Anything wrong?"

"No, no..." Ruggles shrugged. "I'm really glad to meet you."

"Lieutenant, is it gonna bother you that you've got a black man as your platoon sergeant?"

"Absolutely not, Sergeant Trenton." Ruggles tried hard not to sound like he was being obsequious or apologetic. "I just didn't get briefed..."

"Neither did I, Lieutenant, but I figured my new Platoon Commander would be a white guy." Trenton smiled and winked.

Ruggles laughed as the tension between them faded. "Tell me a little about yourself, Sergeant Trenton."

"Well, sir...this third stripe is brand new and temporary. I came over here from Camp Lejeune as a corporal, squad leader in 6th Marines. Enlisted after high school in Little Rock. Been in the Corps since '44. Overseas time with a Shore Party Battalion. Got into the regular infantry when they ordered integration in '48. Guess you could say I'm a Lifer. No wife and no kids, at least none that I know about. Figured I better make my bones with a line outfit in Korea. That's about it. How about you, sir?"

"Not much to tell. From Klamath Falls originally. University of Washington, degree in Forestry. I'm a retread. I only did about a year active duty after OCS and that was right at the end of the war, so no combat experience. I took an early-out and been working in a sawmill up in Salem, Oregon until I got the recall. No wife, no kids either."

"We're gonna get along just fine, Mister Ruggles."

"I hope so. I've been worried about the Marines, you know. Word's gonna get around pretty quick that I'm a relative boot to all this."

"Mister Ruggles, you're a platoon commander in a rifle outfit now. There ain't no need for our Marines to know anything about you except that you're the boss, and that's that."

"And they're gonna snap and pop just because I'm the one wearing the gold bars? That's not exactly how I remember Marines."

"You leave the snap and pop to me, Lieutenant. I'll be right beside you all the way."

Ruggles was feeling much better about his assignment as they walked toward the hut that housed their Marines but that faded quickly when they got closer. It sounded like artillery rounds were exploding inside the hut. There was a riot of shouting and screaming inside, and the corrugated walls occasionally bulged as something slammed into them.

"What the fuck?" Sergeant Trenton sprinted for the door to the hut with Lt. Ruggles hot on his heels. Nobody noticed them enter. All eyes were on a slugfest going on in the aisle between racks. The place was fairly trashed by the exertions of two white Marines who were duking it out with a black Marine at the center of the squad bay. All three were showing damage ranging from bloody noses to rapidly swelling black eyes, but the outnumbered black man seemed to be giving as good as he was getting from his white opponents.

Ruggles was frozen by the spectacle, but Sergeant Trenton leaped into action. He charged into the melee with elbows swinging. "Knock this shit off! Knock it off right now!" He glared around the room and then jumped up onto a footlocker. "All you people stand by your racks, position of attention, mouths shut! Do it!"

At the familiar bark of authority, the second platoon Marines scrambled to stand rigidly at the foot of their double-decker racks. Trenton scrutinized them all with a mean set to his mouth, eyes drilling into each man. "Next one of you clowns says a word or moves a muscle and it's the last thing you ever do!"

Sergeant Trenton took a couple of deep, angry breaths and then jammed his fists onto his hips. "You people call yourselves Marines? Not in my Marine Corps you ain't! This kind of happy horseshit ends today, people...and I mean right fuckin' now. My name is Sergeant Trenton and I'm your new platoon sergeant. I am big. I am black. And I can be your worst nightmare!"

He pointed at the door where Lt. Ruggles stood watching a professional at work hoping his grim expression conveyed the same sort of scorn his platoon sergeant was showing. "Look where I'm pointing." All eyes turned to Ruggles. "That officer right there is Lt. Ruggles and he's our new platoon commander. I am completely fucking embarrassed that he got his first look at you people acting like a gaggle of undisciplined shitbirds. This will be the last time he sees anything like that in this platoon."

Trenton jumped down off the footlocker and stormed toward the door. "You have exactly fifteen minutes to get this area squared away. I want your scuzzy bodies in clean dungarees and standing tall when we get back." He grabbed Ruggles by an elbow to lead him outside, but Ruggles shrugged it off.

"One last thing before we go, Sergeant. Trenton." Ruggles strolled up and down the ranks until he got to one of the white Marines who had been in the fight. He looked the man up and down critically.

"Name?"

"Benson, sir...Robert L. PFC."

Ruggles nodded and walked another pace or two until he was in front of the second white Marine in the fight. He gave the man the same scrutiny.

"And you?"

"Maitland, sir...Lanny J. PFC."

Both men had a distinct down south drawl and Ruggles thought he saw the genesis of the fight. The Corps was shot through with southerners still fighting the Civil War in their minds. He crossed the aisle and confronted the black man in the fracas.

"And who are you?"

"Willis Jackson!" This man was rigid at attention but clearly still furious. Ruggles was about to correct the man's response when Trenton stormed up beside him and did the job.

"Didn't they teach you in boot camp to say sir when you address an officer, Jackson?"

"They taught me..." Jackson was breathing hard through a bleeding nose.

"Well, try it again! And do it right!"

"Jackson, sir...Willis L. PFC."

Ruggles looked around the room and then turned his attention back to Jackson. "Not anymore you're not, Jackson." He turned to point at the two white men across the aisle. "And neither is Benson and Maitland. You'll all three be privates by morning formation. I won't tolerate fighting among members of this platoon. We'll all get plenty of that stuff in Korea. If you men want your rank back, you're gonna earn it." Ruggles headed for the door and nodded for Trenton to precede him. "I'll be back with the Platoon Sergeant in 15 minutes to inspect. Carry on."

Standing in the dark outside the hut, they heard the scrape and thud of furniture being rearranged along with a low roar of very creative profanity. Trenton grinned, and pulled out a pack of cigarettes. Ruggles took one and studied the trembling hand that held his smoke.

"Damn, Sergeant Trenton. I'm shaking like a dog shitting peach-pits."

Trenton laughed and gently punched his officer on the shoulder. "You did just fine, Mister Ruggles. Just fine. Ain't no doubt in anybody's mind who's in charge now."

Third platoon was huffing and puffing in two ranks, one facing the other. They were all armed with M-1 rifles and fixed bayonets in sheaths so they could thrust, jab, and slash without drawing too much blood. Lt. Lopez led his men to the close-quarters combat area right after morning formation, and they'd been trying to kill each other for the past two hours. It had not been going well. For a while it was all a joke, Marines dancing around and gingerly poking at opponents with simulated butt-strokes and sweeping vertical slashes the way they'd been taught in boot camp. Lopez was not happy with that.

"You people better get serious," he shouted as he walked behind the line of sweating Marines. "You won't be laughing and lolly-gagging when some North Korean soldier is trying to kill you. Now...On Guard!" As his men brought their rifles into position, Lopez glanced up at Captain Gerdine who was watching with arms folded across his chest. "Right rank! Advance!"

Marines in the right rank lowered their rifles and charged at the men in the left rank who began to parry and block, maneuvering for space to execute a stab or slash. Rifle stocks and barrels smacked and clanged. Lopez trotted to the far end of the line where Private Abramson was squared off against Corporal Jones, the shanghaied baseball player. Jones was spry and athletic in his defense, but he didn't need to be. Abramson in the attack looked like he was swatting at butterflies.

"Abramson, goddammit! That's a bayonet not a butter knife. You're supposed to try and stick him with it! You two back off and try it again."

Corporal Jones backed off grinning as Private Abramson adjusted the helmet that had slipped down over his eyes, lifted his rifle and charged. Jones parried smoothly and delivered a butts-stroke that sent Abramson's M-1 flying. He was getting set to put in the kill-shot when Abramson suddenly leaped on his back gripping with arms and legs wrapped tightly around Jones' neck and waist. Jones danced and shook, trying gamely to unseat Abramson, but it was no use.

"Goddammit, boot!" Jones swung his rifle over a shoulder and smacked it into Abramson's helmet. "Get offa me!"

"Hold it!" Captain Gerdine trotted onto the field reaching the struggling pair before Lopez could intervene. "Hold on here!"

Other sparring pairs quit their exertions and stared at the strange apparition on the end of their practice line. Most of them chuckled and several laughed out loud. Jones had stopped struggling but Abramson still clung to his back like a leech.

"This guy is hopeless," Corporal Jones panted as Gerdine reached him. "They gotta send him to boot camp before he kills somebody." Abramson was peeking over his shoulder with a wild look in his eyes.

"He's gotta learn...one way or another." Gerdine tapped Abramson on the helmet. "You can let go now." Abramson released his grip and dropped to the ground. He looked at his Company Commander and pointed at the rifle laying on the ground nearby.

"I lost my rifle, sir. I didn't want him to stick me, so I just jumped on his back where he couldn't..."

Gerdine waved off the rest of it. "The key is never losing your weapon, Abramson. Either that or disarm your opponent like Jones did to you." The Captain saw the flush in his young Marine's face. The kid was more embarrassed than he needed to be, and Gerdine decided to build his confidence a bit. "Go get your rifle, Abramson."

With no weapon in his hands, Gerdine coiled into a crouch and faced off with Abramson. "Now suppose the guy you're trying to kill is like you were with no weapon in hand. Easy picking, right?" The third platoon Marines had ambled over to watch the demonstration, and Gerdine thought it might be time for an extracurricular lesson. "So here's this North Korean soldier." He jabbed a thumb into his chest. "And he's got no weapon. You've got that bayonet on your rifle. You got all the advantage. What do you do?"

"I guess I'd just shoot him." Abramson shouldered his rifle as the rest of third platoon laughed and hooted. Gerdine nodded and raised his voice.

"Outstanding, Abramson! That's exactly right! Good thinking. If you have ammo, that's exactly what you should do. But suppose you don't have any ammo? What then?"

Abramson looked warily at the sheathed bayonet on his rifle. "Then I got to stick him with my bayonet?"

"That's what this is all about, Abramson. But you want to be careful." Gerdine spun on Corporal Jones. "Jones! On guard! Attack!"

Jones looked around at the crowd, shrugged, brought his rifle up to a high-port position and charged with the bayonet aimed straight at Gerdine's chest. Gerdine met the charge, side-stepped and batted the rifle away. Jones went stumbling off balance, trying to recover from the unexpected move. Gerdine's hand flashed to his cartridge belt and came up with a Kabar fighting knife. Before Jones could spin around for another charge, the Company Commander had him captured with an arm around his neck and the fighting knife hovering just below an ear.

"The bayonet extends your reach. Take advantage of it. When you charge too hard, you're out of control. You can be caught off balance." Gerdine raised his voice and addressed the other Marines. "He'll use your momentum against you like I just did with Corporal Jones here. You've got to be aggressive but always in control." He released Jones and flipped his knife, catching it by the handle and holding it up for the other Marines to see.

"And you should always have a second blade handy."

That brought a rumble of appreciative laughter. Gerdine grabbed Corporal Jones' shoulder and spoke in a low voice. "Jonesy, I don't think we're gonna be able to get Abramson to boot camp before we go. He's gotta learn and I'm relying on you to teach him."

Lopez got his men back in formation and had them run the drill again with one rank unarmed. Gerdine patted him on the back.

"They'll get it, Baldo. Just keep at it."

"That was pretty slick, Skipper."

"Something I picked up in the last go-round. Japs were big on the bayonet."

"Well, I appreciate the gouge. You gonna stick around and see how we do?"

"Like to, but I can't, Baldo. Top and the Gunny are out at the three-point-five range trying to find us a rocket section leader. I want to take a look at that."

"Yessir. Any word on how soon we go?"

"Nothing definite but between you and me, I'm looking at the end of the week latest. Colonel Murray says the transport ships are in and already being loaded. Won't be long."

Gunny Bates raised his binoculars and watched an anti-tank rocket bounce on the ground short of a beat-up old tank hulk, one of several dotted around the 3.5 Rocket Launcher range to serve as targets. The six men in Weapons Platoon's Rocket Section were undergoing familiarization firing. One man served as gunner, the other loaded the weapon, and then they switched off while Bates and Lt. Boyle who was supervising on the firing line tried to decide who was the most skilled.

"Miss...short fifty." Bates waved at Boyle, held up five fingers and jerked a thumb over his shoulder. "They gotta get better than this," he said to Chief Warrant Officer Trowbridge who ran the range. "Sure as shit we're gonna run into tanks over there."

"T-34s is what I read," Gunner Trowbridge nodded. "And you know they ain't gonna be as easy to kill as them Jap shitboxes we run into last time."

"You goin' on this one, Gunner?"

"Wouldn't miss it for the world. Served with Chesty in the last one. He's saving a slot for me in 1st Marines."

An Able Company gunner sent a round downrange with a bang and the firing line was obscured by a cloud of dust and propellant gas expelled at the rear of the launcher. This one struck armor with a resounding clang. "Better," Bates said. He turned the field glasses on the crew, identified the gunner and made a note. Another rocket team fired but the round dug into the rocky ground just short of the target. "Shit!"

"Aiming point's off," Gunner Trowbridge said. "They got to hold a tad high at this range."

"Yeah," Bates nodded. "And a case of the yips too. Hard for some of them to believe a fucking thing that big don't have any kick, you know? They put too much shoulder into it, anticipating recoil."

"And there ain't none. Takes practice time to get really good with these new tubes."

"We ain't got much time, Gunner. I'm hearing we roll out of this pea-patch end of the week."

"Uh huh...and you've just about run me out of practice rounds, Elmore. I got other outfits want ammo and range time."

"We could maybe get in some practice time at sea," Bates said. "But I need a damn good rocket gunner to teach. None of these yahoos has put more than a round or two through the tubes."

"There was a kid out here a month ago," the Gunner said. "Young corporal. He was a fuckin' crackerjack. Had one of them eyes, you know? Never off more than a couple of yards estimating range, and the sonofabitch never missed. I seen him put three rockets into alternating targets out to three hundred."

"That's the kind of man I need. Remember his name?"

"Marcus was his name. But it won't do you no good to go chasin' after him."

"Why not?"

"Cause he's a fuckin' good piano player is why, Elmore. Base Commander found out the kid was a hot musician and cut him orders to play lounge lizard at the O Club. Primary duty. He's in there every night. Big attraction for the brass and their broads. Even Chesty fuckin' Puller couldn't get him sprung. The Club Manager is under orders to guard him like the family jewels."

When Captain Gerdine arrived at the range, Bates rushed up, tossed a salute and handed him the binoculars. "Sir, I really need to borrow the Jeep."

JOHNNY BASKET'S BAR on North 22nd Street was doing slow business on a steamy summer afternoon. It was an hour or so before the crowd from the nearby Krey Meat Packing plant that made up the bulk of the bar's weekday clientele showed up. Johnny Basket used the idle time to brush up the joint before the rush. He was an admirer of horseflesh and had framed pictures of famous thoroughbreds like Whirlaway, Citation and Man O' War displayed behind the bar where they got clouded by fly-shit and nicotine stains. He was wiping them down and half-listening to a conversation behind him.

Mike Jones and Carl Steiner, both mid-shift workers at the small arms plant over on Goodfellow, were at it as usual, dissecting the news with a copy of today's *Globe Democrat* open between them. While bar talk among the usual crowd ran to sports, mostly what was happening with the Cardinals or the Browns, Jones and Steiner focused on international events, especially what was happening in Korea. Both were WWII veterans and fairly cynical about their wartime experiences.

"See here where it says Dugout Doug visited the troops," Steiner jabbed at an article and hit his draft beer. "He says everything is copasetic in Korea. Believe that shit?"

"I never believed MacArthur when I was in the Pacific last war," snorted Jones. "And I think he's full of shit about this one." Jones pointed at another article on the same page. "Look right here. This guy is writing from the battlefield, right? He says our guys are getting the shit kicked out of them. Pushed all the way down to the ass end of the country. Got a perimeter around someplace called Pusan."

Steiner held up two fingers and shoved their glasses across the bar for refills. "Goddamn MacArthur, sitting on his fat ass in Japan. If everything is hunky-dory in Korea, how come they're putting on a swing shift at the plant? How come we're cranking out ammunition by the ton? All I can say is I'm damn glad my boy is still in training down at Leonard Wood. He ain't likely to go."

Johnny Basket normally steered clear of such discussions. He had a destroyer sunk under him in the Coral Sea and still had occasional nightmares. One war was more than enough for him. Still, he couldn't blame these guys for obsessing. Both of them had kids in uniform. "Heard on Winchell last night, they're sending in the Marines." Basket said as he scooped change off his bar. "Jimmy gonna be involved in that?"

"Yeah, looks that way," Mike Jones said with a sigh. "He called his Ma Tuesday from California. Said they were getting ready to go. She ain't happy about it. Neither am I, truth be told. I seen a few Marine landings in the Pacific. It ain't never pretty."

"Damn shame about your Jimmy," Steiner said. "He should be pitching for the Cards right now."

Jones just nodded and sipped at his beer. "Well, he got himself into it. I'm just hoping he can get himself out of it in one piece."

They were interrupted by a tow-headed kid who wandered in with a handful of change and an aluminum bucket. "My Dad says he wants Stag." The boy dumped a few coins on the bar and stood looking at the horse pictures.

"That's the Davis boy ain't it?" Steiner eyed the kid wearing rumpled jeans and a ratty St. Louis Cardinals t-shirt while Johnny Basket filled the bucket with draft beer. "His old man works gate guard out at the plant, don't he?"

"Too damn lazy to come get his own beer," Jones said as the boy headed for the door with his foaming pail, stepping carefully to keep from spilling. "He should be damn glad his kid ain't old enough to get sent to Korea."

CAPTAIN GERDINE WAS KEEPING the pressure on Able Company which now fielded almost enough Marines to make up three rifle platoons and a weapons platoon. At morning Officer's Call on Wednesday, he announced that there would be a full uniform and equipment inspection for All Hands beginning at 0900. "Nothing formal," he specified. "We don't have time for that. Just check and be damn sure your Marines have all the gear they're supposed to have. It's now 0615." Gerdine buckled on his cartridge belt and checked his watch. "I want it done and dusted, including rosters and a list of any missing gear, by 1400."

That evolution was likely to turn the company area into a zoo, but the platoon commanders, Porter, Ruggles, Lopez, and Boyle, knew better than to bitch about it. They just stood stoically, bleary-eyed, and making the occasional note, as their Company Commander went over another thing he had in store for them: Night Operations.

"After chow this evening, we will move to the San Onofre area and conduct Rifle Platoon in the Attack, Night Infiltration." He saw the jaws drop and Gerdine felt like a tyrant, but his newly acquired Marines needed at least some experience with night operations. And there was rapidly diminishing time to get it done. "This will be a live-fire exercise, so get serious with your guys. All three of you rifle platoon leaders will take your people through the course. Lt. Boyle, your machineguns will do the overhead fire. You go early and set up horizontal and vertical limiting stakes for the guns. I don't want any stupid accidents out there."

Gerdine saw the wounded look on his officers' faces. "Look, gents, I know this is tough on everybody, but we've got to learn to fight at night. Let me tell you something I heard from Colonel Murray yesterday. Concerns the 24th Infantry Division at some place called Taejon. The North Koreans hit 'em with a night attack, and it was a slaughter. Those soldiers never learned about fighting at night and they got overrun. Commies even captured the division commanding general, for Christ's sake! Nothing like that is gonna happen to Able Company."

Lt. Porter, first platoon leader, eyed the training schedule posted on the wall. It was full of scribbles, notes and erasures. "Going to be hard to get much night work in before we go, sir. Any word on when that might be?"

"Still nothing definite. But I'd recommend you have your goodbyes said by the weekend. And you better do it by telephone. No leaves or liberty as of now. Carry on."

Gunnery Sergeant Elmore Bates and First Sergeant Leland Hammond roared off in the company Jeep heading for mainside right after morning formation. They had lots to do and little time to get it done before they needed to be back at Able Company.

Bates dropped Hammond off at 1st Marine Division headquarters where the First Sergeant knew a guy in the G-1 Personnel section that owed him a big favor. And today that favor was being called. Bates next swung by a clapboard barracks building, parked the Jeep and walked inside carrying a bulging knapsack. Corporal Sean Marcus, talented musician and rocket gunner currently assigned to duty at the Officers Club, was waiting for him in the rec room.

"Got your sea bag packed?" Bates led the young NCO into the head and began to pull things from his knapsack.

"Yeah, I'm packed like you said. How's this gonna work?"

"Like fucking clockwork, Marcus." Bates rolled up the sleeve of Marcus' uniform and examined his hand, wrist and forearm. "Here try this on," he said lifting out a plaster cast that hinged open at a taped seam. "Doc Clinton had to use me as a model but looks like it should fit."

Looking distinctly dubious, Marcus fitted the cast to his right arm. "I don't know about this, Gunny. I'm gonna need some kind of chit to show the Club Manager."

"Don't sweat the small shit," Bates said reaching into the knapsack. He held up an official form and showed it to Marcus. "Doc Clinton's got it handled right here. Signed medical chit says you broke your wrist and they had to put it in a cast. And you can't play no piano, with your dick-skinner in a cast, right? So you ain't no use at the O Club. It's perfect."

"Hope so..." Marcus watched as Bates wrapped the cast and then garnished it with bits of cotton and gauze.

"You want out of that bullshit duty, don't you? Duty with a rifle company headed for Korea. Ain't that what you said you wanted?"

"Yeah, Gunny...but they'll be checking for orders..."

"Just leave that to me. First Shirt's got a guy owes him big time over at Division Personnel. The fix is in, and you're covered, Marcus. Just act like this arm hurts like hell when we get over to the club."

Bates parked the Jeep out of sight at the rear of the Officers Club and watched Corporal Sean Marcus limp his way toward the back entry where the Club Manager's office was located. He hoped the kid was as good an actor as he was a piano player. In about an hour, if the scam worked as advertised, Able Company would have a new and talented Rocket Section Leader. He checked his watch and then picked up a copy of the Camp Pendleton Scout base newspaper that he wanted to scan for Korea news.

It was all dismal. Doggies were getting their asses handed to them. No big surprise there. Heavy fighting around the Naktong River with the gooks raising hell. Walker's 8th Army throwing up a perimeter around Pusan and marking time until more soldiers and Marines got there to save his bacon. No speculation about when the Provisional Brigade would hit the road, but everyone knew that was a matter of days if not hours. Bates folded the paper and cranked the Jeep when Cpl. Marcus emerged from the club wearing a grin.

"So, how'd it go?"

"Should have heard him bitch," Marcus laughed as he climbed into the passenger seat. "You'd have thought somebody cut his nuts off. You know he's gonna be making some phone calls."

"And he's gonna find out that you been transferred to Casual Company, Marcus." Bates wheeled the Jeep out onto a base thoroughfare. "And anybody in Casual is eligible for reassign-

ment. Which in your case, means you been picked up by Able
Company, 5th Marines, all kosher and legal."

Right after the company's equipment inspection was complete,
First Sergeant Hammond sat at his desk looking over lists of
discrepancies and shortages. He'd have to make another frustrating trip to Battalion Supply shortly. They wouldn't have
what was needed and the way things were going in the 1st
Provisional Marine Brigade, they weren't like to get what
anyone needed before the unit deployed.

There was a knock on the Quonset hut door and it opened
to reveal Sergeant Steve Petrosky mangling his utility cover
with both hands. The guy looked pitiful like a lost dog.

"Hey, Top. I was wondering if you've got a minute..."

"Ain't you supposed to be out with Lt. Boyle setting up the
guns?"

"Had to pick up the live ammo from the armory, so I swung
by here on my way back. I was wondering..."

"I know what you were wondering, Petrosky." Top Hammond waved a distracted hand at his visitor. "Same shit you
was wondering yesterday and the day before that. Your request
for release from active duty has got to be approved by Headquarters Marine Corps. They got more important shit on their
minds right now."

"Yeah, I know...but I was talking to a guy over at battalion
and he said..."

"I don't give a shit what anyone says, Petrosky. If—and only
if—your request is approved in the next couple of days, you
are on your way back to Pittsburgh. If not you're going to
Korea with the rest of us. Now get lost."

Able Company's second platoon was crapped out near the
entrance to the infiltration course, resting while the third
platoon made their practice run. It was coming on to dusk
when the real show would begin. Lt. Ruggles walked among his
Marines nodding here and there, trading jibes with a few of the

men he'd come to think of as his extended family. He'd compiled notes on them all, working nights with Sgt. Trenton, poring over their SRBs. It was a mixed bag. Some from the Midwest, some from the east coast, lots from the deep south. Two men had some college time, most were high school graduates, and there was a half-dozen who listed no schooling beyond 8th grade. He had two former brig-rats and a few others had nonjudicial punishments for minor infractions. Most of them had clean disciplinary records with conduct and proficiency marks that ranged from substandard to excellent. There were 14 Protestants, 12 Catholics, and one Jew.

And there was Private Jackson, second platoon's only black Marine other than Trenton, the platoon sergeant. The kid had a short fuse, always seemed to have a simmering resentment that made him touchy, but he was solid in his duties. Handled a BAR nicely and seemed to take his fire support duties seriously. Ruggles was thinking of getting Jackson's stripe back before they shipped out. He was still undecided about the other two, Benson and Maitland. Both of them bitched, long, loud, and continuously.

Doc Clinton was a gem. He conducted a survey for bumps and bruises immediately after their practice run. He was always doing stuff like that. The new Doc seemed to think of himself as a country GP and second platoon as his neighborhood medical practice. Ruggles watched Clinton lance a heel blister on PFC Paulson from Albuquerque, gently applying antiseptic, gauze padding, and tape. The Corpsman glanced up at Ruggles and grinned. "He'll be all right, sir. Got new boondockers and they aren't broken in yet."

"Well, shit." Paulson looked up and smiled at his lieutenant. "I was hoping you'd let me skate the infiltration course."

"What are you bitching about, Paulson?" Ruggles watched Sgt. Trenton approach, striding through the line of resting Marines. "No liberty, right? What else have you got to do?"

Trenton squatted and examined the Doc's work. "We got about an hour until it's dark enough to go, Lieutenant." He stood and whispered. "I got a few things I need to say. How about you go somewhere and have a smoke?"

Ruggles just nodded. There were times when he found it best to disappear and leave things to his platoon sergeant. He trusted Trenton completely now and didn't want to interfere with the veteran NCO's leadership style. He'd learned that some things were officer business and many things were strictly enlisted business. "Let me know when you want me to wander back," he said and walked off to watch third platoon straggling off the practice course.

"Listen up!" Sgt. Trenton found a spot at the center of the platoon and began to pace. "A few of you people remain on my shit-list over that incident in the barracks. I want you all to remember what happened to this platoon as a result of that."

Maitland, sitting next to his buddy Benson snorted. "We ain't likely to forget getting run up and down Mount Mother-fucker."

"I ran your dick into the dirt for a reason, Maitland." Trenton stopped in front of his two biggest personnel problems. "I did it because you fucked up way beyond just a barracks fight. You were fighting among yourselves and that ain't the Marine Corps way. Marines got to rely on each other, take care of each other. I learned that in the last war and I want you to understand it before we are up to our asses in this one. Now in less than an hour, we're gonna be running the infiltration course, flat on our bellies, with live rounds fired close overhead. It takes teamwork, people. We rely on each other, take care of each other. Any questions?" Trenton looked around for any sort of discussion but there was none. He nodded. "Good. Now strip your gear down. Helmet, cartridge belt, and weapon only. No packs or canteens. Check to be sure you don't have anything in your pockets that might make noise. When it's time, we go squads on line. First squad on the left, then third and second on the right."

Lt. Ruggles was sitting on a rock near the entrance to the course spooning cold beans from a can. Privates Maitland and Benson approached and stood casually, waiting to be acknowledged.

"Permission to speak freely," Benson said when Ruggles nodded at them.

"What's on your mind?"

"Me and Maitland are requesting transfer, Lieutenant."

"Just before we ship out? You worried about getting killed in Korea? Or have you got a problem with this platoon?"

"Truth is, sir..." Maitland said. "We got a problem with who's running this platoon."

Ruggles took another bite of his beans, to keep him from saying what he was feeling. When he'd chewed for a bit, keeping his eyes locked on both men, he put the can aside.

"I know bullshit when I hear it. You got a problem with me?"

"It ain't you, Lieutenant. It's Trenton."

"I see, and would your problem with Sergeant Trenton be that he's black?"

"We was raised where white people don't take orders from them people is all. It ain't right."

"And if Sergeant Trenton gives you an order in combat, you might not obey it because you aren't used to being ordered around by a black man? Is that what you're telling me?"

"Sir, we just want a transfer to a white outfit!"

Ruggles shook his head and stood slowly. He took his time choosing his words. "Let me tell you two how this is going to go. The only way you're getting out of this platoon is if I decide to shit-can you or the North Koreans kill you."

He took a deep breath and then jabbed a finger under their noses. "The first time you smart-mouth or hesitate to cheerfully carry out one of Sergeant Trenton's orders, you're gonna find yourself in the brig on piss and punk forever. And I don't care if that brig is here, on the ship or in Korea. Just speak up right now if there's any part of that you don't understand."

Maitland and Benson just nodded. Ruggles swept a hand toward the area where the rest of the platoon was strapping on their gear. "Get out of my sight."

Sgt. Trenton stood off by himself at the entrance to the course, eyeing the strands of barbed wire and tangle-foot his platoon would have to negotiate in the dark. Private Willis Jackson approached with his gear strapped on and his BAR over his shoulder.

"Sergeant Trenton, can I talk to you?"

"Anytime, Jackson. What's on your mind?"

"Word is that them two crackers Maitland and Benson went to the Lieutenant and asked him for a transfer."

"So what?"

"Well, I heard Lieutenant Ruggles told them they was staying in second platoon."

"That's what I'd expect him to do. Again, so what?"

"So if them two are gonna stay in this platoon, I want out of it."

"Don't work that way, Jackson. Get back to your squad."

"Then you gonna watch my back?"

"I watch everybody's back, Jackson. I run this platoon without concern for anybody's color or condition as long as they act like Marines. Now you can get that fucking chip off your shoulder and do your duty. How's that sound?"

"Sounds a lot like Jim Crow to me."

Trenton flinched and then locked his eyes on Jackson. When he spoke, his voice was raw and throaty. "You listen to me, Jackson. I was fighting Jim Crow long before you even knew what color you were. I made my way in this Marine Corps by doing my duty better than anyone else. And that's what I expect of you. Now get out of my sight."

Second Lieutenant Art Boyle was showing stress at the objective end of the infiltration course where all three of his machineguns were dug in with crews loading live ammo. Firing real rounds at fellow Marines just seemed to unsettle him, and he was over-thinking. Boyle was pestering the hell out of the gun teams, checking, rechecking, and verifying until Sergeant Petrosky pulled him aside.

"Relax, Mister Boyle. I got it covered."

"I don't mind telling you," Boyle whispered. "This really makes me nervous. Anything goes haywire and we could kill somebody."

"Let me handle it, sir. I done this many times before. Just find yourself a place to observe. Ain't nothing gonna go wrong."

Staff Sergeant Petrosky stood to the rear of his three gun positions as darkness fell and the first platoon to run the exercise mustered at the far end of the course. "All you people have been issued red-lens flashlights. If you hear or see something out there, you are to flash the light. I'll come running and verify. Then and only then will you open fire."

The section sergeant looked up at the darkening sky. "About time to start this rodeo. Now remember, this is training. It ain't combat. Those are Able Company Marines out there and we don't want anyone to get hurt. If you open fire, search and traverse until the barrel of your gun hits a limiting stake, then come back in the other direction until it hits the stake on the other side. Most importantly, your T and E devices are set and locked to keep your rounds eighteen inches over the wire. Don't fuck with them."

Second Lieutenant George Porter's first platoon, containing most of the Able Company originals and a solid mix of NCOs, made their way through the night infiltration course in good time with no serious problems. They did get spotted by the machinegunners about three-quarters of the way to the objective and had to crawl the rest of the way under fire, but they slid safely into the trench at the end of their route hooting and whooping about the stream of colorful tracers that flew overhead.

Capt. Gerdine reviewed the exercise as Lt. Ruggles and the 2nd Platoon got ready to go. "The idea here is to approach an enemy position through his defensive barriers without being seen or heard until you're close enough to overrun him. You're gonna run into concertina, tangle-foot, double-apron barbed wire and all kinds of crap out there. Go slow and steady. If Lieutenant Boyle's Marines hear you or see you, they're gonna open up with the machineguns. And for Christ's sake, remember those are live rounds. If you get hung up or have trouble, just stay put. Do not stand up under any circumstances if you come under fire!" He nodded at Ruggles and Thornton. "All yours. Let's see if second platoon can get through without being spotted."

It was inky dark, the kind of moonless, spooky night that robbed Ruggles and his Marines of much sensory input beyond what they could touch with their hands or feel through bellies and knees as they crawled slowly forward under a low apron of barbed wire. The length of the infiltration course was about 50 yards, and every inch of that seemed to present a new and more difficult obstacle. Sgt. Trenton was crawling in the center of the line with the third squad, and that was intentional. He wanted to keep an eye on Benson and Maitland.

When they reached a line of coiled concertina wire, Trenton felt around for telltales. He'd put in plenty of them himself stringing defensive wire. You tied empty ration cans filled with pebbles onto the wire. Anybody jostles a barrier rigged that way and they're spotted. He nudged Benson crawling on his right and Jackson on his left and pointed at a can dangling in front of their faces. "Pass the word," he whispered. "Stay away from the cans."

In a series of hoarse whispers, the word traveled down the line and second platoon shuttled forward squirming and wriggling deeper into the obstacles. Trenton held back to help one of his men get free of a barb that had snagged the collar of his uniform. Benson and Maitland continued moving forward until they reached an x-shaped steel stanchion that supported a section of razor-wire strung close to the ground. The way to negotiate it was roll over onto your back and crab forward using shoulders and heels. Benson tried it and got caught on the wire. He was snagged at a spot he couldn't reach.

"Lanny!" he whispered to Maitland. "I'm hung up. Gimme a hand."

Maitland slithered toward Benson and began to feel around at the back of his buddy's sweat-soaked uniform blouse. Whatever had Benson snagged was dug in deeply. Maitland felt around for his bayonet and the move sent a shiver through the entire stretch of wire.

The assistant gunner manning the center .30 caliber on the firing line reached for his red-lensed flashlight and snapped it on. Second platoon had just screwed the pooch. He grinned and flashed the light at Staff Sgt. Petrosky who was crouched at the rear of the gun line.

The section leader stood and walked forward. "Got something?"

"Damn sure do," the gunner said and pointed into the dark. "Right out there about eleven o'clock. Somebody's tugging on the wire."

Petrosky closed his eyes and listened. He heard it then.

"All guns search and traverse," he said. "Commence fire!"

Streams of tracers arced over the second platoon. No need to be quiet anymore, Lt. Ruggles decided. He shouted for his men to keep low and continue to crawl.

To his right in the middle of the third squad, Maitland and Benson were still struggling to get clear of the snag that had gotten their move detected. "Sit still!" Sgt. Trenton shouted over the roar of the machine gun fire. "I'm coming to you!"

The darkness ahead was suddenly shattered by a shower of sparks. Trenton cringed as he heard the familiar whine of a ricochet. One of the overhead rounds had struck the steel stanchion where Benson and Maitland were struggling. Maitland yelped and rolled away from Benson. "Sonofabitch!" Holding onto his left forearm, Maitland began to rise. He never made it. His ankles were yanked out from under him and he fell flat.

"Stay down! Just hold still!" Private Jackson yelled for Sgt. Trenton. "Maitland's hit!"

Sgt. Trenton snatched his flashlight from his cartridge belt and switched it on. Reaching carefully up over the wire, he waved it in the direction of the firing line.

"Cease fire, cease fire!" They could hear Petrosky screaming in the distance and the guns fell silent.

Trenton tried to assess Maitland's wound, but it was too dark to tell much, and what he could see with the red lens was distorted by color shift. "Second Platoon," he yelled, "keep crawling. Muster in the trench on the other side of the wire."

Doc Clinton was swabbing Maitland's wound while Captain Gerdine held an unfiltered light for him. The ricochet had scraped a bloody gash just below Maitland's elbow but didn't penetrate.

"Not very serious, sir." Clinton glanced up at the Company Commander and wrapped the wound with gauze. "You caught a ricochet off one of the wire supports, Maitland. Could have been a lot worse."

"Felt like somebody stuck me with a hot branding iron."

"Doc's right, Maitland. It could have been a lot worse."

"Yessir." Maitland examined the Corpsman's bandage and flexed his fingers. "Feels pretty good now."

"You want to take him over to the hospital, Doc?"

"Not personally I don't, Skipper. That Chief is still looking for me. Anyway, I don't think it needs anything but changing the bandage every once in a while."

Maitland stood and began to collect his gear. "Many thanks, Doc."

"You got somebody else to thank, Maitland." Sgt. Trenton pointed to the clump of Marines nearby. "Jackson pulled you down into the dirt or you'd probably be layin' out there dead right now."

Corporal JJ Jones, former major league baseball prospect, was putting on an impressive demonstration of pitching speed and control with Mk II fragmentation hand grenades substituted for baseballs. With Gunny Bates as pitching coach in the pit with him, Jones had put two grenades through the small firing aperture of a bunker 30 yards downrange. He was eyeing the target critically the same way he would facing a slugger at bat and two strikes in the count.

There was serious money at stake. Sprawled on a grassy slope to the rear of Jones, Able Company Marines were watch-

ing intently. Those betting against Jones were hooting and
yelling harassment. Those who had their money on a third
strike were more muted. They'd all been through the grenade
range and knew that the serrated, egg-shaped frags didn't fly
like a round baseball. Still, win or lose, it was nice to sit in the
sun, relax for a while without being hustled to yet another
training event.

Captain Gerdine had decided to give his weary Marines a
couple of hours free of pressure for a couple of reasons. No
question they deserved a little slack. Through exhausting days
and nights, he'd pushed them through one evolution after
another at an intense tempo. They'd completed a long list of
training events in days when a unit operating at normal pace
would have taken weeks to do it. And now that it was done, all
the boxes checked, Gerdine wasn't sure that repetition would
add anything to their skill sets. So he had Top Hammond icing
down some beer and soda back at the company area. And he
intended to cut as many as possible loose to visit the PX and
make phone calls home.

Down below the spectators' hill, Cpl. Jones tossed a grenade
in the air and caught it absently while he kept his eyes on the
target. Gerdine could see Gunny Bates saying something to
Jones, acting like a coach reassuring his man in a clutch situation. And despite his creative profanity and angry demeanor,
Gerdine understood that's really what the Gunny was, a coach
who cared about his players. Able Company was lucky to have
Gunny Bates.

A hush fell over the observers as Jones pulled the pin on a
third grenade. Reaching nearly to the back wall of the grenade
pit with his left arm, and then whirling forward, he made the
critical toss. Gerdine heard a massive intake of breath as his
Marines followed the black speck toward the bunker. Marines
were taught to lob hand grenades, but Jones fired this one like
a big league heater. The grenade disappeared into the bunker
and detonated, sending clouds of dirt and sand into the air.
Gunny Bates whooped and danced around the pit with Jones
in a bear hug. The hillside erupted in a mix of cheers and jeers.
Losers paid the gloating winners.

Lt. Lopez approached his Company Commander wearing a huge grin and extended his hand. "Never bet against one of our own, Skipper." Gerdine reached in his pocket and forked over a dollar bill.

"Didn't think he could do it," Gerdine said. "Hell, I didn't think anyone could do it. That kid has got an arm."

Corporal Jones was mobbed by his backers when he trotted up the hill. Captain Gerdine watched it all with a smile. If he had to evaluate morale, Gerdine thought, he'd have to rate Able Company as a pretty happy bunch by Marine Corps standards.

A Jeep pulled off the road at the top of the hill and Gerdine saw Colonel Murray dismount and walk toward him. He had a pair of binoculars in his hand and waved them at Gerdine. "Saw it from the line shack," Col. Murray said. "Hell of a show! Three grenades right through the firing aperture."

Gerdine and Lopez offered salutes as Murray joined them. He watched the celebrating Marines for a while and then slung the binoculars around his neck. "Your people ready to go, Sam?"

"Ready as I know how to make them, Colonel."

"Better get packing then. Movement orders came in this morning. The Brigade is formed under General Eddie Craig and we go to San Diego Sunday morning. S-4 is typing up shipping assignments right now. We'll be at sea and headed for Korea by reveille Monday morning."

Gunnery Sergeant Elmore Bates punched his second beer with a church-key and wondered if it would be the last one for quite a while. Probably would, at least during time it took to cross the Pacific. Fucking Navy. No booze aboard ship! And every Chief had some stashed in his locker anyway. Well, a few weeks without his nightly couple of cool ones wouldn't hurt.

And who knows about Korea? Most time, Marines in the field, even in combat zones, could find some beer. Or barring that, maybe some local busthead to slake a thirst and calm the nerves. He'd done it with Jap sake a couple of times in the

Pacific. Always seemed to help somehow. Just a taste, enough to kind of slow your breathing and reduce the shakes. You didn't get snot-slinging drunk if you wanted to stay alive. But a little taste always filed an edge off the post-combat jag. And the combat jag was a bitch-kitty when guys around you started dying in all manner of shitty ways. Not likely Korea would be much different.

Bates debated asking the CO to let him go with the advance party down to San Diego in the morning. There was a woman he knew down there thought a lot of him. Good old Doris. Might be he could disappear for a little while and...nah. Best to keep it in his trousers for the duration. Nothing distracts a guy like thinking about a woman. And combat is the last fucking place a man wants to be distracted. Just Top Hammond and a handful of others were married, according to the records. But all the rest of them had some high school sweetie or neighborhood cock-tease they'd be thinking about at the worst possible times. He'd have a few words to say about that when he talked to his Marines aboard ship.

He glanced at the official portrait of Captain Sam Gerdine hanging on the wall across from his desk. He'd met the Skipper's wife—ex-wife now—a couple of times. Della was her name. Seemed like an OK gal. But like a lot of others he'd known, she just couldn't handle the constant upheaval, the cloistered, uncertain elements of life in the Corps. Probably tried to talk Sad Sam into getting out, but a man like the Skipper wouldn't last two weeks lashed to a desk somewhere without a rowdy bunch of Marines to shepherd. The Able Company Gunny knew his CO well and admired him for the capable, squared-away officer he was. He also knew that Sad Sam Gerdine still loved his ex and their little boy. He'd miss them while the outfit was fighting in Korea. And that could be dangerous.

It was yet another thing Gunnery Sergeant Elmore Bates had to worry about and he was thinking about how best to handle it when First Sergeant Hammond walked in with a paper sack containing a fifth of Old Crow. "Thought you and me could kill this tonight," he said unscrewing the cap and reaching for their coffee cups hanging on the wall. "I'm racking here. I already said my goodbyes at home. Don't intend to go through it more than once."

Bates sipped whiskey, winced, and looked at the over-stuffed folder Hammond had placed on the desk. "What's the paperwork?"

"Message traffic, some stuff the Captain needs to see."

"Anything important?"

"Maybe. That kid Abramson? No dice on boot camp. He goes with us. I'm thinking maybe we hold a little graduation ceremony or something for him aboard ship."

"Good idea, Leland. Anything else?"

"Petrosky's request for release from active duty was denied. I saw him on the way over here."

"How'd he take it?"

"Like somebody just shit in his mess kit. Better keep an eye on him."

"I'll handle it. Get our shipping assignment?"

"Yep." The First Sergeant peeled off his uniform blouse and flopped down in a chair with a coffee cup full of bourbon. "Six ship convoy departs tomorrow soon as the fighting 1st Provisional Marine Brigade is all aboard. Then non-stop all the way to Pusan. We're aboard APA-45..."

"What did you say?" Bates nearly choked on a mouthful of booze. "Run that by me again, Leland."

"APA-45, USS *Henrico*."

"Oh, my aching ass! We ain't got a chance."

"What are you bitching about?"

"The USS *Henrico* is what! The fucking Happy Hank. I shipped aboard that rust bucket before, Leland. That ship is a jinx."

"It's just another amphib, a haze-grey hotel like all the rest of 'em."

"Not the Happy Hank ain't. That gator had at least six breakdowns when I shipped aboard her headed for Guam. They had to tow us into Apra Harbor, for Christ's sake!"

Top Hammond poured another drink into their coffee cups. "I'll be sure and let the Commodore know you ain't happy with our shipping arrangements."

"Mark my words, Top! We leave Dago aboard Happy Hank and we probably won't get to Korea."

Combat Zone
Near Chinhae

MASTER SERGEANT PAK CHUN HEE had been following the flow of retreating units for two weeks when he reached a bustling American port near Pusan. He was rounded up along with a large group of stragglers from other scattered and shattered South Korean Army units. All of them were disarmed, searched, and then placed in a holding pen. It was humiliating but necessary, Pak decided. Everyone was worried about North Koreans infiltrators posing as ROK troops. At least they were fed and given access to a shower point.

On the third day, a South Korean major came to visit. He spoke to the transients about efforts to field new fighting units. All would be interviewed to determine where they could best be employed. Those selected would be taken to assembly points where new infantry, artillery, and tank units were being formed. Master Sergeant Pak and five others were singled out for special duty. And that seemed to have much to do with seniority and experience. All six of the men who were escorted from the holding area were NCOs, regular Korean Army soldiers.

They were marched to a large American tent camp, told to line up outside a large canvas structure and wait to be called for interviews. A sign outside the tent said KATUSA. Lettering in *hangul* and English explained the acronym. Korean Augments to U.S. Army.

"So now we will be American soldiers!" The man standing behind Pak laughed and pointed.

"Not likely," Pak said. "They are probably looking for men to serve with American units. It makes sense." Pak pointed at the trucks roaring by filled with American troops. "Look at all the Americans flooding in here. They'll want some of us who know the land and the enemy."

"And you think they will give us rations and weapons, Sergeant Pak?"

"Of course they will," Pak said although he wasn't altogether sure about that. "We are experienced men."

"I would rather fight with my own unit," the man said as the line shuffled forward and individuals disappeared inside the tent.

"And how did that go?" Pak nodded at the American motioning him to enter the tent. "We need these Americans if Korea is to survive."

Pak followed the MP's point and approached a desk behind which sat two Majors, one American and other South Korean. On the collar of the Korean officer's uniform was the brass insignia of the Adjutant General Corps. He eyed Pak suspiciously and then glanced down at a stack of papers. Pak brought his heels together at the position of attention.

"Name?"

"Pak Chun Hee, Master Sergeant, 3rd Infantry Regiment, Capital Guard Command." Pak kept his gaze centered at the back wall of the tent and rattled off his particulars as he'd been taught.

"And how were you separated from your unit? The major was shuffling paper. Pak chanced a glance at the American officer. That man was squinting, as if searching for some fault, but his expression was neutral.

"Wounded in action while conducting a routine patrol along the Demarcation Line, sir. My platoon was overrun on the first day of the Northern assault. I was the only survivor..."

The American interrupted. Apparently he'd understood some of the story. "You are an old soldier," he commented in English. "Do you speak any other languages beside Korean?"

"I speak some English, sir." Pak said in that language and cut his glance over to the American officer who was now smiling.

"That's a big plus," he said. "How did you come to learn English?"

"I spent one year as a driver and orderly for American Observers in Seoul, sir. After the last war and before I joined the Army."

"Well, that's really handy." The American nodded at his Korean counterpart. "Major, I think we'll keep this man around for a while. Put him on the interpreter list." He motioned for the MP who was standing nearby. "Run Sergeant Pak through the drill," he said to the MP. "Get him a KATUSA armband, ID, and some uniforms. Then bring him back here."

JUST AFTER MORNING FORMATION on their first full day at sea, 2nd Lieutenant Art Boyle went looking for his absent Platoon Sergeant. None of the other two Section Leaders, neither Cpl. Marcus in Rockets nor Sgt. Shelton in 60mm mortars, had any idea where SSgt. Petrosky might be. So, officially Petrosky missed a formation which was a chargeable offense, but Lt. Boyle was hesitant to take it that far. There was probably some good excuse, something Petrosky had to do, and he'd just forgotten to let his Platoon Leader know about it. Art Boyle was too new at all this, his first time aboard a Navy ship at sea. There could be a hundred reasons why a veteran like Petrosky failed to make muster. Making a fuss about it could probably just turn into an embarrassment. On his way forward to officers' country with the muster report, Lt. Boyle ran into Capt. Gerdine.

"How are things in Weapons Platoon, Arthur?"

"Good, sir...real good. Just looking for the First Sergeant to turn in my muster report."

"By tomorrow we'll be far enough out to do some live fire training, Arthur. I want you to get up with Sergeant Petrosky and work the gun crews on the fantail."

"Yessir." Boyle chewed on his lip, glancing down at the muster report which listed SSgt. Petrosky as absent. "I'll get it set up."

"What's the matter, Arthur?" Gerdine sensed there was something bothering his Weapons Platoon leader. "You getting along OK with your NCOs?"

"Pretty good, sir. I listen more than I talk. But...you know...sometimes with Petrosky...well, he's a combat veteran and all."

"He's your subordinate. His experience doesn't affect that. Are you having a problem with him?"

"Not really, sir. He's good with the Marines and he knows the guns inside and out. It's just, well...sometimes he gets on my nerves. You know? Always looking for an angle to get himself sent home. Worried about the wife and kids." Boyle was unmarried, but he had a couple of sisters that he missed. "Understandable, I guess."

"Solid NCOs are gonna be critical when we get into action, Arthur. I'll talk to Petrosky. Pass the word that I want to see him when he's got a moment."

"Aye, aye, sir." *And for now,* Boyle decided, *I'll just pencil whip the muster report and mark Petrosky present. He'll owe me one.*

Captain Gerdine made his way aft to do an inspection of the berthing areas two decks below. His Marines were stuffed like sardines into tall tiers of racks, and he'd already been informed that the showers in the after spaces were not functioning. He was compiling a list of such discrepancies to submit to the ship's First Lieutenant. Given the condition of the leaky and creaky old transport, he doubted it would do much good, but he wanted the passage to Korea to be as smooth as possible for Able Company.

As he swung toward the ladder leading belowdecks, Gerdine collided with Sgt. Trenton charging up toward the higher level. Trenton backed up making room for Gerdine to pass.

"Excuse me, sir. Didn't see you coming."

"My fault, Sergeant Trenton. How you making it? Getting your sea legs?"

"Nothing to it, Skipper." Trenton grinned and pointed downward toward the berthing spaces. "Can't say as much for my Marines though. We got maybe six or eight of 'em so seasick they can't get much more than a step or two away from the head."

"Curse of a seagoing service, Sergeant Trenton. I'm headed down to inspect right now. Want to come along?"

"Can't right now, sir. Mister Ruggles wants a count on some platoon gear we got stowed in the forward cargo hold. I told him I'd get it to him before noon chow."

"You two getting along OK?"

"Real good, sir. Lieutenant Ruggles is a good officer. Learns fast. Sometimes he worries too much..."

"Officers get paid to worry, Sergeant Trenton." Gerdine grinned and gave the NCOs bicep a squeeze. "That why we need good NCOs to reassure us."

"Yessir." Trenton mirrored the smile. "I better get moving. By your leave, sir?"

"Carry on...and if you see Staff Sergeant Petrosky, let him know I want to see him when he's got a spare minute."

"Aye, aye, sir. I'll pass the word."

It was hot, dirty and muggy down in the cargo hold. Most of the overhead lights either flickered or burned with a dim yellow glow that made it hard to see what was in the stacks, racks and boxes crammed into the hold. Trenton was needlessly confirming that the second platoon's two GP tents with their issue poles, pegs and guy-lines had made it through the loading process. Trenton was standing right next to Lt. Ruggles on deck when the pallets were sling-loaded aboard, but the Lieutenant wanted reassurance. Trenton clicked on his flashlight to check for tactical marking on a square of canvas and promised himself that he'd hide that damned cargo manifest before long to keep the lieutenant from obsessing over it.

Trenton was climbing atop another pile of reeking canvas when his flashlight beam caught movement. Thinking it might be a bilge rat, Trenton kicked in the direction of the movement and felt his boondocker hit flesh. He heard a groan and saw Staff Sergeant Steve Petrosky sit upright, blinking and drooling. Mixed with the odor of impregnated canvas and bilge refuse, Trenton smelled booze. Petrosky reeked of it.

"Goddammit, Petrosky. What are you doing down here?"

Petrosky sat up and rubbed at his face, blinking in the light. "Fuck...I don't. Who's that? That you Trenton?"

"Yeah, it's me. Where the hell did you get the booze, man?"

"Hey, Trenton." Petrosky rose shakily to his feet and swayed with a grin on his face. "How's it goin' up topside?"

"Never mind that shit. Answer my question. Where'd you get the booze? How'd you get it past shakedown?"

"Don't worry about it. I'm fine."

"You ain't fine, Petrosky. You're fucked up like Hogan's Goat, And the Skipper is looking for you. He finds out you brought booze aboard this bucket and you can kiss them stripes goodbye."

That thought seemed to register. "I can't take a bust, Trenton. Alma and the kids need the money I make."

"This ain't no way to keep it coming."

"It ain't coming, Trenton. That's the goddamn problem."

"What the fuck are you talking about?"

"Called her from Dago. Alma said she ain't got no money. I made out the allotment, but she ain't gettin' no money." Petrosky's ruddy face screwed up and it looked like he was about to cry. "What the fuck am I gonna do, Trenton?"

Sergeant Heywood Trenton didn't know for sure. Petrosky could be a bit irritating when he was sober. Drunk he was a basket-case. Still, the man was a veteran and very good with machineguns. Able Company would need those qualities in Korea. Petrosky's gunners would be firing for his second platoon and a lot of others. He was worth a helping hand.

"Listen up, Petrosky." Trenton grabbed him by and elbow. "You got any more hid-out hooch?"

"Couple of canteens. That's how I got it past shakedown."

"Just follow me back to NCO spaces. Don't say shit to anyone and try not to fall on your ass."

Sgt. Trenton managed to get Petrosky up two decks and forward to a little compartment where he and three other NCOs were berthed. There was no one around as they slipped into the space and locked the door.

"Where's the booze?"

Petrosky pointed at his field gear and two canteens that were hanging from his cartridge belt.

"That's it? You ain't got any more stashed somewhere?"

"That's all," Petrosky said. "All l could get."

"Pour it out. Every fucking drop. Right down the deep-sink. And then get your ass into the shower."

There was a cool sea breeze blowing topside. First Sergeant Hammond and Gunny Bates were chatting on a small observation deck below the pilot house, smoking cigarettes and watching waves ripple on the surface of cobalt blue water. Next to them stood Lt. Ruggles and Lt. Lopez. The officers were engrossed in a sketch Ruggles was making on a thick pad of art paper. It was a seascape dotted with ships like the ones they could see in the distance.

"That's pretty good, Paul. You ever think about doing it for a living?"

"Sent in a sketch to one of those Draw Me deals I saw on a matchbook cover one time." Ruggles snorted and shook his head. "They told me not to quit my day job."

Lopez chuckled and then gazed critically at the other ships in the convoy. Something had caught his Annapolis trained eye. "Do those other ships look different to you? Different perspective...maybe like we're turning away?"

Ruggles looked up from his drawing. "It does seem like it. And I think the deck is slanting a little. Maybe they're just spacing us out a bit..."

"I fucking knew it!" Gunny Bates tossed his cigarette into the wind as everyone on the platform turned to stare at him. "I fucking told you this was gonna happen! Didn't I?" He roared and jabbed a finger at Top Hammond. "We're falling out of formation! It's this fucking Happy fucking Hank! It's a plot. Jesus Herschel Christ, people! This shit-barge is turning around. These anchor-clanker bastards have done it to me again!"

"Take it easy, Gunny." Lopez was about to pull rank but First Sergeant Hammond interceded. "I got this, sir. I'll take him below and get some coffee in him." Hammond opened a hatch and shoved Gunny Bates through it.

Ruggles and Lopez were headed belowdecks when the USS Henrico's 1MC announcing system roared to life.

"Attention All Hands. The ship has experienced a propulsion casualty. We are returning to San Diego for repairs. Delay is expected to be no more than forty-eight hours. All Division Officers and Department Heads muster in the wardroom immediately. Senior Marine officer is requested to attend. That is all."

Sgt. Heywood Trenton sat on a bunk with his legs crossed watching Sgt. Steve Petrosky shiver under an icy cold shower. Petrosky stared out from under the deluge with badly bloodshot eyes. "Feel like warmed over shit, but I think I'm gonna make it."

"Self-inflicted wound, Petrosky."

"Missed muster this morning. Boyle's probably already got me on report."

"Let me deal with that. Anybody asks, I'll tell 'em you were down in the hold with me doing inventory. Don't worry about that shit. Worry about the Skipper. He wants to see you."

"What about?"

"How the fuck should I know? He just said to pass the word you should see him when you've got a minute. Wasn't like he was ordering you to lock your heels or anything."

Steve Petrosky shut off the shower and reached for a towel.

Checking his breath with a cupped hand, Petrosky smelled only Colgate toothpaste. He took a deep breath and knocked on Captain Gerdine's stateroom door. When he heard the Captain's invitation to enter, he opened the door and stepped inside.

"Staff Sergeant Petrosky, sir. You wanted to see me?"

Captain Gerdine was silent for a moment, looking his visitor up and down critically. "You're looking a little rough, Sergeant Petrosky. You feeling OK?"

"Just a little seasick, sir. Been a while since I been on one of these buckets. I'll be fine in a day or two."

"Lieutenant Boyle tells me you're worried about your family."

"Yes, sir. See, I got two kids under ten, and just the wife to handle everything while I'm gone. They refused to release me from active duty and I guess I can understand that. But my wife, Alma...well, she's in a stew over it. She ain't got no money yet."

"You made out the family allotment at disbursing, right?"

"Yessir. Out of my pay and all...but I ain't had no time to get a money order or wire her some dough. When I called her from San Diego, she said the allotment money wasn't coming in. I'm really worried about it, Captain."

"Well, Sergeant Petrosky, you probably heard we're turning around and heading back for maintenance. I'm not authorized to grant liberty while we're in port, but I can make a few phone calls. I'll light a fire under some disbursing people I know. And if you want, I'll personally wire some money to your wife. Come see me after chow, and we'll work out the details. How's that sound?"

"Great, Captain. Thanks a lot."

"Nothing to it, Petrosky. Now you focus on your Marines. I want outstanding machinegunners when we get to Korea."

"Aye, aye, sir...and thanks again."

Feeling terribly hung over but greatly relieved, Staff Sergeant Petrosky went below to borrow as much money as he could from his fellow NCOs.

San Diego

NAVY AND CIVILIAN TECHNICIANS flooded the USS *Henrico* as soon as the captain got her maneuvered alongside and moored at a Navy Yard berth. The push was on to get the engineering problem solved in a hurry, so the ship and the Marines she carried could get churning back out into the Pacific and on to Korea. The captain would need all the speed his engineers could give him to catch up with the convoy now plodding slowly westward, hoping the *Henrico* could catch up somewhere out in mid-Pacific.

Marines aboard the stricken ship accepted the no-liberty policy stoically. They were disappointed with the delay, but going ashore after starting the trip somehow didn't seem right. Getting off the ship, even for a night made most of them feel too much like it was all a cruel joke. They were ordered to stay out of the way but allowed to laze around the weather decks. Most were either napping in the pale sunlight or trading insults with pier-side sailors.

The clank and clang of tools in contact with engine room machinery resounded through open hatches and scuttles, making it sound like the Happy Hank was being torn apart by the snipes down in the engineering spaces. Gunny Bates prowled the decks, snapping and snarling, telling everyone he encountered that the whole thing was a commie plot.

In his stateroom forward, Captain Sad Sam Gerdine was frowning at his image in the mirror and tightening the knot in his field scarf. He had it just about two-blocked properly when there was a sharp rap on his door.

"Come!"

Second Lieutenant Baldomero Lopez stepped in with his cover in hand. He raised his eyebrows quizzically when he saw the Company Commander in service uniform.

"Change your mind about liberty, Skipper?"

"Can't do it, Baldo. I'll be the only one going ashore. I've got to take care of some personnel problems before we get underway again."

"I checked with the Chief Engineer like you asked me to, sir. He's another ring-knocker, so I think I got the straight skinny. Big embarrassment for the captain, so they're pressing hard. He figures no more than one day in port. Likely single-up and get back underway sometime tomorrow morning."

"Good. I talked the captain into showing some movies for our guys and the off-duty crew on the fantail after dark. You honcho that with the other lieutenants. I'll be back aboard before midnight."

Gerdine noted the suspicious glances from his Marines as he paused at the quarterdeck to salute the OOD and then turned aft to salute the national ensign. He was wearing a khaki service uniform with ribbons and badges, so most of them would likely think he'd been called ashore for some kind of official business. He didn't want them resenting him for taking advantage of his rank and status—even if he was.

He stopped first at the Western Union office on base and plunked down $250 in cash with instructions that it be wired immediately to the address in Pittsburgh that Petrosky had provided. Fifty of that was Gerdine's own secret contribution, but Petrosky didn't need to know that. He headed for the main gate where he planned to catch a cab after making a couple of important phone calls. The bank of payphones near the gate was jammed with sailors waiting to make calls. Gerdine checked his watch and then stepped to the head of the line.

"Sorry, gents. Don't mean to pull rank here, but I've got to make an official call."

The sailor being bumped just shrugged and pulled the accordion door open for the Marine officer. Gerdine stepped inside, closed the door, and dug in his pocket for coins. The first call was answered by an officious Corporal who informed the caller that he was in contact with the Marine Corps Base Camp Pendleton Disbursing Office.

"Major Stribling, please. Captain Gerdine calling." It was hot inside the phone booth. Gerdine wiped his brow and waited for his old friend to come to the phone. The man he wanted to talk to had been a battalion staff officer in Gerdine's outfit during the last war. A good man who took care of his Marines and loved the Corps. Charlie Stribling was wounded badly on

Cape Gloucester and took a job in disbursing so he could stay in the Marine Corps.

"Sad Sam! What are you doing on the line? Thought you'd be halfway to Korea by now."

"Been a little delay, Charlie. Damn ship had a breakdown. They're repairing it now."

"What can I do for you, shipmate?"

"One of my NCOs is having a problem with his family allotment." Gerdine read Petrosky's full name and service number from a crumpled slip of paper. "Wife and two kids at home with no money, Charlie. He made out the allotment before we left Pendleton. I'm thinking maybe some kind of admin glitch. Can you track it down and see that it gets moving?"

"Damn sure will, Sam. Just leave it with me. I'll get it squared away immediately."

"Thanks, Charlie. Knew I could count on you."

"Wish to Christ I was going with you, Sam."

"You did more than enough in the last one, Charlie. I'll drop you a line when we get over there and tell you all about it."

Gerdine hung up, dug for more change, and made another call. "Della? It's Sam. I'm in San Diego and I'd really like to see you and Tony. Can't stay more than a few minutes, but I won't have another chance for a while. Is it OK? Great. You still living in the same place?"

The Yellow Cab dropped Sad Sam Gerdine in front of a modest wood-frame house near Balboa Park. His ex-wife worked shifts at the San Diego Bell Telephone exchange. That kept her in shape to pay rent, and her ex-husband's contribution to child support allowed Della Keeler, formerly Mrs. Sam Gerdine, to hire a Mexican lady to watch six-year-old Anthony Gerdine when she was at work.

She was dressed in shorts and a loose silk blouse when she answered the door. And Della, who had always been self-conscious about her diminutive height, had on platform heels that brought her head nearly to Sam's shoulders. He bent to kiss her, but she turned away at the last moment to offer a rouged cheek.

"C'mon in, Sam. I'll mix you a drink."

"Just time for one, Della. I've got to get back to the Navy Base shortly."

She fiddled with an ice-bucket and a bourbon bottle. Sam admired her shape from the back, always one of his favorite perspectives. She had sturdy legs and a beautiful butt below a tiny waist. He closed his eyes, trying not to let his memories get the best of him. *Maybe, if I survive Korea*, he thought, *maybe we can...*

"You really look great, Della."

"Well, that buys you a drink," she said and handed him a highball. He was hoping she'd sit next to him on the couch, but Della took a chair across the coffee table and crossed her legs.

"You still like your bourbon?"

"Nectar of the Gods, right?" He sipped the drink and tried to relax. The way she was bouncing a calf over a knee had him sweating.

"Don't imagine you'll get much of it where you're heading."

"You heard about it?"

"We were married for eight years, Sam. I still hear from people we used to know in the Marine Corps."

"I've got a rifle company now."

"Congratulations." Della smiled. Sam noticed the perfect white teeth he'd always admired. And Della was wearing a shade of crimson lipstick that he'd always liked. She'd put on make-up for the occasion of his visit. Or was it for someone else she'd be seeing later? Della was always careful about her appearance. "I know that's what you always wanted. You must be very proud."

"Losing my wife and son kind of takes the edge off of it."

"Sam, we've been over this before. You made your choice when you decided to stay in the Marine Corps after the last war. With you, everything else runs a slow second to the Marines." Della leaned forward and placed her drink on the coffee table. "Other women might be able to handle it but I couldn't—and I won't."

"You willing to talk about it when I get back from Korea?"

"Anything is possible, Sam. You willing to think about getting out when you get back from Korea?"

She knew he wouldn't answer, at least not answer truthfully right now. And given what she read in the papers, there was a chance Sam Gerdine wouldn't make it back from Korea. "Let me go get Tony," she said standing and tugging at her blouse. "He's excited about seeing his Dad."

Darkness had fallen over the San Diego Navy Yard but nonstop, noisy work continued in the USS *Henrico*'s engine rooms. On the fantail in front of a crowd of Marines and off-duty sailors, George Montgomery was galloping hard and blowing away cattle rustlers as "Riders of the Purple Sage" was projected on a huge sheet of white canvas. Marines in the front row counted the rounds expended from the hero's six-gun and hooted bullshit when he failed to reload.

Watching at the rear of the crowd, Second Lieutenant Arthur Boyle of Weapons Platoon, stood leaning on a stand pipe with his arms crossed. He was a big fan of the genre but less than impressed with the film unspooling as the night's entertainment.

Second Lieutenant Baldomero Lopez of the third platoon arrived, batted Boyle on the shoulder and pointed at the flickering images. "Any good?"

"Never gonna be as good as the book, Baldo. Nobody writes westerns like Zane Grey, and these Hollywood yahoos just don't get his style."

"Skipper's back aboard. He said if I see you to let you know he took care of that allotment deal for Staff Sergeant Petrosky."

"Good. Might stop him whining for a while." Boyle watched a scene for a few moments. "Think we might get any more officers when we get to Korea?"

"We got what we rate, Art."

"I'm hearing George Porter is working his bolt for a slot on battalion staff. He gets it and I'm gonna ask the Skipper to give me first platoon."

"You got your hands full with weapons."

"Some of us don't have the advantages of the Boat School, Baldo. I'm planning on going into politics when I get out. Chest full of fruit salad helps with that. And you get the medals in a rifle platoon."

II. SOUTH KOREA

Pusan

SERGEANT HEYWOOD TRENTON noted a change in the ship's motion about a half-hour before a scheduled early reveille. He got dressed and climbed topside. Word was passed last night that all the other ships in the convoy had already made port in Pusan. This morning it was Happy Hank's turn. *None too soon,* Trenton thought when he reached the midships passageway. After nearly two weeks aboard the plodding troop transport, the Marines were ready for anything other than another monotonous day at sea. Trenton made his way onto a weather deck and squinted in the pre-dawn darkness. He spotted the lights of a port on the near horizon. *Has to be Pusan*, he thought as Navy watch-standers bustled around him. On the far horizon, he could see a line of flames and the occasional flash of artillery rounds impacting. *Hello, Korea. Sergeant Heywood Trenton reporting for duty.* He tossed a morning cigarette over the side and headed below.

Most of the other NCOs were up and sipping coffee at a table on the mess deck. Trenton got his own cup and a bacon sandwich before he slid into an open spot next to Gunny Bates. "Shore lights showing topside. I believe we finally made Pusan."

"Day late and a dollar short," Bates snorted into his coffee. "Swear to Christ if they ever try to send me somewhere in the Henrico again, you can just mark me down as AWOL."

A bosun's pipe trilled over the 1MC. "Now reveille, reveille. All hands heave out and trice up. Give the ship a clean sweepdown fore and aft. Sweep down all ladderways and passageways. Collect all trash on the fantail for dumping. Smoking lamp is lit in all authorized spaces. On deck, set the sea and anchor detail."

"Better get below and shake 'em out," First Sergeant Hammond said as the platoon sergeants rose gulping the last of their coffee. "Muster topside by platoons. Field transport packs and weapons."

Below in second platoon's berthing spaces, Doc Clinton was helping Private Miles Abramson assemble his pack. Clinton pulled a blanket roll strap snug and looked around the crowded space. It smelled particularly bad this morning. Something earthy and verdant mixed with the miasma of sweat and unwashed bodies as muggy air pumped through the compartment ventilators. "Looks like we finally made it, Miles." Clinton helped Abramson wiggle into the pack straps. "I think I can smell land."

"I'll sure be glad to get off this boat."

"Ship, Miles. A boat is a submarine, or a landing craft, or something you take on a fishing trip."

HM2 Arleigh Clinton opened one of the saddle pouches on his own gear and did another quick inventory of his field medical supplies. He had it all plus some extra stuff the ship's Chief Corpsman had offered. He looked around at the Marines he'd come to know so well and wondered who among them would be the first combat casualty, the first one to really need his help.

Private Miles Abramson stood at the foot of a ladder leading topside sweating under the weight of his pack and helmet, waiting for the man in front of him to start climbing. He tugged at the sling supporting his M-1 with one hand. In the other hand was his utility cover, the one he'd soaked in saltwater and dried in the hot sun so it would fade to a pale, salty shade and make him look less like the boot he was. Pinned to the front was a burnished eagle, globe, and anchor emblem. Captain Gerdine said it was one of his own when he handed it over with a handshake during a special formation. Miles treasured it. The insignia wasn't earned in the standard fashion, but it made him feel a lot more like he deserved his place in the ranks.

Captain Sad Sam Gerdine stood on the quarterdeck with his officers and pointed at a Navy motor whaleboat churning toward the *Henrico* as the ship was nudged and shoved by a pair of tugs. "That's my ride, I guess." He looked back toward the fantail where his NCOs were forming platoons and taking a headcount. "Figure it will take an hour or two to get this bucket alongside a pier. Soon as you can, get 'em all ashore and load up the gear. Trucks are supposed to be waiting."

Lt. Lopez nodded and looked out at the line of mountains beyond Pusan. This close to shore they could hear the crack and boom of distant fighting. "Any idea where we're gonna wind up, Skipper?"

"Beats me," Gerdine said as he hitched at his pack and walked toward a companionway that had been rigged over Henrico's port side. The whaleboat was snugged at the bottom waiting for him. "I'll know more after I talk to Colonel Murray."

A flight of four Navy F-4U Corsairs loaded with bombs and rockets roared overhead. The officers looked up at them while their commander disappeared below the deck edge.

"Carrier off shore..." Lopez led the other officers toward the waiting troops. "I've got a feeling we're gonna want as much of that as we can get."

Colonel Ray Murray sat in his Jeep next to his driver watching as the motor whaleboat approached carrying the late-arriving Captain Gerdine. Most of the 5th Marines' other rifle companies were already moving up to the Naktong area. Tardy Able Company by default was now the first battalion reserve unit. A flight of bomb-laden Corsairs passed low overhead and the colonel's driver pointed. "I'd sure like to be up there in one of them Corsairs," he said.

"How tall are you?" Colonel Murray asked as he dismounted to meet Captain Gerdine.

The driver shrugged. "Just a tad under six feet, Colonel. Why?"

"Stick with the infantry, lad." He pointed up at the sky where the aircraft were clawing for altitude. "Get hit up there, you've got a long way to fall. Get hit down here, you'll only have a tad under six feet to fall."

Colonel Murray met Captain Gerdine at the end of the pier and returned the junior man's salute. "Welcome to Korea, Sam. Crossing go OK?"

"Slow and miserable, sir. Like it usually is. My guys will unload as soon as they get the *Henrico* docked."

The rest of the first battalion is with Col. Newton on the way to Masan..."

"Sorry, sir. I've got no idea where that is."

"It's where you're headed shortly. General Craig has a Provisional Brigade CP set up nearby. You'll get a better feel for our deployments once you've had a look at the map. Hop in the Jeep, and we'll get you updated."

"What about my Marines, sir?"

"I'll send the Headquarters Commandant down here to bring them up as soon as everyone is ashore. Your gear will follow in trace as soon as we can get it shoved forward."

Sipping at a canteen cup full of lukewarm coffee, Captain Gerdine tried to follow Brigadier General Eddie Craig's briefing and identify points on the large tactical map in front of them. He was seeing a lot more red than blue, more enemy positions confronting an irregular line of friendly units north of Pusan.

"As expected," General Craig said pointing to a blue square labeled as 8th Army Command Post, "the Brigade has been assigned to General Walker's 8th Army. He's calling us his Fire Brigade. The idea is we go wherever he needs troops to plug gaps and hold this line." The General traced a finger along the stretch of the Naktong River. "The Reds have got the upper hand right now. All UN forces are clustered around the port in what the press is now calling the Pusan Perimeter. It's anchored on the west by the Naktong. That part of the line is now being held by the Army's 25th Infantry Division with their CP at Masan." He tapped a position south of the river and in the center of the perimeter line. "They got hit hard this morning, and we sent Colonel Murray's first battalion up there to reinforce. Baker and Charlie companies will go on line. You'll hold to the rear as reserve element. George Newton or his Three will read you in with more detail when you get up there."

"Aye, aye, sir. Anything else before I hit the road?"

"General MacArthur was down here from Tokyo a few days ago and lit a fire under General Walker's tail. He's had about all the retreat and hold he can stomach. I'm betting we'll be attacking shortly. And we're the freshest troops General Walker has available. I've passed the word throughout the Brigade. Wherever you are right now, don't get comfortable."

Gunny Bates and the other Able Company NCOs were shoving Marines into a long line of Army deuce-and-a-half trucks for the trip forward from Pusan. Waiting for all of second platoon to load, Sgt. Trenton stood with squad leaders Corporals Jones and Thornton counting heads. As they were preparing to close the tail gate and hop aboard, they were mobbed by a bunch of Korean kids who were hawking items pilfered from the supply dumps near the docks.

"Damn, lookee here." Thornton pointed at a little girl who was offering a bottle of Coca Cola. "I'd could damn sure go for a Coke right now." He squatted in front of the urchin. She looked like a little China doll that someone had badly abused with a dirt-smeared face and a tattered dress that barely reached her skinned knees. Thornton pointed at the soda bottle. "How much for that, girlie?" She pointed at the cigarette smoldering between Sgt. Trenton's fingers and held up five of her own.

"Looks like she wants five smokes," Trenton said. Thornton who didn't smoke but chewed tobacco patted his pockets and came up with a pouch of Beechnut. The girl shook her head and pointed at Trenton's cigarette.

"C'mon now, girlie," Thornton pleaded. "You're too dang young to be smokin' anyways."

Private Miles Abramson leaned over the tailgate offering a Baby Ruth candy bar. "Try this, Thornton. "Kids love candy."

"Goddamn; I know that, Abramson." Thornton snatched at the candy bar and pantomimed eating it while making yummy sounds. The Korean girl stamped her foot and pointed at the cigarette.

"Somebody loan me some smokes," Thornton pleaded. While he was collecting cigarettes, a Korean soldier approached wearing a white armband around the sleeve of his U.S. Army fatigues.

Master Sergeant Pak Chun Hee barked something in Korean and all the local kids began to back away. "Orphans," the Korean soldier said, waving his hand at the kids who eyed him suspiciously. "They will just trade the cigarettes for food. If you want the Coke, let me handle it." He reached for the candy bar and Thornton handed it over.

Pak lectured in Korean for a moment, extended the candy bar and held out his other hand for the soda bottle. The little girl snatched at the candy and handed over the Coke. Deal done, the kids scattered.

"Thanks, buddy." Thornton held up his prize. "Ah 'preciate the help." Thornton struggled with the soda until Pak took the bottle and neatly uncapped it with a twist of his bayonet. "Pretty slick," Thornton said guzzling soda. "Thanks again."

"You are U.S. Marines." It was more of a statement than a question. Pak recognized the uniforms from his time with the occupation forces right after the last war. Everyone had much admiration for the Marines. Pak had even been befriended by one during his time as a gofer with the legation in Seoul. He struggled to remember a name and then got it.

"Do you know Captain Connor? He was a Marine. In Seoul, some time ago."

"I don't know my ass from my elbow, pal." Corporal JJ Jones laughed as he climbed into the idling truck. "We're Able Company, 5th Marines and we just got here."

The trucks rolled out of the Pusan port, drivers grabbing gears as they steered northwards. Pak watched them leave and made a note on the clipboard he was carrying. American Marines were known to be ferocious fighters, the sort of professionals he admired. Surely, they would need a reliable professional soldier as translator.

The Bean Patch

IN A RUTTED AND rubble-strewn stretch of disused acres south of Masan, Able Company was pitching tents and unloading gear. Marines involved in setting up camp paused occasionally, looking at each other and showing sheepish grins as long rattles of machinegun fire or the crump-bang of artillery or mortar rounds echoed off the low hills surrounding their new bivouac.

According to what the Captain told them shortly after they arrived, this was supposed to be an area well behind the fighting line where they would be held in reserve until ordered into action beside the other first battalion rifle companies. From what they could hear, none thought *well behind* meant they were very far from a pitched battle on the other side of the hills surrounding the Bean Patch.

With their GP tents erected, Lt. Boyle and Staff Sgt. Petrosky marched the machinegun section across the field to an open area where they intended to ensure all the guns were functional and running smoothly. It was Petrosky's idea. "Hustling up to a firefight ain't no time to discover a gun is on the fritz." He had all three of the .30-calibers unpacked and cleaned then marched off with belts of live rounds draped around the necks of his gun crews. Boyle cleared it with Captain Gerdine who credited it as a good idea.

"All three guns on line here," Petrosky said pointing at a furrow where soybeans had once been planted by Korean farmers. "Load and lock." He pointed at a hill mass in the distance bisected by a long line of irregular boulders. "Target is them boulders out there on the hillside. Range two hundred. This will be free guns, search and traverse."

He paced behind the line as the gun crews popped the feed covers and snapped ammo belts into their feed pawls. "Commence fire on my command. Controlled bursts of five to eight rounds. A-gunners bring 'em on target. Ready on the line...commence fire!"

The guns began to stutter, gunners crouched behind the sights and walked rounds up onto the targets. Dirt and dust began to rise in a cloud on the hillside as .30-caliber rounds pounded the rock. It was like a release for the gunners. No enemy soldiers in sight, but they were in Korea, firing live rounds, what they had trained so long and hard to do. The two Marines manning Gun Three on the line got carried away and blew a long, rattling stream of fire at the distant targets. The barrel began to smoke and glow.

"No, goddammit! Cease fire!" Petrosky charged toward the gun. "You're gonna burn out the barrel."

Petrosky paced up and down the gun line. "How many times I got to tell you people? Short bursts...five to eight rounds. We can't afford to be burning out barrels and over-heating these guns." He paused thinking for a minute. "Let me show you a little trick." He walked over to Gun One. "Now you open fire when I say. Soon as you hear the word JAM, you cease fire. Got that?"

The gunner shrugged and settled down behind his weapon. "Fire!" Petrosky commanded and then he shouted loudly so everyone could hear: PEANUT BUTTER, PEANUT BUTTER, JAM!

The gunner let off the trigger and turned a quizzical glance on his Section Sergeant who told him to count the rounds expended.

"Seven rounds, Sergeant Ski."

"Works every time. Now all you machinegunners repeat after me. PEANUT BUTTER, PEANUT BUTTER, JAM. "Good! Now louder. Everybody." They repeated the phrase until it became a rhythmic chant.

"You keep that in mind when you're on the gun and I guaran-goddam-tee you will fire between five to eight rounds in a burst. Reload, get on the guns, and I want to hear you people sound off!"

They ran the drill, chanting in unison as the guns roared and then fell silent simultaneously as if a cease-fire command had been given. Petrosky strode the gun line.

"Gun One, how many rounds?"

"Six, Sergeant Ski."

"Two?"

"Seven, Sergeant Ski."

"Three?"

"Five, Sergeant Ski."

"Three check your headspace. The rest of you continue the drill."

Lt. Art Boyle was chuckling when Petrosky walked up beside him grinning. "Where in the hell did you learn that, Ski?"

"Guy who showed me was one of Manila John Basilone's gunners on Guadalcanal. Works like a charm, saves ammo and barrels."

ELEMENTS OF THE NORTH Korean People's Army, supported by a battery of captured U.S. 105mm howitzers, were attacking across a broad front south of the Naktong River. The Reds had made a night crossing, brushed by a battered unit of the Army's 25th Infantry Division and run smack into Baker and Charlie Companies of the 1st Battalion, 5th Marines who were just coming on line. It was a running fight at first, with the North Koreans pounding into the Marines' left flank as the battalion commander scrambled to pivot his units and meet the attack. Initial casualties in Charlie Company were heavy until LtCol. George Newton got Baker Company turned and dug in to hold. That's when the artillery on the other side of the Naktong began to drop high explosive rounds all over them.

"We're stuck for a while. Two-Five has priority on the artillery." Newton tossed a handset to his radio operator and glanced at First Lieutenant Tommy Stanton, who was looking up as usual. The sky was Stanton's environment. He was an affable, drawling Texan from Lubbock, a Marine fighter pilot on detached duty as the battalion's Forward Air Controller. "Tex, can we get some air support to hit that battery on the other side of the river?"

"Lemme see what I can rustle up, Colonel." Stanton reached for his own radio, a special set that could talk long distance to the control center at K-1 airfield west of Pusan. As the FAC talked to his fellow aviators, Newton pointed at his own radio operator. "Get the Three and tell him I want Able Company up here on the double."

LtCol. Newton peeked over the rim of the hole as incoming fire buzzed overhead like a swarm of hornets and artillery fire lashed at his positions. Less than two kilometers west, the 2nd Battalion, 5th Marines were struggling against fierce enemy resistance, climbing doggedly up a piece of high ground that was marked on his map as Obong-ni. That meant nothing to the Marines clawing up toward the fiercely defended strongpoint. They just called it No Name Ridge. And that fight had priority right now.

Captain Stanton showed a thumbs up. "Flight of four Corsairs from the Sicily offshore are headed our way, Colonel. Flight lead is an old partner of mine. He says he'll divert two birds to hit our targets."

"Beautiful, Tex. Give me the word and I'll have mortars fire some Willy Pete to mark the target for them."

Ten minutes later, with casualties mounting and ammo running low in the ground fight below Obong-ni, four carrier-based F-4U Corsairs zoomed over the battlefield. "VMF-214," Stanton said as two of the bomb-laden aircraft peeled off and began to circle the Naktong River. "Damned old Black Sheep to the rescue." Stanton listened to a transmission on his radio. "I got 'em on the horn, Colonel. Standing by for us to mark the target."

White Phosphorus rounds from the battalion's 81mm mortars impacted near the North Korean artillery position on the north bank of the Naktong, sending fiery spears of burning chemical and a cloud of white smoke over the target. The Marine aviators rocked their wings and began to dive. Napalm spilled in long scorching runs as the first plane made an attack. The second Corsair followed with high-explosive bombs, and the North Korean artillery fire suddenly ceased. "Nice work, Tex!" Colonel Newton reached for his radio handset. "Give 'em a Bravo Zulu."

Newton contacted his Company Commanders to order a counterattack against the Reds facing them. As costly as this skirmish had been, he knew it was a sideshow. The bulk of the North Korean 4th Division was dug in deep on No Name Ridge and they had to be eliminated or shoved northwards back across the Naktong where they wouldn't present a threat to the port of Pusan. That was the main objective of this push to reduce the Naktong Bulge. There was no doubt in LtCol. Newton's mind that his battalion would soon find themselves climbing No Name Ridge.

Able Company Marines got their first close-up look at war in Korea as the truck convoy carrying them forward passed through villages that had been devastated in earlier fighting around the Pusan perimeter. It was an ugly ride for those that hadn't seen similar things in a previous war. Bloated corpses in grotesque postures lined much of the road. Some were South Korean soldiers, most were civilians—men, women, and kids—burned or blasted in brutal fighting and now blanketed by clouds of black blowflies.

As the rumble of artillery got louder and the stench of decaying bodies overpowered the smell of diesel exhaust blowing over them, Able Company Marines smoked or chewed gum, trying to show a steady demeanor, working hard to hide the effects of an ugly reality check. They were noisy and happy to be on the move when the trucks picked them up at the Bean Patch. After a first hour on the rutted, shell-pocked road winding through the aftermath of seesaw battles that had raged through the area, they were silent, checking equipment for a useless second or third time, fiddling with weapons, looking down rather than out as the convoy rolled steadily northward.

Private Miles Abramson, riding near the tailgate of a truck carrying his squad from second platoon, sat wide-eyed trying hard not to lose the powdered egg meal he'd bolted while they were loading the trucks. He had his helmet clenched between his knees just in case, but he really didn't want to puke right here in front of the other guys who seemed to be taking it all so calmly.

Doc Clinton, sitting across from him, noted the pallor and clenching jaw muscles. Sights like these were shocking to everyone, but for a kid like Abramson, shoved into the sensory horror without the kind of mental prep that comes in boot camp, it was brutal. He dug into his kit for a bottle of Dramamine tablets, shook out a couple, and handed them across with a canteen. Motion sickness was not the problem, but swallowing something against the gorge rising in Abramson's throat might have a calming effect.

Forward of Clinton and Abramson, Gunnery Sergeant Elmore Bates sat across from Sergeant Heywood Trenton. He listened to the rumble and crack of artillery rounds impacting somewhere to the east of the road. "No bigger than fucking seventy-fives," Bates said. "No sweat."

Trenton pushed his helmet to the back of his head, scratched at his scalp, and inclined his head toward the rest of the Marines in the truck. "Tell them, not me." Fighting the jolt and jar of the truck's brutalized suspension, Trenton tried to get a look at the map on the Gunny's lap. "Skipper tell you anything more than he told the rest of us?"

Bates folded the map and shoved it in a pocket. "Ain't much to tell. Second Battalion took an ass-kicking trying to blow the commies off No Name Ridge. We're the next bunch of lucky bastards to take a crack at it. Battalion on line, hey-diddle-diddle, right up the middle."

"And once we get to the end of the road," Thornton said recalling the quick-and-dirty briefing Captain Gerdine had given his officers and NCOs at the Bean Patch, "it's shoe-leather express to wherever the hell Baker and Charlie are."

"That's what the man said," Bates confirmed. "They got into a pissing contest and then pulled back to regroup. When we get there, it's over into the fucking attack."

A guide from the battalion reconnaissance section met Captain Gerdine and his Marines at a staging area with little further information. "Two-five is stuck on the hill," he said. "You guys are supposed to reinforce and take the ridge."

"Just like that," Lt. Lopez said snapping his fingers and smiling at the recon man. "How far to the battalion line?"

Pointing at a road that forked near where the convoy was unloading. "Up that way about two, maybe three miles," the guide said. "Shouldn't take too long."

"Forced march..." Captain Gerdine used his fingers to measure the distance on his map. "Any word on enemy activity along the route?"

"Hard to say, Captain." The recon man waved an arm at the line of low hills that flanked the road. "There's gook units all over them hills, but they haven't moved to cut the road so far." Gerdine smiled at the term. "Gooks." A pejorative for the enemy that everyone seemed to have adopted. The Battalion Intelligence Officer said it was a bastardization of a Korean word for foreigners. And like the terms Nips or Krauts in the last war, it served to dehumanize the enemy.

Gerdine led Able Company, loaded down with all the ammo they could carry, up the road in a long, loose column of platoons. Lopez and third platoon were leading with a squad on point, well forward of the main body. They were followed by weapons with their 3.5-inch rocket launchers and mortars. Staff Sgt. Petrosky's machineguns had been farmed out, one to each rifle platoon. Gerdine and his little command group marched behind weapons platoon with second and then first platoons following. They'd gone about a mile, watching the occasional flight of aircraft in the distance and listening to the increasingly loud rumble of artillery, when Lopez and his third platoon Marines began to scatter, heading for the slime-filled ditches at the side of the road. There was a babble of confused shouts from the head of the column followed by the roar of small-arms fire. Gerdine rushed forward as the rest of the company dove off the road. He saw Lopez waving from a ditch. "Tanks!" Lopez shouted and pointed toward a spot where the road curved sharply. "Two of 'em right up there!"

Gerdine heard them then. The snort of laboring engines and the creak-squeak-clank of tracks chewing into hard-packed dirt. Lopez' point squad came rushing into sight from around the bend dragging a pair of casualties, and Lopez sent a squad up a piece of high ground to the right of the road. Gerdine swerved to follow. Just as the squad got to an area where they could see around the curve and look down on the road, machinegun fire tore into them, forcing Gerdine and the others to sprawl prone. Two of the leading Marines tumbled down the hill. Gerdine rushed by them, desperate to see what he was facing and barely noticing Doc Clinton and another Corpsman rushing toward the wounded.

Gerdine saw from his vantage point atop a little knoll that both vehicles were mud-caked T-34s. The tanks rumbled forward cautiously, raking the road and hillocks with fire from their bow-mounted machineguns. Behind the tanks were maybe 20 or 30 infantrymen carrying rifles or drum-magazine burp-guns. It was hard to tell through a cloud of dust that rose from the tank tracks. Gerdine saw a soldier in the

turret of the lead tank pump his fist for more speed and heard
gears clash as drivers accelerated. He stumbled down the hill
shouting for Lopez to take the rest of his platoon up to the
high ground and engage the Red infantry.

He was rushing back toward Weapons Platoon when he saw
Gunny Bates dragging an anti-tank crew forward toward the
bend in the road. Carrying the tube was Corporal Marcus, the
section leader. *Good choice, Gunny*, Gerdine thought as small-
arms fire erupted on the hill, and third platoon engaged the
advancing infantry. Over the snarl and snap of M-1s and BARs
trading fire, Gerdine shouted for Ruggles to advance with his
second platoon. "Take your people up there to the left," he
shouted, pointing at another line of rolling hills on the opposite side of the road. "Infantry behind the tanks," he panted.
"Soon as you see them open up!"

Corporal Sean Marcus waited behind a boulder at the curve
in the road while his loader crammed a rocket round into the
tube on his shoulder. There was a sharp firefight roaring on
either side of the road, but Marcus ignored that, didn't even
flinch as close rounds kicked up dirt and rock shards around
him and his loader. Marcus was focused on the lead T-34,
trying to decide exactly where to place the round he was
getting ready to fire. For some reason, right up until that very
moment, he'd never really believed that he would wind up
engaging an enemy tank. It was one thing to spit practice
rounds at old hulks on a range but this was the real deal, what
the Marine Corps said his weapon was designed to do.

When the assistant gunner tapped his shoulder and shouted
that the gun was up. Marcus braced his firing shoulder against
the rock and stared through the sight mounted alongside the
tube. He ignored the a-gunner's shout to clear the back-blast
area. If some dickhead was stupid enough to stay behind a 3.5
about to fire, that was just tough shit in this real world. He also
ignored the stadia lines in the lens. That was for figuring lead,
and he didn't need a lead on this fucking monster headed
directly for him with a machinegun spitting and the main gun
swiveling in his direction. Marcus centered his sight right
below the main gun mantlet where the turret fit into the chas-

sis. *That's the sweet spot,* Marcus remembered as he squeezed the trigger.

The 90mm rocket hit the T-34 with a resounding clang, followed by a loud detonation. The tank seemed to bounce once and then flames flickered from the hatches and black smoke billowed. Gunny Bates was suddenly at his side, pulling at his collar and pointing at the hill above them. "Up there!" he shouted, pointing. "Find a spot where you can hit the second one!"

Marcus scrambled up the hill ahead of his a-gunner who was wrestling a second rocket out of his canvas pouch. They tumbled into a spot next to third platoon Marines pumping fire at the enemy infantry. "There's that sonofabitch," Marcus shouted pointing at the second tank maneuvering around the burning hulk of its lead vehicle. "Load!"

The assistant gunner jerked the shorting clip from a round, depressed the contact lever on the rube, and shoved the rocket into the launcher. When it was seated properly, he tapped Marcus to let him know it was ready to fire. Sean locked the center of his sight on an open hatch atop the tank. Armor always thinnest on the top of a tank, he remembered as he tracked the advancing vehicle. The T-34 was almost directly below his perch when Marcus squeezed the trigger.

The effect of the rocket penetrating the tank was spectacular. It must have bored through and hit some ready ammo. Marcus watched the tank erupt in a ball of flame. The turret lifted right off the chassis and fell onto the side of the road. He was marveling at the sight when his assistant gunner pulled him down to avoid incoming fire. "Holy fucking shit!" Corporal Sean Marcus stared at the launcher lying across his knees. It seemed then like some strange, magical device he was seeing for the first time. "Did you see that shit?"

Loss of their tank support sent the surviving Red infantry scrambling back down the road. Gerdine counted 24 of them who wouldn't make the retreat. They'd taken one man killed and five wounded in the encounter, but Doc Clinton said those would probably all survive if they made it to the battalion aid station. Able Company resumed the march toward a much larger fight waiting for them in the distance at No Name Ridge.

As he walked up and down the line, checking on the condition of his Marines, HM2 Arleigh Clinton stopped beside Private Miles Abramson who was holding onto one corner of a poncho supporting a wounded man who couldn't walk. As Abramson struggled valiantly with the unwieldy burden, Clinton noticed a trickle of blood on the young man's wrist and hand. When the CO called for a quick rest, the Corpsman pushed at Abramson's left sleeve. There were four little black dots between his wrist and elbow, two of them still seeping blood.

"Looks like you caught a little shrapnel here, Miles." Clinton pulled some antiseptic and gauze out of his kit and probed around the wounds trying to determine if any of the metal was still in Abramson's arm. "Looks OK...probably some bits still in there...they'll work out eventually." He wrapped a clean bandage around the disinfected spots. "Might just be good enough for a Purple Heart."

Abramson flinched and quickly pulled his sleeve down over the bandage. "Doc, please don't say anything about this, OK?"

"Why not? People get wounded in combat, Miles. Nothing to be ashamed of."

Private Miles Abramson pointed at the man lying on the poncho nearby with two bullet holes in his thigh. "That's wounded," he whispered. "This ain't shit."

Gunny Bates had Able Company's most serious casualty wrapped in a poncho tied with pup tent guy lines and was distributing the dead man's gear and ammo when Gerdine walked up to him. Bates handed over the man's dogtags. "Mason," he said. "One of the guys we sprung from the brig back at Pendleton. Bit of a hell-raiser but he was solid."

"Well, Gunny..." Gerdine massaged the tags between his thumb and forefinger. "He died running toward the fight. Worse ways for a Marine to go."

"That's right Skipper." Bates looked up at his Company Commander. Hard to tell what Gerdine was thinking, but the CO looked exactly like his nickname at that moment. "You know how it goes, sir. It ain't never easy."

"Yeah." Sad Sam Gerdine pocketed the dogtags and signaled for his unit to move. "He's the first, but he won't be the last."

AS ABLE COMPANY BEGAN to ascend No Name Ridge, slowly and cautiously negotiating a series of crags and depressions, they passed battered clutches of exhausted men who had survived three days of brutal clashes on the ridge. Filthy and bedraggled, most showing bloody bandages, survivors from 2nd Battalion, 5th Marines barely acknowledged those sent to relieve them and make another attempt to dislodge the North Koreans from the crucial high ground overlooking the Nak-tong.

Captain Gerdine climbed behind his second platoon with Lt. Ruggles and Gunny Bates who pointed at Corpsmen tending a line of prostrate wounded. "Them guys got the bulldog piss beat out of 'em up here." Gerdine just nodded and pushed on uphill. In their briefing with the battalion commander, Col. Newton admitted some 2/5 units took something like 60 percent casualties in three long days of seesaw battle with the NKPA's 18th Regiment still holding the hill. He expected his first battalion to do better given the pounding that air and artillery had delivered for hours prior to launching their attack.

Able Company paused at an undulating dirt road that circled the ridge just below the military crest. Gerdine watched Baker Company on his right move up to consolidate the battalion line. Ahead about 300 meters on the other side of the road were the battalion's objectives, two distinctive hills, the highest points on No Name Ridge. The road where they were paused marked the rolling point where they would step off into the assault. Able would incline to the left heading for Hill 102 while Baker veered right going after Hill 109.

"Gunny, pass the word to Lieutenant Boyle." Gerdine jerked a thumb over his shoulder where Weapons Platoon was climbing toward them "Have him set his 60 mortars in along this road. Then get a couple of his guys to follow us with comm wire." Each platoon carried a WW II vintage SCR-300 radio, but they were finicky and transmissions were often blocked by terrain features. Gerdine wanted a hard wire into his own hip-pocket fire support. The piddly little mortars wouldn't do much damage, but they did have smoke rounds that would provide concealment if Able Company got into a serious firefight.

A small observation aircraft buzzed over the assault companies waggling its wings. It looked to Gerdine like a Piper Cub but the Forward Air Controller told him it was called an OY Sentinel and as long as it was hanging around, they'd have access to close air support. Gerdine pointed at the slow-moving aircraft. "That ours?"

"That's him," Lt. Tex Stanton grinned and pointed at the huge radio strapped to the back of a beefy NCO who was barking into a handset. "We just been talking to him."

"Ask him to take a look at Hill 102." Gerdine stood and signaled for his men to cross the road and begin their climb. "Let me know what he sees up there."

"Man says he's looked at both hills, Sam." Lt. Stanton led his radio operator up closer to the Company Commander. "He ain't seen much of anything so far. He'll be sure and let us know if he does."

As they crossed the road and continued to climb, Gerdine turned to see Lt. Boyle and his mortarmen digging gun pits in the rocky ground. Stanton strolled past wearing a broad grin and offering a mock salute. "Just sing out when you want Marine Air to save the day."

Captain Sam Gerdine wasn't sure exactly what to think of the cocky aviator. Hard to tell if the attitude was just Texas bullshit or the typical banter between Marine aviators and infantrymen. Colonel Newton said the guy was a gem. Stanton was serious enough underneath the cocky demeanor and seemed to know his business. He'd distributed bright colored squares of silk to each of the platoon commanders and discussed how to mark positions to avoid friendly casualties from close bombing or strafing runs. *We'll see how a grounded fighter pilot does when the defecation hits the oscillation*, Gerdine thought as he continued to climb alongside two Marines who were unspooling comm wire and carrying a Double-E8 field phone.

With aching thigh muscles and empty canteens, Able Company was nearing the crest of Hill 102 by mid-afternoon. They'd been delayed briefly a few times as rifle squads maneuvered to eliminate snipers, but so far they hadn't hit any stiff resistance. Lt. Tex Stanton passed word from an air observer that Baker Company on the right was on top of Hill 109 and digging in to defend after not much more than spotty contact. Captain Gerdine thought maybe the gooks had decided to abandon No Name Ridge. And then the world around Able Company exploded to disabuse him of that notion.

They seemed to literally spring up out of the earth. Machineguns hammered and swept fire into Able Company's leading elements as Marines dove for cover. Gerdine heard the stutter of burp-guns spitting fire from behind what seemed like every rock or fold in the ground. The first casualty in the command group was Gerdine's radio. An enemy gunner popped up out of a camouflaged hide and literally shot it off the back of the Marine carrying it. Gerdine shouldered his carbine, drilled the enemy soldier before he could do any more damage, and yelled for a Corpsman. Doc Clinton came tumbling down the hill, but the radio operator waved him off. The radio was a mangled mess, but he was OK.

When he failed to raise the CO by radio, Lt. Ruggles sent a runner with word that he was facing a broad field of fire coming from camouflaged holes all along his front. And a runner from third platoon on the right said Lt. Lopez was taking casualties from a gook recoilless rifle firing into his right flank. Lt. Porter's first platoon on the left was taking heavy machinegun fire from a couple of caves to their front.

Why hadn't anyone spotted this? Why hadn't the vaunted aerial observers warned them? From behind a big boulder that was being eroded by incoming rounds, Captain Sam Gerdine sat next to Gunny Bates who was cranking the field phone and trying to contact the mortar crews below them for supporting fire. Gerdine felt frustrated with no way to issue orders. He had a couple of runners available nearby, but Gerdine couldn't think of anything he had to say that might help his embattled units. Porter, Ruggles, and Lopez were on their own until Gerdine could get some fire support and room to maneuver.

He'd taught them what to do. Now it was up to them to do it. Gerdine scrunched around looking over his shoulder for his FAC.

"Working on it, Sam! We'll have something shortly." Lt. Tex Stanton looked up from his handset and waved. The stupid grin was still plastered on his face, but there was a different quality to it. *That's how he copes,* Gerdine realized, how Stanton hides his discomfort in this alien infantry world

Next to him on the other side of the rock, Gunny Bates was still trying to reach Boyle's mortar crews on the field phone and having no luck. He was about to run the wire looking for a break when a bad situation got worse. "Tanks!" One of the runners pointed at the road below them. "Fucking tanks—four of 'em!" Able Company had walked into a trap. Fortified positions above them and tanks below them. The T-34s ground to a halt, elevated their cannons, and began to pump high-explosive rounds into Able Company's positions.

Gunny Bates tossed the field phone to one of the runners. "Keep trying!" He sprinted out from behind cover, knowing all the while that Boyle's mortarmen were likely either dead or pinned down by the tanks on the road near their positions. He looked up as he ran, dodging incoming rounds, and saw the little spotter plane buzzing overhead. Maybe the flyboys would arrive and unfuck this very fucked up situation, but the company was getting hurt, and he couldn't rely on that.

Corporal Marcus saw Gunny Bates running toward him, waving and pointing at the tanks. With his loader and another rocket team, Marcus crawled out of cover heading for a spot where he could fire down on the marauding tanks. Reaching a partially covered position, they loaded the tubes. "Get the last one," Gunny Bates shouted as he slid into their firing point. "Hit the last one and then the first one." Marcus got the idea. If they could destroy the trailing tank, the others couldn't back up on the narrow road. And if they got the first one, the tankers couldn't advance. Both rocket gunners cut loose on the rearmost tank and had it burning when Marine air arrived.

Captain Gerdine saw the four Corsairs, loaded with ordnance circling over the ridge and heard Lt. Stanton shouting into his handset. "Get the tanks first," Stanton was yelling to the air controller overhead. Then he caught Gerdine's eye. "Coming in now, Skipper!" Stanton pointed up at one of the Corsairs winging over into an attack attitude. The pilot swooped low over the road below them and pickled a pair of bombs from under his wings. There was a huge blast, and one of the T-34s flipped over onto its side, smoking and burning. Before a second aircraft could follow the first, Gerdine saw another tank shudder and then burst into flames. His rocket gunners were in the fight and doing good work.

"They're wanting to know if you want them to try for the gooks forward of our line." Stanton looked up from his hand-set. "Observer says its right tight, but they'll give it a shot if we can put some panels out."

Gerdine turned to a couple of runners. They might have a chance now that the volume of incoming fire from the tanks was reduced. "Find Lieutenant Porter," he said to one of the wide-eyed Marines. "Tell him to get his guys under cover, and put out some air panels to mark their forward positions." He turned to the second runner as the first one sprinted off dodging bullets. "Same message for Lieutenant Lopez."

Unable to do anything very useful from his covered position, Gerdine decided to take the message to Lt. Ruggles himself. He yelled for his FAC. "Tex, tell 'em we're gonna mark our front with your air panels. When they've got positions fixed, they can go ahead with it."

Lt. Paul Ruggles was squatted among a clutch of wounded being tended by Doc Clinton when Gerdine reached his position. "Two machineguns," he said, pointing to his front. "One of 'em about ten o'clock, the other over there about two or two-thirty. I've got squads trying to get to 'em, but there's gooks firing at 'em from everywhere in between."

"Pull 'em back." Gerdine pointed up at the circling planes. "The FAC is gonna try to hit them from the air. You got those air panels?"

Ruggles shrugged out of his pack-straps and dug around until he found two bright yellow silk squares. Gerdine took the panels and peeked out from behind cover, trying to figure out where second platoon's front was. "Where's Sergeant Trenton?"

"Right over there," Ruggles said, pointing at a shell hole to his left where a machinegun was chattering. "He and Petrosky have been trading fire with the gooks on the left"

"Stay here and be sure your guys pull back," Gerdine said and vaulted out of cover heading for the .30-caliber position where he could see Trenton spotting for Petrosky manning the gun. He was chased by incoming fire as he jumped into the hole and handed one of the air panels to the platoon sergeant. "Air strike coming in," he shouted over the rattle of Petrosky's fire. "Put this out on the left—somewhere it can be seen from the air—as far forward as you can. If anybody's out ahead of you, pull 'em back."

Gerdine turned to Petrosky and the two assistant gunners who were steadily feeding him belted ammo. "I'm gonna put this one in over on the right. Do what you can to cover our move." As Petrosky expertly swept his fire across the undulating ground, Gerdine saw clusters of three or four enemy bodies around holes that Petrosky had hammered previously. Unlike many machinegunners he'd seen, Petrosky believed in precision fire, and it was effective. Gerdine slithered out of the hole and began crawling to his right. He'd spotted a spiky run of rocks out about 30 yards, and that should be well clear of any second platoon elements. As he worked forward ducking enemy potshots, he could see individual Marines hugging the deck and crawling back in the opposite direction.

There was still plenty of incoming small-arms fire, but cannon fire from the T-34s down on the road below the hill had diminished, maybe stopped altogether. It was hard for Captain Gerdine to tell as Red mortars on the reverse slope of Hill 102 were still lobbing shells randomly across his unit's front. When he reached the jagged-rock formation, he slapped the air panel on top and heaved a couple of heavy rocks on a corner of the silk to keep it in place. He looked up as the little observation aircraft passed low overhead and waggled its wings. Gerdine saw several enemy soldiers pop up to spray the little plane with fire, but it didn't seem to deter the pilot and spotter who were directing the attack aircraft. Gerdine flattened and began to crawl back toward the second platoon perimeter, hoping his other two platoons had managed to get their panels in place.

If not, if the runners had been hit, or if any one of a hundred other things had gone wrong, it was too late to worry about it. As he flopped into position beside Lt. Ruggles, the Corsairs dove into the attack. Rockets sizzled from under their gull wings and when those detonated on the rocky sides of Hill 102, the strafing began. No one in Able Company was brave enough—or dumb enough—to crane out of cover and watch the air show. They hugged the ground and listened to the rip and rattle of aircraft cannon and machineguns as the Marine Corsair pilots stitched every patch of ground forward of the air panels. It went on for nearly ten minutes, a lifetime in ground combat, and then there was silence, disrupted only sporadically as Able Company Marines put insurance shots into the NKPA corpses strewn all over the hill.

Around 1800, Able Company reached the summit of Hill 102. Captain Gerdine and his platoon leaders met in a bomb-crater command post to tally the butcher's bill while platoon sergeants and squad leaders roamed around the perimeter setting up defensive positions with the men they had left. Lt. Boyle appeared with his mortarmen around dusk. They were shaken but otherwise unharmed. Boyle had fired a few desultory rounds at the tanks when they suddenly appeared on the road near his mortar positions and then wisely retreated downhill. He was sorry that he'd forgotten to take the field phone with him. It looked momentarily like Gunny Bates might strangle the Weapons Platoon leader, but Gerdine brushed it off and told Boyle to site his mortarmen in along the perimeter to bolster defensive positions.

Lt. Baldomero Lopez and his third platoon were the least damaged. Three dead and double that wounded badly enough to be evacuated off the hill. Porter's first platoon suffered five dead, eleven evacuated due to wounds, and almost everyone else walking wounded in one form or another. Lt. Paul Ruggles had three KIA and 12 wounded, but all of those were able to stay in the fight. Doc Clinton came by just before dark with a string of dogtags draped over his forearm and the official accounting of the wounded including the nature of their wounds. Sad Sam Gerdine tried to keep a straight face, but he was hurting inside. No question, in taking their assigned sector of No Name Ridge, Able Company had a very bad day. And that made the night attack that hit them at 0230 seem almost anticlimactic.

The gook defenders who survived the air attacks and the infantry sweeps during the day emerged in the inky darkness and charged into Porter's thin positions on the left flank of Able's perimeter. Running, shouting, and shooting, the NKPA attackers swarmed through the first-platoon defenders. Porter's Marines, exhausted and bleary-eyed in their defensive positions, didn't see or hear a thing before the gooks were swarming all over them. They fired wildly, spraying the dark with rounds that did little beyond flash-blinding everyone. Lt. George Porter, his platoon sergeant, and their Corpsman barely had time to reach for weapons before a pair of North Korean soldiers killed them by heaving four potato-masher grenades into the platoon CP.

The enemy flowed through first platoon relentlessly, firing bursts into each defensive position as they sprinted past. When they had the perimeter cleared, they consolidated for the next assault on Able Company's position. It was second platoon's turn.

Lt. Paul Ruggles had his Marines spread out just below the company CP. Ruggles and Sgt. Trenton heard the chaos that enveloped first platoon on their left and knew what was coming. They sprinted around the platoon positions to be sure everyone was ready. Staff Sgt. Petrosky grabbed a couple of ammo bearers and displaced his machinegun higher on the hill where he might catch the attackers with enfilading fire from a flank—assuming he could determine where a flank might be in the cloying darkness.

Trenton located newly promoted PFC Lanny Maitland, dropped into the hole beside him, and began to stack M-1 clips within easy reach. Maitland's best buddy Benson was dead and wrapped in a poncho at the rear of the hole. Trenton wanted to ensure the surviving southerner didn't do anything stupid. "You with me, Maitland?" The Marine swallowed visibly and stared into the dark. "I'm OK, I'm OK." He was stacking grenades on the rim of his hole. "No grenades," Trenton said. "Use your rifle. Look for muzzle flashes and then fire into them."

When the rush came, it seemed like muzzle flash was all anyone could see. Bugles blared tunelessly as North Koreans poured into the second platoon line running and screaming. PFC Willis Jackson screamed at his assistant who was crouched in the bottom of their hole. "Feed me magazines," he yelled and began to sweep the dark with a steady stream of BAR fire. He burned through six magazines before an enemy grenade knocked him cold. His assistant, riddled with grenade shrapnel, yelled for a Corpsman, then grabbed the BAR and kept firing at specters in the dark. Staff Sgt. Petrosky's light thirty began to bark in controlled bursts but it wasn't enough to staunch the flood. North Korean soldiers just kept coming in waves, Living attackers vaulted over fallen comrades, tossing grenades and peppering Marine positions as they ran.

Corporal JJ Jones fired his M-1 dry and was digging in a bandolier for another clip when a North Korean soldier swan-dived onto him. The red-hot barrel of the man's burp-gun seared into the flesh of JJ's neck, and he struggled to reach for a knife he'd dug into the side of his hole. The enemy attacker screamed something into his ear, and Jones could smell rancid garlic on the man's breath. Reaching back for a handful of greasy hair, Jones tugged and twisted, trying to wrestle the man into submission when the Korean suddenly grunted and released his hold. Jones rolled away and spotted Private Miles Abramson standing in the hole ramming a fixed bayonet into the man's back.

Sgt. Trenton heard the impact of bodies colliding over the bugles and screams. He knew what the attackers were attempting. He'd seen it before in Japanese banzai attacks. Get in among them, get close as possible where you can't miss, toss grenades, use bayonets. It was designed to shock the defenders, and it was working.

"Second Platoon stay in your holes! Fix bayonets!" Trenton snapped a blade onto the muzzle of his rifle and heard Lt. Ruggles repeating the order down the line. He hoped it wasn't too late. The fight was turning into a savage brawl. Marines stood up in their holes, some firing, most slashing and jabbing bayonets at the shapes dancing around them in the dark.

Some of the enemy attackers had swept up hill beyond second platoon and were rushing at Captain Gerdine's little command post shelter. He ducked a spray of fire, grabbed his carbine, and emptied the magazine into the dark. Next to him, one of his company runners was snapping a bayonet on his rifle. "Take off and find Lieutenant Lopez," Gerdine shouted at the man. "Tell him to bring third platoon up here on the run."

The clash on the slopes of Hill 102 continued. It was basic and brutal. Muzzle flash had nearly everyone night blind, but animal instinct drove the Marines into a different sensory plane. They could feel the presence of a nearby enemy and when they did, they slashed, gouged, kicked, and struck with whatever fell to hand.

Despite the lack of radio contact, someone somewhere down below Able Company became aware of the desperate fight on Hill 102. Mortar illumination rounds began to pop and sizzle overhead. In the eerie, undulating light of flares swinging below parachutes, Gerdine got his first coherent look at the ongoing fight. He was shocked at the carnage, at the sight of his Marines tangling face-to-face with sturdy little men in mustard-colored uniforms. Above the CP, Sgt. Steve Petrosky finally got a look at the battle below his position. He caught a wave of attackers as they bolted from the shadows and cut them down in mid-rush. As overhead illumination faded, Petrosky glimpsed more North Koreans charging but had to hold his fire. They were too close, and in the dark, he couldn't tell friend from enemy.

Below his position, Gerdine saw a man with a bugle lift the instrument to his lips. His cheeks puffed and the horn produced a loud wail. Captain Sam Gerdine blew the bugler backward with rounds from his carbine. He was jamming another magazine into the weapon when three North Koreans suddenly emerged from the dark. Gunny Bates leaped out of the hole and met the charge, swinging an M-1 like a baseball bat and screaming curses. He crushed one man's skull and nearly decapitated a second before the rifle stock shattered. The third man drove a triangular bayonet into his thigh. As Bates staggered backward, Lt. Tex Stanton stepped around him and emptied his .45 pistol into the man's face.

More flares popped overhead as Lt. Baldomero Lopez arrived on the run leading his third platoon Marines. Gerdine waved them on and Lopez led a counter-charge down the slopes of Hill 102 right into the heart of the enemy attack. It was enough to turn the tide. Surviving North Korean soldiers began to scatter and scamper, running hard down the reverse slope of the hill. Supercharged on adrenaline, the third platoon Marines started to give chase, but Captain Gerdine ordered a halt. It was time to consolidate. Able Company had some serious wounds to lick.

By dawn, the ground around the summit of Hill 102 resembled a gruesome abattoir, but Able Company, battered and bloody, was still holding. LtCol. Newton arrived to inspect the battlefield and let Captain Gerdine know the battle for No Name Ridge was over. The Reds had done some serious damage, but the Marine mission was accomplished. What was left of the North Korean 18th Regiment and the rest of their 4th Division had retreated to relative safety on the far side of the Naktong River. No Name Ridge was U.S. Marine real estate. The Naktong Bulge was punctured and deflated. Pusan was safe for the time being.

"WHO'S THE GOOK?"

PFC Lanny Maitland stood at parade rest with a long line of other Able Company Marines with Purple Heart medals dangling from uniform lapels.

"Christ, Maitland..." Corporal JJ Jones standing next to him in formation whispered from the corner of his mouth. "Didn't you hear the briefing? That's the President."

"Don't look like Truman to me." Maitland shrugged and tried to ignore a pair of fat flies that were buzzing his ears. An amplifier squealed before a technician could get it adjusted. The Marines in the parade formation wiggled and squirmed. They'd been standing in middle of the Bean Patch for the past two hours, bored and beset by clouds of gnats, as various dignitaries passed out medals and commendations for actions in the fight for No Name Ridge.

"Syngman Rhee, you dipshit," Jones whispered to clarify, wishing they'd get this nonsense concluded. He had to pee.

The South Korean President's speech began, his words echoing over the 5th Marines regimental formation. The man spoke passable but heavily accented English in a strange cadence as if he were unsure where to end one sentence and begin another. It was flowery oration, full of lofty phrases and thick with praise for the Americans who had come to help rid his besieged nation of the communist scourge. Somewhere in the middle of it all President Syngman Rhee anointed the assembled Marines as "saviors of his country." There was a lot more, but that phrase was what most of the assembled Marines remembered.

At the head of his formation, Captain Sam Gerdine stood still, ignoring the insects swarming around his ears, trying to set an example for the fidgeting men behind him. He'd consolidated his platoons into a single unit for this event. It seemed efficient and helped avoid crowding among the battalions arrayed on the field. It was also a visible reminder that he needed replacements. First Sergeant Hammond was all over that right now, skipping the formation to scour the replacement drafts arriving in Korea.

Syngman Rhee finally concluded his oration to polite applause from the assembled dignitaries on the reviewing stand. *Please God*, Captain Gerdine prayed as Colonel Murray stepped up to the microphone, *don't let him order us to pass in review.* That would be an embarrassing disaster. There had been no time or inclination to review close-order drill. And Gunny Bates, the only man even remotely capable of getting Alpha Company Marines to march in step, was hospitalized at some MASH unit in Pusan.

Colonel Murray apparently understood. He just ordered the commanders on the field to dismiss their units. The 5th Marines CO had more pressing matters demanding his attention. Shortly after the last Naktong battle, Murray got word that the remainder of the 1st Marine Division was at sea and bound for Korea under command of Major General O.P. Smith.

The news flashed through the command like wildfire, and morale visibly lifted. Joining Murray's hard-pressed outfit in a couple of weeks would be the 1st Marines under the venerable warrior Chesty Puller, and 7th Marines commanded by Homer "Litz the Blitz" Litzenberg. General Smith and both of those regimental commanders were seasoned officers with extensive combat experience in World War II. Rumors were flying that American Forces might be home for Christmas 1950 once the vaunted 1st Marine Division tangled with the North Koreans.

Meanwhile, the Provisional Marine Brigade, with his 5th Marines as the ground combat element, remained 8th Army's most reliable quick-reaction force. Colonel Murray had no idea what they might be tasked to do in the time it took the rest of the division to arrive, but he'd learned in Korea to be ready for anything.

There were a lot of empty cots in Able Company's tent camp when Captain Gerdine and his surviving Marines pulled back from the Naktong fighting. It was a bit lonely and depressing at the Bean Patch, despite hot chow and access to showers. Some of the smelly canvas structures that had housed 15 or 20 men stood deserted. Survivors from each platoon quietly moved dead men's gear to a central assembly point and then moved their own things anywhere they could find reassuring company. NCOs bitched and grumbled about the mix but didn't do much to stop it. Until replacements arrived and the veteran Marines turned their attention to absorbing and orienting new men, it seemed best to let them sort out their own living arrangements. Doc Clinton summed it up for some NCOs discussing the situation. "I'd just let them find their own level of comfort," he recommended. "Misery loves company."

There were a few interesting distractions to the routine of weapons cleaning and equipment maintenance. A replacement NCO arrived from Japan with new radios that were supposed to improve communications on the squad and platoon levels. Classes were held so Able Company Marines could learn to use the banana-shaped PRC-6 radio that was being issued to supplement the WWII vintage SCR-300s. It was called a handy-talkie or walkie-talkie, depending on who was doing the describing. Most of the Marines glanced at the nomenclature indicating PRC-6 for Portable Radio Communication Model 6 and promptly dubbed it the Prick Six. Able Company Marines designated to carry it enjoyed walking around the tent camp testing it for range and calling each other by luridly profane call signs.

Newly promoted PFC Miles Abramson was waiting in line to take his turn when he recognized the man issuing the radios. It was a familiar face from his old reserve outfit in Kansas City. Corporal Ron Edison was now a three-stripe sergeant and very surprised to see Abramson looking every inch the grizzled veteran, tanned, confident, and comfortable in a utility uniform that was faded to a salty shade of pale green.

"Good Lord, Miles!" Sgt. Edison batted Abramson's shoulder and shook his hand. "I thought sure they'd wind up pulling you out for boot camp."

Abramson shrugged and ran a finger over the soft bristles under his nose where he was trying not very successfully to grow a respectable mustache. "You know how it goes," he grinned. "First your money and then your clothes." Miles prided himself on a growing command of Marine lingo and catch-phrases. Another of his favorites was *Eat the apple, fuck the Corps*, but that didn't seem to fit here. "They kept trying to get me into boot camp, but no orders by the time we sailed for Korea. And here I am. Got some pretty fucking good OJT up on the Naktong."

"Well, you damn sure sound like an old salt." Sgt. Edison handed over a radio and reviewed the controls. "Take this thing out and play with it for a while."

Abramson extended the antenna and clicked the press-to-talk button a few times. "What's new back in Kay Cee?"

"Damned if I know, Miles. They policed me up at Pendleton and sent me to Japan for a comm course. Gave me a third stripe and then here."

"You gonna stay with us?"

"That's what I hear. Anything I should know?"

"Skipper's a good man. Damn fine outfit, I think. They sure been taking care of me anyway."

"All you can ask, Miles. Come find me after chow. We'll catch up."

PFC Miles Abramson walked around testing the radio, sending cryptic transmissions to Gungy Motherfucker and Shitbird Six before he returned the unit and strolled back to his tent. He had to return the whetstone borrowed from Corporal Bayliss Thornton, but first he wanted to refine the edge on his bayonet. He'd used that 16-inch length of cold steel to kill at least one man up on No Name Ridge, and now it was more than just another piece of gear hanging from his cartridge belt. It was a kind of talisman or good luck charm. It was important to Miles Abramson. Like his salty utility cover, it was a symbol of his passage from boot to combat Marine.

First Sergeant Hammond arrived from Pusan with two trucks and 30 replacement Marines right after noon chow. Six of the arriving men were old Able Company hands returning from hospital treatment. The rest were either fresh from Japan or caught in the churn of personnel within the 1st Provisional Marine Brigade. Hammond showed them around the Bean Patch and then stuck them in empty tents temporarily. He needed to go over assignments with the CO, but Captain Gerdine was busy with another new arrival, the man recently assigned to become the Able Company Executive Officer, or second in command. And First Sergeant Hammond wasn't sure just yet how he felt about having another officer between himself and the CO of Able Company.

"Well, I've got to tell you," Captain Sam Gerdine said to the lanky, trim, and well-pressed officer sitting across from him in the headquarters tent. "After so long without an XO, I'm a bit surprised to see the billet finally filled."

"Tell you the truth, Captain. I'm a little surprised they cut me loose from the Regimental staff." First Lieutenant Rodney R. Solomon was a Rutgers Naval ROTC graduate and a Political Science major, a background which got him short-stopped on his way to a line outfit and stuck for two years with military intelligence duties. "I had to work my bolt pretty hard to get here."

"Don't think I'm not grateful for a helping hand," Gerdine said, shoving a pack of cigarettes and a lighter across the top of his rickety field desk. "But how come you wanted line duty? I mean, staff work is a lot more pleasant...not to mention a damn site safer."

"Sir, I don't want to sound all gung-ho here." Solomon lit his smoke and exhaled. "But I didn't join the Marine Corps to be a staff puke. I understand that stuff is important and all. I got the lectures about blooming where you're planted and the needs of the Corps, you know? But that's just not my...well, Captain, I tried it for a couple of years but I could almost feel the motivation fading. And then Korea, you know? I figured it was time to do what officers are supposed to do."

"And what's that?"

"Lead Marines in combat. Everything else is a sideshow."

Gerdine looked long and hard at his new officer. Was he telling the truth? Was that really how the man felt? Was Lt. Solomon just currying favor, feathering his new nest? If it was bullshit, the man was in for a very rude awakening. If he was really motivated for the reasons he said, then 1stLt. Rod Solomon was Captain Gerdine's kind of officer and a welcome asset. Time would tell.

Gerdine flipped the new man's OQR shut and tossed it on a pile with some others. "Let's give it a shot," he said. "It's your first time in a line outfit, and a lot of stuff doesn't run the way the book says it should—especially in this outfit. Stick close to me. Keep your eyes and ears open. There will be plenty for you to do once you get a feel for Able Company."

Aye, aye, sir." Solomon stood and crushed his smoke into a brass shell casing on the CO's desk. "I've already met First Sergeant Hammond. Who's the Company Gunny?"

"Elmore Bates," Gerdine said. "One of the most competent Marines you're ever likely to meet. Also the most cantankerous but that goes with the territory. He got wounded up on No Name Ridge. In the hospital for a while, but I'm hoping he'll be back fairly soon."

"Looking forward to it, sir. You want me to rack out any place special?"

Gerdine jerked a thumb over his shoulder toward the rear of the headquarters tent. "Move your gear in with mine. There's an extra cot back there. Stop by the battalion armory and get yourself a carbine and pistol. First Sergeant will get you anything else you need."

Captain Gerdine called a meeting right after evening chow with his new XO and the First Sergeant to go over assignments. They'd spent the first hour passing around Service Record Books and listening to Hammond's initial take on the new men. Now it was time to start pencil-whipping the organizational charts.

"Let's start from the top and work down," Gerdine said. "Lieutenant Boyle is jerking my chain to take over first platoon. That leaves us short of an officer in Weapons."

"Glad to take that assignment, sir." Lt. Solomon said.

"Thanks, but no thanks, Rod." Gerdine shook his head. "I finally got an XO and I'm gonna keep you around for a while."

"Shouldn't be a problem," First Sergeant Hammond passed out the cigars he'd brought back from the Pusan PX. "Marcus is about to get his third stripe, and he's proven he can handle rockets. Shelton knows his mortars. I think Petrosky can handle the platoon."

"OK; let him know he's the honcho. Maybe I'll see about a field commission but don't tell him about that just yet."

"Yessir. Mister Boyle's gonna need a platoon sergeant. I'm thinking the new man from Japan, Sergeant Edison."

"Think he can cut it?"

"Six years in the reserves, Skipper, and most of that as a squad leader. No combat experience but I like the way he handles himself."

"Good. So it's Lieutenant Boyle and Sergeant Edison in first platoon. Ruggles and Trenton are solid in second. Lopez needs a new platoon sergeant. Who's ready for it?"

"I like Jones, sir."

"Our star baseball player?"

"Yessir. He's done a hell of a job as a squad leader...especially for a guy who got shanghaied into the outfit by me and Gunny Bates."

"Done. And I'll see about getting him a third stripe. Pass the word to Jones. Have him move his gear and report to Lieutenant Lopez." Gerdine tossed the stub of a pencil he'd been using on the organizational charts and turned to Lt. Solomon. "Rod, we don't do much troop and stomp around here, but we do hold a morning formation. You take it for me tomorrow and introduce yourself around. Top Hammond distribute the non-rated men around to the rifle platoons evenly as you can. Give me a list of who's where when it's done."

"Aye, aye, sir." The XO and the First Sergeant stood. "Anything else for us?"

"Not right now. Shove off and give me some space. I've got eleven letters to write."

Outside the tent, Lt. Solomon stopped the First Sergeant and extended a hand. "Just want you to know I'm really glad to be here, First Sergeant."

Hammond stared for a while and then took the new XO's hand. "Mister Solomon," he said quietly. "You don't know me, and I don't know you. But I do know that man inside the tent back there. Far as I'm concerned he's one of the best Marine officers who ever served. You take care of him and we'll get along just fine."

Captain Sam Gerdine was on number five of the 11 personal letters he wanted to write to the families of the men he'd lost in combat. Truthfully, writing those letters, trying not to be repetitive, trying to inject a little personal detail in each one, was the last thing he wanted to do. But it was a duty he could not bring himself to shirk. Just the thought of those grieving families getting some sort of sterile, bureaucratic form letter made him sick to his stomach. A little personal note to ease that grief was all he could do sitting in a musty tent in Korea, so he pushed through it, grasping for real sentiment, scrawling totally inadequate words on a pad of PX paper bearing the Marine Corps emblem atop each sheet. *If the Sad Sam moniker ever fit*, he thought as he signed the letter in front of him, *it's perfect for tonight.*

Rain was drumming on the CP tent when an NCO dripping water from the rim of his helmet ducked inside. "Excuse me, sir. There's a guy here wants to see you."

Gerdine looked up but he couldn't recognize the man in the faint glow of the battle lantern on his desk. "And who are you?"

"Sorry, sir. Sergeant Edison, Sergeant of the Guard tonight. I'm the one came in with the new radios."

"My fault, Sergeant Edison," Gerdine stepped around his desk and offered a hand. "We haven't met yet. Welcome aboard."

"Thanks, Captain. What about this guy outside?"

"Who is he?"

"Don't know, sir. He's a Korean. He said his name was...well, I can't remember exactly. He says he's a Master Sergeant. He ain't armed or anything."

"Well, probably best not to let him stand out there in the rain. Bring him in and stand by in case I need you."

Captain Gerdine was seated back behind his field desk when a stocky Korean wearing a thoroughly soaked set of U.S. Army fatigues stepped into the tent. The man snapped to a spine-jarring position of attention and saluted.

"Master Sergeant Pak Chun Hee," he barked. "Reporting for duty."

It was a while before Gerdine got over his surprise and returned the salute. He pointed at the chair across from his desk and noted the white armband his visitor was wearing. It showed a block of Korean letters above a term he'd never seen before: KATUSA.

"What can I do for you, Master Sergeant...uh..."

"The Korean is hard for Americans, sir." The man's English was accented but he spoke it better than Syngman Rhee had during the parade ceremony speech. "Easier to call me Sergeant Pak."

"OK, Sergeant Pak. You said you were reporting for duty?"

"I am, sir. I have been anxious for a chance to fight with the American Marines."

"You're gonna have to help me out, Sergeant Pak. Who assigned you for duty with the Marines?"

"It was my choice, sir. I spoke to the commander of the KATUSA headquarters in Pusan."

"What's KATUSA?"

"Korean Augments to the U.S. Army, sir. But the term is misleading. Korean soldiers selected may fight beside any American forces. I wanted the Marines as I know of your fighting spirit. I knew a very fine Marine when I was in Seoul after the Japanese left."

"And how did you find your way to Able Company?"

"I met some of your men in Pusan, sir. Very good men. I made a note of their unit and asked to be assigned here."

Captain Sam Gerdine was completely flummoxed. He had no idea if any of this was legit or maybe some kind of con-job the guy was running. Battalion staff officers who traveled back and forth to Pusan had mentioned Koreans they called Slicky Boys, petty thieves and scam-artists running a black market operation, trafficking in stolen PX supplies. Was the smiling man sitting across from him dripping rainwater a Slicky Boy?

He looked and acted like an old soldier, but Sam Gerdine was in no position to judge that. The only Koreans he'd encountered so far were all trying to kill him.

On the other hand, he thought, if this was the real deal, if South Korean soldiers were being assigned to line outfits, it seemed to Captain Gerdine like a damn good idea. He offered the man a cigarette and lit it for him. "Have you eaten, Sergeant Pak?"

"I had rations before I left Pusan, sir. That was early this morning."

"OK, let's get you fed. I'll have to make some calls about this situation." Gerdine turned to the Sergeant of the Guard. "Sergeant Edison, take this man to see Top Hammond. Tell him I said to get him fed over at the mess tent. And then find the XO. Tell Lieutenant Solomon I want to see him right away."

"So this thing is legit?" Captain Gerdine asked his Executive Officer who had immediately known what KATUSA meant.

"As far as I know it is, sir. Korean Augments to the U.S. Army. The program is being expanded, from what I hear. Originally, it was just older, experienced South Korean soldiers like this man Sergeant Pak to serve as advisors. Now I hear 8th Army has bought into it whole hog. They're forming complete South Korean companies and sticking them into Army battalions as a regular part of the command."

"So a doggie battalion with three American rifle companies and one Korean outfit? All under the U.S. commander?"

"That's what I heard before I left the S-2 shop, sir."

"You hear anything about us adopting that program?"

"No, sir. I don't think Colonel Murray was very keen on the idea."

"Listen, Rod. I think we'll keep this guy around. Won't cost us much, and he might turn out to be a godsend. I mean, there's probably all kind of information we could get from him, about the country, about terrain, about gook units, tactics, that kind of thing."

"As an old Intel hand, I'd say he could be a real asset."

"Good deal. So your job is to keep him under wraps for now. Get him some Marine uniforms and gear. He'll be part of the CP group."

"Give him a weapon, sir?"

"Hold off on that for a while. Let's get a better feel for the guy before we give him any firepower."

"TORE UP SOME MUSCLE and nicked the femur..." The Army surgeon stood at the foot of Gunny Bates' bed and held an x-ray up to the pale sunlight streaming in a nearby window. "But you should regain full mobility. There was some infection, but I think we've got that handled."

"Good," Bates said. "So how soon can I get out of this joint?"

The doctor shoved the x-ray into an envelope and grabbed a chart that was hooked on the foot of the bed. He flipped a few pages and scanned it for a while. "Don't think we'll release you just yet, Sergeant Bates." The Gunny just blinked and waited for the rest of it. He'd tried for a week to teach the doggies what a Marine Gunnery Sergeant was and how he should be addressed, but it was no use. To these clowns, a patient was a patient and a sergeant was a sergeant.

"How long?" He finally said when the doctor remained silent studying the chart.

"I'm recommending you be evacuated to Japan."

"What?" Bates bolted upright and pointed at the thick wad of bandages on his left thigh. "Some little gook shitbird jabs me with a bayonet and you're gonna fucking evacuate me? That's bullshit, Doc!"

The surgeon replaced the chart and sat on an edge of the bed. "Unfortunately, that bayonet wound isn't your only medical problem, Sergeant Bates." He tapped his chest with two fingers. "You've got a little ticker problem. When we did your workup, we found what's called a cardiac arrhythmia."

"I'm a Marine, Doc. You need to speak English."

"It means there's some irregularity with your heart function. Could be a coronary blockage or any number of other things. Thing like that could kill you. Safest bet is to ship you off to Japan where the specialists can evaluate."

"Doc, there ain't a fucking thing wrong with my pump. I need to get out of this zoo and back to my outfit."

"Your outfit is gonna have to do without you for a while, I'm afraid. We've got you on the list to fly out of here on Thursday."

"What's today?"

"Monday. You go in three days. Naval hospital at Yokosuka. Someone from the evac section will be around to provide details."

Gunny Bates didn't acknowledge it when the Army doctor patted his arm and rose to leave. He was running options, developing a battle plan. *I might be going to Japan in a couple of days,* he thought, *but I seriously fucking doubt it. There's gotta be some way to slip out of this dog kennel. It ain't the brig, for Christ's sake. There's gotta be a way out. Just gotta find it.*

By morning mealtime on Tuesday, Gunny Bates had a sketchy scheme of maneuver. He'd asked around and found a guy, an old soldier who was known to ignore regs as long as there was a profit in it for him. Every outfit had a guy like Master Sergeant Kramer of the Quartermaster Corps, who was slippery as snakeshit. You just had to find him, pitch your deal, and meet his price. That posed a problem Gunny Bates had to solve in the next 24 hours. He didn't have a dime or access to anything to trade. And Kramer was not the kind of con-man who did deals on spec.

He was frantically contemplating options when a couple of visitors showed up and solved the problem for Gunnery Sergeant Elmore Bates. Captain Sam Gerdine and HM2 Arleigh Clinton came strolling down the aisle in the center of the ward bearing gifts.

"Damn glad to see you, Skipper." Bates shook hands and nodded at the Corpsman. "Hi, Doc. I'd been hoping somebody from the outfit could find me."

"Wasn't too hard, Gunny," Doc Clinton examined the damaged leg critically. "Just checked with the BAS. They got jammed with wounded and sent you here with some other guys."

"Remind me to toss a fucking frag into that outfit next time we go by."

"Army not treating you right, Gunny?" Captain Gerdine laid a long canvas wrapped package on the foot of the hospital bed.

"Bunch of pansies, Skipper." Bates waved a hand over the bandages on his leg. "Way they fret over this little pinprick, you'd think the gooks had blown a hole in my belly or something."

"Infected," Doc Clinton looked up from paging through the Gunny's medical chart. "But it looks like they got it under control."

"Yeah, figure that fucking gook was probably using his bayonet to scratch his dirty ass before he stuck me with it."

"I want to thank you, Gunny." Captain Gerdine dug in the pocket of his field jacket and produced two padded blue boxes with gold filigree. "You hadn't coldcocked those gooks up on the hill, they'd have had me."

"Nothin' to it, Skipper..."

"Not the way I see it." Gerdine opened the oblong boxes and handed them to Gunny Bates. "Bronze Star and a Purple Heart. You deserve more, but those will have to do for now."

"Damn, Captain. I don't rate this."

"Yeah, you do, Gunny Bates. And they're already entered in your SRB, so that's that."

"Lots of our guys got decorated after No Name Ridge, Gunny." Doc Clinton snapped the medical record closed and replaced it in the holder on the end of the bed. "You should have seen it. Syngman Rhee came and made a windy speech. Called us the saviors of his country."

"I'll be damned. How's it goin' with the outfit?"

"Pretty good, all things considered." Gerdine shrugged. "We took eleven KIA on the hill. A good number of the wounded have come back. And the First Sergeant brought in about thirty replacements—plus I finally got an XO."

"No shit? He worth a damn?"

"We'll see. Right now we're just hanging around the Bean Patch waiting for orders. Colonel Murray says the rest of the division is at sea and headed our way."

"Be a hell of a lot better when we can stop being the Army's butt-boys. I'm ready to get the fuck out away from the doggies."

"They gonna cut you lose pretty soon?"

"Couple of days, Skipper." Gunny Bates smiled to reassure his visitors. He closed the decoration boxes and slid them under his pillow. *Might be telling the truth about that,* he thought, *now that I've got a little collateral.*

"In which case, you'll probably need this." Doc Clinton plopped a mesh laundry bag on the bed. "Clean uniform and your extra boondockers. Top Hammond dug around in your gear for clean socks and skivvies. Weather's changing so he threw in your field jacket."

"Old Leland, mother hen..."

"Sends his best, Gunny. Said for you to stop gun-decking and get back to work."

Bates pointed at the other package on his bed. "Ain't Christmas yet. What else did you bring me?"

Captain Gerdine snapped the twine wrapped around the canvas and pulled out a Soviet Moson-Nagant bolt-action rifle. "It's the one the guy who stuck you was carrying." Gerdine levered the folding bayonet open and handed the rifle to Gunny. "Lieutenant Stanton, the FAC, shot the gook. I picked up his rifle when the dust settled." Captain Gerdine grinned watching Gunny Bates run a finger over the edges of the triangular bayonet and examined a string of Korean characters carved into the stock. "Anyway, I just figured you might want it."

"I really appreciate it, Skipper. Hell, I might just start carrying this thing and get me a little payback with it."

After his visitors left, Gunny Bates wrapped the rifle, picked up his decorations and went looking for Master Sergeant Kramer.

On the return trip to the Bean Patch, Master Sergeant Pak wheeled the Jeep expertly through the Pusan traffic snarl. Captain Gerdine nodded off to sleep as soon as they were clear of the port. Doc Clinton fretted in the back seat, trying to decide how much to tell the Skipper about what he'd seen in the Gunny's medical charts.

Second Battle of the Naktong
8th Army

"THE BASTARDS ARE BACK on this side of the river?" Lieutenant General Walton Walker of the 8th Army swept his eyes over the friendly and enemy symbols dotting all 250 miles of the embattled Pusan Perimeter. Push here, pull there, it was like playing whack-a-mole with the North Korean enemy.

"That's right, General Walker." The G-3 Colonel pointed at a spot on the map where the Naktong River bent sharply. "Elements of their 6th Division crossed sometime earlier in the week."

"And we didn't see anything? Why am I just hearing about this now?"

"These heavy rains have severely limited our air observation, General. They know that and use to it to cover tactical movement. In this case, it seems they came across in commandeered barges. And that sector of the riverbank is held—rather loosely—by a ROK unit. In any case, enemy artillery in this area is a significant threat to our internal lines of communication."

"Yeah..." General Walker said. "And any threat to our LOC makes it hard to coordinate tactical efforts. What's G-2 have to say?"

"Latest intel indicates they have moved one of their general support artillery units onto the high ground here." The colonel tapped a hill mass. "We're calling this Observation Hill. It's full of caves, and the North Koreans have somehow managed to get some artillery pieces into those caves. Shell reps indicate they are likely 122mm howitzers. They've been firing down onto the Main Supply Route to interdict traffic."

"Which explains why the MSR is jammed and all our unit commanders are bitching about a lack of resupply."

"Yessir. Those artillery pieces are wheeled out of the caves and open fire on anything that moves on the hardball that parallels the Naktong. Then they're wheeled right back in, so we haven't been able to get counterbattery fire on them."

"And this goddamn rain that's been pissing down for the past week has grounded all the air support."

"That's correct, General. Until the weather clears air assets will be unable to strike the target."

"And even if we could hit it, there's no guarantee that an air strike would do any damage to guns inside caves. Is that about the situation, colonel?"

"It is, sir. Meteorology predicts that these winter monsoons will continue unabated for the next month. I think our best bet for an immediate solution is to send a unit up there and clear those caves the hard way."

"What's the 25th Infantry doing right now?"

"Tied up with the counterattack you ordered, sir."

"Shit. Get me General Craig on the line."

1ˢᵗ Provisional Marine Brigade

BRIGADIER GENERAL EDDIE CRAIG hung up the phone and walked to a wall map of Korea that his G-3 Officer had recently updated. It was a tactical mess. What should have been a solid arc of UN forces set up to defend Pusan was a wavy line that seemed to shift daily. Push here, pull there, stomp out brushfires and penetrations instead of going over on the offensive. It was damn sure not the way Marines liked to fight. But the Army was driving this bus, and Craig's Marines were just trying to keep it from going over a cliff.

And now another enemy lodgment on the south side of the Naktong was disrupting the flow of supplies to hard-pressed American units. That wouldn't do, especially if MacArthur decided to take a personal hand in the tactical situation. General Craig checked the message board on his desk. There was a personal from CG, 1ˢᵗ Marine Division. O.P. Smith was inbound soon with the other two regiments and all their combat support units. Maybe they'd help break this damn frustrating stalemate at the Pusan Perimeter. Meanwhile, the 8ᵗʰ Army fire brigade had another blaze to smother. He picked up the phone and called Col. Murray at the Bean Patch.

"LOOKS LIKE ANOTHER TRIP to the Naktong." Colonel Ray Murray hung up the phone and led his S-3 Operations officer to the wall map. "Right here," he said tapping a spot. "General Craig says they've got some artillery pieces dug into caves."

"No air in this weather and no Army units available, so send in the Marines. Is that about the situation, colonel?"

"It is. Call LtCol. Newton and get him up here." The regimental commander paused and shook his head. "No, belay that. I'll go see him myself."

"HATE TO HAND YOU a hot potato in this shitty weather, George." Colonel Murray paced up and down in the first battalion Command Post. "But we've been ordered to get rid of those artillery pieces up on Observation Hill."

"So it's back to the Naktong for One Five..."

"Afraid so. Two Five is still trying to recover from the No Name Ridge fight and Three Five is tied up reinforcing the 25th Infantry Division. You're on the spot for this one."

"We know how many tubes are up there? How much security they've got?"

"Latest intel says it's probably four tubes in four separate caves just below the crest of the hill. That makes sense, I guess. Nobody seems to know for sure how many infantry are up there but I'm guessing it's gotta be a company or better."

"I'll refine it once I get a look but my instinct is to set up on the road, then two up and one back for the attack. Able and Charlie probably with Baker on standby to support. Take some engineers with demo to spike the guns and then seal up the caves."

"It's gonna be slick as snot on that hill, George, and it looks like a steep climb." Colonel Murray pointed at his tactical map. The contour lines around Observation Hill were densely packed. Maybe go with one up and two back at first. Get a feel for the opposition and then hit 'em with the rest of your battalion."

"And no air? Is that still the situation?

"It is. Good luck."

CAPTAIN SAM GERDINE sat in the first battalion operations center with his fellow company commanders, marking up the maps spread on their laps as LtCol. Newton and his S-3 issued the order for the attack on Observation Hill. "No air available in this dog-shit weather," the first battalion commander said, "so we're gonna support you with 81 mortars dug in along the road. We estimate four guns in the caves but no one seems to know how many infantry up there as security so we're gonna go slow on this. Able Company goes up first and does what's essentially a recon. Once we know what we're facing, I'll order the appropriate response with Baker and Charlie."

"Engineers have been alerted," the S-3 added. "They'll have a ton of demo to disable the guns and seal the caves."

"Can we get some of that rigged as satchel charges?" Captain Gerdine asked. "Who knows, we might get lucky on the first try."

"I'll see to it, Sam."

"When do we go, sir?"

"Before first light. Call it 0400. Trucks should have you on the road below Observation Hill before dawn. Eighty-Ones will set up on the road. We'll stage Baker and Charlie nearby and bring them up when we hear from you." LtCol. Newton reached for his canteen cup full of rancid coffee. "That's it for now. Issue your orders and let me know if there's anything I need to finesse."

"Better thee than me..." The Charlie Company Commander said to Gerdine as they paused outside the battalion CP looking up at a sky full of pelting rain. "Climb's gonna be a bitch in this weather, Sam."

"And no air support." The Baker Company Commander said. "High angle fire ain't gonna be much help if the bastards are holed up in caves."

"I know...found out all about that in the last one." Gerdine scratched at his chin. An idea was forming. He was thinking about the methods they'd used on the fanatical Japanese defenders hiding in caves on Peleliu.

"Shitty deal." The Charlie Company CO pulled the hood of his field jacket up over his helmet. "Up one hill and then up another. Same tune, different dance. Maybe we could talk the Old Man into waiting until we get a couple of tanks up here."

Sam Gerdine veered off the path leading back toward Able Company. "See you tomorrow morning," he said to the other officers. "I need to see a guy..."

The guy Captain Sam Gerdine needed to see was a pal, a man Gerdine had known well in an earlier assignment at Quantico. The man was a maverick, a former boxer who loved to tangle. Sam Gerdine had pulled him out of a few barfights which the Marine Corps considered undignified conduct for a Marine officer. These days, that buddy ran the 5th Marines Regimental Weapons Company that included a section of 75mm Recoilless Rifles. Gerdine knew from hard experience that the Reckless Rifle was a devastating direct-fire weapon.

STANDING LIGHTS AROUND the hospital compound revealed sheets of rain driven across the area by a chilly wind on a dark night. The saturated hospital tents looked like soggy, sagging canvas lumps. Pooling water made the grounds a quagmire of cloying mud. Anyone who was forced outside on a night like this scampered across a lattice of duckboards and got back inside as soon as possible. But no one was out in the rain at 0200 on a Thursday morning, and that's just the way Gunny Bates figured it.

"Here you go, Kramer." Bates handed over the enemy rifle. "Man can't get laid with that and a good war story ain't half trying." Add to that the Bronze Star and Purple Heart tossed into the deal and Kramer could easily sell his lying ass as a certified war hero. *Piss on it*, Gunny Bates thought when he made the deal. Everybody's got their priorities and mine is getting back to the outfit.

"Jeep's right over there." Kramer pointed at a vehicle he'd struck from the Motor Pool records as lost to battle damage. "Far as anybody around here knows your ass is on a plane headed for Japan. I got it covered."

Bates trotted through the rain and slid into the driver's seat. Managing the clutch with his sore leg was going to be a bitch but he'd deal with that. Thank Christ the Jeep's canvas top was up. Pulling this off was hard enough without dying of pneumonia. He cranked the engine and let the Jeep idle for a while, hoping the heater worked.

"Any paperwork?" Bates felt around on the passenger seat. "How about a trip ticket?"

"You shittin' me, Jarhead?" Kramer waved for Bates to get rolling. "This thing don't exist...and neither do you as far as I'm concerned."

Bates depressed the clutch, feeling a painful pull at the wound in his thigh, and shifted into low gear. "Plenty of gas?"

"Full. Filled it myself."

"You get me the booze?"

"In the back. Three jugs of Old Crow. Now get the fuck out of here."

Gunny Bates released the clutch and felt the rear tires spin in the mud. Great gouts of that mud covered Master Sergeant Kramer by the time the Jeep found traction. "Fuck you, Kramer!" Gunny Bates extended a middle digit and steered for the sentry box at the main gate. He was hoping the man on duty there would see the Jeep with appropriate tactical markings driven by a man in uniform and wave him through rather than step out of his little shelter into the rain.

Unfortunately, the young soldier draped in a poncho and peeking out from under a polished helmet liner was conscientious. Or maybe just bored. There was no other traffic in sight coming or going at the 64th Field Hospital at this hour of a stormy morning. The sentry stepped up to the Jeep and extended a hand. "Trip ticket?"

"Yeah, just a minute." This kid probably has a .45 somewhere under that poncho, Bates thought as he dug around under the front seats as though he was looking for the paperwork. But it would likely take him a few minutes to get it clear of the holster and aimed. He let the Jeep drift forward a bit so that the rear wheels were closer to the sentry. "Must have left it back at the motor pool," Bates shrugged. "I ain't going far."

"You ain't going anywhere without a trip ticket," the sentry said. "You're gonna have to go get it."

"Fuck you, Doggie!" Gunny Bates popped the clutch and hit the accelerator. The gate guard was bathed in slime and heading for the field phone inside his little shelter as Bates grabbed high gear and steered north.

WITH HIS PLATOONS strung out on one side of the road below Observation Hill and a miserable clutch of mortarmen digging their weapons in on the other side in the pre-dawn dark, Sam Gerdine stood in the rain conferring with a Tech Sergeant on loan from the Recoilless Rifle Platoon. "Sorry to drag you out in this, but your platoon commander says you're the best he's got."

The veteran NCO looked up the hill and wiped rainwater from his face. "No sweat, Captain. If it ain't rainin', we ain't trainin'." He jerked a thumb over his shoulder at two Jeeps, each mounting a 75mm Recoilless Rifle and packed with high explosive rounds. "Boss said you're wanting us to do some direct fire into a couple of caves up there."

"That's the drill. Indirect fire from arty or mortars won't work. I've got a Marine up there right now scouting out positions where you can shoot directly into the mouth of the caves. You brought the ground mounts, right?"

"In the Jeeps. We're gonna have to hump them plus the tubes and ammo up to the firing points. Can you spare some guys to give us a hand with that?"

"I'll give you a rifle squad to help and then they can stand by as security for you." Gerdine beckoned to Lt. Baldomero Lopez standing nearby listening to a report on one of the newly issued walkie-talkies. He signed off, slung the radio over a shoulder and plodded over through the thick mud on the roadside. "That was Thornton, Skipper. He says he can see right into three caves from where he is. Nobody moving around in the rain, but he thinks there's a couple machinegun positions below the caves."

"Good. Tell him to get back down here. We got to get the gun crews in position before it gets much lighter." Gerdine glanced up at the top of Observation Hill. The sun was starting to rise, but most of the orb was still hidden behind the crest. "Give the Sergeant a squad to help with the guns and gear."

Lopez unslung the radio and hit the press-to-talk switch. "Hillbilly, Hillbilly...this is Able Three."

"Ah'm here."

Lt. Lopez shrugged off Captain Gerdine's look. "He's from Kentucky, Skipper. Better than the call sign he wanted to use. Horse Cock, seemed a bit much even for Thornton."

"Ah'm here, Able Three...you there?"

"Hillbilly, come on down and pick up your packages."

"On my way. Hillbilly out."

First Lieutenant Rod Solomon walked up as the weapons NCO and his crews began to unstrap the recoilless rifles and package ammo for the climb. "You gonna wait for Baker and Charlie to get in position, Skipper?"

"If this works the way I want it to, we might not need them. You got the drivers briefed?" Both officers glanced down the muddy road at several burned-out vehicle carcasses. The hulks were victims of artillery fire from hill. Solomon pointed at the four six-by trucks that brought Able Company and the mortar crews up from the Bean Patch. They were parked nose to tail alongside the road. "Ready to roll on command, headlights on and engines roaring."

"We'll cut 'em loose as soon as the rec rifles are in position. If the gooks do what they usually do, they'll roll their artillery out and open fire on the road when they hear the trucks."

"That's when the recoilless rifles hit 'em."

"Yep...and then second platoon goes into action."

"They're in position," Solomon said. "Ruggles said he's glad you sent them early. Apparently the climb was a bitch. Slid four feet back for every step forward."

Corporal Bayliss Thornton, Able Company's most accomplished trail guide and mountain man, scrambled onto the roadside. He was caked in mud but grinning when he approached the officers and pointed at the recoilless rifle crews. "Them boys can hit three of the caves from the place I scouted out, Cap'n, but they's a fourth one around a little ridgeline to the right. We ain't gonna be able to hit that one."

"Second platoon will take care of it." Gerdine batted Thornton on a muddy shoulder. "Nice work, Hillbilly. Now get back up there."

Thornton stuffed a wad of Beechnut into his cheek and eyed the waiting caravan. "Better get movin'." He waved at the recoilless rifle crews. "Y'all just foller me."

The gun crews picked up their loads of weapons and tripods. Third platoon riflemen hefted wooden ammo boxes and fell into the conga line behind Thornton. It looked to Gerdine like something out of a Tarzan movie, an African safari with native bearers heading into the bush. "Sergeant," Gerdine said as the senior man passed him, "try to keep the guns out of sight up there, but don't wait on us. When you see those cannons roll out, open fire."

Captain Gerdine watched the struggling men slip and stumble over the muddy ground as they continued to climb past him. After the direct fire element disappeared in the gloom, Gerdine turned his attention to the 81mm mortar platoon. They represented the indirect fire element of a complicated plan that required timing and control What had him worried was an age-old military adage: The best plan rarely survives the first round fired in combat. He spotted a Warrant Officer and another man huddled under a poncho shelter and bent over a plotting board.

"You ready, Gunner?"

"Ready as we can be." The Warrant Officer ducked out into the drizzle and pointed at the hill. "We're gonna be firing on map coordinates, Skipper. It'd help to have an FO up there with your guys."

"Won't need to be too accurate, Gunner. All I need is smoke rounds in the first volley to cover my second platoon's move. If we need HE after that, I'll pass the word and adjust."

"Gotcha covered," the Warrant said and ducked back under the poncho. "We got the firing dope on the tubes. Just let me know when to shoot."

The Able Company XO stopped Gerdine as he headed back across the road. "Can we go over this drill again, Skipper? I got a little cross-eyed when you were explaining it all last night." Gerdine decided it wouldn't hurt to review the bidding while the recoilless rifle crews crawled up the muddy hillside.

"So simple it's complicated, Rod." Gerdine began to tick the major actions off on his fingers. "One, we know the gook arty up there shoots at trucks on the road, right? So we give 'em something to shoot at by running our vehicles loud and proud down the road. Two, the gooks roll their guns out to shoot and the recoilless rifles hit them with direct fire right into the caves. Three, the mortars blanket the hillside with smoke on command and Ruggles with his second platoon already in position halfway up, starts his assault. Four, the engineers sling satchel charges into the caves and problem solved."

"And Colonel Newton bought off on all this?"

"I didn't give him the details exactly."

"Which is why we're gonna go before he gets up here with Baker and Charlie. Is he gonna be pissed off?"

"Maybe—but I'm just not gonna put our guys through another goddamn frontal assault meatgrinder like No Name Ridge. If it works, we're golden. If not, well, you might be Able Company's new CO."

"For what my humble opinion is worth, sir, I think it's a hell of an idea. And I learned a long time ago that sometimes it's better to ask forgiveness than to fuck around waiting for permission."

"Especially if you're asking forgiveness for something that succeeds."

"So, I'm down here with the trucks and mortars. Where are you gonna be?"

"Up there behind second platoon. We'll be in radio contact." Gerdine thumped his chest. "Able Six..." He tapped the XO's helmet. "And you're Able Five."

Captain Gerdine was about to start climbing when he noticed Master Sergeant Pak leaning on a truck fender. Yet another thought struck. "Let's go, Sergeant Pak. You're with me."

The Korean trotted through the rain wearing a smile. "Up the hill, sir?"

"Up the hill..." Gerdine unslung his carbine. "I'm gonna be busy, so you watch my back." He handed over his weapon and dug three loaded magazines out of his pocket. A pale sliver of sun was peeking through the clouds atop the hill. It was time to go. "You ready for this?" Sgt. Pak fondled the M-1 carbine like he'd just been handed a treasure. "At your order, sir."

Captain Sam Gerdine motioned to Private Miles Abramson who was carrying the SCR-300 radio for this mission, checked his watch, and began to climb Observation Hill.

First Lieutenant Rod Solomon heard the squelch break and jammed the radio handset to his ear. "Able Five, Able Six...roll the trucks. I'll call when we need the smoke, over."

"Roger, Able Six..." Solomon twirled a finger over his head and heard the truck engines snarl. "Rolling the vehicles now, out."

He trotted up to the lead truck and jumped up on the step. "Three lengths between vehicles. Loud as you can make it. Move out!"

"Motor T at your service, Lieutenant..." The Corporal in the lead truck grabbed a gear and pumped his fist outside the window to signal the other drivers. "We're rollin'!"

Solomon jumped clear and the trucks began to move. Engines snarled, headlights glared and horns blatted long and loud. It looked and sounded like an olive-drab circus parade. *If the gooks don't react to that,* Solomon thought as he trotted toward the mortar position, *it's flat-ass dereliction of duty.*

Above the noisy bait convoy, two 75mm recoilless rifles stood ready behind a fold in the rocky terrain just about level with the enemy caves. The Tech Sergeant in charge of the gun crews lay half-buried in the mud next to Corporal Thornton. They could hear the ruckus on the road a half-mile below their perch. The driving rain had dissipated to sprinkles and both men were staring through the mists of an early morning ground fog at three caves arrayed in an irregular line to their direct front.

"Here we go," Thornton said. "Gun barrel comin' out of the one in the center."

"Stand by," the NCO shouted to his crews. "When I give the word, haul them guns up onto the crest and open fire." Two more barrels began to emerge from the dark maw of the caves. Pale morning sunlight was reflected off a low blanket of clouds and was slowly illuminating the crest of Observation Hill. The reckless rifle crews could see North Korean soldiers manhandling the artillery pieces, pushing on splinter shields and shoving at rubber tires, rolling them out to open fire.

Thornton had riflemen spread out on either side of the firing position where they'd be clear of back blast. It was going to be rapid fire with no time for textbook drills. The plan was simple. Gun 1 fires three HE rounds into the left hand cave while Gun 2 does the same for the cave on the right. Then both guns concentrate fire on the cave in the center. Twelve rounds total and then haul the rifles back behind cover while the riflemen on either flank open up on survivors.

All three of the North Korean 122mm field pieces were visible now and crews were using hand-spikes to jerk at the trails, working the guns onto a firing azimuth. Thornton and the Gun Section leader could see rain striping the green paint on the cannons and hear Korean chatter. Thornton saw a glint of light above the caves and squinted at it through the drizzle. A Forward Observer was perched up there glassing the road. Thornton estimated the range at 300 yards, dialed a couple clicks of elevation onto his M-1 sight and wrapped his left arm into a hasty sling.

"Let 'er rip!"

"Guns up!" The NCO waved and his crews muscled the recoilless rifles into position. A first round was already loaded, and bearers leaped up onto the ridge with reloads ready. Gun 1 and Gun 2 fired almost simultaneously. Thornton could hear the breeches clank as second rounds were slammed home. He squinted through his peep sight and cranked a shot at the enemy FO. The man disappeared. Thornton couldn't tell if his round had killed the gook or just driven him to cover. And that wasn't really important. The crucial factor was the damage being done by the recoilless rifle crews. The mustard green artillery piece in the left hand cave was mangled and blown sideways. The gun in the right hand cave was emitting gouts of black smoke and the barrel drooped down into the mud.

The recoilless rifle gunners were pouring rounds into the artillery piece at the mouth of the center cave when hidden machinegun positions on the slope below opened fire.

Thornton and the third platoon Marines on either side of him zeroed in and opened up on the muzzle flashes.

Lt. Solomon down below on the road could hear the recoilless rifle fire interspersed with small arms. Hard to be sure, but if the sound of the fight echoing down from the heights above him were any kind of reliable indicator, Captain Gerdine's scheme seemed to be working.

"Able Five...Able Six...smoke, smoke, smoke!" Solomon turned to shout at the mortarmen, but it wasn't necessary. The Warrant Officer had heard the call. The 81mm mortars began to clang and cough as crews dumped long white-painted smoke rounds down the muzzles.

"Able Six...Able Five. Smoke's on the way, out."

Clouds of dense white smoke kept low to the ground by the mist and drizzle formed a long billowing ground fog below the cave mouths. It was perfect screen for the next stage of the attack. Lt. Paul Ruggles swept an arm overhead and stood to lead his men slipping and sliding up the hill. After a few yards of ascent, they spotted muzzle flashes just below the cave entrances and veered in that direction. It looked like the recoilless rifle crews had done their part, as he could see badly damaged artillery pieces surrounded by the mangled bodies of their crews. Now it was up to second platoon to deal with the infantry defenders. And those defenders, in a series of rifle pits and machinegun positions seemed to be focused on different targets. Ruggles looked to his left and saw friendly fire pouring from a ridge line. Shooting at Thornton and the gun positions, Ruggles realized with a grin. Caught 'em with their pants down. He shouted for his men to pick up the pace, urging his mud-caked Marines to push on as fast as the slick terrain would allow. *Big surprise in store for the gooks*, Ruggles thought, *when second platoon emerges from the smoke cloud right up on their asses.*

Captain Gerdine led Pvt. Miles Abramson and Sgt. Pak uphill behind the line of second platoon Marines who had opened fire on the enemy positions below the caves. They were running hard, trying to keep up with the assault line, helping each other up from muddy sprawls. As they cleared the smoke, Gerdine saw that Ruggles had it well in hand. He veered right and led his little CP group toward the long snaky ridgeline that hid the fourth cave. He spotted Sgt. Trenton on a knee jamming a fresh clip into his M-1 and waved at him "Sergeant Trenton, grab some bodies and follow me!"

As a mostly one-sided firefight snapped and cracked to his left where Ruggles' men were storming defensive positions, Captain Gerdine huddled at the ridgeline and peeked. He could see the fourth artillery piece sitting unmanned about halfway out of the cave mouth. This position had yet to come under fire, so where were the defenders? Where was the gun crew?

"Sergeant Trenton, hustle back there," Captain Gerdine pointed at the smoke cloud that was rapidly dissipating behind them, "Bring me an engineer with a couple of satchel charges."

He extended a hand and Pvt. Abramson promptly slapped the radio handset into it. "Able Five...Able Six. Secure the smoke. Tell the Gunner to stand by with HE. If I need it, I'll send a fire mission."

Gerdine kept a wary eye on the fourth cave but he couldn't see any movement from his angle. Miles Abramson tapped him on a shoulder and pointed down the slope below the cave. "Machinegun, Skipper. Three men..."

Gerdine followed Abramson's point. In a hole about 20 yards below the fourth cave's entrance, three North Korean soldiers huddled behind a heavy machinegun that looked to be a captured American .50 caliber. Thing like that could do a lot of damage against assaulting infantry. It didn't look like the gun crew had any idea what was happening on the other side of the ridge. And it didn't look at all like they were willing to leave shelter and investigate. He could see just the one position but Gerdine thought there might be more somewhere out of sight. He keyed the radio handset.

"Able Five...Able Six...put me on with the mortars. Tell 'em fire mission."

In moments he heard the Warrant Officer's croak. "Eighty Ones standing by, Able Six. Send your mission."

Gerdine eyed the ground and did some quick calculation in his head. "This will be H-E, Gunner. From previous plot, right fifty, drop fifty. One round, will adjust."

"On the way..."

Gerdine kept his eyes on the slope below the fourth cave. There was still plenty of firing at his back but it all sounded like M-1s or BARs. The familiar stutter of burp-guns was absent. Sgt. Trenton returned leading a panting combat engineer sergeant as the spotting round impacted on the slope. Gerdine saw the North Korean machinegunners duck down in their hole and sent a correction to the mortars. "Range is good, left twenty and fire for effect."

While he waited for the inbound rounds, he turned to Sgt. Trenton. "How's second platoon doing?"

"Duck soup, Skipper." Trenton flashed a big smile. "Gooks we didn't nail are high-tailing it down the other side of the hill. The engineers are prepping the demo now."

"Casualties?"

"Nary a one, sir." Trenton's grin got bigger. "None at all."

Four 81mm rounds impacted on the slope below the fourth cave. Four more followed almost immediately and the second one in that volley landed right on top of the machinegun position. Gerdine nodded to Abramson. "Tell the 81s to cease fire and stand by—and tell the Gunner Able Six says very nice work."

He stared at the cave entrance wondering what to do about this final position. Assuming the mortar barrage eliminated the covering positions, Gerdine's little detachment might be able to just charge the cave and toss in the satchel charges. On the other hand...

"Sergeant Pak, you got any idea where the gun crew might be?"

"Maybe hiding back inside the cave, sir. Maybe don't want to fight."

He nodded and turned to the engineer holding two demolition bags. "What's your name, Marine?" The engineer pushed his helmet back on his head. "Sergeant Kocs, sir. Eugene Kocs."

"Got it. Sergeant Kocs, we're gonna check out the cave," he said, "then I want you to come up with..."

"Maybe I talk to them, sir." Sgt. Pak stood and peeked around the ridge. "Maybe they surrender."

"You think they might?"

"Smart soldier knows when the fight is over, sir. I will try."

With no further discussion on the matter, Sgt. Pak stepped out of cover and walked cautiously toward the cave with Gerdine's carbine ready at his hip. Just as Pak reached the mouth of the cave, they heard a warning from the other side of the ridge.

"Fire in the hole!" That was followed by a series of explosions and the sound of rock sliding downhill. "That's our demo," the Engineer said needlessly. "Want me to go check it, sir?"

"No, stick around," Gerdine said. "I might need you and your satchel charges here."

Clouds of smoke and rock dust from the detonations on the other side of the ridge blew over them as they watched Sgt. Pak at the entrance to the fourth cave. He was barking something in Korean. He shouted a second time and then fired a couple of unaimed carbine rounds into the cave. This time he got a shouted response. Pak looked back and showed a thumbs up. Then he ducked into the cave. "Let's move up," Gerdine said and led his little assault party toward the cave mouth. "Men on either side," he said to Sgt. Trenton. "Sergeant Kocs, you stay with me and have those charges ready."

When they reached the cave, Gerdine peeked into the gloomy interior. He heard Pak barking commands of some sort but couldn't see anything in the dark. He was about to duck in himself when there was a fusillade of shots. It seemed like an exchange of fire at first, then just a few pops from a carbine.

"Coming out! No shoot!"

Two North Korean soldiers stumbled out of the cave blinking in the pale sunlight with their hands behind their heads. Sgt. Pak was right behind them with his carbine leveled. He shouted a command and both North Koreans dropped to their knees. From the wide eyes and frightened expressions, it looked like they expected to be executed. "Six men," Sgt. Pak said nodding toward the cave. "Four not so wise as these two."

He pointed the carbine muzzle at the kneeling man on the right who had red felt tabs on his collar points. "This one is captain."

"Shit fire," said Pvt. Miles Abramson as he cautiously walked up to get his first close look at the enemy. "Sergeant Pak just strolled in there, killed four and captured two. Man's got some balls."

Captain Gerdine pointed at Sgt. Trenton. "I'm gonna take these two down the hill. Get back to Lieutenant Ruggles and tell him as soon as he's finished with the demo, he can bring his people down to the road—and police up Thornton and the reckless rifle guys on the way."

"Your turn." Gerdine nodded at Sgt. Kocs, the engineer. "Blow the cave and bury the gun. I'll leave a couple of men to cover you."

Sgt. Pak got the prisoners on their feet and prodded them downhill. He was asking questions, and the captured officer seemed quite chatty in response. That much was obvious but Captain Sam Gerdine had no idea what they were saying.

Lieutenant Colonel George Newton stood with his hands on his hips glaring at First Lieutenant Rod Solomon. Strung out behind them on the muddy road were Marines from Baker and Charlie Company just arrived at the base of Observation Hill. The battalion commander wiped rain from his face and pointed at the radio the Able Company XO was holding.

"Captain Gerdine on the other end of that thing?"

"Yessir. He just called. The CO is coming down the hill now."

"I want to see him right away as soon as he gets down here."

"Yessir. I'll pass the word."

"While we wait, Lieutenant, maybe you'll give me your version of what happened here?"

"Well, sir..." Lt. Solomon saw the clenched muscles in the battalion commander's jaw and understood anything he said was probably not going to be well received. He decided to make it simple.

"We took Observation Hill, sir. All four enemy guns have been destroyed."

Col. Newton watched as the second platoon, muddy but smiling, escorted two 75mm recoilless rifles and their grinning crews down a muddy slope toward the road.

"How many casualties, Lieutenant?"

"None, sir."

"None?"

"No sir. Nobody killed or wounded."

"Well, I'll just be goddamned..." The colonel said under his breath. Captain Gerdine leading a small party down the hill behind second platoon was just coming into sight. Newton waited for him, eyeing the POWs and their escort suspiciously. "Captain Gerdine," he said when Sam reached the road. "We need to talk. Over here..." The battalion commander led Gerdine away from the crowd at the base of the hill.

"Let's hear it, Sam—and it better make me happy."

"Sir, I thought maybe I saw a better way to accomplish the mission, so I..."

"Something wrong with my scheme of maneuver?"

"No, sir. I just assessed the situation and sort of made a plan on the fly."

"You were supposed to make a reconnaissance, Captain Gerdine, not conduct an assault all by yourself."

"I wasn't by myself, sir. I had the recoilless rifles and..."

"That's not what I mean, goddammit, and you know it. What if you'd run into an enemy regiment or better up there? I'd have lost a bunch of Marines thanks to a maverick company commander who thinks he's got a better idea on how to conduct..."

"It *was* a better idea, Colonel. I remembered how we used direct fire to blast the Japs out of those coral caves on Peleliu. I mean, no air in this weather, arty and mortars can't get at them in the caves, so I just improvised. It worked."

"And that's the only reason I'm not gonna relieve your ass right now, Sam Gerdine. You get high marks for initiative and substandard for coordination."

"Job's done, sir. Mission accomplished, no casualties."

"Don't get too full of yourself, Sam. It still stinks of insubordination. You should have talked this over with me."

"Yes, sir. I realize that."

LtCol. Newton glanced around at his battalion arrayed all along the road. All eyes were locked on the two officers in confrontation. Rumors and speculation would start flying shortly. "I won't stand here in the rain and discuss it any further, Sam. You come see me as soon as we get to the rear." Newton turned toward his Jeep.

"There's one more thing, sir..."

Newton turned and glared. "Let's have it."

Gerdine pointed at the two prisoners squatting nearby under the watchful eye of Sgt. Pak. "We talked to those two prisoners. One of them is a Captain, guy in charge of these gun positions. He said there's reinforcements due to cross the river tonight. We also found out where they're planning to cross the river. I can show..."

"They speak English?" Newton interrupted, walking over to look down at the prisoners.

"No, sir, but Sergeant Pak speaks Korean. He interrogated them."

LtCol. Newton stared at the Korean NCO dressed in Marine uniform and pointing a carbine at the POWs. "And who in the hell is Sergeant Pak?"

"Volunteer, sir. Part of the KATUSA program. We sort of adopted him. He's been a great help."

"Sam, what the hell? Are you running a private operation these days? Or are you still part of my battalion, subject to my orders?"

"Still part of One Five, Colonel. Hopefully, an effective part."

"We'll talk about that later. Come show me that crossing point on the map. Let's see if we can exploit your intel."

The Bean Patch

THE ENTIRE BATTALION was jubilant at sunrise the day after the bloodless fight for Observation Hill. News flashed around the area that Baker and Charlie Company Marines had killed about a million commies in a night ambush along the Naktong River. That number was slightly exaggerated, but LtCol. Newton confirmed that his Marines had caught the enemy crossing in four barges, sank same, and shot the hell out of a North Korean battalion. Marines who staged the bushwhack had been up until dawn sniping at stragglers in the muddy water. Col. Murray and LtCol. Newton were treated to congratulatory phone calls from 8th Army.

Captain Gerdine endured a 45-minute private harangue from his battalion commander. LtCol. Newton was not one to sour sweet success with bureaucratic bitterness. The meeting concluded with a congratulatory drink and no hard feelings. It amounted to a light slap with a velvet glove. Congratulations on a brilliant plan well executed and don't do anything like it again without prior command approval. Sam Gerdine was humble and contrite, fighting to keep a grin off his face the whole time.

Just before evening chow, a mud-splattered Jeep arrived with Gunnery Sergeant Elmore Bates at the wheel. As Able Company Marines gathered around to admire the U.S. Army Jeep and shout questions, Bates grabbed a willy-peter bag from the backseat and limped into the headquarters tent. The Skipper, First Sergeant, and an officer Bates didn't recognize all jumped to their feet.

"Stand easy," Bates growled. "And you can tell them peckerheads milling around outside to stand by for a ram. Your fuckin' Company Gunny is back!"

"Welcome home, Gunny!" Captain Gerdine shook hands and squeezed Bates' shoulder. "How's the leg?"

"Little sore, Skipper, but not so bad I can't kick ass as required."

"Sight for sore eyes, Elmore." The First Sergeant pointed at the new officer. "This here's our XO, Lieutenant Solomon."

Bates eyed the officer critically and then shook an out-stretched hand. "Nice to meet you, Mister Solomon. These people have probably got you all fucked up, but we'll fix that shortly."

"Heard a lot about you, Gunny," Solomon said with a grin. "Most of it good."

"All the rest is lies, XO." Bates reached into his bag, produced a fifth of whiskey, and handed it to Captain Gerdine. "Little present in return for them things you brought me in the hospital, Skipper. And there's a Jeep parked outside. It's yours—but you might want to run it by Motor T and have them Army tac marks painted over."

After chow, Bates and First Sergeant Hammond sat in the Staff NCO tent sharing a bottle of Old Crow. Staff Sergeant Steve Petrosky sat across from them sipping slowly as he related the story of Able Company's coup on Observation Hill. Petrosky took a small drink and held it on his tongue, savoring the familiar bite, fighting the impulse to ask for more. It had been a long time since he'd been on a toot, and lately he didn't think about it much. "You should've seen it, Gunny. More moving parts than a fucking cuckoo clock, but it worked like a charm."

"Skipper get an ass-chewing for not playin' by the rule book?"

"Minor, Elmore." The First Sergeant waved a hand and re-filled his cup. "He come back from battalion with a smile on his face."

"Thanks for the snort, Gunny." There was still a taste of whiskey in the canteen cup when Petrosky set it down on an ammo crate. He thought maybe, just maybe, he had his booze problem solved. "I got to go check on some new people just come in."

When he left, Bates poured more whiskey and sat back massaging his thigh. "Looks like Ski's in a better temper. Or is he still whining about going home to Mama?"

"Not so much anymore. Mail's been coming through pretty regular. Allotment kicked in, and he's sending most of his pay

home. He's pretty well focused now that he's the honcho in
weapons platoon."

"How's that whiskey, Leland? Your brand, ain't it?"

"Mighty fine, Elmore, mighty fine. I appreciate you thinking of me."

"Yeah, well...turns out I might need your help before too
long."

"Spill it." First Sergeant Hammond took a slug direct from
the bottle.

"I didn't exactly get released from the hospital...more like I
escaped."

"Which explains the Army Jeep you drove up in, right?"

"Bingo. But that ain't the only little glitch. They was gonna
evac me to Japan, and I wasn't havin' any of that shit, so I
talked a guy into coverin' for me and took off. They think I'm
in Japan, but I obviously ain't...which is gonna cause questions
at some point."

"Elmore, you're a fucking piece of work."

"You got buddies up at the head-shed. Think they'd cover
it?"

"Leave it with me. You ain't the only bullshit artist in this
Marine Corps."

"Leland Hammond," Gunny Bates smiled and raised his
canteen cup. "You are a pal, a fucker, a fighter and a heavily-
hung enlisted man that bears watching at all times."

At mid-week, the rains that had been blowing over South
Korea finally abated. Pelting showers driven by chilly winds
gave way to occasional drizzles, and the muddy earth began to
solidify. The 5th Marines serving as Regimental Combat Team-
5 (RCT-5) continued to be the go-to reaction force as engage-
ments all along the Pusan Perimeter intensified. Most of the
enemy attacks that threatened to penetrate were handled by
Army units, backed up by Col. Murray's 2/5 or 3/5. First battalion had it relatively easy, and some said it was a reward for
Able Company's coup on Observation Hill.

The battalion welcomed a trickle of replacements and
worked to repair weather-beaten equipment in relative peace
while the war raged around them. Rumors were rife that RCT-

5 was due to be rotated back to Pusan. Some optimists thought it meant there was a chance they could make it home for Christmas 1950. Most believed more reasonably that the rumored redeployment had to do with the arrival of the 1st Marine Division now said to be docked in Kobe, Japan.

Blue skies over the Pusan Perimeter were suddenly filled with aircraft. Familiar prop jobs festooned with bombs and rockets, even a few flights of sleek fighter jets heading for targets further north, had Marines staring skyward at an impressive display of allied air power.

Private Miles Abramson sat on a soggy row of sandbags and pointed at a jet that roared overhead with wings waggling. On the fuselage in bright white lettering: MARINES. Abramson stared at it in fascination. "Just seems weird," he said to Doc Clinton who sat next to him drying medical supplies in the sunlight.

"It's a jet, Miles…that one is a Panther, F9F, probably from one of the carriers offshore."

"They got Marine aircraft on Navy carriers?"

"They do. Have had since World War II. It's why all Marine pilots are Naval Aviators." Clinton cackled. "Or Nasal Radiators as my Chief used to call them."

"You miss shit like that when you don't go to boot camp."

"Consider yourself lucky, Miles. I never met a Marine yet who had much good to say about the boot camp experience."

"Be funny as hell if they pulled me out and sent me to boot camp after all this."

"Could happen. Word is we're being pulled back to Pusan."

"How come?"

"Joining up with the rest of the division is what I hear. Who knows after that?"

Tokyo, Japan
Dai Ichi Building

SUPREME COMMANDER OF United Nations Forces in Korea General Douglas MacArthur sat with a long-stemmed corncob pipe clenched in his jaws and listened to a final review of Operation *Chromite*. It was mostly niggling detail, but MacArthur listened politely, nodding or briefly commenting as required, while his key players went over their game plan. He was thinking beyond tactical details. Chromite would be a master-stroke, a war winner, nothing short of military magic. It would be a stunning achievement, a world-shaking coup and proof positive that Douglas MacArthur, despite the naysayers and back-stabbers, was the world's premier military commander.

He'd resisted reluctant senior commanders who insisted his plan was too difficult and battled with politicians who thought it too risky. And he'd won. Operation *Chromite*, the amphibious assault at Inchon, the plan he'd been contemplating ever since the first American troops were dispatched to Korea, was going to happen. It had taken iron will and resolve but now the whiners and skeptics could be ignored. MacArthur only had time for the key players, the heart and muscle of Operation *Chromite*, the men gathered around him in his office.

He glanced at the wall-size map of Korea, now marked with broad arrows all pointing at Inchon, the Yellow Sea port city on the western side of the peninsula. MacArthur knew in his soldier's heart that Chromite would accomplish what he intended. Strike at a vital spot where major rail and road networks leading from the north intersected with crucial arteries in the south. Sever the enemy's over-stretched lines of communication. Seize the airfield at Kimpo. Recapture the South Korean capital at Seoul and return it to an overtly grateful Syngman Rhee as the world watched in awe at the sheer magnitude, the sheer audacity of MacArthur's plan.

General Ned Almond, his Chief of Staff as well as designated commander of the newly established X Corps, was updating the current situation in Korea far to the south of Chromite's objectives. As usual, it was frustrating news. Taegu had fallen which threatened the 8th Army with a double-envelopment on Pusan. Walker was dithering, screaming for more troops. Operation *Chromite* would relieve some pressure on his stagnant battle lines, but 8th Army commands had a vital role to play. If Walker failed to break out and link up with the amphibious forces charging in from the Yellow Sea at Inchon, he was finished. Chromite must succeed!

And it will. Perhaps so successfully, MacArthur mused, that he might start sending some troops home for Christmas. He smiled and nodded his thanks to Ned Almond as the Navy representative shuffled through his briefing notes.

"As you know, General..." Rear Admiral James Doyle, Commander of the Amphibious Task Force and the Navy's leading expert on landing force maneuvers, pointed at a set of tide tables projected on a screen. "It's a tricky timing problem with the surges in Flying Fish Channel. Two high tides per day and the depth change is something like thirty feet. We need at least twenty-three feet for the LSTs, so I'm going with the morning high tide for the Wolmi-do operation over Green Beach. Second tide in late afternoon, around 1600, for the primary Inchon landings at Red and Blue Beaches."

Major General Oliver P. Smith, commanding the 1st Marine Division, rose and walked to the wall map. "I'm told there are minimal North Korean forces garrisoned in the city," Smith said, sounding as if he didn't really believe it. "It will be tough enough going right off the landing spots into a built-up area, but my main concerns are the beaches—or lack of them." Smith, a quiet, scholarly Marine with extensive amphibious assault experience in World War II, tapped a finger on two locations marked as Red Beach and Blue Beach. "These landing sites are mud banks and tidal flats at low tide. If we get ashore during a high tide that covers them, we will still have to scale sea walls that run to fourteen feet in most places. We are building ladders at Kobe right now."

"Plenty of air and Naval gunfire to cover you through that, O-P." Vice Admiral Arthur Struble, the overall U.S. Navy commander, was assembling a large task force to support Operation *Chromite*. "Four cruisers and seven destroyers on the gun line. And we fully intend to keep the sky full of strike aircraft from four carriers out over the horizon."

It went on for another hour. Either General Smith, General Craig or one of the two Admirals commanding the Navy elements covered it all. The landing on Wolmi-do, an island that commanded the approaches to the harbor and was connected to the mainland by a long causeway, the landing of the Army's 7th Infantry Division on Yellow Beach to the south of Inchon, the drive to Seoul, all of it, every aspect of Operation *Chromite*. "You all have my complete trust and confidence," General MacArthur said as he stood to end the meeting. "May God grant us success in the execution."

General O.P. Smith was one of the last planners out the door and General MacArthur caught him by the elbow. "I know well what Marines can do in the amphibious assault, General. I saw plenty of it in the Pacific. And now you must do it again. Do this, General Smith, and you will reflect the greatest glory on the reputation of the Marine Corps."

FIRST SERGEANT LELAND HAMMOND sat drinking coffee across a mess table from 1stLt. Rod Solomon. He'd just finished telling the XO about the outfit's last experience aboard the Happy Hank when they left San Diego headed for Korea. "Damn near had to handcuff Gunny Bates to keep him from staging a mutiny." Hammond chuckled and refilled his cup from a porcelain pitcher. "Night we loaded up at Pusan for this cruise, he flat-ass refused to move off the docks. Said he'd shoot any bastard that tried to make him get back aboard this ship. Skipper had to lead him up the gangplank personally."

"Seems to be steaming along OK this time," the XO said, "Maybe the Happy Hank likes the Yellow Sea better than the Pacific."

"Maybe, XO...but we ain't made the rendezvous point yet. And Gunny Bates is still convinced we won't."

Solomon smiled and blew steam off his coffee. "You done a lot of this stuff, First Sergeant? Amphibious landings, I mean..."

"Couple of big ones in the last fracas. I made Saipan and Tinian. Tarawa was the worst. Goddamn meat-grinder that was."

"What do you think of this Inchon thing? Think it's gonna be rough?"

"They're all rough, XO." Hammond watched a Navy messcook stirring a bubbling vat of boiled potatoes. "You been to the same briefings I have. Hard part's gonna be getting our people ashore from the landing craft and up over them sea-walls."

"Uh huh...and right smack into a port city. Ain't we the lucky ones."

"As usual, XO. Love it if we weren't landing within spitting distance of a fucking industrial area with God knows how many gooks crawling through buildings and warehouses, but that port's vital and somebody's gotta take it. Fifth Marines is a solid outfit now—only one in the division with combat experience. No surprise they handed it to us."

Lt. Solomon stood and stretched. "Gotta go retrieve some maps. Skipper wants to do a sand table run through for all hands."

There was a messy pile of maps, overlays, and notes on Solomon's desk in the little accommodation he shared with Captain Gerdine. He rifled through it idly, thinking that for the first time in his life, he was going to be in on something historic. In the wardroom, he'd heard a few senior officers grumble about elements of MacArthur's planned coup at Inchon, but from where Lt. Rod Solomon sat, it looked...well, brilliant. *This one is going down in history books*, he thought. Kids will read about the Inchon landings, maybe even my own kids someday. And I'm going to be right there in the thick of it. It gave him a strange feeling, made his heart thump in his chest. It wasn't fear. Solomon was fairly confident he'd survive, but he couldn't help feeling like some kind of slack-jawed combat tourist. He wanted to absorb it all, remember it all, understand it all.

Solomon pulled the largest scale overlay from an envelope and aligned it with a map of Korea's western coast. Three prime objectives: Inchon port, Kimpo airfield, and Seoul. First Marine Division landing with only two of their allotted Regimental Combat Teams. Seventh Marines still forming in Japan would be along later. Blue Beach to the south was the landing site for Chesty Puller's 1st Marine Regiment, RCT-1. Colonel Murray's RCT-5 would come ashore on Red Beach minus the 3rd Battalion which was designated for the earlier assault on Green Beach, tasked with taking Wolmi-do island and securing the mainland causeway. On D plus 3, the Army's 7th Infantry Division comes ashore, driving inland in hopes of linking up with 8th Army forces advancing north out of the Pusan Perimeter. It was huge and exciting. Solomon ran his hands over the boxes, phase lines, and arrows on the overlay, remembering a phrase he'd heard or read, something attributed to a stuffy British Army officer in World War I: Big hands on little maps, that's the way to kill the chaps.

With his platoons squatted around on an open deck space amidships, Captain Sam Gerdine walked around a section of canvas that had been painted and festooned with ration boxes, lengths of rope and other available scraps. Amateur artist Lt. Paul Ruggles had done an admirable job in providing a mocked-up three-dimensional birds-eye view of their landing area and primary D-Day objectives. As Gerdine talked, he pointed with a yardstick. "We hit Red Beach late afternoon on D-Day. Before we go in, the Navy is gonna plaster the place with air and naval gunfire. Should be entertaining for those of you who have never seen it before. When the supporting fires are lifted, Peter boats will take us right up to the sea walls here...and then we use the ladders. We will be on the left with 2/5 on our right. We've got two main D-Day objectives. First one is the Asahi Brewery here..." There was a roar and hands began to wave in the air. "Yeah, yeah, don't bother volunteering. That goes to Lieutenant Ruggles and second platoon." More complaints as the second platoon Marines stood to take their bows. "First and third platoons will move immediately on the second objective here...called Cemetery Hill." A chorus of boos erupted. "When we secure that high ground on the regiment's left, we advance right through this built up area until we reach this...which they're calling the inner tidal basin. Get that far and maybe I'll get Lieutenant Ruggles and his guys to bring us all a beer."

It went on for another half-hour, and then Gerdine dismissed the troops for detailed instructions from platoon sergeants and squad leaders. He caught Sgt. Pak and pulled him aside. "We're gonna have a battalion of Korean Marines somewhere in this mix, Sergeant Pak. You know anything about them?"

"Very good troops, sir. Very brave..."

"Good. You'll be with me all the way. If we contact them, you'll be my translator."

He found Staff Sgt. Steve Petrosky conferring with Cpl. Marcus and a couple of his anti-tank Marines. "Ski, have you located the flame throwers?"

"They're aboard, sir, scheduled for second wave. I told 'em to look for me or Sergeant Marcus on the beach."

"Don't let them get lost. I've got a feeling the damn things might come in handy."

Operation *Chromite*
Inchon

The USS *Henrico*, steaming slowly alongside her sister troop transport USS *Cavalier*, gave Marines aboard a sobering view as the first phase of Operation *Chromite* commenced just after dawn on 15 September. Able Company Marines and almost everyone else not otherwise occupied crowded the rails in silence, all eyes on the line of warships closing on Wolmi-do Island. Signal lamps flickered and the eerie silence was torn by the drumroll of eight-inch and five-inch naval guns from cruisers and destroyers pounding the operation's first objective. Whispered conversations ceased or turned into shouts as the ear-splitting noise rolled over the waters of the Yellow Sea. The gunfire support vessels raked Wolmi-do unmercifully in a stroboscopic display of muzzle flash at sea and detonations ashore on the crucial island.

When the ships finished and turned away to reform the gun-line, Navy and Marine aircraft roared in from over the horizon and added their explosive weight to the attack. And that was the Marine Corps cue to land the landing force. LCVPs and LSTs churned toward Wolmi-do carrying 3rd Battalion, 5th Marines, and a platoon of M-26 Pershing tanks.

Second Lieutenant Art Boyle watched from the fantail as the Henrico turned away from the island. "Hell of a show," he said to Sgt. Ron Edison standing nearby. "Maybe Three-Five will have it easy."

"Don't see how there could be much left standing on that island," Edison said. "Hope they hit our beaches just as hard."

"They will." Staff Sgt. Steve Petrosky was watching with a foot propped on a lifeline. He was remembering the dazzling, deafening preparatory fire he'd witnessed in the Marianas. "You think nobody can survive something like that—but they always do."

It was late on D-Day afternoon when Act II began. A second high tide had flooded into Inchon Harbor. Cruisers and destroyers returned to the Fire Support Area and erupted in a flashing, roaring display of gunfire support for the big show, the landings on the mainland. Wolmi-do, that critical little mud lump that controlled access to Flying Fish Channel, was secure. The causeway connecting the island with the mainland was open. Third Battalion of RCT-5 was poised on the island to join the fight when landing forces secured the other end of that causeway.

Under murky skies with a stiff wind blowing light rain over the harbor, Able Company struggled down cargo nets and into a line of LCVPs bobbing alongside the Henrico. It was a clumsy operation in the surging swells at the harbor mouth, but the heavily laden Marines all made it into the Peter boats. As the coxswains steered away and headed for the Red Beach control vessel, there was the usual confusion and milling around in an attempt to get the first battalion into position to land in a column of companies. Boats carrying Able Company swung wide onto the far left flank of the assault line.

While the Marines squatted and cursed, soaked by spray and pelted by rain, they looked up into the gloom to see Marine Corsairs and Navy Skyraiders diving on targets inland of the landing beaches. Cruisers and destroyers that had been sending a steady stream of high-explosive shells roaring overhead suddenly went silent. At H-minus 30 minutes, low-slung LCMRs churned into the Fire Support Area to add their heft to the bombardment. The boats were essentially seaborne rocket launching platforms and in 20 minutes, they sent more than 6,000 rockets roaring into high arcs to descend and explode in brilliant flashes all across Red and Blue Beaches. It lasted another 20 minutes, and when it was over, a dense pall of smoke hung over landing sites. Pale light from a setting sun barely shining through low late afternoon clouds limited visibility, but the Marines caught glimpses of muzzle flash from hills surrounding the harbor.

The eight Peter boats carrying Able Company aligned and their engines roared. Assault infantry time had arrived. Captain Gerdine looked around at the other boats running for shore abreast of his own. His Marines were crouched out of sight, but he could see ladders sticking up over the gunwales. It made him think of hook-and-ladder fire trucks rushing to a blaze. Nothing had come their way yet, but Lt. Solomon huddled next to Gerdine pointed to three LSTs on their right off Blue Beach. The ships were smoking, and they could see flames flickering on the decks. Despite the impressive air and naval gunfire prep, the enemy was still in the fight at Inchon.

The landing craft carrying half of Able Company's first platoon bumped into Red Beach, forced in place by a roaring engine as the bow ground into seawall logs. Sgt. Ron Edison checked his watch as Marines in the forward part of the boat pushed ladders into place. It was 1733, a little late but not bad. "Let's go! Up those ladders!" Edison pushed at the heavily laden Marines attempting to climb from the pitching landing craft. He looked back out in the channel where the boat carrying Lt. Art Boyle and the other half of first platoon was bobbing helplessly in the swells, stalled with a crapped out engine. *Half is better than none*, he thought, and started to climb.

Sgt. Edison was looking for landmarks, following the first squad running inland when they were hit by gooks firing submachineguns from a bunker on their left. Edison hit the deck along with the Marines behind him. Four Marines ahead of the first platoon sergeant turned to rush the bunker, but all of them were cut down by fire. Edison shouldered his M-1 and opened up on the bunker. Men lying in the mud behind him joined in with their weapons, but they didn't do much more than chip concrete. Able Company's first platoon was pinned down on their sector of Red Beach not more than 20 yards past the seawall.

The two Peter boats carrying Able Company's second platoon landed at a breach in the seawall. Lt. Paul Ruggles led them ashore and they made good progress, covering about 50 yards before they ran into a shoreside bunker. They could see the muzzle of a machinegun sticking out of a slit on the face of the bunker, but it didn't fire. A few rifle rounds from the rear of the bunker drove the leading squad to ground. Sgt. Heywood Trenton roared up from behind along with PFC Willis Jackson, both unclipping grenades from their web gear. They slammed into the wet concrete wall on either side of a narrow firing aperture. Trenton nodded at Jackson. They pulled pins, popped spoons, and dumped the grenades into the bunker.

The detonations sent a cloud of rocks and dust blowing out of the aperture. Sgt. Trenton waved at Lt Ruggles who led the platoon forward. As the Marines flowed around the obstacle, six dazed and bloody North Koreans emerged with their hands raised. Jackson pulled his BAR Into a shoulder but Trenton waved him off. "Just sit 'em down somewhere and stand guard," the Platoon Sergeant said as he ran off following Lt. Ruggles. "Soon as we get more people ashore, somebody will police them up."

Willis Jackson waved his BAR at the prisoners. "Y'all just sit down right there," he said pointing at the bunker wall. "First one moves is a dead motherfucker." Jackson crouched beside the prisoners and looked back at the seawall where more Marines were climbing ashore. Then he looked at the hills surrounding the harbor where firefights were blazing. *I can guard POWs*, he thought. *There's worse things I could be doing on a day like this.*

Captain Gerdine, his XO, and Gunny Bates landed in the center of their assigned sector and struggled up the ladders with a few Marines from Weapons Platoon carrying mortars and a couple of flamethrowers. There was a deafening amount of noise and confusion, but little fire impacted around them. Gerdine looked up to his left front at Cemetery Hill, their primary objective. He had to get organized and push his Marines in that direction. Sgt. Marcus carrying his 3.5-inch rocket launcher and a canvas bag of spare rounds arrived chased by fire. "First platoon's over there," he said pointing. "They're pinned down by a bunker."

"Let's go." Gunny Bates grabbed the bag from him and turned to Gerdine. "Skipper, you shove on inland. I'll police up first platoon and join up when we clear the bunker."

As Bates and Marcus headed off, Gerdine led his radioman, XO, and some others forward toward Cemetery Hill. They trotted past a low warehouse reeking of rotten fish and spotted First Lieutenant Tex Stanton crouched at a corner of the building shouting into a radio. "Hold up, Skipper!" the FAC pointed overhead. "Better get down. It's gonna be close."

A pair of Marine Corsairs roared overhead and pulled into a tight turn. Stanton shouted into his radio. The pilots leveled their wings and dove with machineguns blazing. Gerdine and his Marines flattened. It was close, damn close. Rounds from the aircraft tore up sections of a road just 50 yards ahead and hot, spent .50-caliber shell casings rained down on the Marines. The air attack shattered a bunker into a pile of concrete rubble, and a pair of North Korean soldiers tore down the road away from the wreckage. Lt. Solomon shouldered his carbine and pumped rounds at the fugitives. Other Marines added their firepower, and both enemy soldiers slammed face forward into the road riddled and bleeding through their khaki uniforms.

"That's a first for me," Lt. Solomon muttered as he slid a loaded magazine into his weapon. "Won't be the last," Gerdine replied. He looked up again at Cemetery Hill. The side exposed to him, the seaward side, was steep, not something he wanted to try and climb, especially if the gooks had any kind of heavy weapons up there backing the mortars. And why wouldn't they? He looked back toward the seawall where more Marines were scrambling ashore. None of them were his. It looked like Baker or Charlie Company and they had their own objectives to take.

PFC Maitland carrying the Company Commander's radio tugged at Gerdine's sleeve. "Able Two, sir... Lieutenant Ruggles."

"This is Able Six. How you doing, Paul?"

"We're held up in a trench, maybe a hundred yards from the beach, sir. I can see the hill off to my left. You want me to head in that direction?"

"Not yet. I'm gonna police up our men and get organized first. You proceed to the brewery. Let me know when you've got that."

Gerdine turned to his XO. "Rod, second platoon's gonna nail down our right flank. I want more people in place before we go for the hill. You get over to the left and round up first platoon.

Lt. Rod Solomon slung one of the handy-talkies over his shoulder and headed toward the landing site with Captain Gerdine shouting at his back.

"And see if the second wave has landed."

Gunnery Sergeant Elmore Bates squatted beside Sgt. Marcus and peeked over a pile of smoking concrete rubble, all that was left of some kind of seaside structure flattened by naval gunfire. To their right front was a machinegun bunker spitting fire at Sgt. Ron Edison and some first platoon Marines.

"Looks like fifty—maybe a tad more—think you can hit it?"

Sgt. Sean Marcus looked over his rocket launcher tube at the Company Gunny. "I can hit it. Can you reload?"

"Ain't my first rodeo, Marcus." Bates pulled a rocket from the bag and jerked the safety arming wire. "Let 'er rip."

Marcus rose from his kneeling position just enough to clear the sight picture, aimed, and squeezed the trigger. The rocket hit just to the left of the bunker's firing aperture, sending a shower of rubble and concrete dust into the air. "Load!"

Marcus felt the Gunny at his back shoving a second round into the launcher. He took another look through the sight and adjusted his point of aim. "You're up!" Bates rolled away to observe the second shot as Marcus squeezed the launcher's trigger blade. The second rocket flew right through the firing aperture, detonated on a back wall, and blew the roof off of the bunker.

Bates stood and shouted. "Edison, get your people and muster on me!" He quickly counted heads and then grabbed the platoon sergeant. "Where's Lieutenant Boyle?"

"Boat broke down out there," Edison pointed back at the water. "He ain't made it ashore yet." As Sgt. Edison assembled his first platoon survivors, Lt. Solomon came trotting down a main road leading through the port. "Skipper wants first platoon up forward," he said pointing up the road.

Bates trotted in that direction past Lt. Solomon who was going the other way. "Where you headed, XO?"

"Gotta find third platoon." Lt. Rod Solomon ran ducking and weaving back toward the landing site. The harbor looked like it was being swarmed by lunatic water bugs. Boats dodged and backed in the chop steering erratic patterns, trying to land Marines while dodging mortar fire from Cemetery Hill on the left and Observatory Hill on the right. Solomon found a covered position near Able Company's landing site and stared out into the harbor. It looked like second wave was coming in from the transports. Third platoon should be in that wave somewhere. He spotted a Peter boat festooned with ladders and bearing a placard showing one of Able Company's assigned numbers. It was towing another boat as it drove forward toward the seawall.

Solomon saw a pair of M-26 tanks clanking across the causeway from Wolmi-do and prayed they would take some of the pressure off the men swarming ashore. The landing area was getting crowded and confused. Enemy fire, aimed or just tossed in the direction of Red Beach, was bound to do some damage.

The Peter boat ferrying Lt. Baldomero Lopez and most of Able Company's third platoon had paused on the way to the beach, tossing a tow line to another landing craft with a disabled engine. In the towed boat, Lt. Art Boyle was soaking wet and steaming mad. He was supposed to be in the first wave, spearhead of the assault on Inchon. But some swab-jockey forgot to lube something or tighten some goddamn bolt and he was stranded offshore while his platoon sergeant led his Marines into combat on one of the most important landings in Marine Corps history. Boyle was bound and determined to make up for lost time and prestige as one of the Peter boat sailors hauled in the tow line and brought the disabled boat into contact with the Red Beach seawall. Ladders went up immediately and Boyle shoved his men out of the way so he could be the first man onto the beach. He looked to his left and saw Baldo Lopez racing up the ladder in his own boat. Boyle skipped a few steps and increased the speed of his climb.

He was just scrambling onto the top of the seawall, maybe a step or two ahead of Lopez, when a bunker on their right erupted with machinegun fire. Second Lieutenant Art Boyle was just sweeping an arm overhead, shouting for his Marines to follow him, when he caught three rounds that blew through his ribcage. He tumbled backward, tripped over the seawall, and fell back into the Peter boat.

Fire from the machinegun in the bunker also hit Baldo Lopez storming ashore. He was stripping out a grenade, pulling the pin, ready to throw it at the bunker when rounds tore into his right arm and hip. Lopez spun with the impact and saw his third platoon Marines rushing forward all around him. The armed grenade fell out of his right hand. When it detonated in just a few seconds, Baldo Lopez knew some of his Marines would be killed. He fell prone, reached out for the grenade, and pulled it under his body.

Staff Sergeant Steve Petrosky, churning inland with two flamethrower men saw Lt. Lopez smother the grenade. He saw the body hump upward when the missile detonated and saw chunks of Lopez' shattered body fly outward in a spray of blood. He knew it was no use, but he flopped down next to the dead officer, waving the flamethrower men forward toward the bunker. He saw the flicker of flame at the end of their launcher tubes as they jockeyed for a firing position. They never had a chance to squeeze the trigger and send flaming fuel into the enemy bunker. Rounds blew through both men and punctured the tanks on their backs.

Sgt. Steve Petrosky pulled a grenade out of the pouch on his webbing and began to crawl toward the bunker through a spreading pool of jellied gasoline.

While Lt. Paul Ruggles tried to raise their CO on the cranky SCR-300 radio, Sgt. Trenton led second platoon Marines on Able Company's deepest penetration. It seemed like they were just taking a leisurely stroll through downtown Inchon. He could hear serious fighting to the rear around the landing areas, but this far in, the little seaside settlement seemed deserted. There was no enemy resistance at the Asahi Brewery building. There was also no beer, so Trenton was creeping forward through the pockmarked buildings and flaming wreckage hoping to get a look at the back side of Cemetery Hill. The forward slope would be a bitch to climb, but the backside looked easier, a gentle rise over a series of small ridgelines.

Trenton signaled his Marines to hold as Lt. Ruggles came trotting up the street dragging PFC Miles Abramson with the radio behind him. "Got through to Able Six," Ruggles said when he reached his platoon sergeant. "He wants us to turn around and head back. They're stuck at the base of Cemetery Hill."

Trenton squinted at the high ground on their left. "And Cemetery Hill is the company objective, right?"

"Yeah, Skipper wants all hands assembled before he starts to climb."

"Borrow your glasses?" Trenton pointed at the binocular pouch on the lieutenant's hip. He carefully looked over the back side of the hill. "You know, sir, I can't see shit up there. I'm betting we could climb that sonofabitch with no problem."

"Captain says we're needed back there..." Ruggles waved a hand in the direction of the landing beaches.

"Yessir, but I bet he wouldn't mind if we got up on top of the hill and handed it to him without anybody having to climb that forward slope."

"Well, shit, Sgt. Trenton, I recall him saying we might be called to help if they were having trouble taking the hill."

"Be some help if we just took the damn hill for him. Right, sir?"

Ruggles turned the second platoon left, crossed the street and led the way up the back side of Cemetery Hill.

Gunny Bates brought Sgt. Edison, Sgt. JJ Jones, and the XO into a little draw at the base of Cemetery Hill's forward slope. Lt. Solomon lit a cigarette and exhaled. "Bad news, Skipper. Lieutenant Boyle and Lieutenant Lopez are both dead. We brought what's left of first and third up with their platoon sergeants."

Gerdine nodded silently, trying hard to retain his composure. He was taking casualties, and that was to be expected. He was mentally prepared for it, focused on the mission, and shoving everything else to the back of his mind where it could be retrieved later when there was time for mourning. Sure, Boyle was a loss—but Baldo Lopez was a favorite. The cheerful Annapolis ring-knocker who'd been with him in the bad old days at Pendleton when there was no third herd in Able Company and not enough Marines in the two platoons they could muster. Baldo loved it, made it all seem like just another bump in the road. Laughing beats whining any day. That was Baldo's outlook. The guy had been like a life preserver found floating nearby when the ship was sinking underfoot. And now he was dead.

"Petrosky knocked out the bunker that killed 'em, Skipper. But we lost the flamethrowers."

The mention of the Able Company machinegun guru brought Captain Gerdine back to his mission. "Gunny, tell Petrosky to find a couple of good flanking positions for the machineguns." He pointed up at Cemetery Hill where they could see the occasional flash of a mortar firing. "We're gonna climb this sonofabitch as soon as second platoon gets here."

With Sgt. Trenton leading and Lt. Ruggles trailing, Able Company's second platoon moved rapidly up the reverse slope of Cemetery Hill. While sporadic fights roared below them and aircraft attacked like a swam or vicious hornets overhead, the Marines were virtually unopposed in their climb. About halfway to the summit, Trenton and four other Marines hit a demoralized clutch of NKPA soldiers huddled in a depression. There were about a dozen of them, and none wanted any further part of the fight. They tossed aside a couple of rifles and a burp-gun or two and raised their hands. Sgt. Trenton pointed at two Marines. "You two take these gooks down the hill. Find the Skipper and Sergeant Pak. They might want to talk to them."

Lt. Ruggles arrived at the summit of Cemetery Hill just ten minutes after they'd started to climb. There were four mortars still standing upright in prepared firing positions, but no enemy in sight. He sent some Marines to scout around the summit, looking carefully into the craters and shell holes that dotted the area and then reached for his radio.

"Able Six...Able Two. You probably ain't gonna believe this but I'm standing on top of the hill. No enemy resistance. We got it secured. Easy climb up the back side. We'll be waiting up here."

Captain Gerdine reported the situation to the battalion commander. Cemetery Hill was in friendly hands, Able Company's initial D-Day objective was taken. That mission complete, the left flank of landing area was secure. It was getting late, darkness was looming, so LtCol. Newton directed Able Company to remain in position around Cemetery Hill rather than advance any further inland. He was worried about a potential counterattack from enemy tanks that had been reported roaming around on the east side of Inchon.

Lt. Rod Solomon spread their depleted first and third platoons around the base of the hill in defensive positions while the Skipper led Gunny Bates and a handful of Marines to the top of Cemetery Hill. Lt. Ruggles was waiting for him, set up in one of the abandoned mortar pits and watching 3/5 and more Marine tanks trundle across the causeway from Wolmi-do.

Gerdine hopped down beside him and offered a cigarette from a rumpled pack. "Nice work, Paul. Colonel Newton nearly choked when I told him one of our platoons had taken the hill in ten minutes flat."

"Sergeant Trenton's idea, Skipper." Ruggles pointed at his platoon sergeant who was walking the defensive perimeter they'd set up on the hilltop. "Did you get the prisoners we sent down?"

"Yeah. Sergeant Pak had a word with them before we turned them over to the Korean Marines. He says you captured the Mortar Company of the 226th Regiment."

"How'd the other platoons make out?"

"We got cut up a bit." Gerdine ground his smoke into the mud. "Art Boyle and Baldo Lopez were killed. Word I got was Boyle never made it more than a couple of steps onto the beach. Baldo was hit and smothered a live grenade to save the Marines around him."

"Sonofabitch. I remember the day Baldo picked me up from the BOQ at Pendleton. Great guy."

"Skipper, we better get back down the hill," Gunny Bates said. "It's gonna be full dark in a little while. Still lots of gooks in the area."

"On the way, Gunny." Gerdine stood up and gripped his second platoon leader's shoulder. "You hold up here, Paul. I'll call for you soon as we get new orders. Keep a good watch tonight...could be infiltrators."

"Got it covered, Skipper. See you in the morning."

Two Marine M-26 tanks arrived at 2100 led by a ground guide with a red-lens flashlight. Gerdine talked with the leading tank commander and then slotted the vehicles into his perimeter at the base of Cemetery Hill. A few Able Company stragglers, including PFC Willis Jackson with his BAR, showed up a short time later. They'd gotten lost in the confusion on Red Beach and fought inland with other units. Corporal Bayliss Thornton was one of those. He'd added his rifle to a depleted squad from 2/5 in the fight for Observatory Hill, the battalion's right flank objective.

"Thought you was our big-time Daniel Boone, Thornton." Gunny Bates led the NCO to third platoon's sector of the line. "Looks like you couldn't find your ass with a ten-man working party."

"It was right confusing, Gunny. I got my bell rung by a close round. Next thing I knew nobody from Able was anywhere around. So I hooked up with some fellers from Two Five. Ran into them tank boys said they was headed for A Company, so I hitched me a ride."

There was more, but a burp-gun blatted and nearby Marines scrambled for cover. A few Marines from third platoon fired into the dark. Gunny Bates scrambled over yelling for Sgt. JJ Jones. The platoon sergeant identified himself and Bates jumped into a hole beside him. "What the hell's happening, Jones?"

"Couple of my people went outside the lines, Gunny. Dipshits were gonna search some gook bodies for souvenirs."

"And they got caught out there?"

"Looks that way. Guys over on the right said there were gooks in a cave."

Captain Gerdine arrived scrambling. "What's the situation?"

"Couple of third platoon peckerheads was out in front of the lines and gooks caught 'em." Gunny Bates batted Sgt. Jones on the shoulder.

"Harris and Gonzalez, Skipper. They're down out in front of the line about twenty or thirty yards. I didn't know anything about it until the gooks opened up."

"What gooks?"

"There's a cave or something up there." Sgt. Jones pointed up the slope of Cemetery Hill. I'm gonna take a couple guys and see if I can retrieve 'em."

"I'll go with you," Gunny Bates said. "Get a couple more and let's move."

It was hard to tell whether the two Marines laying in the mud outside third platoon's lines were dead or wounded. They looked like a couple inert lumps in the gloom. Word was passed down the line that a rescue party was heading out. Gunny Bates grabbed Sgt. Jones by the elbow. "You get the guy on the right. I'll get the one on the left."

The four-man rescue party didn't make it much more than halfway to the casualties before they were driven to ground by a fusillade of fire from the cave on the slope of Cemetery Hill. "Pull back," Bates shouted, and all four Marines started to crawl for the safety of their lines.

"Ain't gonna work, Skipper." Gunny Bates slid panting into a hole next to the Company Commander. "Bastards know we're gonna try and retrieve those Marines. They was waitin' for it. We're gonna have to clear that goddamn cave."

"Maybe not," Gerdine said. "Hustle back to the CP and send Sergeant Pak up here."

Master Sergeant Pak Chun Hee crawled up the forward slope toward a clump of bushes that hid the entrance to a small cave. Everyone on the line below heard him shouting like a demented Drill Instructor. No one could understand, but the Marines recognized the strident voice of an old soldier used to being instantly obeyed. It turned into a shouting match when one of the North Koreans inside the cave responded to Pak's orders.

Captain Gerdine was designating an assault force from third platoon when Sgt. Pak waved from above. "Coming out now," he said as six NKPA troopers emerged into the gloom with their hands behind their heads. Pak marched them stumbling down the slope and then had them squat in a loose circle just inside Able Company's lines. "OK to get your men now." Pak said to Captain Gerdine and Gunny Bates who had wandered over to take a look at the POWs. "They say nobody left in cave."

"How'd you convince them to surrender?" Gunny Bates was pulling each enemy soldier up and searching them for weapons or explosives.

Sgt. Pak pointed at one of the Marine tanks parked nearby. "I tell them they don't come out, we drive tank up and kill them all."

"Probably should have done that anyway," Bates said as he frisked the last POW. "Now we gotta guard these assholes all night."

Sgt. JJ Jones picked a squad and they moved out to retrieve the wounded. Gonzalez was dead. Harris was badly wounded. Doc Clinton didn't think Harris, torn by three rounds in the lower torso, would make it through the night. There was a medical clearing station on the beach that could get badly wounded men out to one of the LSTs that was rigged for emergency surgeries. Captain Gerdine sent the Doc and an escort to carry the wounded Marine back toward the Battalion Aid Station. They were back in an hour. Harris died of his wounds.

Orders for D+1 arrived at about 2100. RCT-5 and RCT-1 would both attack at dawn. Chesty Puller's 1st Marines would advance on the right and Ray Murray's 5th Marines would advance on the left through the southern part of Inchon with a battalion of ROK Marines between them. The ROK Marines were scheduled to make the deepest penetration into the seaport and deal with local civilians. The 1st Marine Division objective was to bring both regiments into a solid line intersecting at Hill 117 which overlooked the Inchon-Seoul Highway. They had about five miles to cover with no solid information about enemy forces.

LtCol. Newton's 1/5 was to follow 2/5 in the move. Able Company was given the right-hand slot in the advance, which put them closest to the Korean Marines. As the move commenced in the pale light of dawn, Gerdine left Lt. Solomon to keep their platoons pushing forward and took Sgt. Pak to see if he could contact the Korean Marine commander. They found the man walking with one of his lead companies, a radio handset in one hand and a Baby Ruth candy bar in the other. Sgt. Pak introduced himself and then Captain Gerdine. The man stuffed the last bits of his candy bar into his jaws, wiped a hand on his trousers, and extended it to shake.

"Major Sun say he is from Seoul," Pak said as the Korean Marine showed a chocolate smile and accepted the cigarette Gerdine offered. "He knows this area well."

Gerdine held a lighter under the Korean officer's smoke. "He got any idea how many enemy forces we might run into?"

There was a rapid exchange in Korean and then the KMC officer waved his hand in the direction of Inchon town as if he were flicking at a pesky fly. "Major Sun say he think all enemy left the town last night. He say civilians coming back to their homes."

"OK; tell him thanks. And tell him if he needs anything to just let me know." More Korean conversation. "Major Sun say he guard flank, no problem." Pak pointed at the bulge in Gerdine's uniform shirt where a pack of Chesterfields rested. "He also say he very much likes the American cigarettes." Gerdine pulled the pack out of his pocket and handed it over.

Major Sun tipped a little salute and then patted the Thompson submachinegun hanging from his shoulder. "More soon we kill all sun-a-beeches."

Captain Gerdine caught up with his outfit feeling a little better about his flank with a battalion of Korean Marines looking to kill all sun-a-beeches. But there was little evidence of the enemy as Able Company advanced into the southern reaches of Inchon. A few frightened civilians peeked from doors and windows as the Marines cautiously trundled past. Beyond those few returning residents, this part of the sprawling seaport seemed mostly dead and deserted.

A Jeep carrying LtCol. Newton's S-3 officer caught up with Able Company before they'd gone much more than a mile into the town. He showed Gerdine a mapboard and pointed at a piece of high ground on the northern outskirts of Inchon. "Our battalion is going into regimental reserve," he said. "You'll set up on this high ground and hold for further orders." Gerdine marked the spot on his own map. It was a good tactical position, near a back road that led out of Ascom City to intersect the main Inchon-Seoul Highway.

"Any chance for an ammo and chow resupply while we're up there on the hill?" Gerdine asked the battalion S-3 officer. His Marines were running short of both necessities. They'd only been able to accomplish a water resupply while they were holding at Cemetery Hill.

"Shore Party is stacking it up back at Red Beach," the S-3 officer said. "Trucks should be up here before dark. Anything special you need?"

"Rifle ammo, radio batteries, grenades...some 3.5 rockets." The S-3 officer scribbled in his notebook. "I'll let the S-4 know. He'll send what he's got."

"My First Sergeant should be ashore by now. Top Hammond. You might send him up if you can find him."

"I'll pass the word." The S-3 officer slid into his Jeep and motioned for the driver to turn it around. Gerdine shouted over the revving engine. "No sense asking about hot chow, I guess?"

"No sense at all, Sam. We'll be on canned beans and weenies at least until we take Kimpo airfield."

Gerdine trotted forward to find Lt. Ruggles and the second platoon leading their advance. He showed them the map and adjusted the company axis of advance toward the new position.

"Bout time we caught a break," Gunny Bates said when he'd caught up with the Company Commander. "Be a good time to reshuffle, Skipper. We ain't likely to get any new bodies anytime soon."

"Ask the platoon commanders for a head-count when we get set up on the hill, Gunny. We'll see who needs what and then make a decision."

While Able Company platoon leaders counted noses and set up on the hill, their reserve position was reinforced. A platoon of M-26 Pershings from the Division's 1st Tank Battalion arrived ferrying a detachment of 75mm recoilless rifles from 5th Marines' anti-tank platoon. Gerdine slotted them in below his defensive perimeter, closer to the road where they'd have good fields of fire if enemy armor appeared. Gerdine didn't think it was likely given the advance of the other two battalions. Enemy armor was unlikely to slip through 2/5 and 3/5, but he wanted to be ready just in case.

First Sergeant Hammond showed up mid-afternoon with a nylon sack of mail. Gunny Bates got a couple of overdue bills and one heavily perfumed letter that left everyone in the CP either gagging or laughing. "Doris," he explained. "Works at a seafood joint in Dago. She douses these things in foo-foo juice so they won't smell like fish."

XO Lt. Rod Solomon looked up from a letter he was reading. "Thought you were married to the Marine Corps, Gunny."

"That I am, XO...but Doris here..." He stuck the letter under his nose and inhaled. "She's special. She's got twin forty-four mounts forward..." He hefted a pair of imaginary breasts and then patted himself on the ass. "And she's about two-and-a-half e-tools across the fantail."

Solomon looked at Captain Gerdine. "Did you understand any of that, Skipper?"

"I think the Gunny means to indicate that Doris is a well-proportioned woman, Rod. That's my best guess, anyway."

There was no mail for Sam Gerdine. He'd been hoping Della might relent and just drop him a friendly line, asking how he was, letting him know how Tony was doing. Nothing. Maybe he'd write her when he had a chance, just a note asking her to keep him posted with news about the boy. She owed him that. Maybe he'd write tonight and send the letter back to the rear with the First Sergeant.

He walked to the top of the hill where he could see Baker and Charlie Companies camped across a muddy expanse in their reserve positions. From his high vantage point, he had a good view of Ascom City out on the horizon. Could be the first battalion was being rested for an assault on that property.

They'd be resupplied and ready once 2/5 and 3/5 linked up with Puller's RCT-1.

He studied Ascom City through his binoculars for a while. If that turned out to be the battalion's next objective, it would be a bitch. It was a disorganized sprawl covering maybe two miles of ground. Mostly residential or industrial storage areas from what he could discern, all intersected by a complex network of streets and alleys. A thousand sniper hides and machinegun positions in a place like that.

"It was once just a little village." Sgt. Pak stood next to him. "Name Taejong-ni. I was there after the second war. Lots of American soldiers there—service command, for occupation forces—after Japs went away."

"Think they'll send us over there, Sergeant Pak?"

"Taejong-ni not so important, sir. More important to take Kimpo and then Seoul."

They distributed supplies, moved some people around between platoons, but for the most part, Able Company passed a quiet night in reserve. Gerdine and Gunny Bates hadn't slept much during the night, busy with regular inspections of the lines, making sure at least one man was awake in each position. Warnings had been issued about North Korean infiltrators hiding among the flow of civilians returning to the little villages and settlements around Inchon.

Just before daybreak, Gerdine was nodding in his little CP next to the hissing SCR-300 radio when Sgt. Pak shook his shoulder. He shrugged the poncho off his shoulders and blinked in the gloom. His watch said 0415. "What's up, Sergeant Pak?"

The Korean pointed down the hill toward the road. "Korea Marine patrol, sir. I talked to them."

"What did they want? More American cigarettes?"

"No, sir. Patrol come from Taejong-ni..."

"Ascom City?"

"Yes, sir. They say enemy tanks and many, many soldiers heading for highway."

"Shit..." Gerdine stood and arched his back against a cramped muscle. "You think it's straight dope, Sergeant Pak?"

"Good man lead patrol, sir. Old soldier like me. I think is true."

"Did they say how far away?"

"Didn't say, sir." Pak pointed at the brightening horizon. "Ascom City maybe five miles from here."

And they'll be moving slow, Gerdine thought, heading for the point where the Ascom City road running by here intersects the Inchon-Seoul Highway. And that would put a force of armor and infantry in position to hit the advancing units in a flank. "Find Gunny Bates." Gerdine reached for the radio handset. "Tell him to round up the platoon leaders."

Gerdine radioed the information to battalion. They didn't seem to be very excited about it after he revealed the report had come from a Korean Marine patrol. First we've heard of it, the battalion S-3 watch-stander said. We'll pass the word. Keep a sharp eye out and let us know if you see anything. Gerdine intended to do a bit more than watch the road. If Sgt. Pak said he believed the recon report, that was good enough to initiate some action in Able Company.

Gerdine briefed his platoon commanders, the senior tanker and the Technical Sergeant in charge of the recoilless rifles. "It's pretty thin," he said, "but I want to be ready if it turns out to be true. Patrol said they've got tanks but didn't say how many—and plenty of infantry."

"I'll need to shift a couple of my tanks," a Staff Sergeant in coveralls said. "We'll find some defilade spots on either side of the road. The AT guys can dig in right next to us."

"Good. I'll leave it with you," Gerdine said and turned to his platoon leaders. "I'm not sure how many are in a shit-pot full, but the Korean Marine patrol reports that's about what we've got headed our way. I want our people in position to hit 'em with plunging fire. It's gonna take some milling around in the dark, but shift your Marines as required to cover the stretch of road in front of our tanks. Be quick doing it. I want everybody ready before dawn."

They came just before full dawn. Back-lit by a rising sliver of sun to the east of the hill, Captain Gerdine counted six T-34s, all of them crawling with infantry hitching a ride. Behind the tanks were columns of Reds ambling along, gabbling and laughing, as if they on some sort of training exercise. Gerdine keyed his radio handset and ordered the platoons perched above the road to open fire. Machineguns, BARs, and rifles blazed. Red infantry were swept off the tanks as the enemy vehicles lurched and roared, steering dizzy patterns and running over many of the infantrymen sprawled on the road.

Gerdine ordered his platoons to shift fire and engage the following infantry that was scrambling into ditches on either side of the road. Plunging fire down into those ditches turned it into a slaughter. Tanks and recoilless rifles engaged the armor pouring anti-tank rounds into the T-34s. Enemy tanks, pouring smoke and flame, lurched to a halt. A few surviving crew members made attempts to bail out, but Gerdine's riflemen cut them down immediately. Only one enemy tank, the last one in the column, survived the initial ambush. That one was rapidly reversing down the road, crushing bodies under its grinding tracks, in an attempt to escape the slaughter.

Corporal Sean Marcus, who had a reputation to defend as Able Company's star tank killer, saw what was happening. The trailing T-34 was using the disabled, smoking vehicles to cover its escape. He grabbed his rocket launcher and batted his loader on the arm. "Hawk, let's get that bastard." PFC Dave Hawkins, who had just been shifted over from 60mm mortars to become Marcus' loader, didn't like the idea much. There were still a lot of gooks squirming around down on the road, but he grabbed a sack of rocket rounds and followed his gunner.

Marcus ran for an angle, stepping over several dead bodies in the roadside ditch before he found the position he wanted. The T-34 was still roaring in reverse, opening the range to about 75 yards, before the first 3.5-inch AT round hit the right track and blew it off the drive sprockets. As the tank swerved left, it provided Marcus with a shot at the engine compartment with a second round that Hawkins stuffed into the launcher. Marcus took that shot and the disabled T-34 began to belch smoke. Two enemy crewmen appeared scrambling out of turret hatches. PFC Hawkins nailed both with his M-1. He was running back up the hill right behind Marcus when a North Korean hidden in the ditch they'd just vacated caught Hawkins with a burst of submachinegun fire. Rounds that tore into his hamstrings crippled Hawkins. Doc Clinton saw it happen and stormed down the hill to help Marcus drag the wounded man into cover.

It was all over in less than an hour. Gunny Bates led a squad from first platoon down onto the road where they put kill-shots into the wounded Reds. It's wasn't much of a chore. Most of the enemy force—it looked like nearly 200 men sprawled around the dead tanks—had been killed in the initial wall of fire from the high ground. It got a bit ghoulish, even for Gunny Bates, when the Marines started digging around in the bloody corpses looking for souvenirs. He called it off and led the squad back off the road. Dead tanks were still smoking and the enemy bodies still warm when LtCol. Newton and his S-3 officer showed up to examine the carnage. It had been a hot fight but completely one-sided. Only one man wounded in the entire skirmish. And PFC Hawkins had already been evacuated. He'd been hit with small-caliber rounds. Doc Clinton said he'd walk like a new man after some treatment and rehab.

"Outstanding work, Sam." The battalion commander said. "If those bastards had gotten past you, they had a straight shot into 2/5's flank."

"Yessir," Gerdine said with a grin. "Not bad for an outfit that was supposed to be resting in regimental reserve." He turned to the S-3 major. "I've got a few commendations I'll be sending your way, sir."

"Send 'em along, Sam. I'll see they don't get lost. And next time you send in a patrol report, we'll be listening a little more closely."

Gerdine walked part way down the hill with his visitors. "Sir, it was Sergeant Pak that alerted us. He's the one talked to the Korean Marine patrol. Can we do something for him?"

"Like what, Sam?"

"I don't know, sir. Maybe give him a medal or something. He's been a hell of an asset."

"Let me ask around, Sam. I can talk to the ROK liaison at Regiment. He might have some ideas."

Captain Gerdine had a few interim ideas of his own. He'd noticed some of the dead North Koreans were carrying U.S.

weapons. There were some M-1 carbines and a few Thomp-
sons among the dead. He remembered the way Pak had admired the Thompson sub-gun that the Korean Marine
commander carried, and he knew the old soldier was a little
embarrassed at having to borrow a carbine. Gerdine picked up
a nice Thompson and dug in a pouch to find three magazines
loaded with .45 ACP ammo. He found Sgt. Pak sitting beside
Lt. Solomon who was heating C-ration coffee. "This is for
you," he said handing over the Thompson and ammo. "It's
about time you had your own weapon to kill the sun-a-
beeches."

Stars came out for Able Company at mid-morning.

A convoy of three Jeeps and a weapons carrier roared up to
the ambush site to disgorge four generals, three admirals, and
a platoon of civilian war correspondents, one of them a female.
As his grimy, disheveled, and unshaven Marines gawked,
Gerdine hustled down the hill. He counted something like 15
stars among the visitors. And five of them belonged to the first
man out of the leading Jeep, General Douglas MacArthur.

The Supreme Allied Commander stood examining the carnage on the road through aviator sunglasses with his hands
jammed in the hip pockets of his khaki trousers. At his shoulders stood Major General O.P. Smith, commanding the 1st
Marine Division, and Brigadier General Eddie Craig, now
Smith's assistant after commanding the 1st Provisional Marine
Brigade in earlier action. Gerdine didn't know the admirals but
suspected they must be involved with the Navy task force that
staged the Inchon landings.

Standing in front of all the ranking officers with morning
sunlight glinting off their gilded insignia, Sad Sam Gerdine felt
like a ratty street urchin. He popped the best salute his stiff and
weary body would allow. "Captain Gerdine, sir. Able Company,
5th Marines."

General MacArthur made a vague motion toward the bill of
his brass-encrusted cap visor and extended a hand. Gerdine
shook the hand and glanced at the two Marine generals who
were wearing big grins. "Marvelous battle," MacArthur waved a

hand at the smoking tank hulls and dead bodies piled up on the road. "Marvelous victory. Did your men do this, Captain?"

"Yessir. My Marines and some tankers and AT crews. Caught 'em by surprise, General."

MacArthur nodded and signaled to a staff officer shepherding the war correspondents. They broke ranks and rushed forward with cameras clicking. "You deserve to be decorated for this action, Captain. I think a Silver Star is appropriate." MacArthur began to dig in the pockets of his leather flight jacket but came up empty-handed. Looking a bit miffed, he turned to a nearby staff officer. "Make a note of that," he said and then he led the correspondents forward for a closer look at the destroyed enemy column.

Generals Smith and Craig hung back to congratulate Gerdine. "Sam came over with us from Camp Pendleton," General Craig said to General Smith. "His outfit was heavily involved in the fighting at the Naktong Bulge."

"Very well done, Captain Gerdine." General Smith gripped Sam's shoulder. "And don't worry about the Silver Star. We'll see it gets into the record."

"Rather it go to one of my Marines, sir. I already got one— on Peleliu last time around."

General Smith chuckled. "And now you've got another one, direct order from General MacArthur. Can't hurt..." The Marine generals walked up the road to talk to the tank and recoilless rifle crews. The road was getting crowded, and Gerdine worried about all the brass this far forward in an active combat zone. He ordered some of his Marines to stop rubber-necking and throw some security out alongside the road. He felt a tug at his elbow and turned to see a short woman with piercing blue eyes smiling at him. She wore a baggy fatigue uniform and had a mop of unruly blond hair stuffed up under a Marine utility cover. "Marguerite Higgins," she said extending a hand. "New York Herald-Tribune."

"Sam Gerdine, ma'am..." He shook the hand and felt a surprisingly strong grip that somehow seemed to fluster him. Gerdine felt extremely awkward staring down at the woman. Maybe it was just the shock of seeing a female at the front; maybe it was a slight embarrassment at being singled out before his grinning Marines. He tried to smile but was fairly sure his expression looked more like a pained grimace.

"Where are you from, Sam Gerdine?"

"The Marine Corps, mostly. Long time ago I came from Michigan, near Lansing."

Higgins was scribbling notes but kept her eyes locked mostly on Gerdine's face. "How long have you been in Korea?"

"Couple of months now. I came over with the first batch of Marines. We were down south of here around Pusan...then Inchon."

She interviewed Sad Sam Gerdine in a clipped, no-nonsense style, firing her next question as soon as she sensed Sam was finished answering the last one. And those questions were appropriate, incisive, and direct. Marguerite Higgins seemed to know a lot about military operations in general. Toward the end, she asked if he was married. Gerdine just shrugged. "Divorced," he said, "but I got a little boy, five years old, lives with his mom in San Diego."

"Well, he'll be reading about his Dad." She smiled, closed her notebook and shoved it into a pouch hanging from a shoulder. She shook hands again and turned to leave.

"Miss Higgins..." Gerdine caught her elbow and pointed at Master Sergeant Pak Chun Hee who was watching the media circus, grinning and puffing on a cigarette. "You should really talk to that man. He's the one who alerted us about the gook...uh, the enemy coming our way."

"Does he speak English?" Higgins retrieved her notebook and started walking toward Sgt. Pak.

"Pretty good at it," Gerdine said. "Learned it from U.S. occupation troops after the last war." Sam introduced the war correspondent to Sgt. Pak who seemed delighted to tell his version of the story.

About 20 minutes after they arrived, the official party remounted their vehicles, spun around and headed back toward the seaport. Gerdine was watching the dust rise from the vehicles carrying departing dignitaries when he heard rifle shots. He spun and trotted up the road where he found Lt. Ruggles, Gunny Bates, and a squad of second platoon riflemen aiming their weapons at a stretch of the roadside ditch. Seven bloody and bedraggled North Korean soldiers climbed out of the ditch, tossing weapons behind them.

"Heard one of 'em babbling when the VIPs left," Lt. Ruggles said as he prodded the prisoners in to a line. "Took a look and there they were, still holding onto their weapons."

"Bastards were down in there the whole time," Bates chuckled. "Not more than 20 yards from where the brass was parked. Had a chance to blow away MacArthur and missed it."

"Thank the Lord for small favors," Gerdine whispered. Getting a bunch of brass-hats killed on a visit to your outfit is not a good career move. "If the subject ever comes up," he warned Bates and Ruggles. "You captured these guys *before* MacArthur arrived."

Able Company's resident radio expert Sgt. Ron Edison, sat in a shell hole surrounded by Captain Gerdine, Lt. Solomon, and Gunny Bates. Edison was putting the finishing touches on an antenna he'd rigged with some comm wire supported by tentpoles. To hide the glow from the radio's tuning dial, the first platoon sergeant had draped a poncho over the little battery-operated RCA set that he'd babied since landing at Red Beach. "Signal propagates best at night," he said, ducking under the poncho to fiddle with dials. "Picked up an LA station last night."

Following a series squawks and static bursts, a deep baritone voice announced that listeners were tuned to the Armed Forces Radio Service broadcasting from Tokyo. "Here we go," Edison said, turning up the volume as an Army Sergeant began the program.

"There's some good news from Korea tonight," the announcer began, sounding perky as if he were calling a ball game from some stateside stadium. "The 8th Army is on the move northward from the embattled Pusan Perimeter. The aim is to link up with allied forces steadily advancing at Inchon. General Walton Walker's command reports several units have crossed the Naktong River. Taegu is in allied hands and the 3rd Republic of Korea Division has captured a second east coast seaport at Pohang. This is truly a united front, a spokesmen for 8th Army told AFRS, with the British 27th Brigade joining with American and South Korean forces in the offensive. American units involved in the breakout include the U.S. 1st Cavalry Division and the 24th Infantry Division. Army Sergeant Bob Lee reporting from Tokyo. More news and stateside sports coming up on the hour..."

Sgt. Edison snapped off the radio and ducked out from under the poncho. "Well, at least we know what's happening south of us."

"Assuming you can believe it." Lt. Rod Solomon stood and stretched. "Notice he didn't say doodly-squat about the Marines."

"What do you expect, XO?" Gunny Bates cackled. "It's a fucking doggie reading the news. We take Seoul, and they'll say the goddamn Army did it."

Early the next morning, First Sergeant Hammond arrived on the hill with ration boxes and a sack of oranges he'd scrounged back at the Inchon port. He reported Marine Engineers were pushing a high-speed road forward from Inchon, making room for a steady flow of supplies as the allied attack pushed toward Kimpo Airfield. "Wheels beginning to turn in the rear," Hammond told his Company Commander. "Marcus is officially a sergeant as of yesterday, and they approved your recommendation for a Navy Commendation for him." The First Sergeant peeled his orange and took a bite, wiping a hand across the juice running down his chin. "And Trenton is getting the Bronze Star you recommended."

"What about Petrosky?" Captain Gerdine tossed his orange idly from hand to hand thinking he'd save it for later. "We wrote him up for knocking out that bunker on Red Beach, right?"

"Yessir. Haven't heard anything about that yet..." Hammond seemed to be holding something back and Gerdine noticed the uneasiness. "What else, First Sergeant? Spill it."

"It's about your recommendation for a field commission for Petrosky. It's still pending, but a guy I know in battalion S-1 says it's gonna be approved."

"Shit, that's great news!"

"There's something else, sir." Hammond leaned in close to whisper. "They also reconsidered his request for release from active duty. See, that's the problem. He can go home to the wife and kiddies as a Staff Sergeant, or he can stick it out with us and become a second john."

Captain Gerdine tossed his orange into the mud. "That's a shitty deal, First Sergeant. He's gonna resent it...and I damn sure won't blame him."

"Let me talk to him, sir." First Sergeant Hammond tapped the stripes stenciled on his uniform sleeve. "NCO to NCO, you know? I'll feel him out on it."

"OK, Top, but I don't want you putting any pressure on Petrosky. If he wants to go, he has my blessing on it."

First Sergeant Hammond found Staff Sergeant Steve Petrosky supervising a squad of 60mm mortarmen who were improving their firing positions. He motioned for Petrosky to join him and walked a bit further up the hill. They sat on the edge of a muddy shell hole and lit smokes.

"What's up, First Sergeant?"

"How's it going, Ski. Just checking..."

"Pretty fair. That kid Marcus is a big help. And he's about to be a three-striper now, so I'm giving him more to do than just hump that three-point-five. You know we lost Shelton in mortars, so I'm having to honcho that, but I've got my eye on a man who can step up pretty soon."

"Yeah, that's good, Ski....and they approved the promotion for Marcus. I just found out about it." Hammond lit a second smoke from the butt-end of his first. "Skipper says you're doing real good up here." The First Sergeant inhaled smoke and lowered his voice. "How are things at home?"

Petrosky looked across at the First Sergeant and his smile faded. "You heard something? Anything wrong with my family?"

"Nothing like that, Ski. I was just askin'. You know? Wondering if the allotment was coming through and all."

"Got a letter a couple days ago," Petrosky said relaxing a bit. "Alma said the kids are fine. Allotment money's coming through regular, and she's getting what I send." Petrosky crushed his cigarette in the mud. "Appreciate the interest and all—but how come you're asking?"

"We got a situation, Ski. Skipper put you in for a field commission. Looks like that's gonna happen before too long."

"Well, damn!" Petrosky grinned. "Marine Corps might not survive making me a fucking officer, but I'll take it."

"You don't have to, you know."

"Why wouldn't I? I can handle it."

"I know you can, Ski. But there's something else." Hammond took a deep drag on his smoke. "They also approved your request for release from active duty. If you want to; you can head home—in grade as a staff sergeant."

Steve Petrosky thought for a moment, staring back to where his Marines were scraping mud from mortar baseplates. "I see," he said softly. "So, I can go home...or I can stay here and become an officer."

"Shitty deal, Ski. But that's about the size of it. Your call all the way. I told the Skipper and he says you're free to go if you want to, no hard feelings."

Petrosky pulled a cigarette out of a rumpled pack and fiddled with it, rolling the smoke between his fingers and glancing back toward his Marines. "You know," he said, "I never expected to be in something like this when they called up the reserves. Thought maybe I'd wind up just dicking around stateside for a couple of months or something. Never really thought I'd wind up in a shooting war."

"Lots of guys in that same boat with you, Ski."

"I know..." Petrosky nodded and lit his cigarette. He inhaled and blew a plume of smoke skyward. "I also know these guys..." He jerked a thumb at the nearby mortarmen. "These guys need a steady hand if we're gonna live through this. I'm pretty good at it...fact is, I like it. Gotta say it's been good for me. I might just stick around in the Marine Corps."

"So...you gonna stay with the outfit?"

"Any way Alma might find out I had the chance to go home?"

"They don't ask wives about shit like this, Ski. It's strictly up to you."

"Any chance they'd put me in another unit when the field commission comes through?"

"No chance. We ain't got the officers we rate right now. They'll keep you here."

Petrosky nodded and stood. "Tell 'em to send me up a couple of gold bars. I'm staying."

THE GOLD BARS MARKING Steve Petrosky as a newly minted Second Lieutenant of Marines arrived two days later. Captain Gerdine pinned them to Petrosky's collar and shook his hand. "I know the story, Steve," he whispered. "So, thanks. You're gonna be a fine officer and a big help in this outfit."

Gunny Bates was the last in a long line of Able Company Marines to shake Petrosky's hand. "If you're expectin' me to salute your dumb ass, you can forget about it," he said with a grin. "And you better hide them butter-bars. Snipers love to shoot officers."

Captain Gerdine had decided to leave Petrosky where he was, running the company's mortar and anti-tank sections. When he got a little time in as an officer, or if the unit somehow got an officer replacement, he'd think about moving Petrosky to a rifle platoon. The XO was still making overtures about taking a platoon, but Gerdine wanted someone familiar with the outfit and its personalities to accede if he was killed or wounded. Meantime, the platoon sergeants were doing well and showing good leadership as they became more experienced and comfortable.

Less welcome news also arrived on the hill that day. First battalion was being pulled out of regimental reserve for the push on Kimpo Airfield. The big picture was relatively simple. RCT-5 with a ROK battalion attached would immediately advance on the vital airfield from the left while Chesty Puller's RCT-1 advanced on line to the right of them.

It kicked off mid-morning, and 2nd Battalion, 5th Marines immediately ran into stiff enemy opposition. They got tangled up in a running fight on the outskirts of the Kimpo complex and stalled. In an effort to help, Murray's first battalion was rushed toward a pair of hills overlooking Kimpo where they could fire in support of the stalled attack. It was a long cautious advance but easy going for Able Company and the other 1/5 units when they finally reached the objective hills. For reasons no one could fathom, there were no defenders on the high ground overlooking Kimpo. The major enemy strength seemed to be down below them stubbornly defending the airstrip in a seesaw battle with 2/5. By 1900, Able Company was set in atop the hill mass marked on the map as Objective Easy. Gerdine spread his platoons across the plateau where they had good fields of fire and sited his 60mm mortars on the reverse slope. Lt. Petrosky strung wire from the mortar position and moved up to act as their Forward Observer.

Throughout the night, the plain below their hill erupted in sporadic blazes as Marines attacked Kimpo and the North Koreans countered. It was difficult to tell friend from foe in the dark, so Able Company couldn't do much in the way of supporting 2/5's attack. Watching it all like a spectator in the bleacher seats of a stadium, Captain Gerdine counted what he thought were three major enemy counterattacks staged by Kimpo defenders. Artillery barrages from several 11th Marines firing batteries halted most of those. It was like watching a spectacular 4th of July fireworks show as Able Company Marines sat atop Objective Easy, wondering when they'd be called to join the fight.

At dawn, Lt. Paul Ruggles spotted another attack coming from the south end of Kimpo's airstrip. It looked like serious business, maybe a battalion on line supported by three T-34 tanks. Gerdine ordered his men to open plunging fire on the enemy concentration. Lt. Petrosky got his 60mm mortars on target after a couple of spotting rounds and ordered them to fire for effect. The cannon-cockers of the 11th Marines added their weight and stopped the tanks. The enemy momentum dwindled after about 20 minutes. As the sun rose higher over the horizon, Ruggles reported survivors running across an expanse of rice paddies in the direction of the Han River. Gerdine got permission to give chase and sent his second platoon down off the hill.

Ruggles' Marines had a field day chasing the fleeing enemy. Sgt. Trenton thought it was something like bird hunters chasing fleeing pheasants across a cornfield. PFC Willis Jackson did some significant damage firing his BAR from the shoulder and cutting down an entire squad. Riflemen fired from hip or shoulder pouring rounds into enemy backs. And the more they killed, the more their speed increased. Sgt. Trenton looked over his shoulder at Objective Easy and estimated the distance they'd covered. They were about to outrun the range of their 60mm mortars. He found Lt. Ruggles jamming a fresh magazine into his carbine and recommended they halt the chase. Ruggles turned his platoon around and led them back toward the Objective Easy, reporting they'd likely killed as many as 30 North Koreans.

The dawn attack appeared to be a last gasp for the Kimpo defenders. With RCT-1 pinching on the right and 2/5 advancing across the runway, the remaining North Koreans abandoned the fight. By noon, the vital Kimpo airfield was in Marine hands.

Waiting for orders atop their hill, Able Company Marines watched as the first American aircraft descended for a landing at Kimpo. Two C-47s touched down and began to unload. "Air wingers," Lt. Rod Solomon said as he watched the airfield activity through his binoculars. "I'm betting by the end of the week the Air Force will have that place looking like La Guardia."

"Hope so," Captain Gerdine said. "We got Kimpo, so you know what's next."

THE MOST SIGNIFICANT obstacles between the advancing elements of X Corps and the enemy-held South Korean capital were the Han River and the urban complex called Yongdong-po which butted up against the river on the south banks. Chesty Puller's RCT-1 was assigned to clear Yongdong-po. The rest of the division was focused on crossing the Han which meandered in a northwest-southeast direction through the Operation *Chromite* battle space. If the Americans crossed the Han River, found strong lodgments on the eastern banks and massed forces, Seoul would inevitably fall.

Planners on both sides of the fight understood the importance of the Han. North Korean commanders had seen the power of the advancing American units and knew they couldn't stop a river crossing. Their next best option was to establish a Main Line of Resistance, using everything they had left to occupy strategic high ground between the river and Seoul.

American planners turned their field forces toward the Han and sited several potential crossing points. The idea was to push assault forces across the river on a broad front, gain lodgments at strategic points, and then leap-frog toward the South Korean capital. More troops were rapidly becoming available for that effort. The U.S. Army's 7th Infantry Division offered the 32nd Infantry Regiment and the battle-weary 1st Marine Division gained a third regiment with the landing in Korea of the 7th Marines under Col. Homer Litzenberg.

Captain Sad Sam Gerdine knew some of this big picture from a combination of battalion-level briefings, Sgt. Edison's radio, and plain tactical logic. What concerned him most was the part Able Company would play as they moved from the Kimpo area toward the river. He found out on 20 September that the 5th Marines would cross the Han at a place marked on the map as Haengju, ferried by Marine amphibian tractors. Able Company would cross in the dark, land on the eastern shore, and then hook hard right to take Hill 125 in a night attack. It was obvious from looking at his map that Hill 125 dominated the main crossing points but no one was able to tell him anything useful about how many gooks were on that hill. It was also obvious to Captain Gerdine that the enemy understood its significance. They wouldn't leave it undefended.

He borrowed Lt. Paul Ruggles' sketch pad and drew out a plan for the XO, Gunny Bates, and his platoon leaders. Night attacks were always difficult in both approach and execution, and he wanted everyone to have a general idea about the lay of the land and his basic plan. "LVTs will get us as close to the objective as possible, and then here's what I've got in mind. We hit the hill from two directions. Sergeant Jones, you take the third herd around to the right up a little spur that parallels the riverbank. Keep the river on your right. That's your guide. You'll turn left to start climbing. Lieutenant Ruggles, you take the second platoon around to the left. Your guide is some railroad tracks that run right past the hill. You'll turn right to start climbing. Lieutenant Ski, you move our sixty mortars up as close as possible. You'll prep the hill when second and third report they're ready to start climbing. You're gonna have to sustain your fire, so take as much ammo as you can carry."

"Any armor reported in the area, sir?" Petrosky stared at the sketch and scratched at his unshaven chin. "I'd like to use Marcus and his guys as extra ammo bearers for the mortars."

"No reports about tanks, Ski, so that should work. Just don't leave the three-point-fives behind. No telling what we might run into over there."

Gerdine pointed at Sgt. Edison and continued. "First platoon stays with me to reinforce the attack on either flank as required. Questions or suggestions?"

"How about illum rounds, sir?" Lt. Petrosky was already computing ammo loads. "You gonna want to light it up?"

"Illum works both ways, Ski. We light it up to see them and they can see us. I don't want to do that unless it's absolutely necessary. There's a battery of 105s from 11th Marines on the other side of the river. I can call them for illumination if we need it, Have your guys concentrate on HE for the mortars."

"I'll go with Jones and third platoon if that's OK, Skipper." Gunny Bates suggested. "He's short-handed."

"Company Gunny's always welcome in the third herd, Skipper." Sgt. Jones was getting comfortable leading his platoon. And the Gunny was smart enough not to assert himself unless it was absolutely necessary.

"OK; one last thing. There's gonna be a lot of dicking around in the dark over there before we go into the attack. Keep your people together on the move to the base of the hill. I don't want anybody to get lost."

They loaded into the LVTs just after sundown. The amphibious vehicles were parked on the western shore of the Han in a long file. Gerdine conferred with a Technical Sergeant in charge to be sure the LVTs would fan out from a file into a line once they were on the water. The sergeant assured him he planned for all of his LVTs to land simultaneously. He had Baker and Charlie Companies to get across the river as soon as he landed Able.

It was a moonless night, but any hope for a clandestine crossing was lost as the noisy LVTs splashed into the Han River with engines roaring and snorting. Halfway across the muddy water, enemy positions on the opposite shore began to fire. Small arms and some mortar rounds impacted, churning up muddy gouts of water or pinging off the armored side of the LVTs, but they did no real damage. Able Company's amphibian transports presented a moving target with drivers swerving and accelerating. Gerdine became disoriented. He could see the hump of Hill 125 to his right, ablaze with muzzle flashes, but it looked to him like they were going to land well to the left of the designated landing point. That meant a longer ride in the LVTs and vital time lost in reaching their jumping off point for the attack.

It turned into an even greater concern when six of the eight LVTs carrying Able Company landed on the east bank of the Han and promptly got bogged down in mud that nearly buried the vehicles. Captain Gerdine had the two assault platoons dismount and begin walking while he transferred Petrosky and his heavily burdened mortarmen to the two remaining vehicles. He waved the drivers on toward the objective and began slogging through the muck and mire toward Hill 125. Baker and Charlie Company on the other side of the river would have a long wait for the bogged down LVTs to bring them across the Han. Able Company was on their own.

Lt. Paul Ruggles found the railroad tracks by stumbling over them. His platoon was spread out in a long line behind him— at least he hoped they were. It was so dark that he worried some of them might not find the tracks. He grabbed at a passing Marine but he couldn't see the man's mud-smeared face. "Who we got here?"

"Abramson, sir. I got the radio..."

"Let me have it," Ruggles said reaching for the PRC-6 slung over PFC Abramson's shoulder. "You plant yourself right here. Be sure everyone finds the railroad tracks and keeps heading for the hill. Don't move."

Abramson found a covered position and squatted in the dark. As Marines emerged from the gloom, he led them to the tracks and pushed them in the desired direction.

Sgt. JJ Jones had easy going as his third platoon approached Hill 125. The ground was soft and boggy this close to the river and most of his Marines were caked with mud to the knees, but they made relatively good speed. Jones looked up into the dark slope, seeing the flare of mortars firing. It looked like there was a bit of a plateau below the summit. That would be his first objective. He could pause to reorganize there and try to link up with second platoon.

When they reached the bottom of the hill, Jones counted heads. All present. Then he found Corporal Bayliss Thornton and sent him on a little one-man recon to find a good path up the slope. The hillbilly was back in just under 30 minutes reporting gooks in several defensive positions below the plateau. He'd been afraid to go any further but indicated the climb shouldn't be too hard. Jones reached for his radio and reported the third herd was in position.

"This is it, sir." Sgt. Trenton was on a knee at the base of the hill when Lt. Ruggles reached him. "I got Maitland and Jackson doing a recon." Ruggles looked around at the lumps in the gloom. It looked like everyone made it. Thank God for the railroad tracks, he thought as he reached for the radio. "Able Six...Able Two is in position, over."

Captain Sam Gerdine estimated he was 350 yards give or take from Hill 125 when the reports from his assault platoons came in on his radio. They'd made faster progress than he could plodding through the sucking mud churned up behind the LVTs. He turned to find Lt. Petrosky helping to unload mortar ammo from one of the vehicles. "We're late, Ski. Get the ammo unloaded and then take your guys forward and find firing positions."

He found Sgt. Edison trudging forward with Sgt. Pak, both balancing ammo crates on their shoulders. "Edison, soon as you've got that gear unloaded," he said, "spread your people out and stand by."

"Behind the mortars or forward of them, sir?"

Gerdine looked up at the hill. The enemy mortars up there were still firing, but there was no incoming around him. Probably still shooting at the crossing points, he guessed, but they'd shift to counterbattery as soon as his sixties opened fire. "Better put them forward of the tubes. I want you as close as possible so you can reach the hill without too much delay. Sergeant Pak, you stick with me."

XO Lt. Rod Solomon was standing near one of the idling LVTs. "Rod, as soon as they're unloaded, send the tractors back to the beach. Then get hold of the assault platoons. Tell them don't wait for a command. They go as soon as our mortars open fire on the hill."

Lt. Steve Petrosky checked the stability of his three 60mm mortars and issued the initial firing commands. They could see the target, so there was no need to complicate it. He figured charge three on the HE rounds would reach the plateau below the summit. He could adjust after the first volley, but his mortar crews were all veterans at this point. They wouldn't need much guidance to keep rounds impacting on target. "Hang 'em up there," he said to his crews who were stripping increments from their first rounds.

"All set, Skipper." Petrosky watched as assistant gunners on each mortar held a high-explosive round above the muzzle, ready to drop it on command. Gerdine checked forward of the mortar pits to ensure his first platoon was in position. "OK, Ski. Let's kick it off."

Lt. Steve Petrosky nodded. "Fire!"

Sgt. JJ Jones and his third platoon spread out on line as they climbed the right side of Hill 125. There was some stumbling and muttered cursing in the dark but the Marines made good progress until they hit a line of machinegun positions below the plateau. Two men went down immediately. The rest went prone on the rocky slope and returned fire. The mortars from Lt. Ski's tubes were hitting well above the defenders. Jones got on his radio and tried to send corrections, but he was having trouble breaking in on the net. Lt. Ruggles was shouting something into his radio from the other side of the hill.

"We're just below the summit," Lt. Paul Ruggles transmitted. "Shift the mortars and we'll go the rest of the way." They'd overrun a couple of enemy positions fairly easily further downslope, and the way to the summit looked clear. Sgt. Trenton was helping a Corpsman haul two wounded Marines down the slope and cursing loudly. He was convinced that both men had been victims of friendly fire from Petrosky's mortars. Three other wounded Marines were making their way downslope from the squad that had knocked out a heavy machinegun position. That gun turned out to be another U.S. .50 caliber and it had done some damage, but when it was silenced, the enemy defenders seemed to lose motivation. Ruggles spotted running shapes ahead as gook riflemen retreated toward the summit of Hill 125. His Marines cut into them with rifle fire.

Gerdine heard the shift request from Lt. Ruggles and looked at his gun line. Petrosky had heard it also and was already ordering the adjustment. "Add 50...right 50," Sgt. Petrosky shouted to his mortarmen. Gunners cranked in the range and elevation corrections as a conga line of ammo bearers passed rounds up to the smoking tubes.

One element of his attack seemed to be going well. He was about to call Sgt. Jones with the other element when the third platoon sergeant broke in on the net. "Able Six...Able Three. I'm stuck below the summit. Machineguns in bunkers. They're below that little plateau. Your mortars are hitting long of them..."

And we just shifted to clear second platoon, Gerdine realized. If Petrosky adjusted again to help Jones, his rounds would likely hit Ruggles' Marines heading for the summit. Ruggles was in the best shape right now. It was Jones on the right that needed help. He shouted into his radio for Ruggles to pull his second platoon back to the plateau below the summit and hold. Then he tossed the handset and shouted at Petrosky on the gunline. "Ski, shift everything to the right side of the plateau!"

He turned to his XO. "Rod, take first platoon around to the right. Pass through third platoon and push for the summit. We need to get moving."

First Lieutenant Rod Solomon vaulted forward yelling for Sgt. Edison to get his men up and running. Gerdine was back on the radio, passing on his new plan, when a North Korean artillery unit on the reverse slope of Hill 125 opened up with counterbattery fire. Three rounds impacted just behind the gunline well behind Lt. Solomon and his charging reinforcements. Four more followed, closer this time, sending the mortar crews and ammo passing detail ducking for cover. More incoming rounds impacted and Gerdine flopped into the mud next to Sgt. Pak as shrapnel buzzed overhead.

When the shelling stopped, he looked up to see Lt. Steve Petrosky lying face up in the mud with several mortarmen kneeling beside him. Gerdine yelled for a Corpsman and saw Doc Clinton sprint forward. Then he reached for his radio and twisted the dial to the pre-set frequency for the 11th Marines artillery battery over on the other side of the Han. He'd memorized the grid coordinates for the summit of Hill 125. Once he had rounds on that plot, he could adjust and hit the reverse slope guns.

"Cannonball, Cannonball...Able Six...emergency fire mission!" Gerdine contacted the battery and began to dictate instructions for the 105mm howitzers to shoot his Marines out of trouble.

PFC Miles Abramson snuggled further into the little hide he cleared for himself near the railroad tracks and wondered what to do. He could see and hear fighting up on the hill. He thought that was where he should be, but the Lieutenant had told him to stay put. Don't move, he said. And Abramson knew a direct order when he heard one. In the first few hours after second platoon disappeared into the gloom, Abramson reassured himself that there must be a reason he was ordered to remain below the hill. Maybe there were other units coming that needed him as a guide. He didn't know. He didn't know anything for sure except that nobody told him anything. He was ordered to say here, so he sat on the railroad tracks staring into the dark.

That's when he heard the gooks gabbling all around him and moved away from the railroad tracks to a spot where he could hide. He clutched his rifle, counted the ammo he was carrying, and watched dark shapes passing by like a circus parade. If he opened fire, he'd be dead before he could reload his M-1. Some of the gooks were carrying mortar components. Abramson could see the tubes in dark silhouette. He counted 34 men in the first batch to pass his position.

Then another group showed up pushing some sort of wheeled gun along the railroad tracks. There were 50 or 60 of them. A third group came by an hour later, gabbling in Korean, and paused not more than 20 yards from where Abramson was hiding. He saw a dull glow as one of them snapped on a flashlight. It looked like some officers checking a map. Fourteen in that group—and one of them squatted to take a shit not more than ten yards away from Abramson. He could hear the man grunt and the sound of runny crap splashing into the mud.

"Here they come." Gunny Bates jabbed Sgt. JJ Jones with an elbow and pointed down the slope below them. He spotted the XO in the lead waving for the Marines below him to increase the speed of their climb. "XO...over here!"

When Lt. Solomon flopped down beside him, Bates pointed at an irregular line of three bunkers to their front. The hard points looked to be log and mud construction. Machinegun muzzles sparked occasionally as the enemy gunners searched for targets in the dark. Petrosky's mortar fire had stopped but there was some heavier stuff impacting on the other side of the hill. It would have to do for now.

"Cover our move," Solomon said to Bates and Sgt. Jones. "I'm gonna try to work around to the right and hit 'em from the rear."

"We're gonna have to shift to keep from hitting you," Gunny Bates said. "How you plan to let us know when you're ready to go?"

"Look for tracers." Solomon unsnapped the magazine pouch on the stock of his carbine. One of the spare magazines was loaded with tracer rounds that he used to mark targets for machineguns or air strikes. "When you see that, shift and we'll go in with grenades."

The XO and Sgt. Edison assigned two Marines to each of the bunkers and began a low, slow maneuver to the right below the plateau where they could remain out of sight. Covering fire from the third platoon snapped and rattled to distract defenders in the bunkers who concentrated their fire on muzzle flashes to their front.

The 60mm mortar crews were dazed and struggling to right the tubes knocked over during the artillery attack. At least two wounded gunners were sitting beside their guns being attended by others but neither man seemed in critical condition. One of the mortar tubes was dinged badly by shrapnel and looked to be out of action for good.

Doc Clinton was working on Lt. Petrosky, sitting in the mud minus his helmet and gear. The Corpsman had stripped away a bloody shirt and was wrapping a battle dressing around Petrosky's ribcage as Captain Gerdine staggered up to the gun line dragging his radioman behind him. "How bad is it, Doc?"

"I'm OK, Skipper." Petrosky was in some obvious pain, wincing with each breath but he seemed lucid.

"Lucky the damn rounds hit in the mud, sir." Doc Clinton said as he prepared a morphine injection. "Shrapnel was mostly funneled upward instead of outward. He caught a bunch in the back. I'll know more when I can see something."

"Ski, you stay down here and try to get the mortars running. I'll call for fire or displace you forward when I know what's happening on the hill."

Captain Gerdine called for Sean Marcus kneeling nearby with his 3.5-inch rocket launcher in hand. "Sergeant Marcus, round up anyone who's not a mortarman and follow me."

Lt. Rod Solomon fired five tracer rounds into the air, strapped his carbine over a shoulder, and pulled a pair of grenades out of the pouch on his cartridge belt. "Go!" He charged downhill behind the nearest enemy bunker as two other teams sprinted for their targets. Sgt. Edison leaped atop the bunker and began to pump rifle rounds down through the thatch roof as Solomon worked around to the front of the bunker. He pulled pins from both grenades. "Fire in the hole!" He shouted and rolled the grenades into the bunker as Sgt. Edison leaped clear.

Captain Gerdine was halfway up the forward slope of Hill 125 when Gunny Bates called on the radio. "Able Six...Able Seven...we got the hill. Able Two is on top and the rest of us are spread out below them. We're checking now but it looks like the gooks have high-tailed it."

Gerdine called the artillery battery and asked them to fire for effect on the reverse slope. Maybe he could catch a bunch of them running. Then he contacted Lt. Petrosky and ordered the mortarmen to displace forward and climb Hill 125.

At dawn, PFC Miles Abramson decided he'd had enough of this Lone Ranger shit. There were no friendly troops in sight and no enemy units had passed since an hour before daylight. *Fuck Lt. Ruggles*, he decided, *and fuck a bunch of orders*. He crossed the railroad tracks and headed toward Hill 125.

Able Company was dug in along the military crest of Hill 125 with a clear view of other outfits below crossing the Han River.

The fight for this important piece of Korean real estate had been costly. Four dead and eleven wounded. The worst of those were being carried down the hill toward the landing site for evacuation. Lt. Petrosky adamantly refused to leave the hill he'd so painfully climbed with his mortarmen during the night. Doc Clinton had pulled a couple of shrapnel chunks from Petrosky's shoulder muscles and tightly wrapped what he suspected were a couple of cracked ribs.

"He ought to go down," the Corpsman told Captain Gerdine, "but he's having none of it, sir."

"He gonna be able to function?"

"Depends on how much pain he can tolerate, Skipper."

"Yeah, Doc. Ski's hard to argue with. Keep an eye on him for me."

Gerdine hoped they'd stay put on the hill for a while. It was crucial high ground now that the Han River crossings were in full swing. LVTs were ferrying ammo and supplies across as well as troops. He'd heard reports that the fresh 7th Marines were already across and Puller's RCT-1 was pushing inland. Colonel Murray's 5th Marines were holding three other nearby hills. Likely General Smith would wait to mass his division forces before he ordered the move on Seoul. Maybe he had a little time to rest and regroup.

He was working on a resupply and replacement request when Lt. Paul Ruggles and Sgt. Heywood Trenton of the second platoon approached.

"Skipper, there's a problem." Ruggles took a knee beside the Company Commander. "One of my guys is missing."

"Missing?" Gerdine looked up from his notebook. "What the hell does that mean?"

"It's Abramson, sir." Sgt. Trenton said. "We spotted him down below as a guide and...well, sir, I don't think he made it up to the hill."

"Jesus Christ! I warned you people to keep an eye on your Marines, didn't I?"

"My fault, sir." Ruggles said removing his helmet and scrubbing at his scalp. "I failed to check and be sure I had everybody before we started to climb. It was so damn dark...and then we got tangled up in a fight..."

Gerdine shook his head sadly. Abramson of all people, the kid who never went to boot camp. All alone in the dark. Likely dead or captured.

"I'm not gonna report one of our Marines missing! He could be wounded, dead, or a POW. I want to know which it is."

"I got a squad mustered, sir." Sgt. Trenton pointed to a bunch of Marines standing nearby. "With your permission, I'm gonna retrace our route and see if we can find him."

"You do that, Sergeant Trenton. Take a radio and Sergeant Pak with you. Don't plan on coming back up on this hill until I've got some answers about Abramson."

Gunny Bates overheard the conversation, squatted by the CO, and lit a cigarette. "Goddamn, Skipper. That poor little turd. Always admired him, you know? No boot camp, no nothin', and he turned into a pretty good Marine."

"Maybe Sergeant Pak can talk to some civilians in the area. They'll find him." Gerdine said a silent prayer. If there was ever anyone who shouldn't die in a shitty deal like this, it was a kid like Miles Abramson.

Bates tossed his smoke and stood. "If they find him dead, I'm personally gonna strangle Ruggles and then Trenton."

The search party was gone less than an hour when PFC Miles Abramson wandered into Able Company's perimeter. Gunny Bates went charging downslope to meet him.

"Abramson, you little shit! Where the hell have you been?"

"Lieutenant ordered me to stay put." Abramson pointed down the hill. "So, I did."

"And you stayed down there all night?"

Abramson shrugged. "It was orders, Gunny…"

Bates grabbed Abramson in a bear-hug. "Listen, you little fartknocker, don't you ever do anything like that again." He released the hug and grabbed Abramson by the shoulders. "C'mon, let's get you some chow and coffee."

Gerdine recalled the search patrol and sat listening to PFC Abramson's description of the enemy forces he saw moving down below Hill 125. Then he called battalion and requested someone from the staff come forward and interview a very observant intelligence asset. He put his XO to work drafting a commendation for PFC Miles Abramson USMCR and went to have a talk with 2ndLt. Paul Ruggles about leadership and responsibility.

They rested on Hill 125 for a couple of days watching distant actions as RCT-7 assumed the burden of advance against retreating enemy formations. Top Hammond brought forward all the resupply items he and a squad of replacements could carry. There were 11 new men assigned to Able Company, all of them fresh off flights from Japan into Kimpo Airfield. No officers in the bunch and only one NCO, a corporal fresh from sea duty. Captain Gerdine and Lt. Solomon met each man and then turned them over to Gunny Bates who gave a very entertaining and colorfully profane lecture about what was expected of them in a veteran outfit like Able Company. Then he doled them out to the rifle platoons.

The new men were sorely needed, but what they carried up the hill behind First Sergeant Hammond was even more welcome. There were boxes full of new boondockers and fresh uniforms. There wasn't enough for everyone, but the First Sergeant made sure the most ragged veterans, some of them showing more skin than cloth in what was left of their utility uniforms, got a first shot at the new gear. And then it turned into mob scene.

Gerdine and the XO stood laughing as their Marines attacked the new clothing like frantic shoppers at a clearance sale. There was a lot of shoving and shouting, boots flew from one man to another as Marines jammed them on remnants of moldy socks in an effort to find a fit. Ragged Marines who hadn't had a change of clothing since Inchon attacked the pile and scampered away with anything that looked like it might fit.

The First Sergeant tossed three pairs of new socks into Gerdine's lap. "Them are precious commodities, Skipper. Plenty of boondockers, but you can't find a pair of socks to save your ass." Gerdine squeezed the soft olive drab material and smiled at the sensation. His first pair had rotted through a week ago, and the socks he was wearing were shot through the heels and toes. He pulled off a boot and noticed Sgt. Pak sitting nearby. He'd noticed that the Korean didn't wear socks and wondered why that was. He reached over and pulled a leg of the Korean's trousers above a boot top. "No socks, Sergeant Pak?"

The Korean just shrugged. "Never issue, sir. Korea army don't have."

"Well, now you do." Gerdine tossed a pair to him. "Try these on for size." Sgt. Pak pulled off his mud-caked boondockers and slipped a dirty foot into a sock. He said something in Korean that sounded vaguely orgasmic and then pulled a sock onto his other foot. He rolled onto his back, stuck his feet up in the air and wiggled his toes. Master Sergeant Pak Chun Hee was in heaven.

And First Sergeant Hammond brought another sack full of mail. Gunny Bates got a pair of reeking missives from Doris that he gleefully jammed under the nose of anyone who couldn't avoid him. Lt. Petrosky showed everyone pictures of his two sons at their First Communion. Alma had word of his promotion and said she was so proud. Sgt. JJ Jones got a letter from his father that said the St. Louis Cardinals were asking about him. They were still interested.

And Captain Sad Sam Gerdine finally heard from Della. It wasn't much, just a few neutral lines asking about his welfare and some chat about her work. There was a picture of Tony aboard a prancing horse on some carousel ride. Sad Sam Gerdine was in his own version of heaven for a few moments on top of Hill 152.

The peaceful interlude ended on the third day. Captain Gerdine and his XO were called to the battalion Command Post with the other 1/5 commanders. LtCol. Newton spread his map and pointed to a line of red to the east of their positions. "This is their MLR," he said. "Last line of defense guarding Seoul. We got the far right sector." The attack was set for sunup the next morning. Three companies in column led by Charlie and aimed at a spot marked on the map as Hill 105 South. It looked to be about 2,000 yards from Able Company's current position.

Story of life in Korea, Captain Gerdine thought as they walked back to pass the word about the new attack. Up one goddamn hill and then up another goddamn hill. It was getting old fast. And this one would be hey-diddle-diddle, right up the middle against who the hell knew what. The good news was that Captain Tex Stanton, the Forward Air Controller, was attached to Able Company, and he promised to keep the sky overheard dark with Navy and Marine aircraft.

They assembled below Hill 152 as the sun was peeking over the horizon. There were none of the familiar little spotter airplanes overhead, but Stanton promised they'd be buzzing around by the time Able Company reached its objective. Gerdine spread his three rifle platoons into a loose skirmish line, and they began to wade through a long series of reeking rice paddies. They were 500 yards from Hill 105 South when Charlie Company at the head of the battalion advance ran into deep trouble. The hill above them was heavily defended, a layered barrier of machineguns, recoilless rifles, and mortar positions that cut into them before they could start to climb the objective. They stalled taking heavy casualties.

Gerdine's radio came to life with orders from battalion. He was to rapidly move forward, pass through Charlie, and press the attack. Baker Company to his rear would swing right and attack the hill from that direction.

Just after they passed through a shot-up Charlie Company, Gerdine's first platoon got hung up in a fight with a line of heavy machineguns. They went to cover and stayed there. Captain Gerdine was in the center of the assault line behind Lt. Ruggles and Sgt. Trenton. They had it a bit easier, facing mostly individual riflemen in foxholes or behind boulders. Third platoon was pressing forward against a recoilless rifle position that they were peppering with grenades. It wasn't too bad, relative to some of the defenses they'd encountered elsewhere. What he needed was some supporting fire to take the heat off his Marines.

Captain Tex Stanton was to Gerdine's rear with an artillery FO and their radios. Gerdine left his XO to monitor the fighting forward and ran back to the fire support party. "I got a flight of four two minutes out," Stanton said when Gerdine reached him.

"Biggest hang up is on the left." Gerdine pointed toward his pinned down first platoon. Heavy machineguns." Stanton consulted his map and Gerdine pointed at the trouble spot. "Corsairs are packin' napalm," Stanton said. "You want that? Might be a tad hot for your boys."

"Hell, yes." Gerdine said. "I'll pull 'em back and you can burn the whole damn hillside." He turned to the artillery FO. It was a man from 11th Marines that he knew vaguely. "I'll want to push forward right after the air strike goes in," he said. "Can you give us some kind of follow up fire and advance it as we move?"

"Can't shoot until the airplanes clear the space, Sam. But soon as they're off the target, I can start the battery firing a rolling barrage ahead of your guys."

"That'll do. Set it up and I'll pull my guys back."

"I better go with you," the FO said. "Be a damn site more effective if I'm up there to call the adjustments."

When he got back to his position behind second platoon with the artillery FO in tow, Gerdine contacted each of his platoons telling them to pull back and find cover from the air strike that was coming. Gerdine looked up to see a flight of four Marine Corsairs circling overhead with bulbous napalm cannisters hung under their wings. The jellied gas in those tanks would splash everywhere. "XO, get over to first platoon and make damn sure they're under cover." He pointed Gunny Bates in the other direction. "You do the same with Jones and third platoon, Gunny. They're gonna be dropping napalm, and I don't want any of our people caught by it."

Second platoon to his direct front was already moving, some crawling some rushing down the hill to find cover. Lt. Paul Ruggles stood to wave them back and Gerdine saw the man's head snap backward. His helmet flew off and Ruggles crumpled to his knees before he pitched forward on his face. Sgt. Trenton was up and running toward the downed officer but Gerdine cut him off. "I'll get him," he shouted as the first aircraft winged over to dive on the slope to their front. "Get the rest of them under cover!"

Sgt. Pak ran forward to assist with Ruggles, and they dragged him down the slope. The platoon leader's face was covered in blood. He was either unconscious or dead. Hauling the man was like pulling a floppy toy over rugged ground. Ruggles' arms and legs flopped loosely as Gerdine and Sgt. Pak dragged him behind a line of boulders. Gerdine shouted for a Corpsman and saw Doc Clinton sprinting in their direction as the first napalm cannisters tumbled from under the attacking planes. They heard a prolonged whoosh as the napalm splashed in long runs over the hillside. And then an intense wave of searing heat hit them.

"Goddamn, Tex! Too close...too close." Gerdine waved at the Forward Air Controller further down the slope but Captain Tex Stanton had his eyes fixed on the sky. The second pair of Corsairs were making their run. It felt like a blazing tornado tore over them when the second napalm strike went in on the hill. Breath was sucked out of Gerdine's lungs and the blast of heat seared his forearms making the hair sizzle and curl. Gerdine had seen plenty of napalm runs in Korea, most of them high in the hills against distant targets, but he'd never been this close to one. He was dazed and panting as he looked around him. The artillery FO and his radioman were curled in fetal positions behind the rocks. Sgt. Pak sat up staring with wide eyes at the flames cracking and roaring to their front. Doc Clinton had fallen across Lt. Ruggles body and was just beginning to move.

"Send your fire mission," he shouted at the FO and saw the man reach for his radio handset as he pulled a map from his uniform pocket. Then Gerdine got on his own radio to check on his platoons. Responses were a bit muted as if everyone were shocked, mumbling and nearly speechless by the close pyrotechnics they'd witnessed, but everyone had survived. When the arty FO began to send his fire request, Gerdine turned to check on Lt. Ruggles. Doc Clinton had him propped against a rock and was pawing through a shock of the man's matted hair, dabbing at a stretch of bloody scalp with a gauze pad.

"Lucky day..." Doc Clinton broke a vial of smelling salts under the wounded officer's nose. "Round just tore a gap in his scalp. Gonna need a few stitches." Ruggles batted at the vial waving under his nose and stared around vacantly. "Might have a concussion. He ain't going any further up the hill today, Skipper."

The first 105mm howitzer rounds struck the slope above them. The FO peeked over the boulders and sent a correction to the battery. "We can go after the next round," the FO said to Gerdine. "I'll keep it moving ahead of you."

Able Company started up Hill 105 South stepping gingerly through a scorched and smoking landscape. There was nothing more than sporadic resistance. Marines snapped shots at a few dazed enemy riflemen who sat in their holes, so traumatized that they couldn't shoulder their weapons. They passed some truly horrible sights as they slowly followed the artillery barrage toward the summit of the hill. Enemy dead sat or lay prone looking like badly charred lumps of meat. Flesh had burned completely off some of the defenders, revealing bones and skulls. Some of the dead seemed to be grinning at the advancing Marines, burned faces revealing teeth in a rictus of charred flesh. And all across the hill as Able Company advanced, the odor of petroleum mixed with the cloying stench of burned flesh formed a low hanging mist that caused some men to puke as they climbed.

They held at the summit, watching while the FO walked his rounds all over the reverse slope. Captain Gerdine reported his objective taken and then walked around his Marines to see how badly they'd been hurt. It turned out to be four killed, including two of the replacements, and 11 wounded. Doc Clinton sent eight of those down the hill and then flopped down next to his Company Commander. The Corpsman wiped idly at bloody hands that shook visibly as he struggled with the cigarette Gerdine offered.

"You OK, Doc?"

"Weary to the bone, Skipper." Doc waved at a line of poncho-wrapped bodies. "But better than some."

"Don't let it get to you, Doc. I know that's a hell of a lot easier said than done, but you've saved a lot of lives, you and the other Corpsmen. There ain't a Marine in this company don't know that and appreciate it."

"You seen Sergeant Jones, sir?"

"Not since we got up here. Why? Is he looking for me?"

"More likely he's looking to avoid you, Skipper."

"Why's that, Doc?"

"Worried you might send him down, I think."

"He get hit?"

"Yessir. Caught a burst of grenade shrapnel."

"Is it bad?"

"Depends on how you look at it. It was in his arm—the left one—his pitching arm."

Sergeant JJ Jones was sitting in a hole with one of his squad leaders when Captain Gerdine found him late in the afternoon. The left side of his utility blouse was shredded and bloody. His left arm was completely swathed in bandages. Gerdine nodded at the squad leader to leave and then sat down into the hole next to Sgt. Jones.

"How bad is it, Jonesy?"

"Hard telling, Skipper. Stiff as a fucking board. Doc says there's still a couple of good-size chunks in the arm yet."

"Had to be your pitching arm."

"Yeah, I been thinking about that. Might be no problem at all. Might be my baseball days are over." He sighed and squinted at the darkening horizon. "At least I ain't dead."

"Jonesy, maybe you ought to go on down, you know? See some good doctors. At least they'd tell you what the damage is."

"Captain Gerdine, I ain't going down off this hill." He waved his good arm at the Marines swinging e-tools nearby. "I ain't leaving these guys while I can still hack it."

"Nobody's gonna blame you for having it looked at, Jonesy. We can get along without a third platoon sergeant for a while."

"Remember Lt. Lopez, sir?"

"Of course I do. He was one of our originals, from back at Pendleton."

"When we were on the ship one time—day before we landed at Inchon—he cornered me for a talk. Seemed like he knew something was gonna happen to him. Anyway, he made me promise to take good care of third platoon Marines if it did."

"And?"

"And I aim to keep that promise, sir. If it costs me a baseball career, well, that's the way it goes. I ain't leaving these Marines."

IT SEEMED TO CAPTAIN Sam Gerdine that half of his Marines
were walking wounded. Many of them were limping or sport-
ing wads of bandage as the company entered the southern
outskirts of the South Korean capital. Able Company was
assigned to sweep a section of the Inchon-Seoul Highway,
covering the third battalion's rear and right flank as that unit
pushed into the city proper. The roar of firefights deeper in
the built-up area and the crack of tanks firing ahead had everyone on edge.

"Glad its them and not us," Gunny Bates said to the captain
walking beside him. "I seen some of that house-to-house shit
on Saipan, Skipper. It's a bitch."

They were entering what looked like a residential stretch
with two and three-story buildings on either side of the road. A
major thoroughfare cut the highway just ahead on their line of
march. Sgt. Pak said that street ran to the South Korean government complex which was one of 3/5's initial objectives.

"We'll hold at the intersection, Gunny." Captain Gerdine
pointed at Sgt. Trenton leading the advance with second
platoon. "Get up there and remind those people to keep looking up, heads on a swivel." Gerdine had briefed his Marines
that Seoul's urban sprawl would demand different tactics and
concerns. A city is sniper heaven, he reminded them. They're
gonna be in there up high, shooting down on us. Look up and
watch the roofs.

He heard a Jeep approaching from the rear and the man in
the front passenger seat was waving at him. The battalion
operations officer jumped out when the Jeep slid to a stop.
"Hey, Sam..." The major jerked a thumb over his shoulder. "I
brought you a replacement." Gerdine watched Second Lieutenant Paul Ruggles hopping out of the vehicle and gathering
his combat gear. His head was wrapped in bandages, but he
was smiling.

"Reporting for duty, Skipper." Ruggles shrugged into his
gear and held out a steel helmet. "Take a gander at that. Ser-

geant Trenton picked it up after I was hit." There was a deep dent and a bullet hole in the front. Gerdine turned the helmet and examined it. There was no exit hole. "Round still in your head, Paul?"

"Nah, I think it ripped a gap in my scalp and then ran out of steam. Maybe rattled around in there a little bit and then dropped out." Gerdine nodded and handed the helmet back. The operations officer was waiting with a map in hand.

"We need you to make a left up ahead, Sam." The S-3 Major pointed at the intersection. "Company from 3/5 has reached the Government complex." He jabbed a dirty finger at some black rectangles on his city map. "You'll provide security on the street while they clear the buildings."

"Yessir..." Gerdine pointed up the street. It sounded like a major tank battle going on up there. He could hear the clatter of tracks on pavement and the periodic crack of heavy rounds hitting concrete. The whole horizon over the city of Seoul was roiling with a cloud of smoke and concrete dust. "Any word on what's happening up ahead?"

"Defended roadblocks on most of the main thoroughfares. Some T-34s roaming around. First Tanks are having a field day."

"How deep you think we'll go?"

"You'll get pinched out about here." The major pointed at a black box marked Middle School. "Don't go any farther than that. Three-Five takes it from there. We'll be pulling back."

"Aye, aye, sir."

The major remounted his Jeep. "Take it easy, Sam. It's almost over. Army's on the roll, and we'll probably be pulled back to Inchon when Seoul falls."

Gerdine watched the Jeep roar back up the street between his Marines and then turned to look at Lt. Ruggles. The shoulders of his uniform were stiff with dried blood.

"You OK? Seems like they'd have kept you for a while."

"Looks a lot worse than it is, Skipper. I'm gonna have to start parting my hair on the other side, but I'm fine."

Captain Gerdine sent Ruggles forward toward second platoon and got his company up and moving toward the intersection. With Gunny Bates shouting and pointing, Marines in the lead platoon were taking occasional anti-sniper pot-shots at windows in buildings along the route. Air strikes were hitting targets in the gut of the city when Able Company made the left turn at the intersection. Sgt. Pak wandered over to talk to a clutch of frightened Korean civilians who crouched in an alleyway guarding bundles of their belongings.

"They say some enemy ahead, sir." He waved a hand down the highway toward the city center. "Most strong that way. Plenty people lose their homes."

"Maybe that won't last long," Gerdine mumbled. He was watching a flight of airplanes swooping in to drop bombs which sent huge plumes of smoke and dust over the city when they detonated. Gerdine didn't say so, but he thought there wouldn't be much left for the displaced civilian residents by the time Seoul fell.

The South Korean government complex was mostly secured by the time Able Company reached the area. Gerdine found the CO of George Company 3/5 and then slotted his Marines along the street fronting the complex. There were a few civilian correspondents in the area who suddenly started running toward the complex with their cameras poised.

"Here we go...gotta see this!" The George Company Commander sprinted off after them. The Marines in the courtyard of the complex were lowering a North Korean flag and unfurling the Stars and Stripes to raise in its place. There were still a few desultory shots being fired inside nearby buildings when the American flag was jerked up the flagpole. First platoon Marines closest to the gate stood gawking. A couple of them even saluted.

"It ain't no Iwo Jima," Gunny Bates said. "But it'll do for this fuckin' place."

"Yeah..." Captain Gerdine watched the 3/5 Marines pose for pictures with the enemy flag. "Good to see that after all we been through."

"Skipper, I'd like to get a closer look at that place. Can I take Sergeant Pak and a couple of rifles and do a little exploring?"

Most of the buildings in the South Korean government complex had been fairly well trashed by NKPA troops who occu-

pied the area before 3/5 drove them out of it. Gunny Bates led
Sgt. Pak with PFCs Jackson and Maitland toward the domed
building at the center of the concrete sprawl. "Looks a little bit
like the Capitol back home." Willis Jackson was from Washington, DC. "If you close one eye and squint a little."

"Guess you'd know, Willis." Lanny Maitland was from Birmingham, Alabama, and had never seen Capitol Hill. "Bet it
was full of the same kind of asshole politicians too." He gave
Jackson a shove as they climbed the steps. Despite their earlier
differences at Camp Pendleton, they'd become close friends,
often sharing rations and news from home when letters arrived. Gunny Bates referred to them as the Bobbsey Twins.

They wandered the cavernous building, gawking at mar-
bled tile fixtures and intricate carvings on wooden moldings.
The air smelled musty and rancid. Several stretches of flooring
were scorched where North Korean soldiers had lit cooking
fires. Fuel for the fires appeared to be stacks of South Korean
won. Bates picked up a few charred bills and examined them,
while Sgt. Pak poked around for as many as he could find and
stuffed them in his pockets.

Kicking at a pile of rubble and trash near the entrance to an
office, Maitland found a little desk set featuring small South
Korean flags. "Called Taegeuk," Sgt. Pak told them pointing at
the red and blue circle. "Good, bad, life, death...all one." Maitland gave one of the little flags to Jackson and pocketed the
other one. "What's these here?" Jackson pointed at sets of three
black bars that surrounded the colorful circle at the center of
the flag. "Means nature things," Pak said. "Heaven, earth, water,
fire...all things like that."

They wandered into what looked like a formal courtroom.
"Leaders sit here," Sgt. Pak swept his arms around the space,
his voice echoing off the high walls. "Sometimes vote," he
laughed. "Mostly argue and shout at each other."

"You're right, Lanny." Jackson looked at the seats in tiers
around a podium. "Same as back home. Asshole politicians
yelling and screaming."

Bates opened a door near the podium at the back of the
room. "Jesus Christ," he laughed. "I just died and went to
fuckin' heaven!"

The others stared over his shoulder into a western style bathroom. There were mirrors, gold faucets and fixtures over marble basins, but Gunny Bates ignored them. He headed directly for a gleaming white porcelain toilet and dropped his trousers. He flopped down onto the toilet bowl and sighed. "Ain't had a proper indoor shit since we left Pendleton," he said with a huge grin. "I'm gonna enjoy this."

Able Company was halted by a roadblock just short of their final objective at the Seoul Middle School. A line of North Korean riflemen opened fire from behind the barricade formed by old furniture and slabs of concrete they'd dragged across the street. Fortunately, there was plenty of cover as Marines scrambled out of the line of fire into doorways or alleys between buildings lining the street.

Gerdine peeked out of an alley trying to get a sense of how tough the roadblock would be to crack. No machineguns or anything else much more deadly than a couple of standard burp-guns, but there could be tanks or something heavier backing the play from further down the street. Standing above him, Gunny Bates suddenly opened up with his M-1 rifle. He fired eight rapid shots and pulled back to reload. "Sniper up high across the street," he said as he shouldered the rifle and swept the muzzle left and right. "Think I got him."

Gerdine spotted Lt. Steve Petrosky kneeling across the way beside Sgt. Sean Marcus. Couple of AT rounds ought to bust up the roadblock. He waved and shouted, pointing at the roadblock. "Have Marcus put a few rockets into that damn thing."

Sgt. Marcus, ducked from cover, knelt and fired. The rocket blasted a huge chunk of concrete into rubble as the gook defenders ducked. The second round sent most of them scurrying away down the street, chased by Marine rifle fire.

Lt. Steve Petrosky stepped into the open and waved for his men to advance on what remained of the barrier. A single shot rang out from someplace high across the street. It hit Petrosky in the juncture of his neck and shoulder and drove down through his chest. He crumpled like a marionette whose strings had been cut. Marines on both sides of the street began to pump rounds into the upper reaches of the surrounding buildings. Bates and the platoon sergeants sent riflemen into the buildings to look for other enemy shooters.

Doc Clinton was kneeling over Petrosky's body when Captain Sad Sam Gerdine sprinted across the street. The Corpsman just looked up and shook his head.

Operation *Chromite* was all but over for the 1st Marine Division by the end of September. Seoul was a wreck, but at least it was a South Korean wreck as opposed to a North Korean propaganda claim. General MacArthur flew in from Tokyo to declare the city liberated and returned the capitol to Syngman Rhee in a farcical ceremony even as Marine units were still fighting in the streets around him.

In the weeks following the fall of Seoul, Able Company got some replacements, but there never seemed to be a net gain. They took more casualties as they hammered at North Korean forces in and around the capitol. Captain Sam Gerdine followed orders but he did it judiciously, sparing his men as much pain and suffering as possible. They listened nightly to Sgt. Edison's radio and speculated about what new nightmares they might have to endure.

The 7th Marines under Col. Homer Litzenberg stayed hot on the tail of retreating North Koreans confirming the regimental CO's nickname: Litz the Blitz. Elements of the Army's 7th Infantry Division pushed north pursuing enemy formations back toward the 38th Parallel. Murray's 5th Marines and Puller's 1st Marines were kept busy with assaults and sweeps to disengage stubborn enemies that either refused to retreat or just didn't get the word that it was all over in the south now that Walker's 8th Army had finally linked up with X Corps forces after their steady advance northward from Pusan. And the South Korean Army was improving vastly now that the Americans had firmed them up a bit, providing advice, supplies, and inspiration.

Able Company and the rest of the 5th Marines were trucked back to Inchon in the second week of October. A few of them attended ceremonies and heard some dignitaries speak at dedication of the temporary 1st Marine Division cemetery. As a bugler blew the sad notes of Taps, there was a cold wind sweeping down out of the north, and the surrounding mountains all wore caps of snow. Captain Gerdine, Lt. Ruggles, First Sergeant Hammond, Gunny Bates, Sgt. Trenton, Doc Clinton, and a few others among the surviving plank owners from the old Provisional Marine Brigade walked the long, perfectly aligned rows of crosses. They saw the markers for Art Boyle, Baldomero Lopez, Steve Petrosky, and too many other Able Company Marines buried at Inchon where they'd rest a while waiting for a last ride home.

"Name, rank and service number," Ruggles whispered. "That's all she wrote."

"Ain't much else to it." Sgt. Trenton stared across the field of markers and shook his head. "You gotta know going in that it could end up this way."

Gunny Bates pulled a big olive drab handkerchief from a pocket and wiped at his nose. "Just nine is all you need..." He took a deep breath and sighed into frigid air.

"What's that mean, Gunny?" Doc Clinton wiped at tears he was trying to hide. He'd been with so many of the dead buried here in the last seconds of their life. "Nine what?"

"When a Marine dies..." Bates turned away and stared at the Korean hills. "All he needs is nine men: Six for pallbearers, two for road guards and one to count cadence."

They wandered apart then, except for Captain Sad Sam Gerdine who knelt to have a quiet conversation with Lopez. "It probably don't mean much to you now, Baldo, but we're putting you in for the Medal of Honor. I think you'll get it. You damn sure deserve it." He stood and patted the grave marker. "Rest easy, you old ring-knocker."

While Able Company was waiting for orders at Inchon, they lost a loyal Korean ally. Master Sergeant Pak Chun Hee came to visit Captain Gerdine and announced that he was duty-bound to return to his old unit. Pak had discovered that a reformed ROK Capitol Division was nearby, advancing with the U.S. 8th Army from Pusan. He was very sorry to leave the Marines and hoped they wouldn't think he was abandoning men who had given him a second home. Pak hoped Captain

Gerdine and all the others he'd grown to know and respect would understand that an old soldier must do the right thing. And he said the right thing for him was to lend his experience and combat skills to the reconstituted Capitol Division.

He spent hours visiting each platoon explaining at each stop why he must leave and expressing his gratitude. Before he left Inchon, Able Company Marines put together a duffel bag full of rations and whatever else they could spare, anything they thought might be useful to Sgt. Pak and remind him of the U.S. Marines who considered him one of their own. Many of them wrote their names and home addresses on slips of paper to include in his bag. Captain Gerdine scrambled around to find a Bronze Star Medal and pinned it to Sgt. Pak's uniform at a little formation.

They were lined up near a temporary quartermaster store where some winter clothing was being issued when First Sergeant Hammond told them they were due to embark in amphibious shipping shortly. He didn't know where they might be bound. There was some talk about the division being relieved by another unit, possibly the 2nd Marine Division from the states. Nobody believed that. There was rumor about another amphibious landing, over on the other side of Korea. That seemed more plausible. Speculation was rampant, but none of Able Company's veteran Marines tolerated any suggestion that they might be home for Christmas.

When shipping assignments were posted, Able Company discovered they'd be going back aboard the USS *Henrico*. Gunny Bates didn't even bother to bitch about it.

"I'M ASSUMING Y'ALL have read this letter from General Mac-Arthur?" President Harry S. Truman tossed the document on his desk and looked around at two of his most trusted advisors gathered in the Oval Office. Retired General George Marshall, now serving as Secretary of Defense after Louis Johnson was summarily dismissed, and General Omar Bradley, the current Chairman of the Joint Chiefs of Staff, both nodded wordlessly. They sat stiffly on the other side of Truman's desk, formulating responses to the question they both knew was coming. Both men had crossed professional swords with Douglas MacArthur, the man most clearly on the President's mind at this crucial point of the ongoing war in Korea.

President Harry Truman wanted straight talk, unvarnished opinions about, El Supremo, the man the newspapers were calling a military genius after Inchon. Truman picked up the letter again and snapped it with a fingernail. "It seems to me," the President said, "once you get past all the flowery phrases, MacArthur is patting himself pretty soundly on the back."

"No surprise there, Mr. President." General Bradley had been a major MacArthur critic concerning the disposition of American bombers in the Philippines at the opening stages of World War II in the Pacific. "General MacArthur is his own best cheerleader."

"Regardless, he's got something to cheer about," George Marshall admitted. "Inchon was brilliantly conceived and executed."

"Yes, it was." The President polished his glasses and slipped them back on his face. "But I'm leery of what he's asking now. He wants to chase the Reds back across the 38th Parallel and take their capitol at Pyongyang."

"Got 'em reeling," General Bradley said. He was suspicious of many things about MacArthur, particularly the man's purported interest in running for President. "I understand he wants to maintain the momentum, press his advantage."

"I'm all for beating the hell out of 'em," Truman said. "They deserve that for invading the south in the first place." He kicked back in his chair and pursed his lips. "But my original concept for Korea didn't involve what he's wanting to do now. I envisioned pushing them back where they came from and reestablishing the status quo ante bellum."

"And MacArthur wants to push all the way to the Chinese border." The new Secretary of Defense stared at a painting on the Oval Office wall. It was a copy of an original by Emanuel Leutz showing Washington crossing the Delaware. Likely Douglas MacArthur imagined himself standing in that boat like General George Washington.

"I'm thinking he wants a picture of himself peeing in the Yalu the way Georgie Patton did at the Rhine." General Omar Bradley, the simple soldier, had never been a fan of military showboating, by George Patton or Doug MacArthur.

"Well, I need to respond to this." Truman pushed the MacArthur letter around on his desk blotter. "Do I tell him to back off, or do I tell him to push on into North Korea?"

"There's the concern about China, Mr. President." General Bradley sipped coffee and shrugged. "Seventh Fleet is reporting Chinese vessels shadowing our ships in the Yellow Sea just off the Korean coast. MacArthur gets to fighting close to their border and they might just decide to take a hand in this."

"You mean come across and fight with the North Koreans? When we met on Wake, MacArthur assured me that was most unlikely. Didn't seem worried about it at all."

"It could happen, Mr. President," George Marshall said. "You've seen the reports of our fliers tangling with Migs over Korea, and my information is that most of them were flown by Chinese pilots."

"Just hard for me to envision," Truman mumbled. "Our fight has been with the North Korean communists. We've got 'em on the run. I'd just like to end this..."

Secretary of State Marshall ran a hand through his thinning white hair. "I'm of the opinion that we will never get a working peace settlement with Pyongyang," he said, "unless we're dealing from a position of overwhelming strength, and they're dealing from a demonstrated position of weakness."

"It's the way of war, Mr. President." General Bradley nodded. "Always been that way. Doesn't matter who the enemy is."

"Well, OK. I guess we let the dog off its leash. But let's do it the right way." President Truman stood to conclude the meeting. "I'll send him the official orders. He's OK to pursue the enemy into North Korea—but I want him to be damn careful about the Chinese."

III. NORTH KOREA

Wonsan

ABLE COMPANY WAS BACK aboard the Happy Hank in mid-October, steaming south through the Yellow Sea, aiming for another amphibious landing at Wonsan on the east coast of Korea. There was talk about an Operation *Tailboard*, but after a zinger like Operation *Chromite* at Inchon, that just sounded too weak to be real. And it really didn't matter to Captain Gerdine's Marines who were happy enough to eat some chow that didn't come from a can and sleep through the night without having to worry about an enemy attack or climbing another Korean hill.

They were seriously shorthanded, almost as bad as they had been at Camp Pendleton when the balloon went up and they had to beg, borrow, or steal people to fill the ranks. First Sergeant Leland Hammond said they were due for a block of replacements at Wonsan. Captain Gerdine and XO First Lieutenant Rod Solomon were hoping there might be a few officers in that block. Second Lieutenant Paul Ruggles, a Reservist, was the only officer left commanding a rifle platoon. The others were led by Sergeants. A handful of Corporals remained, but most of Able Company's rifle squads were being led by veteran PFCs or privates. Gerdine asked for official sanction to make some sorely needed field promotions. While they waited to hear from regiment about that, they were making a list of worthy individuals.

"It don't mean a whole lot in combat," Gunny Bates advised. "When the shit hits the fan, a Marine will follow the man he trusts to get the job done. Don't matter what's on his sleeve."

"On the other hand," Lt. Solomon said, "a promotion is a way of recognizing a man's performance of duty. We've got a bunch that should be recognized."

"If I had my way," Captain Gerdine said, looking over the proposed promotion list, "every damn one of them would get a medal."

"You mean other than the Purple Heart?" Gunny Bates snorted into his coffee cup. "Damn near all of 'em got that one already."

"Let me work on it." First Sergeant Hammond folded the list and stuffed it in a pocket. "I know a guy in S-1."

"Damn, First Sergeant," Lt. Solomon laughed. "You know a guy nearly everywhere in the Marine Corps."

"Comes with the territory, XO." Hammond pointed at his chevrons. "Hang around a while and you find out the Marine Corps is really just a small club of regulars who run the show."

As the ships carried the 1st Marine Division around the southern foot of the Korean Peninsula and into the Sea of Japan, commands got warnings about cold weather that they would face in the coming operations. Forecasters said the winter of 1950 would be a cold one, but not unusually so. The climate was loosely compared to winters in Minnesota or North Dakota.

"That's pretty loose," Lt. Ruggles complained. "It says here there's a place in North Korea called Hagaru where temps have been recorded as low as thirty-five degrees below zero." Ruggles had a little experience with cold snaps in Oregon, but he couldn't remember any days when temps dropped below zero.

"It's gonna be a cold sonofabitch," Doc Clinton said. "But on the bright side, we'll probably have a white Christmas."

The warning order sent First Sergeant Hammond into the service record books to see if any Able Company Marines were from typically cold areas or had any winter weather expertise. There were just three. Two city boys from Minneapolis and one former ski instructor from Vermont.

He set them to work refining notes they received from General Smith who had deployed to Iceland at the start of World War II. It never amounted to much more than warnings about getting wet and some advice about layering their clothing, but it was something. More winter gear was said to be stacked on the docks at Wonsan waiting for them. And apparently it was quite safe to stockpile vital gear there. South Korean Forces had taken the port earlier. The Marine landing would be strictly unopposed.

The ships of the amphibious task force arrived on schedule but Wonsan was closed. Enemy mines had been sown in the harbor and the Navy was busy clearing them. Thus began a dreary period of offshore steaming that the Marines called Operation *YoYo*. While Navy minesweepers dredged the harbor for explosive devices, Marines aboard ships steaming back and forth and back and forth and back and forth had little to do but watch and cheer every time one of the ships in the harbor exploded a mine sending huge gouts of muddy water skyward.

Gunny Bates loudly reprised his theory that the USS *Henrico* was part of a dark scheme to kill Marines with boredom. "It's a fuckin' commie plot," he claimed when the landing delay was announced. He waved his hand at the other ships waiting for clearance to enter Wonsan Harbor. "There all in on it now."

Right after morning chow on their third day at sea off Wonsan, Hospital Corpsman 2nd Class Arleigh Clinton took Sgt. JJ Jones to see a Navy surgeon from the division's 1st Medical Battalion who was aboard the Henrico. They x-rayed the left arm and then stood looking at it in the ship's sickbay.

"Most of this is minor stuff," the Doctor said pointing at several dark blotches above and below the elbow. "Probably work itself out eventually. The big concern is right here." He tapped a finger on the x-ray. "You've got a pretty good chunk in the elbow, and it's in the humeral trochlea where the upper arm joins with the lower arm bones. You probably feel it grinding when you flex the arm."

"Yeah, I do, Doc." Jones flexed his left arm and twisted it as he would in spinning a baseball. "It's kind of a click or a little catch in there."

"Well, we can probably dig it out once we get set up at Wonsan."

"That's a little dicey isn't it, Doctor?" Clinton had spent some time researching in the ship's small medical library. "Jones is looking at a major league baseball career based on that arm."

"Honestly, it's always a little dicey when you get to digging around in the area where two big bones meet," the Doctor said. "Elbow is kind of like the knee. Sometimes when we open it up, we wind up doing more harm than good. Depends a good deal on how skilled the surgeon is. You really ought to see an orthopedic man. He'll be able to tell you more than I can."

"Thanks, Doctor." Sgt. JJ Jones offered his right hand to shake. "I appreciate the advice."

They walked out of the sickbay and headed for the mess decks where a second meal was being served. "What do you think, Doc?" Jones asked as they fell into a long chow line.

"If you can live with it," Clinton said, "I'd let it ride, JJ. Let me scout around when we get ashore. Maybe I can find a bone man, and we'll get an expert opinion."

After chow, HM2 Arleigh Clinton went looking for the Company Gunny. The outfit had lost two of its four medical Corpsmen during the Inchon-Seoul fighting, and Clinton wanted to be sure there would be a medic or two among the replacements at Wonsan. He found Bates sitting alone, leaning against a ventilation scuttle near the fantail with his eyes closed. There was a chilly breeze blowing across the decks, but Bates was perspiring. "You OK, Gunny?" Clinton knelt and reached for a wrist to check his pulse. "You don't look so good."

Bates jerked his arm away and sat up straighter. "I'm fine, Doc. Just a little woozy."

"Something you ate at chow didn't agree with you?" Doc Clinton wrestled the Gunny's arm and felt the pulse. It was a little slow but strong.

"Ain't my gut."

"Well, it's something." There was a pasty pallor showing through the deep tan on Bates' neck below the ears. "Come below and let me check you over."

"Go away, Doc. I'm fine."

"No, you're not, Gunny. I know about the cardiac arrhythmia."

Bates struggled to his feet and shook a finger under Clinton's nose. "You don't know shit, pecker checker!"

"Yeah, I do, Gunny. I saw your chart when we came to see you in the hospital at Pusan."

"Goddammit! That's my private business."

"It's the kind of private business that can kill you if you don't do something about it."

"Listen up, Doc Clinton. You say anything about this and I'll write your ass up for a court-martial. I swear I will!"

Doc Clinton laughed. "On what charge? Doing my job?"

"Dopery, mopery, and felonious grunge! I don't fuckin' know, but I'll find something to put your ass in the brig!"

"Calm down, Gunny Bates." Doc Clinton offered a cigarette and his lighter. "I'm just trying to take care of you. It's in your best interest..."

Bates inhaled, winced and shook his head. "No...no, it ain't." He stared out across the sea at the ships steaming nearby. "I been doin' this shit for sixteen years now, Doc. It's what I know, what I'm good at. Nothin' means squat to me except this rifle company. I ain't gonna cry the poor-ass and leave 'em cause I got a little ticker problem."

Clinton saw the fervor in the man's eyes. Gunny Bates honestly didn't much care one way or the other, but if he was going to die, he wanted it to be while he was doing what he loved to do. It was a hard thing to understand for anyone who hadn't seen the man in action, seen how he truly cared for his Marines underneath all the shouting and screaming, seen the uncle, the father, the teacher and mentor that he really was. Taking that away from a man like Gunnery Sergeant Elmore Bates would be the cruelest kind of medical treatment.

"I've been looking into it," Clinton said. "There's this stuff called Trinitrin. It's a compound of nitroglycerine, good for some cardiac patients. I'll try to get some for you at Wonsan." Doc Clinton walked away, hoping he wouldn't be complicit if Gunny Bates died in the next couple of days.

They waded ashore or rode in landing craft when the ships were finally cleared to enter Wonsan Harbor. There were plenty of Korean and American soldiers milling around the docks waving and jeering at the combat loaded Marines. A Quartermaster Corps NCO told Hammond and Bates that they'd just missed a USO show featuring Bob Hope and a bevy of Hollywood starlets. They stood in lines outside dockside warehouses to receive the promised winter clothing. There were long johns, sateen winter trousers, mufflers, field jackets, and gloves. Each man got a long, heavy Navy parka with a hood and fleece lining. The most welcome item was a sleeping bag with a heavy liner. In place of the bulky horseshoe blanket rolls wrapped around the top of their haversacks, the sleeping bag was lighter and could be neatly rolled and strapped to the bottom of their packs for easy access. Some Marines—either wily traders or just plain lucky—even managed to secure one of the Army's fur-lined winter caps with earflaps.

And there were shoe-pacs, boots with waterproof rubber bottoms and laced leather uppers. They were issued two pairs of heavy woolen boot socks and told to change them often. They were instructed to keep one set next to their body where the socks would dry before being switched with a wet pair. It all seemed like manna from heaven until they tried marching in all the heavy gear and their feet started to sweat through the felt insoles of the shoe-pacs. What appeared to be a minor inconvenience when they were just getting the feel of the new gear would turn into a serious impediment as frigid winds began to blow and snow blanketed North Korea.

Able Company got 26 replacements at Wonsan, mostly men who had been called to active duty with reserve units from across the U.S. There were no officers available, but a couple were promised in the near future. Two of the new men were NCOs, one of them a Staff Sergeant retread with some combat time toward the end of World War II. Gerdine discovered that he had some mortar experience and made him the new weapons platoon leader. The other Sergeant went to third platoon to assist JJ Jones who was still nursing a gimpy arm.

The others were fresh-minted Marines out of boot camp. Gunny Bates created a battle-buddy system assigning each new man to an experienced one and dividing the replacements as evenly as possible throughout the platoons. The Able Company veterans received the new men with the typical disdain a veteran has for a man who has yet to face the crucible of infantry combat. The Able Company veterans, many of them younger than the replacements, were standoffish at first. They spoke of dead men and past battles in salty jargon and short-hand reference, ensuring the new men were listening when they related wildly exaggerated sea stories. It was short-lived. Burdens of life in a rifle platoon are easier when shared, even with new men who had yet to pay the price of admission to the show.

Gerdine and his XO met each man and did their best to gauge attitude, motivation, and relative value, trying to avoid superficial judgements. It looked like a pretty fair crop, but only time and experience could be the ultimate judge. Until that time passed and that experience was gained, they had to trust that any Marine who survived his training and reached a combat outfit was a good Marine until he proved otherwise.

Captain Sam Gerdine attended a big-picture briefing just before Division units began to move out of Wonsan. Apparently, General MacArthur had obtained permission for a full-scale pursuit of North Korean forces steadily retreating north of the 38th Parallel. His scheme, to be engineered on the ground by General Ned Almond's X Corps, was to advance toward the Yalu River, 135 miles distant across the mountainous sprawl of North Korea all the way to the Manchurian border. General Walton Walker's 8th Army was to attack toward the North Korean capital at Pyongyang on a western axis of advance. General O.P. Smith's 1st Marine Division would lead an attack northward along an eastern axis and guard the Army's right flank. The staging area for the Marine attack was a little place marked on their maps as Hamhung, an intersection for most major roads crisscrossing the area.

On the first of November, General Smith ordered Col. Murray to get moving northward. One of his RCT-5 battalions was to relieve a company of the 7th Marines that had been pushed up to stand guard over a recently captured airstrip near a place called Yonpo, five miles southwest of Hamhung and 60 miles north of Wonsan. LtCol. Newton's first battalion got the call. Gerdine explained as much of this as he thought his Marines needed to know and then shepherded them aboard a narrow-gauge Korean train for a rattling ride north. Most of the drafty, rattletrap railroad cars that carried 1st Battalion, 5th Marines had been used at some recent point in their history to haul pigs or cattle. The smell was nearly overpowering at first, but cold winds blowing through the wooden walls of the cars made it tolerable after a few miles.

Charlie Company got the enviable assignment to guard the airstrip while Able and Baker were sent on long patrols to probe for enemy forces around Hamhung. Baker went east of the railroad tracks. Able went west with two platoons. Gerdine left his mortars with third platoon emplaced near the road, deciding he'd go no further into the countryside than the max range of his mortars.

It was a relatively easy slog at first with second platoon leading the way across rapidly freezing rice paddies and traversing gentle slopes covered with a light layer of fresh snow. His Marines fidgeted with the new winter clothing, experimenting with the handiest ways to maneuver in the bulky outfits. They stopped a couple of times to change socks as Doc Clinton and two new Corpsmen walked the line on sock patrol. They were about a mile north of their starting point when Sgt. Trenton, walking with the second platoon's lead squad, tripped an ambush.

There was something different about it from the first shots. Unlike the North Korean enemy they'd encountered around Inchon, this outfit knew how to maneuver. They liked to move and shoot, pinning elements down with machinegun fire while squads moved rapidly to close on the flanks. Captain Gerdine pushed his first platoon up through the second and the melee rapidly turned into a running gunfight. Ruggles and Trenton were doing everything they could to get a handle on the fight, laying down a base of fire with light .30s and BARs, while directing Sgt. Edison's Marines to sweep wide and feel for a flank. But the enemy flanks seemed to disappear before they could be engaged. Gerdine got on his SCR-300 radio and called for 60mm mortar fire. That was helpful. When the rounds started cracking in all across the front, the enemy began to congeal into a few positions that could be attacked.

Sgt. Trenton, PFC Willis Jackson, and PFC Lannie Maitland overran one of those positions and took four prisoners who were trying to repair a malfunctioning machinegun. The rest of the enemy retreated over the horizon. Gerdine adjusted his distant mortars in an attempt to cut off their retreat while his Marines swept the area looking for stragglers. They found three or four and killed them on the spot, much to the shock of the new men in the unit. Only two first platoon Marines were wounded, and Doc Clinton said neither required evacuation.

"Skipper, you better come look at this." Lt. Paul Ruggles was standing near a hole with his carbine aimed at the four prisoners his platoon had captured. "Could be mistaken," he said when Gerdine joined him, "but I don't think these are Koreans."

The prisoners, sitting bunched in the bottom of the hole with their hands behind their heads, did look different. And they smelled terribly—an odorous mix of excrement and garlic wafted up from each of them. Their faces were plump, almost cherubic, as they stared up at their captors through dark eyes. But there was no resentment, fear, or venom in their expressions. Two of them were actually smiling. They wore fur-lined caps with earflaps above bulky padded uniforms. Their feet were stuffed into what looked like an Asian version of gym sneakers.

"Them are Chinks," Gunny Bates said as he pulled the jammed machinegun out of the hole. "And this here is a Chinese machinegun. I seen 'em before when we was on occupation duty in Shanghai." Bates unclipped the circular drum magazine from atop the weapon and rattled it. "Horseshit design. These drum magazines jam too easy."

"You really think these guys are Chinese?" Other weapons being pulled out of the hole by Jackson and Maitland looked more familiar, including a couple of bolt-action rifles and one of the PPSh-41 burp-guns that was intimately familiar to the Marines after Inchon.

"And look here," Bates said pulling a mustard-green ammunition cannister out of the hole. "Does that look like Korean writing to you?"

It didn't. In fact it looked entirely different from the Korean *hangul* that Gerdine had seen ever since he'd been in Korea. He wished Sgt. Pak were still around to advise him. He'd certainly know the difference between Korean and Chinese lettering.

"Pack this stuff up," Captain Gerdine ordered. "Let's get these guys back to battalion and turn them over to S-2."

By nightfall, the prisoners Able Company brought in from their patrol had been thoroughly interrogated. "Definitely Chinese," the S-2 officer told Gerdine, "and downright chatty. Claim to be proud members of the Chinese 370th Regiment."

"What the hell are they doing here?"

"More pertinent question is how many more of them there are. These guys claim they crossed the Yalu with the rest of their division a couple of weeks ago. One of them claims a political officer told him there are something like six Red Chinese major formations in Korea. Given what we know about their organization, that would be a couple of Army-sized commands."

"You believe that? I mean, what would that be...something like twenty divisions?"

"Twenty-four to be exact. And I don't know whether it's true or just propaganda he's spouting. He damn sure believes it."

"What are you gonna do with them?"

"Send 'em to the rear—far back as we can—all the way to X Corps, if I have my way. General Almond and his ilk have been claiming the only Chinese in North Korea are a little bunch of volunteers, advisors to the North Koreans. I'm thinking he might change his mind if he gets a load of what these bozos have to say."

But General Arnold, backed by General MacArthur who was regularly reassuring the White House, continued to insist there were no large, organized Chinese Communist Forces fighting in Korea. Nobody in the 1st Marine Division believed a bit of it. As the Division continued to move north, heading for a tadpole shaped splash of blue on their map called the Chosin Reservoir, the field commanders all expected to meet Chinese formations sooner or later.

The division's northward move seemed to be going in fits and starts. RCT-7 had advanced furthest toward Koto-ri. RCT-1 was steadily trekking up the main road with a huge logistical tail plus most of the tanks and artillery. Murray's RCT-5 was delayed by forays east and west of the main road leading north as they patrolled to guard the flanks. Given Able Company's running fight on Nov. 2, Colonel Murray ordered a reconnaissance in strength to the west of the main road. The entire first battalion hooked left while the other two battalions advanced up the road or combed the flanking hills.

Captain Gerdine's company, familiar with the area, was in the lead. Gerdine and Gunny Bates were walking with Sgt. Jones and the third platoon at the head of the battalion advance. A small spotter aircraft zoomed low overhead waggling its wings.

"What the hell's his problem?" Gunny Bates looked up at the aircraft and saw an arm waving from the cockpit.

"Wish I knew," Gerdine said. Captain Tex Stanton and the Forward Air Control Party were well to the rear with the battalion CP group. It was pretty obvious that the pilot in the little aircraft was trying to communicate something. He decided to halt the advance and spread his men out to wait for word from the battalion commander.

The small aircraft continued to zoom low over Able Company. At times it was so low that Gerdine thought he might be able to reach up and touch the landing gear. The squadron identification painted on the fuselage was clearly visible. The plane was from Marine Observation Squadron-6 or VMO-6, but neither Gerdine nor Gunny Bates had any idea where that outfit was based. On his next pass, Gerdine saw the pilot point excitedly waving his arm toward a hill mass to the right. He banked hard to fly back over the Marines on the ground and Gerdine saw a sign the observer in the opposite seat was holding. GOOKS!

"Well, that's pretty clear," Gerdine and Gunny Bates turned the third platoon and began to climb the high ground. Their radio was silent, so Bates had the operator do a comm check to be sure it was working. It was, and reception on the SCR-300 was loud and clear by the time they reached the top of the hill.

"Sonofabitch," Gerdine whispered as he swept the western horizon toward a spot the map labeled Huksu-ri. He handed the binoculars to Gunny Bates and reached for the radio handset. "That's gotta be at least a battalion." The horizon seemed to be teeming with enemy movement. Some were advancing and others were sweeping outward as flank guards.

"There's a couple hundred of 'em or better," Bates said as he glassed the enemy formation. "Looks like North Koreans to me, but they could be Chinks."

Gerdine keyed the radio and sent the observation report to his battalion commander. "Airborne spotters confirms your count," LtCol. Newton responded. "Hold your position. We're gonna hit 'em from the air."

The rest of Able Company climbed the hill to reinforce third platoon and be in a good position to watch the air show. It was long and spectacular. It was also an impressive display of allied airpower from every available source. The huge enemy formation was caught in the open, and everyone with an armed aircraft wanted in on the strike. As the little VMO aircraft circled overhead, they saw Marine and Navy Corsairs run on the target dropping napalm and then returning to strafe with rockets and machineguns. When they pulled off, a flight of four Air Force P-51 Mustangs appeared over the target with superchargers whining. More rocket and machinegun runs went in and by the time the Air Force pilots turned for home, there was nothing moving on the horizon. Gerdine reported that, but Able Company was ordered to hold while Marine artillery pounded the scorched battlefield.

"Well, they ain't fucking around this time." Sgt. JJ Jones said to Gunny Bates as they watched the impressive firepower display.

"Sending a little message," Captain Gerdine said. "I'm thinking the colonel wants them to know they aren't tangling with amateurs."

"Hard to use shit like that when you're in a close firefight," Gunny Bates said. Gerdine just nodded. If he were an enemy seeing that kind of firepower, he'd be damn sure every fight was close enough that an enemy couldn't bring it to bear. He fully expected orders to advance into the scorched area for some sort of body count or damage assessment, but Able Company was ordered to turn around and serve as the battalion rearguard when 1/5 marched back toward the main road.

"Straight north without delay," LtCol. Newton told Captain Gerdine and the other company commanders when they reached the road. "Getting pressure from above, I guess." Newton shrugged. "Anyway, we head for Hamhung beginning tomorrow morning." He pointed at several points on his map, wide spots along the road leading to Chosin Reservoir. "From there we go straight up the road—Sudong, Koto-ri, and Hagaru at the south end of the reservoir. At that point, we go up the east side and 7th Marines advance on the west side."

"Then what, Colonel?" one of the commanders wondered. "We still looking to link-up with the Army?"

"That's what they tell me," Newton said. "Apparently, General Walker's people are on a roll toward the Yalu. The scheme seems to be that we turn west once we've cleared the area around the reservoir."

Captain Sam Gerdine stared at the miles and miles of wide open terrain between the Chosin Reservoir and the Yalu. "That's a hell of a lot of terrain to cover, sir. Gotta be a pot-full of North Koreans and Chinese between here and there."

"No doubt." LtCol. Newton folded his map. "And the weather is getting worse. Just between us girls, General Smith is not too happy about splitting us up at Chosin. But General Almond and his wizards at X Corps are calling the shots."

A winter storm hit as Able Company was gearing up to move north. Temperatures plummeted and a cold wind blew snow into a frigid funnel formed by hills on either side of the main road leading north. Gunny Bates walked the column of Marines in the first pale light of dawn as they waited for orders to move. Most of them had cut their loads down to a reasonable size. The crew-served machinegunners and mortarmen had spread ammo and components out among the rifle platoons.

Sgt. Sean Marcus stood with his back turned against the wind. He was still carrying a 3.5-inch rocket launcher even though he'd been instructed to turn the weapon over to someone else and concentrate his efforts on running the AT Section of Weapons Platoon. Bates didn't bother to mention it again, just nodded as he passed by Marcus. The man was proud of his reputation as Able Company's reliable tank killer. And since

RCT-5 would be hugging the road most of the way north, they just might run into enemy tanks.

Riflemen all carried what the Corps called a basic unit of fire: Cartridge belts full of clips and at least one bandolier draped over a shoulder or tied around the waist. Each man was supposed to have four hand grenades, but there was no way to check on that underneath the bulky parkas and other winter clothing. The Inchon veterans knew the value of grenades and would have as many as they could comfortably carry. And those vets would have pre-checked the new men before they fell out on the road. They looked a little miserable huddled against the wind, but Bates knew they'd endure and respond as required. He was proud of Able Company, proud to be their Company Gunnery Sergeant.

He saw Doc Clinton standing next to a shapeless blob near the rear of second platoon. Somewhere under all that clothing and gear there had to be a Marine. Whoever it was looked more like an olive-drab version of the Michelin Man with an M-1 slung over a shoulder. Gunny Bates jerked at the strings holding the parka hood, opened the flaps, and found PFC Miles Abramson grinning at him. "Got enough gear to keep you warm, Abramson?" Bates chuckled and poked at the padding on the man's body.

"I hate the fucking cold, Gunny." Abramson's cheeks were raw, red, and chapped despite the hood surrounding his face. "Doc got me an extra parka from one of the wounded guys."

Bates draped an arm over what he imagined must be Abramson's shoulder and led him away for a private conversation. "Listen, fartknocker, I ain't no big fuckin' fan of winter either." The Gunny felt around Abramson's body searching for the man's combat gear. "But you gotta be able to reach your gear and ammo, right? You been in enough fights to know that."

"Thought we were just gonna road march..."

"That's what we're gonna do, Miles. But this road we're standin' on is as important to the gooks as it is to us, right? They're not gonna just let us march along countin' cadence, are they? We're bound to tangle assholes, and I don't want you standin' around digging under all that crap for ammo. Now go give the Doc back the extra parka."

He stopped by Sgt. Edison at the head of first platoon. "You bring them cupcakes, Edison?"

"In my pack, Gunny." Edison jerked a thumb over his shoulder at the bulging haversack on his back. "Couldn't find no candles."

"First Shirt will come through. Always does," Bates said. "Now don't tell anybody anything, and take care of the cupcakes."

"They're already in rough shape," Edison said. "Wife did the best she could, but they got a little damaged in the mail."

"They'll do..." Gunny Bates caught the Skipper's signal from the middle of the formation. "Off and on, Able...we're movin'."

Able Company trudged forward, leaning into the wind. Two trucks on loan from the division's 1st Motor Transport Battalion ground behind them carrying tentage, extra rations, water, and a few clandestine items like Sgt. Edison's radio and a Chinese war sword the First Sergeant had borrowed or stolen somewhere.

Gunny Bates turned around and looked back through the formation at the trucks following Able Company. The First Sergeant was standing in the first one bundled up behind a .50 caliber machinegun. He waved and showed a thumbs up.

"Fuckin' Leland..." Gunny Bates grinned and shook his head. They had 16 miles to cover before an overnight stay at Oro-ri and a little surprise Gunny Bates had for Able Company Marines.

They had a series of tents erected alongside the MSR on the morning of 10 November 1950. Orders said they would strike the overnight camp and continue the march as soon as possible. Gunny Bates said that would be possible only after they'd appropriately marked the 175th Birthday of the United States Marine Corps. And Able Company did that three times on that frigid morning in North Korea.

One platoon at a time was brought out of the cold and wind to stand gathered around a rickety little table where a dozen badly battered chocolate cupcakes were arranged to look like

numbers 1 and 5—loosely. Each little cake had a candle burning in its center. First Sergeant Hammond read the message
from former Commandant General John A. Lejeune as required on the occasion, and Captain Gerdine used Hammond's
rusty old Chinese war sword to hack one of the cupcakes in
two. The first little handful of crumbles went to the oldest
Marine in the platoon. The next bit went to the youngest,
marking the passage of heritage and tradition from one gener-
ation to the next. There was some argument about which men
deserved that recognition, but XO Lt. Solomon had checked
the records and put an end to it quickly. Doc Clinton was
drafted to work out the geometry, and each man got at least
one little bite of improvised birthday cake. And they were all
singing the *Marines' Hymn* as Able Company started north once
again.

It took nearly three days for RCT-5 to cover the ten miles
to their next destination at Koto-ri. The road-bound formation
and accompanying vehicles stretched and expanded like an
accordion, but that wasn't the reason for the slow progress.
Snipers continually took pot-shots from high ground on either
side of the road. Rifle platoons, roaming those hills as flank
guards, had to chase them away, and that robbed the northbound formation of momentum. And the North Korean
weather was steadily deteriorating. Much of the march was
made into the teeth of frigid winds that snapped and whipped
at the Marines, forcing them to lean and stagger.

Able Company was dispatched up a snow-covered hill
when lead elements of the formation were hit by machinegun
fire from the east of the road. Pushing up toward the crest, Sgt.
Edison's first platoon encountered a bunker that halted their
climb. It was a fairly elaborate defensive position, a large,
heavily sandbagged bunker surrounded by rifle pits, each
containing a Chinese soldier. Sgt. Sean Marcus was called
forward to deal with the bunker, and he put two well-aimed
rocket rounds right into the entrance. Other defenders were
dispatched fairly quickly after that.

At least three of the enemy riflemen were discovered frozen nearly to death in their holes. They could not have run
even if they had wanted to when Edison's Marines assaulted

them. Their feet resembled big lumps of black ice and their ungloved hands were so swollen that they could barely pull a trigger. Shooting these pitiful creatures was both a tactical necessity and an act of mercy. Edison and two of his Marines dug through the bunker rubble and found a portrait of Josef Stalin that they presented to Captain Gerdine as a souvenir.

A more pressing problem presented at nightfall when temperatures dropped to zero. First platoon was ordered to hold their recently captured piece of high ground overnight to guard against infiltrators. At sunset, frigid air covered them like a sheet of ice. It was a still, shocking cold. There was no wind, but the drop in ambient air temperature seemed to engulf the Marines like a painful weight pressing in from all sides. Some of Sgt. Edison's men swore they could actually see the cold descending on them, and none bitched too loudly about orders to hack fighting positions out of frozen rocky ground. The work warmed them if only temporarily. Sergeants Edison and Marcus toured their little perimeter reminding everyone to change socks and work the actions on stiff, balky weapons. If the gooks valued this hill enough to defend it, Sgt. Marcus told his squad occupying the right side of first platoon's perimeter, then the bastards might just try to take it back.

"You can break out the sleeping bags," he told them as he ordered a 50-percent alert for the night, "but only stick your feet and lower legs into them. I don't want to catch anybody on watch with his bag pulled up higher than the knees."

Three times during the night, gooks were spotted moving below first platoon's perimeter. Or Marines on watch swore they saw something moving. Each time, the night erupted in rifle fire, grenades were rolled down the hill. It lasted a few minutes. If there was any return fire—and no one could be sure there was—it did no damage. What it did do was keep everyone jumpy, including Sgt. Sean Marcus who was constantly up and checking his men. During that long frigid night, he found three of them who should have been sitting up on watch nodding with bags clutched tightly around their shoulders. He kicked them awake and screamed for a while, feeling like a hypocrite. He'd also fallen asleep twice sitting with his back to a boulder at the center of their position.

Sgt. Sean Marcus stumbled forward to sit on a rock where everyone in his squad could clearly see him. He was fully exposed and wanted to be. "I'm gonna be right here all night," he said, his voice echoing and his breath steaming in the freezing night air. "I'll be awake. And you bastards on watch better be, too." As he sat staring into the dark with his carbine across his knees, Marcus worked his toes in the shoe-pacs. In the turmoil of the fight, he'd neglected to change his socks. He was losing feeling in his feet and he thought about changing his socks, but he didn't think his frozen fingers could manipulate the boot laces. He should probably walk a little, move around, stomp his feet, but that didn't seem right. He had to be a rock out here like the one he was sitting on, solid, unmoving, alert and ready for anything just as he expected his Marines to be.

In the morning, Sgt. Sean Marcus could not walk back down the hill.

They carried him to Doc Clinton who cut the boots off his feet and assessed the damage. Marcus' feet were black, swollen, and bruised nearly to the ankles. He could march no further on those decaying clumps of icy flesh. He would likely lose a couple of toes and possibly other parts of each foot where the frozen flesh had died from lack of blood circulation. He would need to be evacuated.

If there was any good news that morning as Able Company resumed the march north, it was that Chesty Puller's RCT-1 with the division's logistical tail was not far behind. Sgt. Sean Marcus, the tank-killer, was left with First Sergeant Hammond to wait for better medical attention when Puller's outfit passed by on the way to Koto-ri. With tears freezing on his cheeks, Sgt. Marcus tried at least twice to stand and walk. Each time, the First Sergeant pulled him back down and eventually tied him securely in a sleeping bag.

"Not your fault, son." The First Sergeant sat beside him and helped Marcus smoke a cigarette. "You did what you thought you had to do up on that hill. And that's all we can ask from any man."

BY THE MIDDLE of the month, Litzenberg's RCT-7 had advanced up what now was known as the MSR or Main Supply Route all the way to the Chosin Reservoir. Units of his 7th Marines were stretched along the southern reaches of the frozen reservoir and well to the west of it at a site called Yudam-ni. It was the furthest reach of the 1st Marine Division's advance. Now, Major General O.P. Smith, resisting constant chivvying by X Corps, paused to consolidate. Fearing an enemy counter stroke that could cut the MSR behind him and catch the division with combat power dispersed, Smith wanted to marshal his forces, establish a firm combat and logistical base at Hagaru, and build an airstrip there. His supply line from the south was tentative and vulnerable. And Smith wanted an air route to resupply and to evacuate an increasing number of casualties from both enemy action and cold injuries.

General Almond thought the Marines were being balky and skittish. Under pressure from MacArthur in Tokyo, he wanted to hook the Marines hard left, and have them reach out for contact with 8th Army operating far to the west. The vaunted 1st Cavalry Division was poised to assault the North Korean capital at Pyongyang and still the dreaded Chinese hordes, those huge swarms of soldiers everyone said were lurking in the shadows, had not engaged in any sort of organized resistance as allied forces drove toward the Manchurian border. Almond was frenetic. Smith was cautious.

Caught in the middle of it all at the Chosin Reservoir with 7th Marines ahead of them and 1st Marines behind them, Murray's 5th Marines were ordered to begin sweeping to the east of the reservoir. "I don't like it one damn bit," Murray told his three battalion commanders. "I think we should keep our combat power massed on the west side, but orders are orders."

"Colonel Murray's not too happy about it." LtCol. Newton stifled a yawn as he briefed his company commanders. "But we start moving east of the reservoir shortly." He pointed at a spot on the map, a site about a third of the way up the eastern bank of the solidly frozen lake labeled Sinhung-ni. "It's about seven miles northeast of us here at Hagaru."

Captain Gerdine studied his Battalion Commander as the briefing continued. Newton was a shadow of the man who drove the battalion through Inchon and on to Seoul. He looked like he hadn't slept in weeks. He chain smoked, hands trembling as he lit one butt from another in a distracted ritual. Like everyone else up and down the division chain of command, Newton had too much to do and too few men to do it with, but Gerdine thought there was a deeper problem with the battalion CO. These days, exhausted by mission creep and steadily deteriorating weather, Newton's fire seemed all but extinguished. He appeared pained by the orders he issued, as if he believed they weren't wise or simply too painful to contemplate beyond the necessary broad strokes of what he had to do with his command.

Apparently, others had noticed LtCol. Newton's deteriorating condition. Just before they moved east, word came down to the rifle companies that they had a new Battalion Commander. LtCol. George Newton was being transferred stateside. His replacement was LtCol. John Stevens, formerly the XO of 2ⁿᵈ Battalion, 5ᵗʰ Marines.

Captain Gerdine and the other rifle company COs met him at a briefing on the Sinhung-ni movement the day before it was scheduled to commence. On the one hand, the COs thought as they watched Stevens issue orders, he's an old 5ᵗʰ Marines man with experience at Inchon and not some stateside replacement. On the other hand, he was an unknown quantity to the men who would have to carry out his orders. They left the briefing wondering whether Stevens was a cautious, level-headed tactician or a gung-ho field grade officer out to prove he could handle a battalion in combat. LtCol. Stevens gave no indication at first blush that he leaned one way or the other.

When artillery batteries from the 11ᵗʰ Marines were in place for fire support, RCT-5 began to swing around the south end of Chosin Reservoir and hook north headed for their first objective at Sinhung-ni. Able Company was in the lead, forging forward through blowing snow as they crossed a set of landmark railroad tracks. The ground sloped steadily upward, and Captain Gerdine was worried about getting his Marines silhouetted on the crest as they crossed that high ground. He sent Lt. Ruggles probing to the right, looking for a passage on lower ground to the east. Sgt. Edison, leading his first platoon, swung off in the other direction toward the banks of the reservoir. It was a costly move.

Sgt. Edison, walking with the lead squad, thought he saw movement through the blinding snow to his left, somewhere out on the frozen surface of the reservoir. He halted his unit and went forward to look. The ground seemed to fall out from under his feet as fire erupted all around him. He seemed to have fallen into some kind of snow shelter or cave with his parka hiked up around his armpits. His rifle was buried in snow to his right. He was digging around for it when an enemy soldier jumped into the pit, stabbing at him with a bayonet fixed on the end of his rifle. The blade struck just under Edison's armpit, piercing layers of clothing but missing skin and bone. The enemy soldier jammed a sneakered foot on Edison's chest to extract the bayonet, but Edison grabbed the rifle barrel and fought for leverage. He kicked hard and reached for the holstered pistol on his hip. There was a round in the chamber. If he could dig the .45 out and cock it with a thumb, he had a chance.

Captain Gerdine heard the firefight erupt on the left. All he could see through the blowing snow was muzzle flash. He couldn't raise anyone on the radio to find out what was happening, so he sent Lt. Solomon rushing through the storm to retrieve Ruggles and second platoon. Gunny Bates came trotting by him with remnants of the trailing third platoon. "I'll check it out, Skipper!" Bates rushed through the snow blowing off the reservoir leading Sgt. JJ Jones and others off to the left. Gerdine looked up into the overcast sky. There would be no air support on a day like this. He switched to the artillery observer frequency on his radio and began to set up a fire mission.

Sgt. Ron Edison kept kicking at his assailant who continued trying to clear his bayonet. The shoe-pacs made a satisfactory thud on the man's chest, but the padded uniform absorbed the impact. He heaved himself to the left and managed to locate his pistol in the jumble of snow, ice, and winter clothing. When he finally had it clear of the holster, he cocked the hammer and stuck the .45 under the gook's chin. The shot snapped the enemy's head back and blew a fur cap full of brains and gore into the air. Edison struggled up to a sitting position and put another pistol round into his dead assailant. The firefight was still snapping around him, and when he looked up out of the hole, he could see tracers lancing through the snow and mist. He rolled the dead man away and found his M-1. He clicked off the safety and fired a round into the air to clear the action. *Thank you, John Garand*, he thought as the M-1 cycled to load another round into the chamber.

Peeking over the edge of the hole, he saw a few lumps in the snow, jerking with recoil as they fired at targets he couldn't see. He shouted for his platoon to pull back and saw a few of them begin pushing backward over the snowy ground. He heard firing to his rear and thought at first he might be surrounded by an unseen enemy. Then he heard a familiar voice shouting curses. It was Gunny Bates. No mistaking that. Someone was coming to pull him out of this mess. Sgt. Edison poked his rifle over the rim of the hole and began to fire. He didn't have identifiable targets, but he did have firepower and ammo.

Gunny Bates paused the counterattack behind a rolling ridge of hard-packed snow and tried to assess how badly first platoon was hurt. He could see a BAR and a few rifles firing to his front. He could also see three or four Marines lying in the snow where they'd either been killed or wounded. From the muzzle flashes he could see forward of them, it looked like the gooks were in a sort of L-shaped position with the long leg dug in along the banks of the reservoir. There was a machinegun hammering at the short leg of the L. "Open fire on the left flank!" Bates yelled at Jones and the third platoon riflemen. Then he began to maneuver to the right where he could work himself closer to the machinegun.

Lt. Solomon and Lt. Ruggles were pushing their men back over the terrain they'd covered in the flanking patrol. Hearing the firefight in the direction of the reservoir, Ruggles wanted to head in that direction, but the XO cut him off. "Not until we know what's happening," Solomon said, pointing to where he'd left Captain Gerdine. "Keep going in this direction." Sgt. Heywood Trenton caught sight of a Marine crawling on hands and knees through the snow as he ran back with the second platoon. In the sleet and wind, he couldn't tell for sure who it was. Maybe a straggler? Somebody lost and looking for direction? He shouted for the man and took off in that direction.

Gunny Bates heard the shouting at his back, shouldered his rifle, and spun. It was another Marine, parka flying in the wind, kicking up flurries as he plowed through the snow. Bates waved and pointed at the machinegun blazing away to his left. Trenton tumbled in beside him at the snowbank that hid them from enemy observation.

"You lost?" Trenton was gasping after his run through the snow.

"Not yet, I ain't, Trenton. Machinegun up there is cutting into Edison and his guys. I'm about to put a stop to that shit."

Sgt. Trenton peeked up over the snowbank. "Looks like he's in a hole with a couple of others. Hard to see..."

"I'm countin' on that," Bates said, digging into a pouch on his cartridge belt for a grenade.

"They're gonna see you sure as shit when you move." Trenton spotted a long line of rocks to their left front. They were small, probably eroded over time by reservoir waters, but they'd provide some cover. "Let me get around to them rocks and distract 'em a little. When I open up, you make your move."

"I'll buy that for tactics, Trenton. Shove off."

Sgt. Trenton began a slow, cautious crawl toward the line of rocks. The machinegun was firing in short, controlled bursts. *And right into first platoon's flank*, he thought, trying to ignore the snow that was jamming up his sleeves and down the front of his uniform as he crawled. When he found a position that gave him a clear line of fire at the machinegun position, Trenton tumbled a few spare M-1 clips into the snow where they'd be handy and then began to squeeze off rapid fire at the enemy position. By the time he had burned through the first clip, he saw a huge looming shape rise like a startled pheasant out of a winter cornfield. Bates was running hard, knees pumping high, snow flying, a rifle in one hand and an armed grenade in the other.

Gunny Bates might have been able to get a grenade into the machinegun position from the snowbank without breaking cover, but he didn't have an arm like JJ Jones, and he didn't want to take chances. He saw the assistant machinegunner turn toward him when he was about ten yards from the hole. The man's dark eyes went wide, and he reached for a rifle, but Bates ignored that. He heaved the grenade as hard as he could right at the man and then rolled away. The enemy soldier shouted something and leaped out of the hole just as the grenade detonated with a sharp crack, blowing snow and shrapnel into the machinegunners. Bates killed the man who tried to escape and then crawled forward to put insurance shots into the others.

He spotted Sgt. Trenton peering from among the rocks and waved. "I'm gonna police up first platoon and pull 'em back," he shouted. "Get back to the Skipper and let him know we're comin' in!"

Gunny Bates crawled forward until he found Sgt. Edison and ordered him to pull back while he kept the enemy on the reservoir banks busy. Edison crawled out of the hole and began shouting for his men to withdraw from the ambush. He saw one of his squad leaders struggling with blood covering one side of his face. Sgt. Ron Edison ran to help and but never made it. A wicked burst of fire cut into his thighs and he lay bleeding into the snow on the banks of the Chosin Reservoir.

"Get back up there and cover the withdrawal," Gerdine said to Sgt. Trenton when he got the situation report about his first platoon. He turned to Lt. Ruggles. "Paul, take a squad and go with him. Get everyone back here. I've got a battery standing by. When you're clear, I'm gonna have 'em fire."

In a running gunfight through the blowing snow, Lt. Ruggles, Gunny Bates, and Sgt. Trenton got most of first platoon clear of the ambush site. They had to carry three men including Sgt. Edison and leave seven dead in the snow. The supporting battery took care of everything else with a steel curtain of artillery fire.

Baker and Charlie Companies advanced through Able later in the day heading for Sinhung-ni. Badly chewed up in the fight, Captain Gerdine's Marines held position along the eastern banks of the Chosin to serve as battalion rear guard. Seven dead men lay wrapped in their sleeping bags, while the three wounded men from first platoon waited with Doc Clinton for Jeeps coming up from Hagaru to evacuate them. PFC Miles Abramson knelt next to his old reserve unit friend sharing a cigarette.

"You're gonna be OK, Sergeant Edison," he said. "You'll be back in Kansas City before you know it."

"Do me a favor, Miles." Edison's words were slurred from the morphine administered by Doc Clinton who kept vials of the drugs in his mouth to keep them from freezing. "My radio—I want you to have it."

"Sure," Abramson said. "I'll take good care of it. Bring it back home to you if I can."

"And one more favor, Miles..."

"What's that?"

"If they try to send you to boot camp when this is over, you tell 'em they can kiss your ass—and mine too."

Thanksgiving Day

CAPTAIN GERDINE'S Able Company had pulled back from the eastern side of the reservoir for Thanksgiving at Hagaru. It was a crowded place and vulnerable to enemy attacks from the surrounding high ground, so Gerdine was ordered to set up as security on a hill overlooking a valley where Marines from 1st Engineer Battalion were attempting to blast, carve, and scrape an adequate airfield out of the frozen ground.

Tanks arrived, leading a convoy of trucks from Koto-ri, just after dawn. Willing hands helped unload the vehicles which were jammed with what Marine cooks and bakers needed to prepare an adequate holiday meal in completely inadequate conditions. Able Company watched it all, bitching profanely, cleaning gear and changing into dry socks and felt shoe-pac insoles that the First Sergeant had issued before they climbed the hill.

Hacking and wheezing with a croupy cough, First Sergeant Leland Hammond climbed up later in the day with a small sack of mail and a copy of the 1st Marine Division Thanksgiving menu. According to that mimeographed document, embellished with turkeys wearing helmets and Marine insignia, the feast was to include shrimp cocktail, stuffed olives, roast young tom turkey with cranberry sauce, candied sweet potatoes, fruit salad, fruit cake, mincemeat pie, and hot coffee. The Marines on East Hill passed the document around, laughing and speculating about what little bit of that Thanksgiving largesse they might expect to see stuck out of sight and mind up on East Hill. First Sergeant Hamond tramped back down at mid-morning, promising to do everything he could to ensure they'd get a share in the feast. He knew a guy.

Leland Hammond also knew this might be the last time he'd see his company for a while. He was due to depart for Koto-ri on a southbound convoy right after Thanksgiving chow. HM2 Clinton, whose medical opinions were now gold standard in Able Company, had listened to the First Sergeant's lungs and diagnosed early stages of pneumonia. When he told the Skipper about it, he added that a condition like that was particularly dangerous to an older man who had smoked constantly most of his life. Despite the First Sergeant's best efforts to convince the Skipper that it was only a bad cold, Captain Gerdine ordered him to the rear. "Can't afford to lose you for good, First Sergeant," he said. "Get back to 1st Med Battalion and let them treat you. And that's an order. You can rejoin us when you're better."

HM2 Arleigh Clinton looked over the Thanksgiving menu with Able Company XO 1stLt. Rod Solomon. "Hope we get some of this stuff, XO."

"Me too, Doc." The XO was chewing on a lump of laxative gum the Corpsman had just given him. "If this stuff works, I might even have room for a solid meal."

"How long's it been, sir?"

"Three, four days, I guess."

"XO, we gotta do something about getting people to shit around here..." They both snickered at the thought but Able Company like many other units was having serious problems with impacted colons. For some men, it was just too difficult or daunting to dig through all the clothing and bare their ass to the frigid wind and cold.

"Maybe we should line 'em up," the XO laughed, "and have Gunny Bates order them to do it by the numbers."

"Whatever works." Clinton shrugged. "It's getting ridiculous. Yesterday Jackson came to see me..."

"Black guy? BAR man in second platoon?"

"That's him. He tells me his dick has disappeared."

"What?"

"It's the goddamn weather, of course. Man's dick shrivels up with the cold and he has to dig so hard trying to find it to take a leak..." There was more, but neither man could stop laughing. Able Company had its share of problems, but morale wasn't among them.

Gunny Bates passed out a skimpy collection of letters, periodicals, and packages while letting everyone at Mail Call know loudly and profanely that his failure to get a perfumed missive from Doris was part of a larger communist plot to destroy his morale. There was a very nice letter for Captain Gerdine in the mail. Della had seen an article from a New York paper that mentioned him. She wrote that she would miss him on Thanksgiving, miss his expertise in carving their turkey. There was a subtle play to her words that made Sam Gerdine believe she might consider a reconciliation. He'd leap at that chance if it were ever seriously offered. He wasn't ready to quit the Corps, but maybe he could cook up some kind of staff assignment. Maybe Della would be OK with it if he weren't constantly in the field, bouncing around the world with the infantry. When all this was over, he wanted to play a larger part in raising their son. Captain Sad Sam Gerdine had seen too many kids from screwed up families using the Marine Corps as a surrogate father. It rarely worked well.

Sitting across from Captain Gerdine in a little rocky cleft that served as their company CP, 1stLt. Rod Solomon was chuckling and shaking his head. The Company Commander saw him snapping a fingernail on a letter he was reading.

"Win the sweepstakes, XO?"

"Better in some people's view." Solomon handed across a nicely typed letter bearing the Rutgers University logo. "I'd forgotten all about that."

"Says here..." Gerdine read a few paragraphs, "You've been accepted at the Rutgers Law School. Congratulations."

"Ain't that a bitch?" Solomon shook his head in disbelief. "I applied while I was marking time in a staff job. Never thought it would come through..." The XO leaned back against the rocks and began to laugh. "And here I am in Korea freezing my ass off!"

"Korea won't last forever. You can go when it's over."

"Maybe so—assuming I survive."

"You'll survive, Rod. And you'll make a damn fine lawyer, if that's what you want to be."

"Skipper, I'm not sure what I want to be...except maybe warm, or half-drunk, or elsewhere."

They chuckled and Gerdine handed back the acceptance letter. "Reminds me of a guy we had in my outfit on Peleliu," the Captain said. "We're sitting up on some damn rock with Japs shooting at us, and this guy comes up with a letter he got at Mail Call. It's his draft notice. You know, ordering him to report for induction. He wants us to send him home immediately so he can comply with his draft orders."

"What happened?"

"First Sergeant tore it up and kicked the guy's ass all the way down the hill."

"Which is what a good First Shirt does when one of his peckerheads comes up with something stupid." Gunny Bates slid into the CP and lit a cigarette. He nodded at the letter. "You get drafted, XO?"

"Sort of, Gunny. I got accepted to law school."

"Well, fuck that, XO. You're a Marine and Marines hate fuckin' lawyers...who are always tryin' to put their asses in the brig. You don't want to be no fuckin' shyster, XO."

"I'll take that under advisement, Gunny."

Bates nodded, pulled out his notebook, and riffed through a few pages. "Skipper, I been wonderin' if you heard anything about a promotion for Abramson?"

"I did, Gunny. S-1 officer caught me on the way up here. Abramson and Jackson both approved for promotion to Corporal, effective first of the month."

"Well, wonders will never cease. Desk jockeys finally got off their fat asses. I'll let 'em know right after chow. If fuckin' chow ever gets up here."

Fucking chow did get up to Able Company on that Thanksgiving Day 1950, but it was a little short of what the menu advertised. Each man got a dollop of fruit cocktail that was mostly icy slush and a slab of half-frozen turkey meat. And they had to improvise eating it. They'd thrown away their mess-kits long ago. The coffee was cold.

Major General O.P. Smith sat behind a rickety field desk stuffing his old briar pipe with Sir Walter Raleigh tobacco. A fresh supply had come in with the Thanksgiving supplies, and Smith did his best thinking when he was wreathed in aromatic tobacco smoke. He squinted at the situation map in front of him contemplating the orders he'd have to give at the evening briefing.

According to X Corps plans, he was to push west rapidly and devil take the hindmost. And that devil was the Red Chinese Army. Smith could feel it in his soldierly bones. Everyone knew the CCF was out there in strength. And no one seemed to know why they hadn't yet made their big move. *That's the worrisome thing*, General Smith thought, relighting his pipe. When they make that big move, as everyone with an ounce of combat sense knows they will, the last thing he wanted was to get caught with his Marines scattered all to hell and gone, stretched so thin that they couldn't mutually support each other.

Smith just didn't know how much more delay General Almond would tolerate now that he'd relieved the Marines of responsibility for the east side of Chosin Reservoir. Almond had cobbled together an Army regimental combat team from the 7th Division's 31st Infantry to assume operations to the east. Task Force Faith, named after the officer chosen to command it. Well, good luck to them. With the frozen stretches of the reservoir between his Marines and Task Force Faith, Smith couldn't be much help if they got into serious trouble.

The Commanding General made a few notes on the margin of his map. He'd have to push Litzenberg and his 7th Marines up to Yudam-ni post haste followed by Murray's 5th Marines and then order the attack to the west across miles of open terrain and torturous hills, feeling for 8th Army units that seemed to be fluid and scattered all over western North Korea. Meanwhile, he'd order Chesty Puller's 1st Marines to close up from the rear and occupy positions along the MSR while they struggled to get an airfield in operation at Hagaru.

Smith knocked the dottle from his pipe and stood to stretch. It wasn't ideal in his view, but it would keep his combat power intact. It was the best move he could make—until the Chinese made theirs.

The Chinese made their move two days after Thanksgiving. Shortly after 8th Army elements crossed the Chongchon River pushing for the Yalu, hundreds of thousands of Chinese troops who had been lurking in North Korea since October launched a mighty offensive. There was no practical way for the Marines to reinforce across miles of rugged, mountainous terrain, but that didn't deter planners at X Corps from ordering them to attack west as the 8th U.S. Army retreated in bitterly cold weather.

Major General O.P. Smith and his field commanders didn't know much about the situation to the west of Chosin Reservoir beyond the fact that it was bad and deteriorating rapidly. It would be a few more days until the Chinese in their battlespace made a move to surround the 1st Marine Division, cut the MSR, and trap the Marines in a lethal encirclement. While the 8th Army fell back in disarray, the 1st Marine Division reluctantly continued with plans to attack in their direction. The 7th Marines were dug in at Yudam-ni, mustering combat power for an attack that no one thought was anything like a wise tactical move. Fourteen miles southeast at Hagaru, the 5th Marines were loading up to rush forward and join them.

The Chinese offensive was the major international news story of the day as Captain Gerdine and Able Company loaded trucks for their move to Yudam-ni. They'd heard a bit about it via Sgt. Edison's radio, now being guarded and monitored by newly promoted Corporal Miles Abramson. There were lurid reports of human wave attacks staged by Chinese troops advancing with red banners flying as U.S. Army units were shattered and dispersed.

Those reports had drawn gaggles of reporters and war correspondents to Korea from Japan. One of the places they could land close to the action was the rough but functional airstrip at Hagaru. A visiting correspondent approached Captain Gerdine as he was checking rosters and manifests with Gunny Bates at the head of a truck convoy.

"Sam Gerdine, right?" Marguerite Higgins waved her hand and smiled. "Got any room on those trucks?"

Gerdine turned to stare at the woman with blond hair blowing in a cold wind. He'd been warned that some of the reporters might try to hitch a ride north. And he'd been told under no circumstances was he or anyone else involved to let that happen.

"Might be room, Miss Higgins." Gerdine peeled off a glove to shake her hand. "But not for you, I'm afraid. Orders were pretty clear. No civilian passengers on this run."

"I might just stow away under a tarp or something." She was smiling, but it looked to Gunny Bates like she was thinking of doing just that.

"Don't try it, lady," he growled. "I'd just have to toss your butt out into the snow."

Higgins eyed the Gunny for a while and decided he meant what he'd just said. "Shit!" She took a look at a couple of other correspondents interviewing Marines aboard the trucks. "I'm sick and tired of briefings and map studies."

"You probably know more about what's going on than I do," Gerdine said, tossing his pack and gear on the truck.

"I know the damn Chinese are running wild all over the place."

"We heard something about that." Gunny Bates gave the Skipper a hand climbing up over the tailgate and then turned to Marguerite Higgins. "Can I ask you a question?"

"Usually works the other way around," she said, "but go ahead, shoot."

"You got the straight dope on the Chinese, right?"

"I got some information on that, yes."

"Well, we been wonderin' and maybe you can tell me. How many fuckin' hordes are there in a Chinese platoon?"

If there was an answer, no one heard it. Engines roared and the trucks rolled northward, taking Able Company to the Chosin Reservoir.

THEY REACHED THE MOST advanced position around dusk and were assigned to an area on the outskirts of the village. It didn't look like much to fight about, just a few ramshackle huts and animal pens surrounded by Marine tents. Temperatures were falling rapidly and snow flurries were blowing, but Captain Gerdine decided not to erect their own tents. There seemed to be frenetic activity everywhere at Yudam-ni, and he had no idea what lay in store for his unit. Sleeping bags would have to do until he got some idea of how long they might be here. Gerdine left his Marines looking for shelter from the cold wind and went to find the battalion commander.

An attack west was scheduled for the next morning, LtCol. Stevens told his company commanders, and the 5th Marines were scheduled to lead it. "The big idea," Stevens said, "is to link up with the Army at Mupyong-ni." He tapped a spot on the map well to the west of the reservoir. "That's about fifty-five miles from here, so we take it a step at a time. Tomorrow at dawn we step off up this road and pass through forward elements of 7th Marines. There's a little spur just here..." He pointed at a squiggle on the map beyond a box labeled 1/7. "It's about five hundred yards beyond their perimeter. Then we develop the situation depending on enemy resistance. We'll have a spotter plane overhead, and he'll have some Corsairs on call."

Able Company led off at dawn the next morning, but they didn't get far. They were stopped cold, well short of the battalion objective, by stiff Chinese resistance. Charlie Company came forward, then Baker, but the Chinese refused to move out of well-defended positions. With his rifle companies stalled, Stevens called in Marine air. Corsairs pounded the enemy with bombs and rockets but it didn't amount to much more than an extravagant display of air power. Orders arrived at mid-day for 1/5 to break off their assaults on the Chinese defenders and look for night defensive positions.

Captain Gerdine's Marines didn't know it as they banged entrenching tools into the rocky ground, but they'd run head-on into elements of the Chinese 89th Division. And there were plenty of other formations of the CCF 20th Army roaming the area around them. So many, in fact, that Chinese troops seemed to appear everywhere, as if rising from the snow-covered ground like wraiths hovering over the Marines. It didn't take Colonels Litzenberg and Murray long to realize the tactical situation had changed drastically. Prisoners claimed to be from three or four different Chinese divisions.

Informed of the situation, General Smith called off any further westward movement. His two regimental commanders up at the reservoir mutually agreed they must shift from offensive to defensive combat if their units were to survive. The massive Chinese counter-offensive plaguing 8th Army to the west had now rolled east. The Marines holding along the banks of the Chosin Reservoir were either already surrounded or would be shortly.

The temperature at Yudam-ni dropped below zero on the night Able Company was recalled from the abortive attack. This time they pitched tents, but the effort was agonizing. What usually took ten or 15 minutes became hours of fumbling with frozen hands and fingers. They passed a bitterly cold night by rotating platoons off the perimeter at two-hour intervals and bringing the frostbitten men in out of the frigid winds. Lt. Solomon managed to scrounge diesel fuel, and they got some space heaters going. At dawn, the Marines were staggering into the cold, barely able to ignite C-3 explosive or unused mortar increments in an effort to heat canteen cups of coffee. Doc Clinton gave a few of the most chilled little nips of the medicinal brandy he'd scrounged from pals at the 1st Medical Battalion.

A hot fight broke out shortly after sunrise. Easy Company, 7th Marines was barely holding a few meager positions on Hill 1240 north of the Yudam-ni complex. Able Company was ordered to relieve them and secure the reverse slope of the hill. It was a crucial mission. If the Chinese managed to take three critical hills between the banks of the reservoir and the

MSR, they could flow troops directly into the Marines' shaky perimeter. Hill 1240 was one of those critical hills.

Sergeant JJ Jones was tied in with Lt. Ruggles' second platoon on his left as his third platoon began to climb the hill. Wounded men from the 7th Marines flowed downhill past them as they advanced. Able Company Marines bounced up and down into the snow as Chinese mortar fire blanketed the slopes. When second platoon got tangled up and stalled in a hot firefight, Jones moved his men forward to a line of abandoned holes and inclined them left to fire support for Lt. Ruggles and Sgt. Trenton who were taking casualties. Focused on the action to their left, Jones and his Marines missed the Chinese who swarmed out of snow caves and drove into their flank.

The Chinese were on them quickly, and the fight became a close-quarter deadly struggle between individual Marines and bayonet-wielding Chinese soldiers. Sgt. Jones fired all 15 rounds in his carbine magazine at two men charging his position, but the underpowered rounds barely caused the Chinese to stagger. What little kinetic energy carbine rounds imparted seemed to do nothing more than blow dirt or dust off their padded uniforms. Jones was fumbling for another magazine when Corporal Bayliss Thornton in the next hole dropped both attackers with rounds from his M-1 rifle.

When Corporal Doug Bland got his .30 caliber machinegun working and swept the area to third platoon's front, the Chinese began to fall back. Survivors dropped into shell holes, and the fight on the forward slope of Hill 1240 became a whack-a-mole game with Marines popping up to fire at Chinese soldiers who popped up to fire back at ranges that were rarely more than 20 or 30 yards. Jones reached for his radio and contacted the Skipper for support. He didn't trust the damn carbine anymore, so he discarded it and reached into his haversack for hand grenades. He had six of them and he intended to burn each one right over the plate and into the face of a gook.

With his left arm clicking at the elbow and throbbing with pain, Sgt. JJ Jones threw a pair of perfect strikes and struck out two, a rifleman at 15 yards and another at 20 yards in front of his position. He was just releasing a third toss when the burp-

gunner at bat emptied his drum magazine and blew Sgt. JJ
Jones' pitching arm out of the park. Cpl. Thornton saw the
severed arm fly off in a spray of dark blood and scrambled
from his hole screaming for a Corpsman.

Over on the left of third platoon, Sgt. Heywood Trenton
was charging uphill behind Lt. Paul Ruggles as Chinese defenders melted away toward the summit of Hill 1240. Behind
them, Lt. Solomon was leading first platoon up to relieve Jones
and his Marines. To cover their retreating troops, Chinese
mortarmen on the other side of the hill began to drop high-
explosive rounds on the charging Marines. Sgt. Trenton caught
a burst of shrapnel in the calf of his right leg but managed to
limp up to the summit with blood oozing into the top of his
boot.

By nightfall, Able Company and a reconsolidated company
of the 7th Marines were holding Hill 1240. On the slope below
the summit, Doc Clinton had mustered three Marines from
Able's 60-mortar section to help him carry Sgt. JJ Jones down
the hill to a battalion aid station. Jones was loopy on morphine
when they picked him up, but he tugged at the Corpsman's
parka with his good hand and pointed at the bandaged stump
of his left arm.

"Solves the operation question don't it, Doc..."

Doc Clinton just nodded and pushed the stretcher-bearers
downhill, trying not to notice the freezing tear-streaks on the
wounded man's cheeks. Captain Gerdine met the stretcher
party near the base of the hill and said a few innocuous words
that may have comforted Sgt. Jones but left the Company
Commander feeling like a blustering relative at a family funer-
al. Gunny Bates stood nearby recalling the day back at Camp
Pendleton when they'd drafted Jones into a combat-bound
rifle company from a comfortable stateside billet. Big League
baseball lost a hell of a prospect, but much more importantly
in the view of Captain Gerdine and Gunny Bates, Able Company lost a hell of a good Marine.

EL SUPREMO SEEMED to be in a somber mood as he listened to reports, projections, and plans from his two senior Army combat commanders. He'd said little beyond standard greetings when the two men arrived at his residence in the U.S. Embassy. Generals Almond and Walker had been summoned from Korea to appear in person before General MacArthur, and despite the short notice, both men came with updated maps, field reports, and what they hoped were plausible explanations for the disastrous situation developing in North Korea.

General Walton Walker, commanding the 8th Army, felt sweat running down his ribcage as he poked at the wall map with his cigar. "Obviously, sir..." He cut a glance at MacArthur sitting with fingers steepled under his chin. "our thrust in this area northwest of the Chongchon River has been blunted." *Best vague word I can think of,* Walker decided. Better than smashed or shattered, both of which are more accurate. "We essentially ceased offensive operations on 25 November when the ROK II Corps collapsed thus exposing my flank..." MacArthur sat stone-faced, no reaction, impossible to guess what the man was thinking. "Our IX Corps units in this area..." Walker stuck the cigar back in his mouth with one hand and swept the other across a broad area that included Pyongyang, "have fallen back and we're working to consolidate a line right now..." There was more but, MacArthur interrupted.

"How many Chinese are you facing?"

"Estimates are running in the area of two-hundred thousand CCF, sir." Walker cleared his throat and stood silently puffing his cigar. He'd wanted to avoid dropping this bombshell in front of MacArthur and Ned Almond who had insisted for weeks that there were only small, isolated units of Chinese volunteers fighting in Korea. Both men had been pilloried by the American press when the truth about CCF's strength became blatantly obvious in the last days of November.

General Almond, ever the MacArthur sycophant, waved a hand in the air. "Of course those are rough field estimates, General."

Maybe, thought General Walker, *but I believe the estimate is correct, maybe even a bit short of what my troops are facing.* He'd seen the evidence, swarming attacks by large formations in padded uniforms that left piles of bodies bleeding into the snow. He kept his eyes on MacArthur as Ned Almond prattled reassurances. MacArthur looked petulant as he fiddled with a long-stemmed corncob pipe. *Hurts to be wrong when you're El Supremo*, Walker thought.

"Well, in the back of my mind..." MacArthur said when he got the pipe lit and drawing satisfactorily, "I always thought there was a possibility of something like this..."

General Walker nearly choked on a mouthful of cigar smoke. *What in the hell? Does he really expect me to believe that? He knew this might happen all along but insisted on telling the press, not to mention the White House, that it wouldn't?*

"Uh...yes, sir." Walker said when he finally found his voice. "But I think it's painfully obvious that we underestimated the Chinese forces in North Korea." *And by we,* General Walker added silently, *I mean you, General MacArthur.*

MacArthur stared at Walker blankly for a few long seconds, then pointed his pipe at General Almond. "And what are your estimates of enemy strength in the east, Ned?"

General Almond didn't answer the question directly. He wanted to get a few things on the record first. "General MacArthur, X Corps is facing a bit of a different situation in the east. To facilitate the link-up with General Walker's forces, we've had to spread ourselves fairly thin over a battlespace of some four hundred miles. Now that said, I expect the Marines up near the Chosin Reservoir and our 7th Infantry Division can continue an attack to the west..."

"Hold onto that, Ned..." MacArthur waved it off with his pipe. He stood, jammed his hands into the back pockets of his khaki trousers, and moved to the map. It had recently been updated with the allied positions in blue and the enemy formations in red. The map looked like it was bleeding from the Yalu across to the Sea of Japan as MacArthur scrutinized it. He shook his head as if he doubted what the map was telling him. The chiseled planes of MacArthur's face seemed to sag as he turned to look at Almond.

"How many Chinese did you say in your area, Ned?"

General Almond riffled through some papers in front of him trying to obfuscate. "Well, we've identified at least four distinct divisions..."

"A number, Ned. How many do you estimate?"

There was no masking or obfuscating now. "Six figures, General. About the same as those facing Walton's forces in the west."

MacArthur's eyes closed and his face twisted as if he was trying to run the numbers in his head. "Half a million Chinese," he whispered. "Half a million..."

When he opened his eyes again, the old war horse had returned. MacArthur strode across the room and picked up his pipe. "I'll not play the Chinese game, gentlemen—not in this debilitating winter weather. We will shift from the strategic offense to defense. Order a withdrawal of X Corps across the board. We will consolidate into a perimeter defense around the Hamhung-Hungnam area."

THERE WAS A DWINDLING number of company-grade officers in the two rifle regiments holding against increasing enemy pressure on the last days of November 1950. An ad hoc mix of platoons and companies from both 5th and 7th Marines where constantly seizing, holding, and then re-seizing a string of strategic hills as fresh Chinese units swarmed all over the Chosin Reservoir area. At this point unit integrity was becoming thin veneer among the Marines at Yudam-ni.

Survivors who didn't know each other from previous service or campaigns got friendly and familiar as their units intersected, crossed, or reinforced against an ever-tightening noose. And all of them agreed the only bright aspect of their situation was the order from X Corps to cease and desist any further attacks to the west. That had been nonsense from the start. At this point everyone who thought beyond yes-sir-no-sir-three-bags-full was grateful to General Smith for delaying, dithering, and low-crawling before he made any attempt to carry out those attacks. His foot-dragging had kept 5th and 7th Marines together at the far northern extent of the division advance, and that gave the vastly outnumbered Marines at Yudam-ni a chance against the Reds.

And the Reds encircling Marines on the west side of the reservoir and soldiers on the east side kept pushing hard. Information from POW interrogations and radio intercepts indicated there were something like six Chinese divisions packed in the hills and valleys. Everyone at Yudam-ni knew they'd have to retreat, withdraw, fall back, or attack in a reverse direction. The descriptive varied, but the reality remained constant. The Chinks had the strong hand, and the Americans would have to fold. It was just a matter of time.

FIRST SERGEANT LELAND HAMMOND heard the hospital gossip about Chinese hordes swarming all over Marines up at the Chosin Reservoir. There was talk of brutal combat and heavy casualties. Some of it was embellished sea stories told by wounded men, but enough rang true to convince Leland Hammond that he needed to get back to Able Company.

Of course, he knew a guy that might help. In fact, he knew at least three influential guys at Koto-ri, so First Sergeant Leland Hammond began jerking chains and calling in favors. The guys were all steady pals, old salts and slick operators who understood why a man who was visibly feverish and barely dodging double pneumonia would insist on returning to a line outfit in combat. A Chief Hospital Corpsman, a shipmate from sea duty aboard the cruiser USS *Boston*, arranged discharge from the hospital and issued a load of antibiotics for the road. A Technical Sergeant and drinking buddy from Parris Island days opened his supply tent and let Hammond fill a sea bag with socks, knit caps, mufflers, and other goodies including a box of the Tootsie Roll candy that everyone seemed to crave. And finally, a Chief Warrant Officer from 1st Motor Transport Battalion, a man who remembered Leland Hammond fondly for rescuing him from a barfight at Quantico, got his old friend a warm seat in an ambulance that was headed north up the MSR.

Actually, the ambulance was just one of a long line of trucks and other vehicles ferrying resupply and reinforcements to the 1st Marine Division headquarters at Hagaru. Chesty Puller lashed it all together under the command of a Royal Marine officer named Drysdale who was bringing in his 41 Commando, RM, to fight alongside the U.S. Marines. Also along for the ride was George Company, 3rd Battalion, 1st Marines from Puller's command, a rifle company of soldiers from the Army's 31st Infantry, and a load of cats and dogs, staff officers, and headquarters people, all under orders to report for duty at Hagaru.

First Sergeant Hammond spotted about a dozen field grade officers and about double that number of senior NCOs when the convoy loaded up to move at 0645. Not much for him to do amid all that horsepower, so he tossed the sea bag into the rear of the ambulance along with a nylon sack of long-delayed mail for Able Company and settled in next to a chatty Corporal who wheeled their vehicle into a slot near the rear of the convoy. The First Sergeant handed the corporal a Tootsie Roll, took one for himself and then shoved the box under the seat for safe-keeping. Eleven road miles to Hagaru and then he'd find a way to reach the company further north at Yudam-ni. There would be a guy. There always was.

The Chinese halted the convoy's progress after a mile or two, pouring plunging machinegun and mortar fire onto the MSR. The convoy stretched and contracted like an accordion, drivers bitching and engines burning precious fuel as the Royal Marines and George 3/1 assaulted Chinese forces on a couple of hills to the east of the MSR. The fight was hot for a while with too many casualties and not enough progress. Colonel Drysdale called it off and waited for a unit of M-26 Pershing and M-4 Sherman tanks to arrive. When the armor came roaring up the road, tank rounds silenced the enemy on the high ground, and Drysdale pushed on with the tanks in the lead.

They covered another three miles before things really got rough. The Chinese began to pound the road with heavy mortars and machineguns on both sides of the convoy route. Under withering cover fire, they plunged down onto the convoy line, cutting the road and separating elements into little packets of resistance. Most of the infantry at the head of the unit managed to break through and pushed on toward Hagaru following the tanks. The others were left to fend for themselves until help could be summoned.

First Sergeant Leland Hammond and his driver were in one of those little marooned groups toward the tail end of the convoy. When their ambulance was shot full of holes by a machinegun that raked the vehicle from radiator to rear bumper, blowing out all the tires on the left side, Hammond ordered a bail-out into the snow. The chatty driver barely got his door open when the machinegun cut him nearly in half. Hammond crawled across the bloody seat and retrieved the man's M-1. He pulled the driver's door shut, rested the rifle on the window ledge, and opened fire on Chinese soldiers, kicking up gouts of snow as they charged downhill.

Other drivers and defenders retreated to the opposite side of the road dragging wounded men into a drainage ditch. They didn't last long against burp-gun fire that swept the ditch as the Chinese poured down onto the road. First Sergeant Hammond saw several shocked troops lift their hands in surrender. In a few minutes, the Chinks had a slew of prisoners lined up along the side of the road. He thought they'd be summarily executed, but the Chinese lost interest in the POWs and began looting the stranded trucks.

It was chaos around the crippled ambulance where Hammond was hiding. More American prisoners with their hands on their heads were being shoved into little clumps, poked, pushed, and harassed by laughing Chinese troops, but their main concern seemed to be ransacking the trucks. Hammond saw a pair of them with burp-guns slung around their necks heading in his direction. His rifle was empty, and if the dead driver brought along any spare ammo, Hammond couldn't find it. He tried hard to control a hacking cough as he crawled over the seat to reach the back of the ambulance. No way was he going to be captured by these bastards. He knew a guy—big strapping buck sergeant when he was captured by the Japs on Wake Island in the first days of the last war. A skeletal, toothless, and shattered wreck when he was finally liberated in 1945. First Sergeant Leland Hammond was not going to be that guy.

His plan was to get out the back of the vehicle and hide somewhere until help arrived or the Chinese finished their looting, and he might be able to walk back to Koto-ri. He reached for the interior handle of the rear doors just as they were jerked open. A pair of Chinese soldiers pointed their weapons at him and motioned for him to get out of the ambulance. He nodded and raised one hand, acting as if his other hand was injured. They screamed at him and made threatening gestures with their weapons. Hammond shuffled a bit, keeping his right side facing away from the Chinese while he fumbled under his parka for the .45 pistol in a holster on his hip.

He jerked it clear, thumbed the hammer and shot the closest man in the face just before the second man squeezed the trigger of his PPsh-41. The muzzle flash from the little sub-gun lit up the inside of the ambulance and about half the rounds in the drum magazine slammed into First Sergeant Leland Hammond's chest.

The Chinese soldier dragged the dead Marine out into the snow and then began to dig through the blood-stained duffle bag he found.

"OUCH! GODDAMMIT, DOC..." Sgt. Heywood Trenton sat in a warming tent with his right leg exposed while HM2 Arleigh Clinton probed for chunks of shrapnel. Clinton pulled a fingernail-size chunk of Chinese mortar out of Trenton's leg and dropped it with a clink into a nearby canteen cup.

"Just one more, Heywood." Clinton picked up a surgical probe and went back to work on the swollen calf muscle. "You should have let me send you over to the BAS for this."

"Just do what you gotta do, Doc. I go over there and they'll wind up sending my ass down to Hagaru."

Doc Clinton shrugged. "Way I hear it, we're all heading that way shortly."

"Yep. Probably start tomorrow morning." Second Lieutenant Paul Ruggles picked up the canteen cup full of shrapnel and rattled it. "Skipper's getting the word right now. We bid a fond adieu to beautiful Yudam-ni as of 1 December."

"And that's tomorrow...the day after?" Doc Clinton swabbed disinfectant on Trenton's leg and unwrapped a battle dressing. "I can't remember what fucking day it is."

"You lose track of time when you're having fun." Trenton bounced on the bandaged leg and reached for his rifle. "Thanks, Doc."

Around noon that day, Sgt. Trenton was selecting an M-1 for his lieutenant out of a stack of discards. Lt. Ruggles was insisting on carrying a rifle after a harrowing experience on the perimeter during which he failed to stop a charging Chinese with ten rounds from his carbine. Ruggles had to dodge a bayonet and use his .45 pistol to keep from getting skewered. That was it for the second platoon leader. He disassembled the carbine, tossed the pieces into the snow, and asked Sgt. Trenton to find him an M-1.

When Trenton got back to the platoon area, the Bobbsey Twins—Cpl. Jackson and PFC Maitland—were huddled together working on Jackson's BAR they had disassembled on a poncho in front of them. It was Maitland's position that the

296 Dale A. Dye

bottle of Vitalis hair tonic he was holding worked better as a lubricant in freezing weather than the issue weapon oil, which tended to turn sludgy as temperatures plummeted.

"I'm telling you, Willis..." Maitland said as he sprinkled some hair tonic into the BAR receiver. "This shit is fuckin' magic. I use it on my M-1. Never fails."

"You are just topped off with horseshit..." Jackson laughed, wiped at his weapon and looked up at their platoon sergeant who was limping past. "Hey, Sergeant Trenton! Will you tell this fuckin' cracker that weapons ain't meant to be oiled with Vitalis hair tonic?"

"Weapons are meant to be lubricated with whatever the hell keeps 'em functional, Jackson. If it works on an M-1, it'll work on your precious BAR."

Trenton paused to give his wounded leg a rest and watch the pair argue. It brought a smile to his face. He remembered the day he'd met both of them in a barracks brawl, the first day he and Lt. Ruggles took over the platoon back at Pendleton. Both of them full of prejudice and preconceptions. Combat in Korea knocked that bullshit for a long loop. Now Willis Leon Jackson from Washington, DC and PFC Lanny Jacob Maitland from Birmingham, Alabama were virtually inseparable.

Trenton heard the rattle of a firefight and looked in the direction of Hill 1282, one of three strategic spots north of the perimeter. Aircraft were circling, and heavy mortars began to fire in support of whatever the hell was going on up there. It was about a half-mile distant, but Trenton could see muzzle flashes and the black puff of impacting 81mm rounds. *It was miserable enough sitting up on one of those wind-blasted hills*, Trenton thought, *without having the Chinks hammering at your ass*. He recalled a long sub-zero night Able Company spent on Hill 1240, just to the right of 1282. Colder than a well-digger's ass up there.

"Get 'em up and moving, Heywood." Lt. Paul Ruggles approached and pointed up at the distant battle. "Just got the word from the Skipper. Some 7th Marines got their tit in a wringer, and we're gonna spend the night up on that bastard."

"Yes, sir." Trenton handed over the M-1 and a bandolier of clips. "Might want to test fire this before we leave."

"Can't be second-guessing my platoon sergeant..." Ruggles worked the action and jammed a clip of eight rounds into the rifle. "If you say it's good, it's good. And it's gotta be better than that piece of shit carbine."

Sgt. Trenton didn't bring along a bayonet for the lieutenant's new rifle, and Ruggles didn't ask for one. It was a mistake.

They reached the foot of Hill 1282 in mid-afternoon. Captain Gerdine was ordered to drop one of his platoons on adjacent Hill 1240 where another hard-pressed position needed reinforcement. He selected the tough-luck third platoon, now just two short-handed squads led by Cpl. Bayliss Thornton, and sent them off to the right while he led the others to the foot of their objective. He was pleased to note the furious firefight was tapering off to a few desultory rifle shots.

Lt. Rod Solomon, now for all intents and purposes the weapons platoon leader as well as Company XO, remained at the foot of Hill 1282 setting up mortar tubes while Captain Gerdine reorganized his understrength command. Combining about a squad and a half from first platoon with two squads remaining in second platoon gave him a best combination of mass and firepower. It made sense, so he turned it over to Lt. Ruggles and Sgt. Trenton as they began to climb. Not much of a rifle company left, he thought, and I'm back to being an under-loved and under-appreciated platoon leader.

It got noticeably colder the higher they climbed up the forward slope of Hill 1282. Probably another sub-zero night. They passed through a chopped up unit of Dog Company, 7th Marines, anxious to get the hell off the hill, and Gerdine found a first lieutenant in charge for a situation report. "Damn site better now than it was an hour ago," the lieutenant said pointing to a row of corpses under snow-covered ponchos and sleeping bags. "They beat the crap out of us."

"Know how many are left up there?" Gerdine pointed toward the summit.

"Best guess is a shit-pot full, Skipper. Air boys say they disappeared down the reverse slope, but they'll be back. That's for damn sure." The lieutenant was slack-jawed and mumbling. "They hit us three times...just come swarming over the crest and right into us like a fuckin' steam-roller."

Gerdine eyed the military crest of Hill 1282 which looked to be around 50 or 60 yards below the summit where two tall rock projections poked skyward, forming a little dip in the ridgeline. Right and left of that were steep ascents. They'd come through that little draw. He could see clumps of dead Chinese surrounding the holes Dog Company had dug to set up a defensive perimeter. Higher ground was scorched and pock-marked by air strikes. He tossed a little salute by touching the rim of his helmet.

"I relieve you, sir." It was probably unnecessarily formal. The lieutenant knew he'd been relieved and was already pushing his surviving Marines down the hill carrying their wounded and dead, but it was the way Sad Sam Gerdine was taught to effect a relief, the way Marines did such things no matter what. Speaking the words made him feel a bit better. Now the hill and the responsibility for holding it was officially his. At least he wouldn't have to order his guys to dig fighting holes. They just jumped into the vacated positions and waited.

At dusk, the Chinese had not reappeared to make another try for Hill 1282. Gerdine sat looking up at the little dip in the crest with a sense of foreboding. He had about a platoon of Marines, two .30 caliber machineguns, and his mortars at the base of the hill. Not much. And the air cover that had been buzzing overhead earlier would shortly be gone for the night. The Chinks would be back. He knew it. Just a question of when and in what strength against his puny little band of defenders. He could hear other units on nearby hills exchanging fire with attackers. In some of the lulls, he heard the Chinese pumping themselves up with great waves of shouting and bugles blowing before the rattle of gunfire and the crack of mortar fire drowned it all out. He walked uphill to find Lt. Ruggles with Sgt. Trenton in one of the abandoned holes.

"I want some kind of early warning, Paul." Gerdine crouched beside the hole and pointed up at the summit. "Put a fireteam up there as an OP before it gets much darker. Don't let 'em get silhouetted. Maybe a couple of yards down the reverse slope. And tell 'em to get the hell back here if they see movement."

Sgt. Trenton peeked over the summit of Hill 1282. In the gloom he spotted a row of boulders about 15 yards down from the crest. Those should provide adequate cover and concealment. "Right down there," he whispered to the three Marines with him. I'll take Semple off to the left side." He pointed at Cpl. Jackson, who had handed off his BAR to an assistant when he got tapped for the OP and was cradling a borrowed M-1. "You and Maitland find a spot on the right. You see or hear anything, you let me know, and we bug out back to the perimeter." A snowstorm with high, whistling winds blew in over the crest of Hill 1282 as the four Marines crawled carefully down into their listening posts.

About an hour later, half buried by the blowing snow, PFC Ken Semple elbowed Sgt. Trenton. "Think I hear something down there," he whispered, nodding toward the blackness below their position. Trenton scooted closer, closed his eyes and listened. He heard nothing but blood coursing through his veins.

"Down there, Willis..." PFC Maitland whispered to Cpl. Jackson. "There's something moving down there." Jackson looked, shifting focus, searching for movement with his peripheral vision. He saw nothing but moonlight on fresh snow. The only sound was the whistle of wind that seemed to rise and fall in tone as gusts blew over the hill. "Give it another minute," Jackson whispered. He quietly pulled a bayonet from the scabbard and snapped it onto his rifle. Maitland nodded and fixed his own bayonet.

The Chinese platoon crawling slowly up Hill 1282 was the vanguard of a night attack ordered by the commander of the 325th Regiment. They were specially selected for their ability to move silently and wore white padded uniforms that blended with the snow-covered ground. They'd been in position long enough to watch the Americans take posts behind the boulders to their front. Just four men, no obstacle. They would kill these four and then signal for their comrades spread out below to commence the attack. The platoon leader dug under the snow and found a small rock. He tapped it once on the stock of his burp-gun, and his platoon rose like white ghosts to charge the Americans above them.

Sgt. Trenton saw them first and fired his M-1 empty, screaming for the others to pull back. He expected to be shot in the back as he dragged PFC Semple toward the crest, but the Chinese fire passed overhead. He reloaded at the crest while Semple pumped rounds down at the attackers. And then they ran for the platoon perimeter.

Cpl. Jackson and PFC Maitland didn't get more than a step or two toward the summit before the Chinese were swarming all over them. Jackson crumpled to a knee as a bayonet pierced his thigh. Maitland shot that man off his friend and then emptied his M-1 at three more charging uphill. He was fumbling to reload when a round caught him in the shoulder.

"Lanny, follow me!" Cpl. Jackson realized there was no way they could escape now. He growled, pointed his bayonet, and charged into the Chinese. And then they stood back to back in the snow and wind, slashing and jabbing with bayonets on empty weapons they had no chance to reload. Between them during that short, brutal fight, Cpl. Willis Jackson and PFC Lanny Maitland killed nine Chinese soldiers either with bayonets or bare hands. They were fighting back toward the crest of Hill 1282 when a burst of fire from the follow-on attackers killed them both. They dropped into the snow, still back to back, as the Chinese soldiers jumped over their bodies and swept over the crest of the hill.

Just as Captain Gerdine predicted, the Chinese attack came flowing through the dip in the crest of the hill. He'd put both of his light .30s on either side of that feature where they had converging fields of fire, and the gunners were doing serious damage along with his riflemen and BAR men blocking the path of the assault. Cpl. Doug Bland and the machinegunners had been so well-trained by Steve Petrosky that they were exchanging bursts in what the old timers called "talking guns," alternating bursts from one then the other as if the .30s were having a conversation.

The enemy continued to surge through that constricted little draw like water flowing through a funnel. In just a few minutes, attackers had to leap over stacked bodies, but they just kept coming. There seemed to be no end to the supply of screaming Chinese firing and falling, tossing grenades, and tumbling down toward his Marines with bayonets flashing in the moonlight. Every few minutes Lt. Solomon at the base of the hill sent mortar illumination rounds popping over the fight, In the eerie, shifting light, Gerdine noted the carpet of dead Chinese seemed to flow closer and closer to his positions. Chinese charging downhill were stumbling and staggering over the corpses.

"Fix Bayonets!" He shouted over the roar of gunfire. He heard the command repeated tentatively, as if his Marines couldn't believe what they'd heard. *Probably the last thing I ever do and likely the dumbest,* Captain Sam Gerdine thought as he reached for his bayonet and snapped it onto the muzzle of his rifle. *But something's got to stop their momentum. And nothing does that better than a counterattack.*

"Follow me!" He leveled his rifle, pointing the bayonet at a padded form, and charged uphill. Most of Able Company followed their leader, smashing into the charging Chinese like football linemen at the snap. Some of them stabbed, hacked, and slashed with their bayonets. Those who didn't have a rifle or a bayonet just charged anyway, swinging entrenching tools or whatever was at hand at anyone within reach. Able Company's blood was up and boiling.

Gerdine was too busy to look right or left, but he could hear the fighting clearly. There were odd shots and submachinegun bursts, but most of those came from the Chinese. His own machineguns had ceased fire for fear of hitting Marines. The gunners waded into the fight with pistols and fighting knives. Gerdine heard the unmistakable voice of Gunny Bates screaming colorful profanities. There were other screams in English and Chinese, but the sound that carried over it all was the meaty thud of blades or blunt objects smacking into bodies.

Lt. Paul Ruggles tossed his new M-1 when the stock shattered against an enemy skull. He was using his steel helmet to swipe at two Chinese soldiers who were dancing around Sgt.

Trenton, trying to avoid the platoon sergeant's bayonet thrusts. He dropped one man into the snow and fell on him, bashing at the man's face with his helmet. He felt something like a hot lash tear across his back and thought he might be on fire. Ruggles rolled away from the dead Chinese, hoping the snow would extinguish whatever was burning his back. Another Chinese soldier fell on him heavily, and Ruggles looked up to see Sgt. Trenton pulling his bayonet from the man's back. Trenton's eyes were wide and red-rimmed. He looked like an insane, homicidal ghoul grinning in the flare light.

"Get up, Lieutenant! Get the fuck up!" Trenton reached down and pulled his officer upright as Ruggles shoved at the dead Chinese soldier. Ruggles got to a knee, but pain shot through his back muscles when he tried to stand. Trenton tossed him one of the Chinese burp-guns and reloaded his own rifle. They began to blaze away at running forms. But at this point, the Chinese were running in the opposite direction. They heard bugles blaring from somewhere on the other side of the crest.

"Pull back! Everybody back in the holes!" They heard Captain Gerdine shouting and saw 60mm mortar rounds detonating in the little saddle at the crest of the hill.

Captain Gerdine and Lt. Solomon checked on survivors at dawn. Probably dumb luck as much as anything, Gerdine thought, when they discovered only three men were killed and just six others wounded. He walked up to the summit where he and Lt. Solomon helped shove the bodies of Cpl. Jackson and PFC Maitland into their sleeping bags.

"Couple of really good ones," Gerdine sighed as they carried the corpses over the summit. "Couple of our originals from Pendleton."

"Don't beat yourself up, Skipper." Lt. Solomon squeezed the captain's arm. "They gave you an early warning that saved a bunch of our Marines." Solomon took a look downslope at the Chinese bodies. "And they killed a bunch of Chinks while they were at it."

"The Bobbsey Twins," Gerdine said as they gently laid the bodies in a hole with Able Company's other dead. "The hair tonic twins. We're gonna miss these two."

Doc Clinton was working on Lt. Ruggles who sat shirtless and shivering while the Corpsman bandaged a long gash on his back where a round had cut a painful furrow between the shoulder blades. No serious damage done, Clinton reported. Sgt. Trenton brought his lieutenant his battered helmet plus a new rifle, a bandolier of ammo—and a bayonet.

"Day late and a dollar short, Lieutenant." Sgt. Trenton pulled the bayonet from the scabbard and started to fit it on the rifle.

"Don't bother, Heywood." Ruggles shrugged into his shirts and parka. "If I ever use that thing after this, it's gonna be to carve open a ration can."

Cpl. Abramson was nursing a bandaged left hand and colorfully cursing the Chinese soldier that had bitten him during the fight for no better reason than Abramson was trying to strangle him. Abramson flexed his fingers and looked up at the officers. "That little commie cocksucker bit me! Think I'll have to get a tetanus shot like they give guys who get bit by rabid dogs?"

Captain Gerdine told him not to worry about it as he eyed the four dead Chinese Abramson had dispatched during the fight. If there was a mad dog here, it was Abramson. The befuddled kid who came to Able Company in civilian clothes carrying a little cardboard suitcase had become a solid Marine, a determined killer.

They found Gunny Bates lying in a hole with his feet propped up on an ammo can and his eyes closed. He didn't open them when the CO and XO approached. Only the little puffs of steam from his shallow breathing told them the Gunny was still alive. *Maybe he's just exhausted*, Gerdine thought as he slipped into the hole beside his Company Gunnery Sergeant. After what he did last night, the Gunny had every reason to be dead tired. Still, it was unlike Gunny Bates not to be up and charging around the area, checking on their Marines.

"Gunny..." Captain Gerdine shook him gently by the shoulder. "You OK?"

Bates opened one red-rimmed eye and rolled it around to take in his visitors. "I'm all right. Just feels like some asshole shot me with a shit-pistol." Gunny Bates was not about to mention the more frequent pains in his chest. Nor was he about to ask for more of the nitro pills which might tempt Doc Clinton to mention it to the Skipper. He propped himself up on an elbow, opened his other eye, and glanced at the piles of dead Chinese carpeting the slope.

"Jesus Herschel Christ," he chuckled. "I can't fuckin' believe we did that."

"Clearly you did," Lt Solomon said. "A goddamn bayonet charge, Skipper? What the hell were you thinking?"

"I wasn't..." Gerdine just shook his head. "I've got no idea..."

"Well, who gives a big rat's ass?" Bates struggled to his feet and took a deep breath of frigid air. "We stopped them fuckin' Chinks dead in their tracks. That's what counts."

The count was staggering. There were 60 or more dead Chinese soldiers layered in frozen postures on the forward slope of the hill when LtCol. Stevens arrived to take a look. He'd heard about the fight and wanted to see it for himself. The battalion commander had his XO take some statements from survivors of the bayonet attack. He thought Captain Sad Sam Gerdine might just be good for a Medal of Honor recommendation, but he kept the idea to himself. There was a lot of fighting left to do before they got clear of the Chosin Reservoir.

By the time Stevens and his party returned to the perimeter, the pull-out order had been issued by General Smith at Hagaru. Beginning at 0800 the next morning, Marines would abandon the positions on the west banks of the Chosin Reservoir and march south. Litzenberg's 7th Marines would move overland guarding the flanks and clearing high ground parallel to the MSR while Murray's 5th Marines stuck closer to the road. First Battalion, 5th Marines would serve as rear guard. Able Company, covered by a section of tanks, would be the last Marine unit to leave Yudam-ni.

It took a couple of hours for the slow-moving train of infantry and vehicles to clear Yudam-ni. Captain Gerdine's battered Marines watched them roll south, keeping sharp eyes on the high ground they'd fought for prior to what everyone was calling The Big Bug Out. They could see Chinese troops milling around atop the hills to the northeast of Yudam-ni. Glassing those hills with binoculars, Lt. Rod Solomon swore he saw some smiling Chinese waving goodbye.

By the time Able Company finally moved south, covering low ground to the east of the MSR, units of the 7th Marines were already engaging Chinese forces on a series of hills to the west of the road. Gerdine's Marines pushed steadily south, listening to the fights on their right and glancing cautiously at air strikes plastering enemy targets. It was obvious that the Chinese were trying to cut the road behind the withdrawing Marines and in front of them if possible. Gerdine halted his command that first night next to a column of artillerymen from 1st Battalion, 11th Marines. Fresh snow was blowing in, and the 105mm howitzers parked in a star-shaped configuration alongside the road were nearly covered in lumpy white blankets.

The last thing Gerdine or the battery commander expected was an attack from the rear, so that's exactly what happened. Around midnight with about half of the Marines huddled in sleeping bags and the other half on watch and shivering beside them, Chinese came skating and skidding across the frozen reaches of the Chosin Reservoir and attacked in a shouting mob.

The infantry Marines scrambled for covered positions and opened fire while the tankers cranked balky engines to power up their turrets. The enemy tactics were familiar and frustrating. They just kept coming, leaping over the bodies of fallen comrades, shouting and shooting in what looked to be an uncoordinated mad dash. Corporal Bayliss Thornton, with his short-handed third platoon, was farthest from the road and closest to the enemy attack. He set up a line of grenadiers, passing, arming, and heaving a shower of grenades at the enemy line as a couple of his BAR men fired into the Chinese flanks. After about a half-hour, they ran short of grenades, ammo, and practically everything except Chinese attackers.

Thornton led his men in a withdrawal toward the road where he'd sited a .30 caliber machinegun. He jumped into the position beside Cpl. Doug Bland and his assistant. "Just keep crankin' on that thirty!" Thornton shouted and organized a chain of porters who ran back and forth from the road with belts of ammo for the machinegun.

Making no progress against Thornton's stiff defense backed by fire from the tanks, the Chinese swept around in a huge fan and then turned toward the artillery positions. Thornton saw it happening and sprinted to the rear in an effort to warn the gun crews. "Comin' yer way!" He screamed, but the gun crews were already uncovering the howitzers and cranking the tubes down to zero elevation.

Gunny Bates and Sgt. Thornton organized a few Able Company Marines to work as ammo passers, running high-explosive rounds up to the cannon crews as the battery began to fire directly at the Chinese. Artillery wasn't at its most effective in direct fire over open sights at a charging enemy, but the situation was desperate, and the artillerymen were skilled. The howitzers leaped and bounded as they fired, shedding snow as the crews slammed in round after round. Cannon fire cut long bloody swaths through the enemy formations as Gerdine's machinegunners and riflemen picked off fleeing survivors.

Thus passed the first night of the withdrawal from the Chosin Reservoir. At dawn when the Marines began to roll south again, airborne spotters in observation aircraft reported that the Chinese had cut the road behind them and were sitting astride it. There was only one direction left now, straight south until they reached Hargaru. About 10 more miles—if the enemy didn't manage to also cut the road in that direction.

The southbound convoy was moving slowly, irritated by snipers who had learned to target the Marines at the wheel of trucks and Jeeps. Each time a driver fell, the convoy stopped to find a replacement and sweep the adjacent high ground with fire. Marine aircraft appeared overhead just a few hours after dawn. Little grasshopper aircraft circled the MSR and called the Corsairs down each time a target was spotted. And there were a lot of targets. Each time a flight of four attack planes expended all their ordnance and pulled off heading south, another flight appeared. A couple of Australian Air Force P-51s joined the fight, dropping napalm cannisters and the snow-covered hilltops west of the road were wreathed in fire and smoke.

The air strikes allowed Able Company to speed up its advance through the deep snow drifts on the east side of the road. They soon passed the slow-moving trucks towing the artillery pieces. A few of the artillerymen who had fought off the enemy attack during the night recognized some of Captain Gerdine's Marines and shouted for them to join up.

"Some of you shit-birds might make good cannon-cockers!"

"Fuck that." Cpl. Miles Abramson waved his bandaged hand at the trucks. "Man could get a goddamn hernia hauling them arty rounds."

"On the other hand," Lt. Rod Solomon said as he walked past, "a 105 howitzer packs a bit more punch than an M-1 rifle."

"All the same to you, XO," Abrams said, trying to catch up as Able Company strode past the arty unit's trucks. "I'm good just being a rifleman."

"Never can tell what might happen when they send you to boot camp, Abramson."

"Fuck that too, Lieutenant."

Able Company continued to move at a fairly fast clip. They passed heavily laden trucks and Jeeps, some of which had corpses piled on top of other cargo. Naked feet and arms blackened by frostbite jounced and flapped like long planks fresh from a sawmill as the vehicles slowly ground over the bumpy road. Orders from the regimental commanders had been absolute and firm. No Marine dead were to be abandoned on the battlefield.

On the morning of the third day marching south beside the division trains, Able Company arrived at the Toktong Pass. They were held up while Marines from 2/5 ahead of them assisted in carrying dead and wounded men down a steep incline from a finger of high ground that overlooked the MSR. While Doc Clinton and another Corpsman walked the line of weary Marines ordering sock and insole changes, Captain Gerdine spotted Gunny Bates kneeling beside one of the stretchers that had just been carried from the top of the pass. Bates was sharing a smoke with the man on the stretcher and nodding occasionally, glancing up at the top of the ridgeline.

"Stand by to move, Sam!" LtCol. Stevens came marching up the road with his battalion staff officers. "We're gonna pass through second battalion and take the lead."

"Aye, aye, sir..." Gerdine spotted Lt. Solomon and signaled for him to get the men up onto their feet. "Any idea how much further to Hagaru?"

"Seven miles...give or take. But we can only move as fast as the 7th Marines can advance clearing the high ground. Don't let your people get barn-sour and start double-timing."

"No chance of that, sir. We're dragging ass as it is."

Gunny Bates fell in beside Gerdine as they passed details of men loading casualties onto idling trucks. Bates looked up at the pass and shivered. "Poor bastards..."

"Us or them?"

"Them poor bastards," Bates said jerking a thumb over his shoulder. "Guy I was talkin' to is a *panyo* I knew back stateside. Name's Barber. Mustang who did Iwo with 26th Marines...commands Fox Two-Seven. They stuck his ass up on that hill when we was headed for the reservoir. Told him to hold Toktong Pass and keep the fuckin' Chinks from cutting the road."

"Never knew we had people up there..." Gerdine eyed the high ground on either side of the pass. It was a hell of a long way from the reservoir and any kind of support.

"Yep. Barber and his outfit had to hold up there getting the shit knocked out of them by half the goddamn Chinese Army until Litz the Blitz sent a unit to relieve 'em. That's gonna be one for the history books."

Chinese forces still harassed the convoy as it ground steadily south toward Hagaru, but it was mostly small-arms, pot-shots and stray mortar rounds. The heavy-lifting in the effort to keep the Chinese at bay fell to the 7th Marines who were sweeping over the hills that ran parallel to the road. Their efforts, always involving sharp fights over one hill or another, kept the enemy from blocking the road as the convoy closed on Hagaru. At least that's what Able Company Marines speculated as they plodded past a line of prime movers towing a battery of 155mm howitzers. The prime movers, big tractor-like vehicles that ran on tracks like tanks, were out of gas and artillery Marines were milling around them waiting for fuel trucks to come up from Hagaru.

The big cannons, the primary weapon of 4th Battalion, 11th Marines, were the largest artillery pieces in the division arsenal, good for targets out to 10 miles or so. Those long-range weapons gave the infantry Marines, fighting much closer to the enemy, a little reassurance that high-explosive help was available. Apparently, the Chinese in the hills overlooking the MSR also understood the value of the big guns. They opened lethal machinegun and mortar fire on the stranded battery.

Ahead of it all, Able Company suddenly got the order to face about and rush to the rescue. Bitching and grumbling about having to turn around when they were so close to the Hagaru perimeter, Able Company Marines unslung their weapons and started back in the opposite direction.

Captain Gerdine found most of the artillerymen taking cover under or behind the prime movers. The big cannons were useless for returning fire at close range, so he had Lt. Solomon set up the 60mm mortars and begin a counter-battery fire on targets that he figured must be on the reverse slope of the adjacent hills. Then he sent Sgt. Trenton and a couple of rifle squads up to clean out the machineguns and snipers.

They made quick work of it, and the punishing enemy fire ceased around noon. The artillerymen were grateful for the rescue, and when the fuelers arrived, they offered Able Company a ride the rest of the way into Hagaru. Gerdine had seen enough of his Marines shuffling and stumbling on half-frozen feet to know a good deal when it was offered.

Able Company rolled the rest of the way into the perimeter at Hagaru waving and cheering in blowing snow, straddling the big cannons and bouncing like birds on a wire.

CAPTAIN SAM GERDINE'S MARINES—now really a rifle company in name only—were assigned to a northern stretch of the perimeter, a spot that was less than a mile from the southern foot of the Chosin Reservoir. The position was near the truck park maintained by the division's 1st Motor Transport Battalion, and their rolling stock was varied and impressive. It was also crucial. General Smith had made it clear and unequivocal. His 1st Marine Division would emerge from the costly Chosin Reservoir fighting intact, carrying their wounded and dead. Nothing of use to the enemy was to be left behind.

Able Company's orders were also clear. If the Chinese attacked, they were to protect the vehicles at all costs. While Lt. Solomon and the Gunny got tents pitched and space heaters blazing, Captain Gerdine paid a visit to LtCol. Olin Bell, CO of the Motor T outfit. Sam knew him from the Pacific and from service at Camp Pendleton. The man was a minor legend in the division, a mustang officer that many swore had enlisted in the Marines back when Christ was a Corporal. He was a decorated WWII vet with a big, frequently broken nose plastered on his face between dark eyes that actually seemed to twinkle when Olin Bell laughed, which he did more often than not.

"Sad Sam Gerdine!" Bell roared when his visitor ducked into the command tent. "I been looking through the casualty lists but never found your name. Thank God for small favors." Bell pulled a couple of canteen cups from a tent pole and dropped them next to a bottle of Johnny Walker in the middle of his field desk. "I expect you're as road-weary as I am. Let's have us a little snort."

"Damn, that's good..." Sam Gerdine sipped the liquor and savored it. "I guess when you run a fleet of trucks, you can find a little space for whiskey."

"Damn straight." LtCol. Bell laughed. "You call, we haul—anytime, anywhere."

Bell was a favorite of General O.P. Smith although they were polar opposite personalities. Smith was reserved, studious, and taciturn. Olin Bell was loud, raucous, and full of sea stories that he loved to tell. That access to high command was part of the reason for Gerdine's visit. He wanted to see what kind of useful information he might be able to wheedle out of the gregarious LtCol. Bell.

"Big picture remains the same, Sam." Bell poured another inch of whiskey into their canteen cups. "We high-tail it out of here with everything we can carry. Down to Chesty Puller's patch. He's holding the back door at Koto-ri and Chinhung. We police his people up and then roll on down to Hamhung."

"And after that?"

"Shit-fire, Sam...who knows? Ain't that enough?"

"Enough for me. I barely got a platoon left in Able Company."

"Well, you ain't the Lone Ranger in that regard. This division took a licking, and there's more to come."

"Figure they'll hit us here...chase us all the way south?"

"Don't see why they wouldn't, Sam. Talked to a guy in G-2 this morning said there's the whole damn 26th Chink Army between here and Koto-ri."

Gerdine drained his whiskey and stood. "I appreciate the drink and the skinny, sir. I've got my people tied in with yours on the perimeter. We'll keep it buttoned up tonight..."

"You might encounter a few beat-up Doggies trying to get through, Sam. Tell your people to make sure it ain't some lost and lonely soldier before they open fire."

"What's the Army doing back behind us?"

LtCol. Bell kicked back on his stool and swirled the whiskey in his cup. "What do you know about the situation east of Chosin?"

"Not much, sir. Some Army outfit relieved us over there..."

"Yeah, Task Force Faith—31st Infantry out of the 7th Division. Chinks hammered the outfit right down to parade rest and they broke, scattered, most of 'em killed or taken prisoner. A few that managed to escape have been straggling in here— just a handful—but I'm gonna run a little recon up there before dark to see if I can rescue any of the poor bastards that make it across the reservoir."

"Anything I can do to help, sir?"

"Sam, I know you're short-handed but I could use a few of your Marines as security up there."

Staff Sergeant Heywood Trenton, Corporal Miles Abramson, and Corporal Bayliss Thornton piled into a three-quarter ton weapons carrier that was idling behind LtCol. Bell's Jeep. They were volunteers for the rescue mission to the south end of the Chosin Reservoir. They were also about all Captain Gerdine could afford to send and still man the company's extended stretch of the Hagaru perimeter.

Abramson was fiddling around trying to load a pintle-mounted M-2 .50 caliber heavy machinegun with one gloved hand and the other bandaged into a clumsy stump. Cpl. Thornton looked up from his seat next to the driver and laughed. "Ain't nobody never showed you how to load ol' Ma Deuce, Miles?"

"It's a fucking machinegun. How hard can it be?" Abramson finally got the feed cover raised and was contemplating a long belt of linked ammo.

"Get down from there before you hurt yourself." Sgt. Trenton elbowed Abramson out of the way and efficiently loaded the weapon. He pulled the charging handle twice to bring up a ready round and then set the safety. "We survive this dumbass trip, and I'll give you a block of military instruction."

A pale sun was dropping toward the snow-covered ridges west of the reservoir when the slow-moving vehicles braked to pick up a disheveled pair of shivering soldiers stumbling down the road. When LtCol. Bell hopped out of his Jeep, the men just stood slumped with heads hanging, looking like a couple of half-frozen hobos. They had no weapons, helmets, or other equipment. One of them finally raised his hands as if he wanted-ed to surrender.

"Them boys are flat fucked up," Thornton said as he climbed out of the truck to lend a hand. The soldiers followed him toward the tailgate, shuffling and sniffling. Neither man seemed able to climb aboard the weapons carrier, so Abramson and Staff Sergeant Trenton helped, one lifting and the other shoving.

"There's a pile of blankets back there," LtCol. Bell said. "Wrap 'em up and give 'em a drink of water." He hopped back in his Jeep and signaled the drivers to push on toward the reservoir.

"What the fuck happened to y'all?" Thornton handed over the canteen he had tucked in his belt next to his belly to keep it from freezing.

"They're all dead..." One of the soldiers mumbled with water dripping down his bearded chin.

"Who is?" Thornton retrieved his canteen and passed it to the second man. "You ain't dead—leastwise not so you could tell."

"They killed everybody..." The second man was a little more coherent. "Except us, maybe a couple of others. We escaped..." Abramson draped OD blankets over their shoulders and both men promptly dozed off, their heads bobbing lifelessly as the weapons carrier bounded its way north.

Parked at the edge of the reservoir with the sun starting to set, LtCol. Bell swept his binoculars across the ice. A chill wind blew snow into little whirls, but he couldn't spot anything moving out on the frozen surface. Maybe two was all he'd get this trip. Maybe that's all that was left of Task Force Faith.

"Over to the left, sir!" Sgt. Trenton had a higher and broader perspective behind the machinegun. He spotted several dark shapes staggering in their direction. "About 10 o'clock, Colonel. Looks like about half a dozen or more."

Bell pointed at Abramson, Thornton, and a couple of his own Marines. "You people hustle out there and help 'em in. Be careful out on that ice."

The first two little groups were nearest to the shoreline. Six men, arms wrapped around each other, were stumbling on frozen feet. Abramson and Thornton reached them fairly quickly. When the soldiers realized they were being rescued, two of them began to cry. Another soldier, apparently made of sterner stuff, shrugged off Abramson's help.

"I made it this fuckin' far," he growled. "I'll make it the rest of the way."

A third group much farther out on the ice was slower, and several of them appeared to be badly wounded. The party halted when a couple of them fell, lying motionless on the ice. LtCol. Bell eyed the distant group of survivors and then shouted at Sgt. Trenton. "See any more out there?"

"No, sir...just that bunch that fell down." They were helping the first six into the weapons carrier and wrapping them in blankets when Trenton swiveled the machinegun and opened fire. Tracers lanced across the ice over the prone survivors and chopped at the opposite shore. "Chinks on the other side!" He shouted and fired another burst. "They're trying to get to those guys!"

LtCol. Bell looked across the frozen stretch of water and saw forms in padded uniforms sliding down a snow bank toward the surface of the reservoir. "Keep those bastards busy," he shouted and ran for his Jeep as Trenton and others opened fire across the ice. Bell shoved the driver aside and started the engine. He had no idea how thick the ice was at this point or whether it would support the weight of his vehicle. If it didn't hold, he wanted to be the only one taking a lethal bath in the frigid water. Regardless, there was no way Bell was going to let those soldiers die out there or become POWs.

He jammed the Jeep into gear, popped the clutch, and headed for the shoreline. Abramson and Thornton ran alongside and then hopped in back. "Get out!" Bell shouted, but he didn't hit the brakes.

"Nossir!" Thornton squirmed into the passenger seat. "You cain't get them fellers all by yerself. Gonna need a hand."

The conversation ended when the Jeep hit the icy surface and began to slide in and out of drifts. Bell handled it expertly, correcting without over-steering. The Chinese out on the ice dropped prone and began to fire at the skidding vehicle. Abramson shouldered his M-1 and blazed through a clip, rounds going everywhere as the Jeep bounced and jolted. Tracers and ball ammo from Trenton's machinegun cut into the Chinese and a few scrambled back toward cover on the far bank.

LtCol. Bell thought he felt ice shifting under the wheels of his Jeep. If the surface cracked and swallowed them up, it was over. He stared around, trying to spot any cracks forming on the surface, but it was hard to see anything but blowing snow. Best bet, he decided, is just keep going, don't stop, keep the weight moving from place to place, and hope the ice was thick enough at each of those places. He steered the Jeep with tires spinning to the other side of the survivor party, using the bulk of the vehicle to shield them from the Chinese fire. When they were clear of the four prone men, he whipped the wheel and hit the brakes. The Jeep slid to a stop as Abramson and Thornton leaped down to help the wounded men into the rear of the vehicle. One of them was unconscious, and Thornton had to heave the man over his shoulder and then dump him onto the others. "That's all she wrote, Colonel!" Thornton hopped up on the hood and began to fire his rifle. "Let's get the fuck out of Dodge!"

"Got about a dozen of them," LtCol. Bell reported to Gerdine when they returned to the Hagaru perimeter. "And your boys were terrific. I'm gonna write all three of them up for commendations."

Trenton, Abramson, and Thornton weren't the only Able Company Marines about to be decorated. LtCol. Stevens came to find Gerdine the next morning and let him know General Smith intended to pin a Navy Cross on him at a little ceremony planned for later in the day. It was in recognition of the action on Hill 1282. "It's an interim decoration, Sam. We put you in for the Medal of Honor, but that might take a while."

"Sir...I don't..."

Stevens help up a hand to stop the protest he knew was coming. "Don't even start, Sam. This is important for a bunch of reasons. Folks at home need a bit of good news from Korea right now, and you're part of that. Colonel Puller's coming up from Koto-ri, and there's a bunch of press due to land at the airstrip in about an hour. Smile politely and be humble for them." Stevens turned to duck into the snow blowing outside the tent. "And try to clean yourself up a little."

Doc Clinton and Lt. Solomon heated some water in a helmet so he could shave and run a wet cloth under his reeking armpits. It took two blades to cut through the matted crud on his face. Captain Gerdine emerged from the ordeal nicked but clean-shaven as Gunny Bates came in with a clean utility uniform. "Had to do a little guessin' about sizes, Skipper." Bates shook out the trousers and shirt. "But these ought to make you half-ass presentable." Gerdine had lost considerable weight in Korea as had all of his Marines, but with a little tucking and belt-tightening he felt confident enough to head for the ceremony.

"You know I don't deserve this," he said as he shrugged into his parka.

"Skipper, please..." Gunny Bates shoved him toward the tent flap. "You been a fuckin' hero to me and all our Marines ever since this dance started. Ain't nobody on God's green earth deserves it more than you do. Now go get that medal. I'm gonna round up something we can wet it down with when you get back."

Hagaru's improvised airstrip was busy as Captain Gerdine approached the division command post. He could see civilians milling around one of the C-47s—Marines called them R-4Ds—parked nearby. The press had arrived. A couple of other aircraft were disgorging passengers to be replaced by wounded men on stretchers. A helicopter clattered overhead and pivoted to land. Gerdine paused to watch. He'd heard about the whirlybirds being used for the first time by Marines in Korea, but he'd only actually seen one a time or two before this. He imagined what it would be like if those helicopters could be used to land Marines on hills, ready to swoop down on an enemy rather than having to fight their way up against defenses.

Given some seriously inclement weather, the Adjutant told Gerdine when he reported as ordered, the small ceremony would be held indoors in a briefing tent. "You will stand to attention at a designated spot during the reading of the citation. General Smith will do the honors by pinning on your decoration. At that point, visiting dignitaries will be given the chance to congratulate you. You may then take a seat for the CG's briefing, after which you will make yourself available for press interviews. Do you have any questions?"

Captain Sad Sam Gerdine had about a million of them, but he reckoned the Adjutant wouldn't have any satisfactory answers, so he just shook his head and let the Sergeant Major lead him to the briefing tent. It was warm inside the tent with space heaters blowing in four corners. Sad Sam Gerdine stood at a rigid position of attention where the Sergeant Major planted him, trying to focus on a billowing tent flap rather the dignitaries and reporters who all seemed to be studying him as though he were an insect under glass. As the military dignitaries took seats on wooden chairs at the front of the crowd and the civilian press jostled toward the back, Gerdine tried to shape his wind-chapped and freshly-shaved face into some semblance of a smile.

General Smith entered from somewhere behind him, and the Adjutant barked for attention to orders. The military crowd rose, and he began to read the citation. "For extraordinary heroism while serving as Commanding Officer, Company A, 1st Battalion, 5th Marines, in action against aggressor forces in the vicinity of Yudam-ni, Korea on 30 November 1950. While defending a crucial hill, Captain Gerdine's unit came under a massive assault by enemy forces who launched a night attack against his vastly outnumbered unit in an attempt to recapture Hill 1282, a key position guarding the Marine perimeter. Vastly outnumbered and nearly overrun, Captain Gerdine led a valiant counterattack, charging the enemy with fixed bayonets..."

There was more, but Sam didn't comprehend much. At times is seemed like he was listening to some oily voiced announcer over a badly tuned radio. At other times he thought the Adjutant sounded like a duck quacking mindlessly. During dramatic pauses in the narration, he heard his blood pumping. *They have to be talking about someone else,* he thought. Maybe there was another Captain Sam Gerdine, the kind of guy who would actually do something like what was being attributed to him.

He flinched visibly when a smiling General Smith approached to pin the medal on his chest. The general put a reassuring hand on Gerdine's shoulder to steady him. "You're a credit to this division, Captain. All of us are very proud of you."

Gerdine fought a mental fog, smiling and nodding as one man after another passed through a line to shake his hand and offer congratulations. He didn't recognize most of them. Toward the end of the line was the legendary Colonel Chesty Puller, who pumped Sam's hand vigorously, smiled and pulled him closer. "Relax, Old Man..." Chesty's whisper was a raspy growl. "I've been through this a time or two. It gets easier with practice."

When the briefing began, Sam sat quietly trying not to stare down at the medal pinned on his chest. During all his years of service, he'd never actually seen a Navy Cross, the nation's second highest decoration for gallantry in action. And now there was one hanging on his jacket. He looked down at the padded box and copy of the citation the Adjutant gave him. When the press stuff was over, he would mail it all to Della in San Diego—something for Tony, something to show for a missing father.

General Smith stood before a large mapboard and did the situation report on his division personally. Normally, that chore fell to the Assistant Division Commander, but Brigadier General Eddie Craig's father was dying, and he'd been sent home to be with the family. Smith used the well-chewed stem of his pipe as a pointer, calmly narrating positions and dispositions. Some of it Captain Gerdine knew, but a few things came as a surprise. It was obvious that the 5th and 7th Marines had executed a fighting withdrawal from their furthest point of advance at Yudam-ni. He'd been part of that. And there was no revelation in the announcement that both regiments plus all other division elements were gearing up to head south shortly.

But it came as news to Gerdine that Chesty Puller's 1st Marines, holding strategic positions further south along the MSR against intense pressure from the Chinese 60th Division at Koto-ri and their 89th Division at Chinhung-ni, were involved in a very nasty fight. Up north, he'd been oblivious to all that. He'd also been unaware of just how many Chinese they were facing. An entire Red army—the 26th with four divisions at hand—was poised on the east side of the MSR between Hagaru and Koto-ri, along the path the division would traverse in the move to Hamhung.

At last, General Smith opened the floor to press questions. Smith answered most of them openly and honestly deferring often to his superior, General Almond at X Corps. His demeanor changed when a reporter with a British accent asked him how he felt as a Marine about retreating in the face of the enemy. Smith bristled a bit chewing on his pipe. Gerdine could see anger building, but the general's voice was calm when he eventually responded.

"Let me make one thing clear," he said. "The 1st Marine Division is *not* retreating. We are simply attacking in another direction."

When the tent cleared, Gerdine remained behind to answer questions from the press. There were about ten of them, nine men and Marguerite Higgins. Sam deferred big picture questions, reminding the reporters that he was simply a company commander, one of many in the division. Marines at that level didn't have much opportunity or inclination to be concerned with large-scale tactical or strategic questions. After that, it was standard fare to which Captain Gerdine tried to offer standard answers. How bad was it up on that hill? Pretty damn bad. What did you think when you saw all those Chinese coming at you? I thought I'd better do something to stop them. Did you actually charge with a fixed bayonet? I did. How many do you think you killed? I wasn't counting.

The only reasonable queries came from a correspondent for the Chicago *Daily News*. Keyes Beech had been a Marine Combat Correspondent in the Pacific during World War II. He wanted the names and some description of the actions taken by the enlisted men of Able Company. Beech understood who did the heavy lifting in close combat. Gerdine gave him a few names and said he'd be glad to make them available for interviews.

Marguerite Higgins didn't pepper him along with the others, but she caught him outside after the interviews ended. "There's hot coffee," she said pointing at a nearby mess tent. "If you've got a few minutes for me."

They sat at a bench table with steaming porcelain mugs between them. "I'd like to talk a little bit about the action on that hill," she said. "And I don't have a lot of time. General pipe-puffing, hard-ass Smith says I've got to be out of here by nightfall."

"OK by me, Miss Higgins..."

"We've met before, Sam. I think you can call me Maggie."

"What's on your mind, Maggie?"

"I want to know what was on *your* mind, that night up on the hill at the Chosin Reservoir."

Gerdine shrugged and sipped at his coffee. "Nothing..."

"What?"

"There was nothing on my mind...at least nothing that I can remember. I just knew—or maybe I just felt—that we had to stop the Chinese before they killed us all."

"And you thought a bayonet charge was the way to do that?"

"Like I said, it was more feeling than thinking. You know, instinct...I...well, I just did it and thought about it later, I guess."

"And your Marines just followed?"

"That they did."

Maggie Higgins paged through her notebook. "I talked to a couple of them earlier." She read from her notes. "He ain't like other officers. The Skipper cares about us. I'd follow him anywhere."

"Gotta be Thornton...or maybe Abramson."

"It was Thornton...who wanted to be sure I got his name right for the folks back home in Paducah, Kentucky."

"Good man...good Marine."

Higgins riffled through her notebook and found another quote. "How about this? Sad Sam Gerdine is one of the best goddamn Marines ever shit between a pair of boondockers. He ain't just an officer. He's a leader."

Gerdine chuckled. "That would be Gunnery Sergeant Elmore Bates."

"Check..." Maggie Higgins snapped her notebook shut. "It seems your guys are pretty fond of you."

"I'm damn sure petty fond of them."

"What's this Sad Sam business?"

"Damned if I know. Somebody called me that out on Peleliu in the last war. Can't seem to shake it."

"Are you sad?"

"In general? No. Went through a divorce and that was depressing. Still is. Lost a bunch of really good men. That hurts. But all things considered, I'm a pretty lucky guy. I'm happy doing what I'm doing."

"What makes a man like you, Sam Gerdine? That's what I'm after."

"Hard to say, Maggie. I guess I see myself as a little more than just an officer in charge of a bunch of men. You know? There's gotta be discipline sure, but I think you should be a sort of...I don't know...a teacher or mentor, as well as their commanding officer."

"That the way you're going to raise your own kids?"

"Only got one, and I haven't seen him in a long time." He tapped the box containing his Navy Cross. "You could do me a favor by helping me mail this stuff to him."

Maggie Higgins took the medal and citation, jotting down a mailing address in San Diego. "I'll see it gets safely in the mail." She stood and extended her hand. "Well, Sam Gerdine. I've gotta run before your General Smith sets the MPs on me. You're a good man. I'll remember you when the others piss me off."

Gerdine sat with Lt. Solomon, Lt. Ruggles, and Gunny Bates toasting the decoration. Bates had somehow procured a bottle of medicinal brandy, and they were sharing a drink. Bates swore he meant every damn word when Captain Gerdine told them about his quote for Maggie Higgins. "Can't wait to see that in the New York *Herald Tribune!*" Lt. Solomon laughed and clinked his canteen cup with the Skipper.

"Don't worry about that, XO." Gunny Bates said. "She'll clean it up for decent folks."

The tent flap whipped open, and a tall officer ducked in. "Sorry to interrupt, gents." Colonel Homer Litzenberg nodded as everyone stood. "But I'd like to talk to one of your Marines."

"Anyone in particular, Colonel?" Captain Gerdine lifted the brandy bottle and shook it offering the CO of the 7th Marines a drink.

"Just a short one," Litzenberg said, "and then I'd like to talk to Corporal Trenton."

"We've got a Trenton, sir." Captain Gerdine poured a shot of brandy into a canteen cup and handed it to the senior officer. "But he's a Staff Sergeant."

"Colored man?" Litzenberg swallowed his drink and returned the canteen cup.

"That's him, Colonel." Gunny Bates nodded. "I recall him saying you served together at Camp Lejeune."

"How's he been doing?"

"Top notch, Colonel." Captain Gerdine said. "One of my very best. Brave, smart and a damn fine leader."

"Is he around somewhere?"

"Yessir…" Bates threw on his parka and headed for the tent flap. "I'll go get him for you."

"Just show me where he's hiding," Litzenberg smiled. "Don't want him to think he's being called on the carpet."

"Out walking the line, sir." Lt. Paul Ruggles said when Gunny Bates and an unfamiliar senior officer asked for Sgt. Trenton. "I'll send someone to get him."

"Not necessary, Lieutenant. I'll find him." Colonel Litzenberg walked off bending into a cold wind.

"Who was that Gunny?"

"Litz the Blitz, Mister Ruggles. Colonel Homer Litzenberg, CO of the 7th Marines."

"What's he want with Sergeant Trenton?"

"Apparently, they're old buddies…"

Colonel Litzenberg spotted a tall figure bundled in a parka with an M-1 slung upside down over a shoulder. The man was talking to a couple of Marines huddled behind a .30 caliber machinegun and pointing out at the near horizon. He couldn't see the man's face, but it had to be Heywood Trenton.

"Sergeant Trenton…" Colonel Litzenberg approached and returned the salute that Trenton instinctively snapped.

"Colonel Litzenberg?"

"I told you I'd be checking on you."

"Just a little surprised to see you here, sir."

"Well, they had to bring us down out of those damn mountains sometime." Litzenberg crossed his arms and stared at the NCO. "Looks like you've lost a little weight—and gained a couple of stripes. Congratulations."

"Thank you, sir. I'm doing just fine."

"That's what I hear, Trenton. Your CO thinks highly of you."

"It's mutual, sir. Captain Gerdine is tops in my book."

"So, I can rest assured you're not pissed off at me for letting you go to Korea?"

"Colonel..." Sgt. Trenton laughed and shook his head. "Believe it or not, there ain't a place on earth I'd rather be right now."

"You know, Sergeant Trenton, there's more and more colored men coming into the Corps these days. What do you think about that?"

"I think a good man is a good man, sir. And the color of his skin don't matter if he's a good man. If he ain't a good man, black or white, he won't last long in this Marine Corps."

Colonel Litzenberg smiled and pulled off a glove to shake hands. "My sentiments exactly, Sergeant Trenton. If we don't cross trails again, I want you to know I'm proud of you. And if you ever want to get out of this pogey-rope outfit, you're welcome in the 7th Marines."

The big move south to Koto-ri was set to begin at dawn on Wednesday that week in blustery winds and blowing snow. Plans called for the 7th Marines to lead off, sending rifle companies and platoons up into the deep snow covering the adjacent high ground to sweep for enemy formations. They were paralleled down on the MSR by all the supporting units, artillery, armor, and the division headquarters. Colonel Murray's 5th Marines, plus the Royal Marines 41 Commando, and George Company, 3rd Battalion, 1st Marines on loan from Chesty Puller's command, were to hang back at Hagaru to keep Chinese Forces from storming into the rear of the division trains.

Almost everything that could be moved was aboard trucks, tanks and other vehicles as the long lines of marching men and grinding vehicles snaked out onto the road. Demolition crews from the 1st Engineer Battalion were rigging charges all over

Hagaru to destroy anything and everything that couldn't be moved. What could not be destroyed by explosives was being torched. Huge clouds of thick, black smoke rose over Hagaru.

There was still some fighting left to be done by the rear guard. Patrols searching along the town perimeter made sporadic contact with Chinese or North Korean probes. Air spotters reported a concentration of Chinese forces in and around East Hill overlooking the abandoned airstrip. Golf Company, 3/1 got the initial call to clear the hill, but there was some confusion, and LtCol. Stevens sent Able Company to clear it up.

"What's the problem?" Captain Gerdine asked a first lieutenant at the base of East Hill. If there were Chinese up there, they were well hidden.

"I was told to wait for air support." The lieutenant shrugged.

"Candy-ass 1st Marines..." Gunny Bates said. "How about you people stand back and let a real rifle company show you how to take a hill."

Gerdine likely couldn't have stopped it if he wanted to at that point. His Marines flowed into an assault line like the practiced professionals they were and started to climb. Lt. Ruggles and Sgt. Trenton were leading the pack. There were a few desultory shots fired when his Marines ran into some Chinese in fighting holes, but it was a relatively easy ascent. At the military crest of East Hill, about 50 yards from the summit, Gerdine ordered his men to fan out and find any Chinese defenders. There were a bunch of Chinese on East Hill, but they were in no mood to defend.

"Skipper! Look at this shit!" Cpl. Miles Abramson appeared cresting the hill and pushing about 20 Chinese captives, limping and stumbling with their hands on their heads. And then Sgt. Trenton appeared on the right flank pushing about 30 more dispirited Chinese soldiers. Gunny Bates and Cpl. Thornton brought in another 50, and before mid-morning, Able Company had a head-count of 200 Chinese soldiers squatting in a big clump below East Hill. Doc Clinton took a cursory look at many of them and reported their sad state.

"No damn wonder they don't want to fight, Skipper." He said to Captain Gerdine. "Most of 'em are half-frozen, the rest are sick as dogs from one thing or another. From the smell of it, I'd say it's mostly dysentery."

"Well, hell..." LtCol. Stevens said when he came up to look at the bag of POWs Able Company had captured. "It's tempting, but we can't just shoot 'em. And we're due to roll out of here tonight."

Colonel Murray was consulted and the decision made to give the Chinese some medical supplies and leave them behind at Hagaru. "Be sure none of them have weapons and then we'll just leave them here for their buddies to police up after we're gone."

Able Company spent the rest of the day collecting enemy weapons and stashing them in big piles for the engineers to destroy. And then they spent a long, cold night watching the Chinese watching them. The move from Hagaru by the 5th Marines was delayed until the following morning due to jam-ups on the MSR.

They finally got moving the next morning at around 1000 when Able Company came down off East Hill and flowed into the column moving south. By the time they were a half-mile down the road, rear-guard formations reported enemy forces were flowing into Hagaru, but they seemed much more interested in looting anything left behind in the little town than they did in pursuing the Marines.

After about five miles of stop-start progress while patrols trudged up high ground on either side of the MSR to engage enemy units firing down on the Marines, the convoy halted at what appeared to be a roadblock. American vehicles of all descriptions were parked pointing in all directions. Most of them were shot full of holes. At a couple of points they were jammed together, tilted and bent, some nearly on top others. It looked to Captain Gerdine like a car-chase scene from one of those cops-and-robbers movies, one vehicle wrecks and the pursuers pile up behind in a mad jumble.

Later in the day, Able Company was perched in deep snow on a spike of high ground after routing a Chinese platoon.

During that short, sharp fight, they'd killed eight and captured a 75mm recoilless rifle. It was a U.S. weapon and Captain Gerdine was contemplating taking it with them as his Marines sat around in the snow watching the convoy below them crawling past the wreckage.

"Look at those fucking trucks," Cpl. Abramson said. "We got people down there can barely walk, and the trucks are all loaded with rear-echelon shit."

Corporal Bayliss Thornton spat and watched as the globule turned to ice. It made a distinct pop in mid-air which made him grin. He pointed at a truck piled high with tent frames, wooden doors, space heaters, and stacks of canvas. "Remember what I told you before? In this here Marine Corps it's mind over matter..."

"They don't mind and you don't matter," Abramson finished and struggled to his feet as Sgt. Trenton passed the word. Able Company was being called down onto the road.

"You want us to haul this goddamn reckless rifle along, Skipper?" Gunny Bates was against the proposal and Gerdine decided he was probably right. The last thing his beat-up, weakened, and shivering Marines needed was more weight to carry. "Just leave it, Gunny. Figure some way to disable it."

As Able Company staggered and slid down the slope leading to the road, Bates armed a grenade and tossed it into the weapon, slamming the breech closed behind it. The resulting detonation bent the rifle into a useless shape. XO Lt. Rod Solomon kept a small working party behind on the hill to destroy other enemy weapons while Gerdine and Gunny Bates led the rest of their men down onto the MSR.

By the time they reached the road, Marines were push-starting some of the abandoned vehicles. So far, they'd managed to add two functional weapons carriers and a Jeep to the convoy. It was a help as many of the Marines on the march were suffering so badly from frostbitten feet that they could barely walk. And there was an increasing number of walking wounded from fights in the adjacent hills that could use a ride.

"You hold here," LtCol. Stevens ordered when Gerdine reported in to him. "Security on both sides of the road. There's a couple of tanks running rear guard. When they pass, you can join up on us."

"Aye, aye, sir." Gerdine looked around at the jumble of wrecked vehicles which were being unceremoniously shoved to the side of the road. "Any idea what happened here?"

"What's left of a northbound convoy," Stevens replied. "Royal Marines and some others that Chesty Puller sent up toward Hagaru. Some of them got through, but a lot of them got trapped and left behind. Bunch of them were captured. Puller sent men to recover the bodies."

"Yessir. How we doing up ahead?"

"It's a damn snail's pace, Sam, but I'm expecting to be at Koto-ri tonight."

As the convoy ground past, Able Company Marines not otherwise occupied began to dig through the abandoned vehicles. The Chinese had thoroughly ransacked most of them, but Cpl. Bayliss Thornton had some luck inside a bullet-riddled ambulance. He found a box of Tootsie Roll candy under a blood-crusted front seat. A vaguely familiar smell wafted over him when he opened the rear doors looking for more treasure. The sweet odor was coming from a red nylon sack full of mail. Thornton opened it and pawed through the letters. He couldn't read some of the handwriting, but he immediately recognized the cloying smell emanating from one envelope.

"Hey, Gunny!" Thornton carried the redolent letter and the rest of the mail toward Bates who was directing Marines into security positions. "You ain't gonna believe what I found."

"Sonofabitch!" Bates said when Thornton waved the envelope under his nose. "Doris! Where the fuck did you find this?"

"Ambulance back there a ways," Thornton said handing over the sack of other mail. "I think most of the rest is for our guys."

Bates pawed through the envelopes. It was all addressed to men in Able Company. Somebody in the ambushed convoy had been carrying mail for them. "I'll turn this over to the XO so he can hold Mail Call," Bates said tucking his own letter into his parka. "What's that under your arm?"

"Tootsie Rolls, Gunny. Found 'em in the ambulance."

"Gimme a couple. Take a few for yourself and give the rest to Doc Clinton."

"Shit-fire, Gunny. That's a waste of good candy."

"What the fuck are you talking about, Thornton?"

"Candy is meant to be eat..." Thornton handed over a few rolls and stuffed a few more into his pockets. "Damn ole Doc uses 'em like they was medicine or something. Remember that new guy...Maynard was his name, I believe."

"Yeah, so what?" Bates was anxious to get to his letter from the lovely Doris.

"Well, damn ole Maynard gets shot—took a round in the leg when we was in that night fight with the arty boys—and damn ole Doc chewed up a good Tootsie Roll and stuck it in the bullet hole."

"Shut the fuck up, Thornton...and go give that candy to Doc Clinton."

An unexpected Mail Call and candy issue improved Able Company morale considerably. As the tanks ground past and they fell in behind to continue the march toward Koto-ri, Gunny Bates was smiling despite painfully chapped lips. Doris still loved him. She'd gotten some sexy new underwear that she wanted to model for him when he got home from Korea.

There were more stops and starts as the convoy accordioned its way south but nothing very serious. Able Company had it fairly easy through most of the day, marching on the road while other units trudged through the snow above them. Most of the 1st Marine Division's dwindling combat power and all of its logistical tail was tucked safety inside the Koto-ri perimeter by midnight on 7 December.

"Pearl Harbor..." Lt. Solomon said to Gunny Bates as they supervised setting up the company's tents. "World War II started on this day in 1941."

"Not so's anybody gives a shit..." Gunny Bates said as he tugged on a guy line.

Captain Gerdine sent Bates off to find First Sergeant Hammond. The last they'd heard, he was still at Koto-ri. It was late on a miserable night when they arrived, but somehow Captain Gerdine had expected his rock-solid senior NCO to be waiting for them. He might be in the hospital or he might have been evacuated. Bates would find out.

At around 0300, Bates returned and shook Captain Gerdine out of his sleeping bag. "Skipper...you better come hear this."

Bates led his Company Commander to an idling Jeep where a tall, rawboned Chief Warrant Officer waited with his boot up on a fender. "Gunner Trowbridge, 1ˢᵗ Marines," the man said introducing himself. "Sorry for the early reveille, but Bates asked me to come along. I'm an old *panyo* of Leland Hammond's."

"Where is he, Gunner?"

"Ain't no easy way to say it, Captain. Leland's dead."

"No...what the hell happened?"

"Connived his way out of sick bay and joined up with a task force Chesty sent north to Hagaru last week. They got ambushed at a place they're calling Hell Fire Valley. You all passed through it on the way down here."

"And that explains the mail we found in that ambulance on the road." Gunny Bates wiped a sleeve across his face. "Leland was trying to rejoin us up at the reservoir, I'd bet. Just like him. Sick as a fuckin' dog, but you couldn't get him to sit one out."

"I found out about it when they brought the bodies back in," the Warrant Officer said. "I knew him for a lot of years. Man and boy, we went back a bunch, him and me. If I'd known he was here, I'd have strapped him down and kept him in sick bay. I'm heartily sorry, Skipper. Leland was a good man and a solid friend."

"To all of us, Gunner. Thanks for letting me know." There wasn't much else to say. Gerdine followed Gunny Bates back to the tents feeling hollow, as if something vital had been ripped from his chest. Certainly, someone vital had been ripped out of Able Company's guts with the death of their loyal First Sergeant. Sad Sam crawled back into his sleeping bag, truly sad this time, thinking about how often First Sergeant Hammond had cajoled, scolded, and guided him through rough patches, always deferential but always firm, pointing the way forward.

Gunny Bates sat next to Gerdine, propped up against a tent pole, unable to sleep. When he spoke, there was a catch in his voice. "Fuckin' Leland...he was a rock."

"We've got to continue the march, Gunny."

"I know, Skipper. I know...but I just feel...goddammit...I just feel like some asshole blew a hole in my belly." Bates drew a deep breath. When he exhaled, Gerdine heard a sob. "Fuckin' Leland. He was a damn fine Marine, best ever First Shirt...fuckin' good friend."

Making his rounds with Gunny Bates the next morning, Captain Gerdine kept the information about the First Sergeant relatively quiet, mentioning it only to those few survivors who remembered the man, either from Camp Pendleton or from the Inchon campaign. And every one of those said First Sergeant Leland Hammond would be sorely missed.

They spent most of the morning thawing out and trying to eat. On the road or struggling up and down frozen hills, eating was just too hard. They existed on candy or any part of the ration that could gulped down without preparation. When they did have a few quiet moments, most of them promptly fell asleep. There was no fuel for fires if any could be lit, and fumbling to open ration cans with frozen fingers or a sharp knife was both futile and dangerous. The rations inside hardly made it worth the effort anyway.

Doc Clinton was worried about malnutrition and decreasing strength levels that made the bitter cold an even greater health threat. That morning at Koto-ri, he became the unit's official nutritionist and sous-chef. Working inside a tent, he set a few Marines to opening ration tins. Didn't matter what they contained. It all went together in a steel helmet to make a sort of slumgullion. When he had five or six helmets full, Doc Clinton set them all to heating over a fuel burner. Each surviving man in Able Company had a full belly as they broke camp and got ready to move. The hot meal was welcome if not very tasty.

"Not so's anybody gives a shit." Gunny Bates used a ration cracker to scrape stew remnants out of a helmet. As usual he was the last enlisted man to eat. Captain Gerdine insisted that the junior Marines ate before anyone else. Officers always ate last and the CO only after that. With chow consumed, Bates supervised packing up the tentage in trucks and waited for word from Captain Gerdine and the XO who were at a morning briefing.

There were 10 miles to cover between Koto-ri and Chinhung-ni. General Smith said he expected that stretch to be the toughest yet, a downhill march through ravines with sheer cliffs on either side and the Chinese 60th Division occupying the hilltops. Assuming we get everything and everyone that far, the General told his officers, we've got to start climbing again, up to the Funchilin Pass where the Chinese have blown a vital bridge for the third time.

"And this time they did it right," the Division Engineer said. "We're gonna have to figure out a way to bridge a thirty-foot gap to get the vehicles across."

On the first day of marching south of Koto-ri, what had been a series of small unit skirmishes in the hills overlooking the MSR—squads, platoons or companies engaging Chinese or North Korean forces who seemed to be paralleling the route— suddenly morphed into a bigger fight. Air spotters reported a large Chinese unit digging in atop Hill 1457, about a mile northeast of the road. It was crucial terrain that overlooked stretches of the MSR that included the Funchilin Pass.

Taking Hill 1457 fell to LtCol. Stevens and the bone-weary riflemen of his first battalion. Captain Gerdine's Able Company set up to climb in concert with Baker Company on their right and separated from Able by a ragged ridgeline. They started trudging uphill through deep snowdrifts. Charlie Company and a provisional outfit of soldiers swept around to catch any defenders that were driven off the slopes. There were plenty of Chinese for everybody on Hill 1457.

Baker Company was the first to make contact. They were halted and pinned down by enemy defenders in a series of snow caves and bunkers. There were at least three heavy machineguns firing and while Baker Marines tried desperately to maneuver, mortars rounds from tubes on the reverse slope began to impact.

Captain Gerdine was in the process of swinging Able Company around to assist when a pair of Chinese recoilless rifles began firing into his exposed flank. It looked like the enemy gunners had a good supply of ammo as they kept up a constant rate of fire assisted by riflemen who peppered the dodging and ducking Marines as they ran for cover. Cut off from each other by a long, boulder-strewn ridgeline, Able and Baker Companies were fighting two separate battles, and losing both to stubborn defenders.

Lt. Paul Ruggles was crouched beside Sgt. Trenton in a stand of large rocks when a 75mm round blew apart one of the bounders and stung both men with rock shards. The blast knocked Trenton unconscious. Ruggles checked him for serious wounds but found nothing worse than some cuts where either shrapnel or sharp rock had sliced into the man's face and neck. Peeking up over the boulders, he spotted Doc Clinton and screamed for the Corpsman.

Chinese defenders were heaving a shower of grenades down on the Marines, and Doc Clinton had to dodge explosions as well as incoming rounds in his run for the ridgeline where Lt. Ruggles was waving at him. He vaulted over some large rocks and slid down to find Sgt. Trenton unconscious and Lt. Ruggles dripping blood from his face and neck. He immediately examined Trenton, reporting that the platoon sergeant was in no immediate danger. "Just had his bell rung real good." Clinton shouted at Lt. Ruggles who was wiping blood off his own face with a parka sleeve. "Hang on, Lieutenant and I'll take a look at you."

"Don't bother." Ruggles was inching forward along the ridgeline in the direction of the recoilless rifle positions. "I've had just about enough of this shit."

Corporal Miles Abramson was on the opposite side of the ridgeline lying next to a BAR gunner in a slight depression. The ground ahead of him leading to a pair of snow-covered bunkers was level with only a slight rise. He thought if he could do a little broken-field running up that incline and if he jinked and jived on the way, he might have a shot at reaching the bunkers alive. "Cover me..." He reloaded his M-1 and waited for the BAR man to fire. When he did, Cpl. Abramson took off running up the slope, firing his rifle from the hip.

Lt. Ruggles wiped blood out of his eyes and decided his position just above and to the right of the recoilless rifles was about as good as it was going to get. He snugged his hips into the snow and shouldered his M-1. It looked like there were just two men on each weapon banging down at Able Company, but several others popped in and out of a snow shelter passing ammo. The range to target was about 75 yards. Ruggles felt he couldn't miss, or if he did, he could easily and quickly correct his aim.

Cpl. Miles Abramson flopped into the snow next to the lowest enemy bunker, catching his breath and jamming a fresh clip into his rifle. The enemy position was just a hole dug into the snow and fronted by an old culvert through which a water-cooled machinegun was firing. Abramson recognized the bulbous water jacket and conical flash hider on a bit of the exposed barrel. He'd seen the North Koreans using similar weapons at Inchon. *Probably no more than two or three of the bastards in there*, he thought as he armed a grenade. The second bunker was above this one and looked to be open front and rear. One thing at a time, Abramson reminded himself, and looped the grenade into the bunker. He rolled aside and when his grenade detonated sending up a shower of snow, Abramson struggled to his feet and charged the second bunker.

Lt. Ruggles had cleanly picked off the nearest two-man recoilless rifle crew which brought a flood of others out into the open where they opened up on him with rifles and burp-guns. Their return fire was close and effective. He was pinned down so firmly that he couldn't even look up much less use his rifle.

Doc Clinton had a groggy Sgt. Trenton propped up and nearly revived. Trenton's face was swollen into a grotesque mask, but he'd be OK. Clinton had been keeping an eye on the Lieutenant's progress along the ridgeline. He saw the two enemy gunners drop and the firing line of enemy soldiers reacting to the flanking attack. There were five or six Chinks peppering Lt. Ruggles and no return fire. Doc Clinton couldn't tell if Ruggles had been hit or just immobilized. He reached for

Trenton's M-1 rifle and checked to see if there was a ready round chambered.

It had been a long time since Doc had fired an M-1, maybe not since boot camp. He couldn't remember. What he could remember was how to aim and fire a rifle, any rifle. He'd grown up in the Louisiana bayous plinking squirrels and game birds. The Corpsman squinted through the rear sight aperture and found the front sight blade. Not much different than the old Remington .22 he used to carry in the swamps. Then he brought that sight picture onto a Chinese soldier and squeezed the trigger.

Miles Abramson poked the muzzle of his rifle into the second bunker and emptied the clip. A wounded man crawled out right beside him dragging a burp-gun by the sling while Abramson was fumbling to reload. Miles bashed him behind the neck with the butt of his rifle. That took the man was out of the fight, but the impact damaged Abramson's rifle. The operating rod jumped out of track. While he was struggling to repair the malfunction, a Chinese soldier popped out of the bunker's rear entrance. Cpl. Abramson dropped his damaged rifle, grabbed the burp-gun and emptied the drum magazine, blowing the Chinese soldier back into the snow in a bloody lump.

Effective fire from somewhere below him took the pressure off Lt. Ruggles. He peeked up from under the rim of his helmet and saw Chinese soldiers falling like ten-pins. He got his rifle back into action and nailed the two Chinese firing the second recoilless rifle.

Enemy resistance confronting Able Company dwindled rapidly then. The hottest part of the fight was over in a matter of minutes, and Captain Gerdine herded his survivors uphill to finish it. On the other side of the ridgeline, he could hear Baker Company still fighting, but he wasn't sure what he might do to help. Able Company had taken some serious casualties. Gerdine needed to see what he had left before he worried about Baker Company. As usual, Gunny Bates had a plan.

"I'm gonna move one of them reckless rifles up onto the ridgeline," he shouted as he trotted uphill leading a couple of men from the 60mm mortar section. "Give them commie bastards a little taste of their own medicine."

Lt. Ruggles was gasping for breath, kneeling beside one of the weapons when Bates and his drafted gun crew arrived. "Give us a hand, Mister Ruggles..." Bates began to break the 75mm recoilless rifle down quickly and expertly into portable components. "Grab as many rounds as you can carry and follow me."

While surviving Able Company riflemen mopped up enemy positions below them, Bates and his Marines carried the weapon to the top of the ridgeline where they could see the fight Baker Company was having with a line of three machinegun bunkers. Bates selected a spot and jammed the tripod down into the snow as Lt. Ruggles arrived with his arms full of high-explosive rounds. "You know how to handle that damn thing?"

"It ain't hard, Lieutenant..." Bates showed the men carrying the barrel and breech how to lock it to the tripod and squatted to the left of the weapon, peering through the sights. "This here opens the breech," he said pointing at a knob affixed to a lever. "Open her up, shove in a round, and then close it again." The gunny flopped down into the snow and began to shift the weapon onto target with the elevating and traversing hand-wheels.

Ruggles slammed a round into the rear of the weapon and closed the breech. Bates looked over his shoulder. "Clear the back-blast area!" Marines behind the gun holding ready ammo jostled out of the way. Gunny Bates made a couple of sight adjustments and then jammed the knob on the elevation hand wheel to fire the weapon. The blast of propellant gas escaping from the rear of the weapon raised a storm of snow and rocks. The blast on the other end was equally spectacular. An enemy bunker seemed to heave like a wounded animal shedding snow and then collapsed.

"Reload this sonofabitch!" Bates cranked the weapon around to aim for the second bunker. As Ruggles jammed another round into the breech, he could see Baker Company Marines rising from the snow. Bates put his next round into the second bunker just as a squad of Chinese soldiers were abandoning it. Most of them went down in the explosion which collapsed the bunker. Those that didn't were picked off by Marines who dropped their ammo load and reached for their rifles.

When Gunny Bates called for a third round, Ruggles told him to ceasefire. He could see Baker Company Marines storming the last remaining enemy position. It would fall without further help.

Doc Clinton handed the M-1 back to Sgt. Trenton who was groggy but functional and went to check on other wounded Marines. His brief foray as a rifleman was over for now. And there were plenty of wounded Marines scattered along the slope. Maybe as many as a half-dozen that needed medical attention. And there were three dead men to be carried down the hill. HM2 Arleigh Clinton was headed down with one of the dead Marines slumped over his shoulder when he kicked the grenade. Stumbling and struggling in the deep snow, Clinton didn't see it, or maybe he did and decided it was a dud. It wasn't.

The detonation blew Doc Clinton off his feet and face down into the snow. His butt and hamstrings were painfully peppered. The wounds felt like someone was jabbing Clinton's backside with a red-hot poker. Snow funneled the shrapnel, he thought as he tried to assess his mobility. *Could be worse...a hell of a lot worse...I could be dead.* He rolled over and spotted the dead Marine he'd been carrying. Someone else would have to complete that chore.

"Corpsman! Corpsman!" Doc Clinton sat bleeding into the deep snow which was numbing his painful wounds. He chuckled. It was the first time he'd ever issued that summons. Usually it was the other way around.

Royal Marines of 41 Commando came up the hill after the fight to relieve the American Marines and hold the crucial high ground against a counterattack that everyone knew was coming. LtCol. Stevens walked up with them and found Captain Gerdine.

"Nice work up here, Sam." The battalion commander squatted in the snow and offered a cigarette. "Baker Company is damn grateful. How is Able Company looking?"

"Pretty rough, Colonel. Three dead and eight wounded bad enough they'll have to come down off the hill."

"What's your count of effectives?"

Gerdine looked up at Lt. Rod Solomon who was listening nearby. The XO held up two gloved fingers on one hand and three on the other.

"Looks to be about 23, sir..."

"OK, that's enough for your people." LtCol. Stevens stood and pointed down toward the MSR. "Police 'em up and get back to the road. I'll have my XO meet you there."

"Aye, aye, sir. Got anything special in mind for us?"

"Engineers are trying to get a bridge built over the gap at Funchilin Pass. They're gonna be too busy to worry about security. Your Marines will provide it for them."

Gunnery Sergeant Elmore Bates sat slumped next to the captured recoilless rifle. Blood was pounding so hard in his ears that he could barely hear anything else. Every time he tried to take a deep breath of frigid air it felt like someone was squeezing him in a painful bear-hug. And when he blinked against the glare of the snow, fireworks exploded in his eyes. *Little technicolor bugs crawling around in my eyeballs,* he thought. *Should have made a couple of them young fartknockers carry the tripod. Heavy sonofabitch. Forgot how heavy it was. My ass is wore plumb out.* Adrenaline only carries you so far. He fumbled in the pocket of his parka and retrieved a little lump of tinfoil. Four nitro pills left. He popped one of them under his tongue. Might be time to see Doc Clinton about getting some more...

"Gunny! Skipper says we're leaving...muster on him."

It was news to Gunny Bates. He hadn't heard, seen, or done much after destroying the second bunker. When his firing party left to help with the mop-up, Bates sat frozen in position next to the gun. Lt. Ruggles shouted for him again, and Bates waved a hand over his head. Then he pulled his canteen out from under his parka and swallowed cold water to chase the cottonmouth. He leaned on the recoilless rifle to lever himself up onto his feet and stood swaying for a moment, fighting for balance.

"You OK, Gunny Bates?" Lt. Ruggles put a hand on the Gunny's shoulder. "You don't look so hot."

"I ain't never looked hot, Mister Ruggles..." Bates shook his shoulders and smiled. "Not in my nature. Just a bit tuckered, that's all." The Gunny saw Able Company Marines helping to position Royal Marines on the slope. "What's up with that shit?"

"Royal Marines are relieving us. We been ordered back down onto the road. Skipper says we're gonna pull security for the engineers."

"Well then, Mister Ruggles..." Gunny Bates slung his rifle and shrugged. "We better get down to the road and protect them peckerheads."

Huddled with two other Corpsmen in the back of an ambulance, Doc Clinton lay on his stomach, smoking and drifting on a morphine shot. "Gotta be a ton of scrap-metal in your hamstrings," the man doing the probing and picking said. "And we ain't even started on your ass."

A second Corpsman was swabbing shrapnel wounds with disinfectant. "Arleigh, you really ought to let us tag you and send you to BAS for this..."

"Negative." Doc Clinton lit another smoke and shook his head. "Just do the best you can for now. I'll see a surgeon when we get to the end of the road."

"Well, it's your ass...and I mean that literally. But how you gonna walk?"

"Very carefully."

"We can probably get you a ride, Arleigh."

"No thanks. I can walk a damn site better than I can sit right now."

THE 1ST MARINE DIVISION'S long logistical train was jammed solid on the road to the north of the Funchilin Pass. And it would remain that way until the hard-pressed Marines from their 1st Engineer Battalion accomplished what many said was impossible. Gerdine was told in a quick-and-dirty briefing from his battalion S-3 that an Army element moving up from Hamhung had pushed the Chinese off the high ground south of the pass, but there were still a lot of them roaming the hills on the north end. And all of them wanted to stop the engineers from bridging the gaping chasm they left by destroying the bridge at Funchilin Pass.

It took only one truck to carry Able Company survivors up the road to the pass. They were halted short of the actual work site where they met Major Dennis Lindsey, an engineer officer in charge of site security. Captain Gerdine and Lt. Solomon left their Marines with Gunny Bates to get some hot coffee at a roadside field mess and drove up a steep incline in the Major's Jeep. The area directly adjacent to the gap had been cleared of idlers and kibitzers so the engineers had room to work. Their bulldozers and other heavy equipment were parked alongside the road waiting for the call. There seemed to be a lot of milling and head-scratching at the edge of the deep canyon. Gerdine noted a couple of Air Force officers conferring with the Marine engineers and asked about it.

"They may be the answer to some very tough questions," Lindsey said. "We're trying to get an M-2 Treadway Bridge in here. The colonel thinks maybe the Air Force can air-drop the stuff we need from their C-119s. The Army's got a bridge company Koto-ri with trucks big enough to carry the sections. If the air-drop works—and if the sections come down where we need them—and if they land in one piece—we might just be able to get you guys on the move again."

"Lot of ifs..." Lt. Rod Solomon said as they walked forward to get a closer look at the problem. "That there are," Lindsey replied. "But we're running a little short of better ideas."

The engineer walked them as close as they could get and outlined the problems facing his battalion. "There's a hydro-electric power plant down there," Lindsey said pointing down into the valley below the pass. "Water from the Chosin Reservoir up north flows down to the pass through a system of tunnels. And then its funneled into those things..." He pointed at an array of four huge concrete pipes dug into the hillsides. "They're call penstocks, and they carry the water down to spin the turbines in the power plant.

"As you can see," Lindsey continued, pointing at the sheer cliffs running down the mountainside. "There's no way to bypass or work around the pass, not if we want to get all our rolling stock out with us. And General Smith insists on that. Chinks have blown the original concrete bridge at least twice before, but this time they went whole hog." He pointed at tangled abutments on either side of the gap. "There's about a thirty-foot traverse to cover. And right now we just don't have the right stuff to get it done."

"Chinks been giving you much trouble?" Gerdine looked up at the frozen hilltops and silently prayed he wouldn't have to climb them.

"Mostly snipers and the occasional machinegun they maneuver into position. We work all night, and they've got good targets with all the lights burning. What we need is a kind of rapid-reaction force. When they start that kind of shit, you guys take them under fire and chase them off so we can concentrate on the work instead of jumping for cover."

Gerdine eyed the terrain. There was a broad ledge running across a knoll at a point where the ground plunged downward toward the valley. It looked like just about enough room to dig his few remaining men in on line. "How about if we set up over there?" Gerdine pointed at the knoll. "From there we've got good observation and we'd be firing over your heads if we have to engage."

"You're the experts." Major Lindsey shrugged. "Long as you keep the bastards off of us, I'm happy."

"Might get a little noisy," Lt. Solomon commented. "That gonna bother your guys?"

"With all the noise we make?" Lindsey laughed. "We'd be lucky to hear a bomb go off."

"Can you run us back down the road?" Gerdine nodded at the Jeep. "I want to load up on ammo and borrow some extra firepower."

They borrowed two extra BARs and a .50 caliber machinegun to supplement the two .30 calibers that were still functional. They begged or stole all the ammo they could fit aboard a truck and loaded it beside the two remaining 60mm mortars and several cases of HE rounds. By the time it was all loaded and assignments made to crew-served weapons, it looked to Captain Gerdine like nearly everybody in his short-handed command was either a machine gunner, a mortarman, or some variation of those roles. There would be some on-the-job training involved when they got back to the Funchilin Pass, but at least they wouldn't be climbing hills.

Able Company couldn't see the air-drop from where they were dug in at the Funchilin Pass, but they noted a flight of ungainly looking Air Force C-119 Flying Boxcars passing overhead just after dawn. Those aircraft roared over Koto-ri, and crewmen pushed huge 2,500 pound Treadway bridge sections out the clam-shell doors between their tail booms. LtCol. John Partridge, the Division Engineer, needed four of the steel sections to bridge the gap at Funchilin, but he ordered eight dropped by huge cargo parachutes just to hedge his bets. It's fortunate that he did. One section fell right into Chinese hands, and another landed so badly damaged that it was useless.

The U.S. Army's Bridge Company of the 58th Engineer Battalion at Koto-ri got the Treadway sections loaded on specially built trucks and started them up the long grade toward Funchilin Pass escorted by elements of the 7th Marines. Other C-119s followed and dropped plywood for use as center sections to support vehicle traffic once the engineers had the Treadway Bridge constructed. The wood was manhandled aboard trucks and they followed along the three-and-a-half mile trek to the work site.

With the arrival of the bridging materials, Funchilin Pass turned into a beehive of construction activity. Marines manning dozers, caterpillar tractors, and truck-mounted cranes began the slow and laborious chore of carefully pushing the sections into place. It took nearly a day of frustrating work in bitter cold to get the first sections across the gap. Engineers rode them across and set up a work site on the south side where they could begin locking the support structures in place. The work progress did not go unobserved by the Chinese overlooking the pass.

Generators were still roaring, winches whining, and work lights blazing at 2200 on the first night of construction work when a pair of enemy heavy machineguns swept the area. Rounds sparked and sang off steel as engineers scrambled for cover. Able Company had been waiting for it. Lt. Solomon was on duty atop the knoll and quickly spotted muzzle flashes to the south. Able Company's firing line roared to life. Their 60mm mortars pumped illumination rounds over the hillside opposite the pass. Gunny Bates crouched behind the .50 caliber and pumped tracers up at the enemy gunners as everyone else opened fire along the line. The incoming stopped, but Captain Gerdine ordered his Marines to keep pounding the area for a while as the engineers went back to work.

On the second day, trucks carrying the plywood planking arrived at the work site, and Lt. Paul Ruggles, the former sawmill manager, got excited. "Skipper let me go down there and bear a hand," he asked as engineers fired up saws to cut and fit the wood. "I know my way around stuff like that." An hour later, Ruggles found himself covered in sawdust, working beside a section of engineers who were measuring and cutting plywood with everything from hand saws to chain saws.

"Careful, Captain..." Gunny Bates said as he watched Ruggles work down below the knoll. "Them fuckin' engineers will be wantin' to hold on to Mister Ruggles."

"I'll go down and see he doesn't get too comfortable." Gerdine picked up his map case and headed down off the knoll. He wasn't worried about losing Lt. Ruggles. He wanted to spend a few minutes near a work light where he could see to handle some admin chores he'd been neglecting. Scribbles in his notebook reminded Gerdine that he eventually needed to write up some decoration recommendations for his surviving Marines. Ruggles, Gunny Bates, Sgt. Trenton, Doc Clinton, Abramson, Thornton, and few others were going to finish the Chosin Reservoir Campaign wearing Bronze Stars or better. He was determined to see to that.

The Chinese tried again to disrupt the work that night, but Captain Gerdine barely rolled over in his sleeping bag when the return fire started. His XO had it on auto-pilot by this time, and his Marines were enjoying shooting without being directly shot at in return. It was good for their sagging morale. Marines love to shoot, anything and everything that goes bang and tears shit up decisively.

And for the most part they didn't have much better to do as they watched and marveled at the engineers working below the knoll. Even the eternal kibitzers and sidewalk supervisors among them who always had a better idea kept silent. They knew a marvel of engineering expertise when they saw one. Marine infantry and rolling stock began to cross the bridge at the Funchilin Pass on the third day of construction. Exhausted engineers waved or just nodded to acknowledge the cheers they got from the Marines who tromped or drove over their structure. The march south to the next objective at Chinhung-ni was underway at last.

Captain Gerdine and his handful of Able Company Marines were assigned to accompany Colonel Murray and the 5th Marines as security for the command group. They weren't in shape to do much more hill-climbing along the route south. Captain Gerdine and Lt. Solomon constantly walked back and forth among the Marines, offering encouragement to men who shambled along with their heads down against a biting wind. Corporal Abramson walked beside Doc Clinton, offering help when the Corpsman stumbled with the pain in his legs and backside. Other Marines lent hands and shoulders to walking wounded, often relieving them of gear or other burdens. Able Company was dinged and depleted, but there was no quit in any of them, not this close to the end.

"We're a pretty picture, aren't we?" Lt. Rod Solomon eyed the Marines passing by him. They were filthy, ragged, and bleary-eyed, but they kept putting one frozen foot in front of the other.

"Prettiest picture you'll ever see," Captain Sam Gerdine said. "These men are the absolute best..." And their Skipper loved them, each and every raggedy-ass one of them.

They were rounding a twist in the road when Sgt. Trenton in the lead shouldered his M-1 and signaled for the men following to take cover. Unslinging their weapons, Able Company flopped into the snow as Trenton cautiously moved forward a step or two. He made a come-along motion with the muzzle of his rifle and a line of limping Chinese soldiers came into sight with their hands raised. There were 15 or 20 of them, probably the remnants of a platoon or maybe a company, all wind-chapped and limping on frozen feet. None carried weapons. Most of them bowed or bobbed their heads as Able Company Marines rose from the roadside and approached.

Gunny Bates had them assembled in a ragged formation when LtCol. Stevens arrived with this CP group. "Pat down for weapons," he said. "and just keep an eye on them. Those that can walk can follow us. The rest can just stay here and freeze."

Unsure of what the orders meant and feeling a bit sorry for the sad specimens gathered at roadside watching American firepower roll past, Able Company Marines offered cigarettes and a Tootsie Roll or two. When they moved out a bit later, the Chinese meekly followed, limping along as though they were just another Marine unit on the march.

Up to this point in the brutal campaign around the Chosin Reservoir, Marines mostly fought Chinese Army units. They were the largest and most looming threat, but there were still some NKPA units milling around and some of them were spoiling for a fight. On a late afternoon north of Chinhung-ni as Able Company spread out around the 5th Marines CP, the North Koreans took a final shot at them. Colonel Murray had paused to rest his exhausted troops when marauding T-34 tanks roared around a bend in the road and opened fire with cannon and machineguns.

Captain Gerdine, Lt. Solomon, and Gunny Bates were closest to the road and first to react. They had long ago lost their remaining AT weapons, so they gathered as many hand grenades as they could carry and began to stalk the T-34 which was idling in the middle of the road with all weapons blazing. Everyone in the CP group who hadn't been wounded in the initial fusillade was firing whatever weapon they had at the tank.

"More coming around the bend!" Lt. Solomon was on a little ridge above the lead tank. He could see two more T-34s grinding forward.

"Get back and bring our people up here!" Gerdine waved at his XO and then led Gunny Bates up under the lead tanks guns. "Hit the tracks," he shouted as he armed a grenade. "I'll go for the driver!" As Bates jammed grenades between the T-34's road wheels, he ducked under the barking machinegun on the bow and crawled across the vehicle's forward glacis plate. The driver had his vision slit open and Gerdine could see a pair of wide, white eyes staring from under a fur-lined helmet. A pair of Bates' grenades detonated on the opposite side of the tank, and Gerdine made his move. He shoved the muzzle of his M-1 directly into the driver's vision slit with one hand and triggered two rounds. Then he dumped the grenade into the tank with the other hand.

The remaining North Korean crewmen bailed out through the top turret hatches, but they never made the ground. Marines following Lt. Solomon up to the bend in the road killed them in a blaze of rifle fire. The second T-34 ground forward and opened fire as the third one reversed back down the road. Half of Gerdine's Marines were crouched around the disabled tank ducking ricochets, and the other half were buried in the snow trying to avoid fire from the second vehicle. At that point, Baker Company came roaring up the road to rescue Able Company and return the favor done them on Hill 1457.

They brought a couple of 3.5-inch rocket launchers and a 75mm recoilless rifle that promptly took the second marauding tank under fire. The T-34 was a smoking hulk in short order. Marines rushed around the bend chasing the third vehicle as a pair of Corsairs appeared overhead and dove into the fight. Baker Company's CO ran past Gerdine who was watching the show from atop the first T-34. "Many thanks," he yelled at his fellow Company Commander.

"We're even..." The man smiled and waved as the Corsairs took out the remaining North Korean tank with a volley of rockets.

"The shit just keeps on comin' don't it, Skipper?" Gunny Bates stood below Gerdine's perch shaking his head. He examined one of the dead tankers and snapped an insignia off the man's fur cap. "North fuckin' Koreans. I thought them assholes was out of this fight a long time ago." He pocketed the insignia and pulled out a small wad of aluminum foil. He spread it, found what he wanted and popped a pill into his mouth.

"You OK, Gunny?" Gerdine climbed down off the tank and watched their Marines forming up on the road to continue the march.

"Just a little headache is all. Coupla aspirin..."

The convoy was moving around them, and they saw Colonel Murray's headquarters commandant waving them forward. They were tucked into a tight perimeter at Chinhung-ni by dark. Chesty Puller's 1st Marines had the area encircled tightly, and just a few of the arriving units had to plug gaps in the perimeter. Able Company caught a rare break and drew security duties deep inside the base camp. Captain Gerdine rotated sentries around the CP on two-hour watches in blowing snow followed by two hours in a warming tent. There was some concern when S-2 reported prisoner interrogations revealed the Chinese 89th Division was operating in the area. If they were out there in the dark maneuvering in the snow and wind, the Chinese were not inclined to attack. The night passed quietly.

It was an easy march the following morning but slow and plodding with most of the infantry Marines stalking and stomping on half-frozen feet. Some sympathetic drivers offered rides, but the men who walked into the Chosin Reservoir campaign mostly wanted to finish it the way they started—on their feet.

What remained of Able Company loaded on trucks at Sudong-ni for the final legs of their 80-mile journey from the northern reaches of the Chosin Reservoir to the Sea of Japan. Nobody was doing much math as the survivors rolled into Hamhung where they got a rare hot meal, but Able Company had lost three-quarters of its combat strength along the way. All Captain Sad Sam Gerdine knew for sure as he nodded over a steaming cup of coffee and a cigarette was that he'd lost a lot of good Marines. And with every one of them, he thought as he silently recalled names and faces, he'd lost a little piece of his heart.

They rode the same rickety railroad cars down to the seaport at Hungnam that had hauled them north at the start of the action back in October. The cars were still drafty rattletraps, and they still reeked of manure, but no one complained or even mentioned it. Discomfort had taken on an entirely new meaning for the survivors of the Chosin Reservoir campaign.

They cleaned up a bit at Hungnam and loafed around, scrounging gear and sympathy from the soldiers who manned the seaport, waiting for the sailors manning the troopships moored at the docks to put them aboard for the trip to Pusan. Gunny Bates laughed until there were tears in his eyes when Captain Gerdine informed him that Able Company would load up the next morning—aboard the USS *Henrico*.

Gunny Bates missed a specially prepared and sumptuous meal set out for the Marines by the sailors aboard Happy Hank. It was just one short day of steaming to Pusan, and he could eat then. He was too tired to bother right now. As he lay in an isolated rack up near the forecastle, feeling the ship pitch under him, Elmore Bates decided he was more than a little lucky to be alive. He'd spent ten minutes under a hot shower shortly after they came aboard ship and discovered dings, dents, rents, bruises, and shrapnel wounds from his scalp to his heels. Damn right. Lucky to be alive. He'd felt that way after combat before a time or two, but this time, this fuckin' Korea mess...well, that was a certified sonofabitch, and any man who survived it was a lucky sonofabitch beyond the average lucky sonofabitch.

His entire body hurt, but he ignored it. Pain was a familiar signal. It meant you were still alive. He took the deepest breath he could manage and smiled as images and memories unspooled before his eyes. Able Company. What an outfit. What a fuckin' wonderful gaggle of hard-ass Marines. His chest spasmed painfully. He'd have to see Doc Clinton, that good-as-gold pecker-checker with an ass full of Chink shrapnel, when they reached Pusan. And then he'd continue the march. Meanwhile, he'd just rest a bit, think a little, maybe sleep if he could.

Gunny Bates thought about Doris. Wonderful woman, truth be told, with a huge heart underneath those massive boobs of hers. For some reason he'd never quite understand, and despite all his nonsense, Doris loved him. He knew that just like he knew his name and service number. Maybe he'd let her make an honest man out of him when he got back Stateside. Maybe he'd make some time for something besides the Marine Corps. Maybe he'd just throw a big-ass party and invite the Skipper and all the Able Company jarheads to a wedding. It would be fun...but not quite the same without Leland Hammond. Fuckin' Leland.

Gunnery Sergeant Elmore Bates took a long, deep breath, closed his eyes and went to sleep.

"Died in his sleep, Skipper." Doc Clinton wiped at the tears streaming down his cheeks. "I went to check on him...and he was gone. Heart just stopped."

The news hit Captain Sam Gerdine like a paralyzing electric shock. Gunny Bates gone? After all we've been through? Now? Aboard the Happy Hank? Nothing kills the Gunny. It simply can't be true.

But it was. Gerdine and Lt. Solomon followed Doc Clinton toward the forecastle. The Corpsman was sobbing and wiping his nose with a sleeve. "Goddammit! I knew he had a heart problem. He made me promise not to say anything. I killed him."

"No, Doc...you didn't kill him." Captain Gerdine stood staring down at Bates stretched out peacefully in just his skivvy drawers, old wounds, and scars obvious all over the man's body. He put his arm around the Corpsman. "Even if we'd known about it, Gunny Bates would never have let us send him off the line. He just reached the end of a long road he loved to travel. That's all..."

"You could order Gunny Bates to do a lot of stuff," Lt. Solomon said as he pulled a sheet over the dead man's face. "And he'd still do exactly what he wanted to do, exactly what was right for his Marines."

When Doc Clinton and Lt. Solomon went to fetch the ship's surgeon. Captain Sad Sam Gerdine pulled the sheet back off the Gunny's face and knelt by the rack. "I'm sure gonna miss you, old fartknocker. Thanks for being our Gunny. Thanks for guiding me and teaching me. Thanks for being such a damn fine Marine."

NOT MUCH HAD CHANGED. It was still a sprawl of tents and milling Marines as replacements flooded in and veterans rotated out, headed home or to new assignments within the division. Christmas was coming, and there were make-shift decorations sprouting up throughout the area. Rumors were coursing through the 1st Marine Division that Bob Hope might bring his USO Show to Korea for a special holiday performance. New uniforms, new gear, and refurbished weapons were being issued to replace the lost, damaged, or just combat-worn implements carried back from the Chosin Reservoir campaign.

There was a great deal of speculation among the replacements about what would come next. Allied forces were now safely back on the south side of the 38th Parallel, but there was still a lot of war to be fought. The Chinese were still pushing and the North Korean People's Army was rapidly regrouping. No one really knew where, but all understood the fight would continue in Korea. Among the veteran survivors still serving with division units, no one much gave a shit. Whatever came next for them couldn't possibly be as bad as what they now called the Frozen Chosin in the Freezin' Season.

"Company formation at 0800 tomorrow, Skipper." Newly minted Captain Rod Solomon ducked into the tent and watched as Sam Gerdine packed his sea bag. "Right after colors OK for the change of command?"

"Be fine, Rod." Gerdine snapped the bag closed and sat on a sagging cot. He reached into his map case and extracted a bottle of Old Crow. "How about we have a little drink to the new Able Company Commander?"

They sat passing the whiskey bottle for a while, smiling and smoking to fill the silence that hung between them. There just didn't seem to be much to say. Sad Sam was on his way Stateside, and Rod Solomon was tapped to be the new boss based on Gerdine's strong recommendation.

"Old Crow..." Solomon sipped and smiled. "This was First Sergeant Hammond's favorite."

"Yeah...the Top Sergeant said it was appropriate. An old crow drinking Old Crow."

"I hear the new First Sergeant knew him."

"Leland Hammond knew damn near everybody."

"He always said the Marine Corps was really just a little club run by regulars."

"Stick around for a while and you find out just how small and tight that club really is. Your new First Shirt for instance...Master Sergeant Jack Butts served with Hammond in the Pacific. Before that at Parris Island, I think. Butts hears about Hammond and works his bolt to get Able Company so he can carry on for his old buddy."

"I'm guessing he's a good man."

"You'd be guessing right, Rod. Listen to him; let him guide you."

"Think he'll be OK with Trenton as our new Company Gunny?"

"I think so. If he's not, Heywood Trenton will disabuse him of the notion. Hard to argue with a man wearing two Silver Stars and a couple of Purple Hearts."

"Saw Doc Clinton this morning up at the BAS. Promotion came through. He's gonna be a surgical assistant, he says."

"We had some damn fine Corpsman, Rod. But none of them was as good as Arleigh Clinton. Man saw Able Company as his own private medical practice."

"Paul Ruggles also got his promotion. He seems to be getting a handle on things at Baker Company. Said to thank you for recommending him as the new CO."

"He'll do fine. He took Thornton with him, so he'll have at least one solid squad leader."

"You get your orders yet?"

"I did. Headed for the recruit depot at San Diego. Staff job." Gerdine had written to let Della know about the new assignment, a job that would keep him desk-bound, out of the field and right there in San Diego. He was hoping she would reconsider their divorce and was preparing to pitch that proposition as soon as he got home.

"Anyplace other than Korea, I guess..." Rod Solomon shook the bottle and took a little nip. "San Diego will be nice this time of year."

"Yeah...and guess who's going with me?"

"Who?" Captain Solomon passed the bottle.

"Corporal Abramson."

"No shit? They actually gonna send him to boot camp?"

Gerdine laughed and shook his head. "Even the hidebound Marine Corps knows better than to try that with a man like Miles Abramson. He'll wind up at Pendleton—Infantry Training Regiment—until they cut him loose and send him back to Kansas City."

Captain Rod Solomon stood and extended his hand. "Thanks for everything, Skipper. Thanks for trusting me and teaching me. I'll try to make Able Company as good as you did."

"Don't do that, Rod. Make your new Able Company your own. Mold it to reflect your own style and personality. They'll respond to good leadership from a good Marine officer. That's you in spades, my friend."

Solomon smiled. "I guess it's about this time that a good Marine says Semper Fi."

"Semper Fidelis—and good luck."

About the Author

DALE DYE is a Marine officer who rose through the ranks to retire as a Captain after 21 years of service in war and peace. He is a distinguished graduate of Missouri Military Academy who enlisted in the United States Marine Corps shortly after graduation. Sent to war in Southeast Asia, he served in Vietnam in 1965 and 1967 through 1970, surviving 31 major combat operations.

Appointed a Warrant Officer in 1976, he later converted his commission and was a Captain when he deployed to Beirut, Lebanon with the Multinational Force in 1982-83. He served in a variety of assignments around the world and along the way attained a degree in English Literature from the University of Maryland. Following retirement from active duty in 1984, he spent time in Central America, reporting and training troops for guerrilla warfare in El Salvador, Honduras, and Costa Rica.

Upset with Hollywood's treatment of the American military, he went to Hollywood and established Warriors Inc., the preeminent military training and advisory service to the entertainment industry. He has worked on more than 50 movies and TV shows including several Academy Award and Emmy winning productions. He is a novelist, actor, director and show business innovator, who wanders between Los Angeles and Lockhart, Texas.

Printed in Great Britain
by Amazon

41529716R00195